Praise for THE BODY MAN

"'The Body Man' is a spectacular political thriller with multiple intriguing subplots to build the mystique for a huge bang! A fan-favorite kickoff to an exciting new series!"

— Kashif Hussain
Best Thriller Books

"'The Body Man' is a bold, fast-paced story that blurs the lines between fact and fiction. The unique plot and the strong characters will have you turning pages late into the night. There is no doubt about it: Eric P. Bishop is the real deal!"

— C.E. Albanese
Former US Secret Service Agent
and author of *Drone Kings*

"I loved 'The Body Man'." Eric has written a taut, torn-from-the-pages thriller that takes readers into a world of secrets and power ... packed with compelling characters who are so authentic I feel I've met them."

— Adam Hamdy
Author of *The Pendulum Trilogy*
and the forthcoming *Private Moscow*
with James Patterson

"'The best intrigue novel of the year! It's the plausible meeting of two entities—Deep State and Top Secrecy—that ensures and instills uneasiness in the national intelligence community. It sends readers on a roller coaster ride!"

— Julie Watson
Julie Watson Reviews

THE BODY MAN

A THRILLER

ERIC P. BISHOP

FORCE POSEIDON

DETROIT

President Carter #39

Thank you so much for your service to our great nation. I hope you enjoy my debut novel The Body Man.

All the best

FORCE POSEIDON

Published in the United States of America by Force Poseidon
forceposeidon.com

Library of Congress Control Number: 2021942447

Force Poseidon hardcover edition – September 2021 ISBN-13 978-1-7366214-6-2

Force Poseidon eBook edition – September 2021 ASIN B098DDWN6Y

Force Poseidon trade paperback – September 2021 ISBN-13 978-1-7366214-5-5

This book was produced in Adobe InDesign CC 2021 using Literata Book 10/17 for body copy and DIN Condensed for chapter headings. For information about special discount bulk purchases of paper or ebooks, please contact Force Poseidon Direct Sales via email at reachout@forceposeidon.com

Author images by Brandi Fugate @ Full Nest Photography

Oil rig photo by Zachary Theodore

Manufactured in the United States of America

@ForcePoseidon · ForcePoseidon.com

For mom
My most ardent supporter.
I love you, always.

In Memoriam
My Nanny
Hilda Dewhurst
11/11/1917 – 03/08/2010

THE BODY MAN

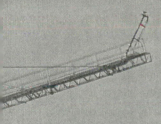

"In every powerful organization there is always someone who knows where the bodies are buried."

Chapter 1
Washington, DC

The Body Man closed the front door of his townhouse and crossed the tiled landing. A stiff breeze pushed against him approaching the top step. His eyes looked down at his Ares Diver-1 GMT watch, a gift from the most unlikely of sources.

Fifteen minutes. Plenty of time.

Cast iron gas lamps stood like sentries in front of each residence, dotting the tree-lined street. He habitually looked left then right, keen eyes probing both sides of the road for anything that shouldn't be there. The meticulous stare searched for the slightest anomaly but revealed nothing out of place.

Habit led his right hand to slide under the black leather coat. His fingertips brushed against the smooth belt he bought last year in Italy until his thumb bumped into the reassuring polymer frame of a .40-caliber Glock G23 Gen5 MOS.

Confident of his surroundings, he descended the steps to the sidewalk and approached his silver Nissan Maxima, the daily driver he drove in town when keeping a low profile. In a suburban Maryland rental garage was a gorgeous black 1973 BMW 3.0 CSL homologation special he drove when he didn't care who saw him.

Tonight, invisibility was an ally, discretion a trusted friend.

Without breaking stride, he climbed into the vehicle, started the engine, and pulled away from the curb.

The Body Man accelerated quickly to make a meeting he preferred not to attend with a reporter from Politico. He knew what he was about to do was necessary, but at the same time he was also keenly aware of the firestorm that would erupt once he brought the media into the mix and revealed the damning intel only he possessed. This move also went against everything he had always held sacred, personally and professionally.

Yet he had no choice.

The drive from Vienna to McLean paralleled Route 123 and should only take ten minutes at this time of day.

Still, the Body Man ran heavy on the gas to shave off a precious minute or two. His eyes darted from the rear view to side mirrors.

All clear.

Up ahead, the traffic light turned yellow and then red as he braked hard to slow the vehicle. With a slight chirp, the Maxima came to a sudden stop just short of the crosswalk. His fingers struck the steering wheel in a rhythmic beat that sounded like drumming. Next to him another vehicle, a black 1963 Chrysler Imperial in decent shape, idled at the white line and inched forward like an impatient toddler not keen on being told no. The heavily and probably illegally tinted window glass concealed the occupant.

The black Chrysler powered forward as the light turned green. It shot into the intersection at the same moment as an older Ford F-150 pickup truck blew through the red traffic light from the right. The sound of shrieking metal pierced the still night as the two vehicles collided and bounced off each other with enormous force. Glass shotgunned into the air across the intersection as both vehicles came to a sudden and violent stop.

The Body Man was out of his car and moving toward the vehicle closest to him, the black sedan, even before all the flying debris had hit the ground. His role of protector was always worn just under his skin.

As he approached the driver's side door of the Chrysler, a male figure was visible through the crazed fractures of the windshield. He was slumped against the steering wheel and appeared unconscious but unbloodied, and no other passengers were inside. The Body Man yanked at the door, but it didn't give with the first pull. He gripped the door handle harder and strained his muscles as he jerked with more force. On the second tug, the door groaned and pulled free with a sharp metallic creak.

With the door open, he leaned into the car and reached to the driver's neck to check for a pulse. As his index and middle fingers pressed against the carotid artery, the driver's head jerked up from the steering wheel and the closed eyes sprang to life.

The Body Man knew that look. Only darkness, empty and devoid of emotion.

Survival instinct and years of training took over as his hand pulled away from the driver's neck and went for his weapon. However, before he reached under his leather coat to pull the Glock, the driver's balled fist shot out from the steering wheel and struck him hard in the solar plexus. The unexpected blow caused him to stumble back from the car.

Still upright, he felt another presence behind him. He now understood none of this was an accident.

It was a takedown—and he was the target.

His brain was still connecting the dots as a white box van stopped to the right of the Chrysler. Its side door slid open with a high-pitched squeak indicating the track needed lubrication. The van focused his attention as he turned to face a towering figure.

At close to six feet seven inches tall, the imposing man wore all black and a face mask with slits revealing dilated eyes.

The Body Man gripped the butt of the Glock from under his coat and drew his weapon.

Target acquired, but he didn't get the chance to pull the trigger. His attacker delivered a swift roundhouse kick, striking his wrist and sending the Glock clattering across the asphalt, landing twenty feet away.

Surprised by the move but undeterred, the Body Man dropped to the ground and twisted in midair to face the pavement. He did what looked almost like a squat thrust as his body went perpendicular. His right foot shot out and the sole of his shoe met his attacker's left knee, causing a loud snap and popping sound as heel met cartilage.

Not surprisingly, the heel won.

The sound made a sickening crunch like a wishbone pulled apart. The man in black yelled in pain as he dropped to the ground, grabbing his knee and writhing in agony.

The Body Man jumped to his feet to face his attacker as two muscular arms reached around his chest. The driver of the sedan was on him and squeezed his torso like a python. Using his height and weight advantage, the Body Man pushed off with the balls of his feet, propelling both bodies back toward the car's door frame. Flesh met steel and an exaggerated grunt came from the driver as he collapsed into the car.

The Glock lay less than twenty feet away, and the Body Man made his move toward it—the weapon was his only chance of survival. He closed the distance in less than two seconds as his hand swooped down and touched the polymer grip with his extended fingertips. Searing pain caused his arm to recoil from the weapon as a chunk of lead tore at his flesh between the wrist and elbow. A stream of crimson flowed out his sleeve as blood droplets splattered on the ground in a circular pattern. Undeterred, his eye darted toward the Glock as it lay just out of reach.

He saw the muzzle flash from within the dark interior of the van, the bullet whizzing by his ear.

A warning shot.

Don't go for the gun.

As he considered his next move, the force of a body slammed into him like an NFL linebacker sacking a quarterback and drove his body to the asphalt. Disoriented by the sudden blow, he felt a piercing twinge as a needle entered his neck near the seventh vertebrae.

A burning sensation followed that moved from the base of his skull to spread fast through his whole body, first inducing slight paralysis. He was still aware but felt like a heavy shroud suffocated him. Then he was turned over, face up.

Two burly men stood over his immobilized body for just a moment before grasping his arms and dragging him to the rear of the Maxima.

They the hunters, he the fresh kill.

The drug was working faster now, and unconsciousness was coming. The last thing the Body Man remembered was being stuffed into the trunk of his own car and one of the men wrapping the arm wound with a long length of white gauze, ripping the end in two and tying it off. The other man placed a thick hood over his head.

Then the trunk was slammed shut with finality.

Lights out.

Chapter 2
FBI Washington Field Office
Washington, DC

Eli Payne hung up the phone, a look of disgust plastered all over his face.

"Can you believe this horseshit?"

His squad supervisor and assistant special agent in charge, Wes Russell sat across the field office bullpen. He looked up from case files spread across the desk, rolled his eyes, and turned back to his paperwork.

"What is it now, Payne? Your team lose another wide receiver?" He asked it with a hint of amusement.

Payne pursed his lips. "Not funny. They want me to head out to Vienna for some damned missing-person call." An annoyed expression clung to Payne's face like graffiti.

"Sounds like a Virginia State Police matter."

"That's what I said just now. VSP phoned in a Request For Assistance to HQ because the missing person is supposed to be federal, so of course HQ dumped on the field office. I was the moron who picked up the phone. The woman who called it in says the missing person is a federal agent."

This caused Russell to perk up. "One of ours?"

Payne shook his head. "Naa, White House."

"Well now, that could be interesting."

"Hardly. It's a divisional match-up tonight. *That's* interesting."

The squad supervisor rolled his eyes. "Of course, it is."

"Can I dump this thing back on the state turds?" Payne pleaded.

"No, and I doubt the Staties would like to know you call them turds. I think this one is all you."

Payne responded with a pleading look. "Come on, Wes. There's gotta be someone else around here who can take this." He paused for a moment before adding, "How about Miller?"

"Nope, wife has an ultrasound and she's been sick, so he's on paternal leave. The baby is due any day."

"Not fair."

"To him or to you?" Wes said. "Stop whining, man. It should be quick. After all, Vienna isn't far away. With any luck the woman has dementia, and nobody is missing." Russell paused. "You know what? Take Stone with you. She needs more field experience."

Payne rolled his eyes. "The new chick fresh out of Quantico? Do I look like a babysitting service?"

"She's not a 'chick.' Jeezus, Payne, you're a walking sexual harassment lawsuit. Yes, she's new, but that's more reason to get her feet wet. She doesn't have a field training agent yet. Be better than the complaint desk agent she's working this week. Just don't screw her up on her first assignment."

"What's that supposed to mean?"

"You don't have a stellar track record with the newbies."

"You're crazy. I'm a great teacher."

"Guess you forgot all about Special Agent Calvin."

"Oh, I see how it is. You're going to bring that up forever?"

Russell laughed. "You'll never live down the noodle incident."

Payne shot his boss a dirty look before heading to the far end of the bullpen, where Probationary Agent Katherine Stone sat typing on her computer. Her back was to him, and she had white earbuds firmly implanted in her ears.

"Stone?" he said from a few steps away so as not to startle her. When she didn't respond, he cleared his throat and tapped her on the shoulder. Startled anyway, she turned around and locked eyes with him, removing one of the earbuds.

"Yeah. What's up?"

"Eli Payne. We met on your first day."

Kat Stone was attractive, not magazine-cover, but she radiated a wholesome girl-next-door quality that wasn't diminished at all by a killer figure. Long auburn hair was pulled back in a ponytail to reveal a lean face, small nose, high cheekbones, and large brown eyes.

She regarded him in recognition. "Yeah, I know who you are. I thought your rule was to avoid new agents like the plague."

Payne accepted that he had a reputation within the office for being a jerk. Something he did little to dispel. He'd readily admit that playing nice, especially with the new agents, wasn't his forte.

"Well, today I'm bending the rules."

"Lucky me, I guess …" she said as her voice trailed off.

Payne just looked at her, his face expressionless.

"Also heard you're a big football fan," Stone said.

His stoic glare faltered and a slight smile appeared at the corner of his lips.

"Guilty as charged." Payne's mood ticked up thinking maybe Stone would work out after all, especially if she liked football.

Stone shrugged. "Not me. I think it's barbaric."

"You hate apple pie and your momma too?" he asked in a sharp tone as his smile faded.

"Excuse me?" she asked. Her eyebrows raised and she removed the second earbud. Her body visibly tensed.

Payne decided getting into a pissing match with the newbie wasn't a good training technique.

"Never mind. Topic for another time. Listen, I got a case. Wes told me to bring you along."

"You mean I get to stop taking these complaint calls?"

"That's right. At least for a few hours."

"Count me in," she said. "I've never talked to this many crazy people in my life."

Payne smiled in appreciation. People would be shocked to know how many crazy people called the FBI every day all over America.

"Grab whatever you need and let's hit it."

Stone opened the bottom desk drawer and removed her purse. "What kind of case?" she asked without looking up.

"Missing person."

"Isn't that for the police?"

"Already tried that line of reasoning and it didn't work."

"Where we headed?"

"Vienna. The missing person reportedly works at the White House, so we're going to interview the elderly lady who called it in before we shitcan it back to the state police. Let's go."

Payne turned away as Stone rose and double-timed after him.

They passed through the glass doors of the FBI field office with a wave to the civilian receptionist.

"On the radio or text if you need us, Ellen," Payne said, and led Stone to the bank of elevators without looking back.

They stepped inside and the metal doors closed as Stone asked, "Victim's name?"

Payne frowned. "Well, he's not a victim. At least not yet—let's find out first if anyone's even missing. But the name the caller gave is Ralph Webb. He's supposed to live in the townhouse across the street from the caller."

"Did you call the White House? Confirm he's missing?"

"Easy, girl," Payne said as the elevator came to a stop in the federal building's basement garage and the doors hissed open. He stepped aside and gestured for Stone to exit first.

"Your Grace."

She was not amused and rolled her eyes. "Funny." But she stepped out followed by Payne.

"First things first—FBI 101, I know you had this. We need to interview the woman and if her story's convincing, we'll figure out what to do next. Calling the White House on routine investigatory matters isn't something we do out here on our own. And listen, probie—you ever need something from the White House, you call the liaison downtown and let them take it from there."

"And if it's nothing?"

"Well, she goes back to feeding a bunch of cats, you go back to the complaint intake desk, and I scoot home to watch football." Payne pointed her to his G-car.

Stone opened the passenger-side door of Payne's government car and climbed in, letting out an audible, drawn-out whistle. The seat and floorboard were covered in layers of receipts, crumpled napkins, paperback books, Rite-Aid coupons, and discarded fast-food wrappers. She brushed trash off the seat and tried to find a bare spot on the floor with her foot.

"What's the whistle for?" Payne asked.

"Your car is an absolute pigsty."

"Says who?"

"Says me." She made a face and shook her head in disgust.

"Well, I'm used to working alone."

"I take it there's no Mrs. Payne?"

"That's kind of personal, isn't it, special agent?"

Stone looked down and stirred burger wrappers with her shoe. "*Aaaand* there's my answer."

"I like my stuff just the way it is, thank you very much."

"Pretty sure the Bureau has some rules about keeping the appearance of your car presentable."

"And I'm pretty sure I've got a finger on the issue," Payne said as he raised his middle one in her direction before slamming his car door shut.

Stone laughed out loud and pointed toward the mess on the floor. There were several hardcover books among the trash.

"I see you like to read thrillers."

"You noticed?"

"I'm surprised I saw them with all the garbage on the floor but I'm relieved you can read something not filled with pictures of adult women."

"Yeah, that's funny, because I keep the nudie magazines at home under my mattress where my Mom won't find them."

"You're a classy guy, Payne. But you still need to clean out the car once or twice each year."

"Uh-huh." Payne started the car and depressed the gas pedal enough to give the engine a not-too-subtle roar as the revolutions jumped. Whitesnake's *Here I Go Again* picked up from where it left off, erupting from the speakers at an ungodly level.

Stone's hands automatically rose to cover her ears. "Jeez, this is my Dad's music," she yelled, reaching over and turning off the music.

Payne cocked his head, his eyes narrowed, and his lip curled into a scowl. "Well, at least your Dad has good taste in music."

He dropped the car into Drive and powered out of the parking space, squealing tires and narrowly avoiding a nasty scrape against a concrete column.

Payne didn't lift his foot off the gas as the vehicle rocketed out of the underground garage.

Chapter 3
Washington, DC

Merci De Atta settled into the comfortable first-class Air France seat, her exhausted body sinking into the embrace of rich imported leather. She had already slipped off her shoes, her standard custom when settling into a flight.

The hours after a hit were often tough on her. During the physical act of taking a life, she was focused, determined, and nothing distracted her from finishing the job.

However, once the task was complete and the adrenaline rush abated, she needed to let go. Now on a plane soon to be at cruising altitude leaving the United States, she had reached that place mentally where she could lean back and breathe.

A flight attendant in a dark blue skirt and white blouse with a silver crucifix dangling from her neck stopped at her row long enough to take a drink order before disappearing into the front galley. Two minutes later, the woman reappeared and placed a glass in the cupholder. Merci nodded to the woman and picked up the tall crystal filled with brown liquid.

She took two sips from the Long Island Iced Tea. As the alcohol entered her bloodstream, she relaxed, and her mind turned back to the events six hours earlier.

A husky male voice came from the transceiver deep within Merci's right ear. "He's about to emerge from around the curve. Be ready. You've got about ten seconds."

Along the Mt. Vernon Trail, the Potomac river glistened blood-red with the reflection of the sunrise. To Merci's right was the river and to her left the George Washington Memorial Parkway moved steady, the morning traffic not yet at a standstill.

The mark loved his early morning run on the trail. Predictability would soon be his death sentence.

Merci knew what to do. Like an Olympic gymnast who'd spent years honing her abilities, Merci's skills were natural and regularly exercised. Keeping a steady pace, she picked out the spot further down the trail.

The voice crackled again in her ear.

"He's visible. I say again, he can see you."

Merci counted to ten. At the designated spot, she pushed her right foot to her left. The unnatural motion caused her to miss a step as her body weight shifted to the right and sent her down hard in an apparent stumble on the running trail. At the last moment, she raised her arms just so, and it disguised a softer impact and rolling depletion of energy that prevented injury.

As Merci hit the ground she artfully slid several feet along the dew-soaked grass, rolling onto her stomach.

She lay motionless on the ground, slowed her breathing, and waited. Merci had studied Danny Frazier's file closely and she anticipated his reaction. He didn't disappoint, stopping and helping her up, brushing wet grass and leaves from her arms and making sure she wasn't hurt.

They talked for a minute after he helped her up. Unlike many of her marks, Merci sensed Danny wasn't just some self-absorbed asshole. He appeared to genuinely care for her well-being after she took the faked hard fall. A pity.

After a minute of flirtatious back and forth, Merci assured Frazier that she would survive, and she insisted he continue his run. He went to one knee to retie his shoe and as soon as he knelt, Merci's left hand moved across her body in one smooth motion and reached inside the fanny pack. A suppressor would have been preferable, but speed trumped stealth. She took a final look around and raised the weapon toward Danny's back, taking a measured breath.

Merci carefully applied initial pressure to the trigger but waited until she'd completed her exhale. At the end of the breath, she made two smooth consecutive trigger pulls without the slightest hesitation.

The first slug struck Frazier's spine like a sledgehammer hitting thin concrete and he collapsed to the ground, gasping for breath and not finding any. The second round penetrated with equal concussive force an inch from the first, and he went still.

As Frazier crumpled to the ground, his face landed flush against the gravel of the trail. Merci stood over him with the barrel of her 9mm Sig Sauer P320 pointed at the back of his head. Out of the corner of her eye, Merci saw movement atop the Arlington Bridge and a piercing banshee scream disturbed her trigger pull. Her imperceptible flinch a moment before the slide lurched back caused the third bullet to miss its specific target by millimeters. But it didn't matter. The shot had still drilled a hole in the back of Danny Frazier's skull.

Confident the mark was dead, she took off in a dead sprint toward the roadway, sure to keep her head down and not give the frantic woman screaming on the bridge a look at her face.

Merci darted into the open door of the waiting van as it came to a skidding halt. She slammed the passenger door shut and the driver accelerated away, leaving lines of rubber on the asphalt as it powered away from the scene.

The man driving the van said nothing. A mile down the road, he slowed and blended into routine traffic, and only then did he look over.

"We good?" The man asked.

"We are good," she said.

"You sure he's dead?"

"Two in the back, one in the head."

"Good girl."

Merci's body stiffened at his comment. *You sanctimonious asshole.* "Take me to Dulles," she said.

"Not yet." The driver shook his head. "We have an additional stop."

Her eyes narrowed, and she gripped the Sig in her right hand tighter. For the briefest moment, she considered putting a bullet in his head as the car darted among traffic.

"That isn't part of the arrangement," she said through gritted teeth. "Do I need to call my handler?"

"No, he doesn't know anything about this. Look, I'm just the messenger telling you the plan's changed. That's it. I don't call the shots."

"Like hell the plan's changed. By whose authority?"

The driver raised his bushy eyebrows. "By *his* authority."

Shit. Things just got complicated.

Her reverie over, Merci sensed the person next to her even before she opened her eyes.

"You pressed the call button," said the attractive flight attendant who now stood at her side. She pointed to the illuminated light on the bulkhead above Merci's seat.

Merci smiled and held up the crystal glass. "I did. Would you be so kind as to pour me another? Maybe a half this time?"

"Hard day, girlfriend?"

A narrow smile emanated from the side of her lips.

"You have no idea."

The flight attendant smiled and removed the glass from Merci's extended hand.

Five minutes later, with the second glass of liquid emptied and the alcohol pulsing through her bloodstream, Merci closed her eyes once more. This time her mind focused on the new task. She had a job, one she was told to do, not requested, a big difference from her typical practice. Merci never liked being told what to do. It rubbed her all the wrong way. She agreed to do it but only because the man who summoned her never asked anything, only told, and she felt like she had no choice. Merci was cornered, trapped.

And an animal only responds one way when backed into a corner.

Chapter 4
Manassas, Virginia
Manassas Regional Airport (HEF)

The Body Man awoke with a metallic taste in his mouth. He knew it was his own dried blood. Darkness engulfed him, but he felt the vibrations of a moving vehicle. He felt an extreme desire to throw up, but swallowed hard, pushing the bile down with a forceful gulp.

The car came to a halt with a shudder then and the engine stopped. airstairs

A moment later the trunk lid opened, and two sets of strong hands yanked him out. The hands let go of him and he struck the concrete hard, making the same sound as a bag of flour hitting a tile floor.

He saw a glimmer of light from where the hood gapped his chest. The light became short-lived as a vicious beating commenced.

The Body Man had received his fair share of ass whoopings in his younger years, but more often he had given them out. Even during his darkest of times, he'd never dared beat anyone with the ferocity his abductors railed on him.

This was calculated. Personal.

At first he'd tried to deflect and block the strikes, but they came from every direction, plus he couldn't see because of the hood and his hands were restrained behind him anyway. Instinctively he curled up in a ball and waited for more strikes to come. And they did, one after another. He suffered for minutes before blacking out.

The unmistakable smell of piss and shit greeted the Body Man when he awoke hours later. Lying in his filth, he shuddered at his own stench.

Two men came for him. He knew they were men by the sound of their steps. Men walk with a different gait than women, which he knew from years of experience on the job watching people, studying them.

One of them shuffled his feet, while the other walked with a discernible limp. One foot came down with a different intensity than the other. The two men arrived on either side, yanked him to his feet, and carried him down a flight of stairs. Neither man said a word.

His clothes were cut off and a garden hose sprayed ice-cold water over his body. The chilly water felt good on his skin, although it burned in places where open wounds covered his body. With fresh clothes pulled over his damp, naked body, the shirt and pants clung to his moist skin.

A pair of oversized hands lifted the hood high enough to force-feed him Vienna sausages, a strawberry Pop Tart, and a Snickers candy bar. Contrary to the advertisements, the Snickers did not satisfy.

Five minutes later, someone led the Body Man to an adjacent bathroom, pulled down his pants, and sat him on the toilet. He didn't like pissing like a woman, but it was far better than the alternative of warm urine running down his leg.

After he finished, still in the hood, the Body Man was shoved back inside a vehicle. He was relieved it wasn't a car trunk. The door sounded like a van's as it slid along a crooked track and slammed closed. Someone pushed him to the floorboard and the vehicle sped off.

The Body Man started to count. He reached 420, which meant only about seven or eight minutes had passed when the vehicle came to an abrupt stop.

Once the door slid open, he knew they were at an airport because he recognized the distinct sound of an auxiliary power unit plugged into a waiting plane. An APU meant the plane was a jet, and a jet meant the Body Man's trip was going to be longer than a prop plane could manage.

It must be late. The tower is probably closed unless the field is too small for FAA control. Perfect time to get someone on a plane without anyone seeing. I'd do the same thing.

Strong hands grabbed him, pulled him out of the vehicle, and led him onto the waiting plane.

One word came to mind. *Rendition.*

Spooks? A foreign agency?

The Body Man's mind raced. He knew he'd die before any secrets escaped his lips. *The capsule.* His tongue went back to the top right molar.

The capsule was gone.

But how did they know about it?

Then a realization struck him like a roll of quarters in a sock. *I may be well and truly fucked.*

With the capsule missing, the matter of his life and death no longer rested in his own hands. Others with unknown intentions held his fate. That pissed him off more than knowing he might die soon. Death was a part of life, and he didn't fear it. What he did fear was the lack of control.

For the first time since his youth, he felt vulnerable, and the taste of bile filled his mouth.

Geoff Watson heard a noise. He left the office in the rear of the building and made his way through the darkened hangar. His boots squeaked on the freshly polished floor.

It was late, and nobody should have been around.

His wife, Ann, had spent most of the day on all fours over the porcelain pony. A nasty stomach bug had made its way through the family and Geoff was hoping it would continue to skip him. With Ann unable to clean the offices at Dibaco Aviation, the responsibility had fallen to him.

The vibration caused by jet engine start-ups near the metal building shook the walls. The high-pitched noise from the turbines filled the hangar even with the big bay doors closed, and the sound startled him. Geoff walked quickly through the vast space, and the noise grew louder as he reached the front of the building.

Near the hangar doors, he moved toward the large window that overlooked the tarmac. With the blinds drawn, only the faintest amount of light from the exterior motion sensor lamps made its way through the gaps in the vertical blinds.

Geoff pulled aside one of the wide slats and peered outside.

Less than thirty feet away, an executive jet sat on the ramp. With the airstair lowered, Geoff could see part of the interior of the plane. Ann had told him she rarely saw anyone on the nights she worked, and here someone was preparing to take off.

Two bulky men descended the airstair and waited on the tarmac as if expecting an arrival. They didn't look friendly. The hairs on Geoff's arms stood up as a shiver ran through his body.

A set of headlights pierced the darkness beyond the idling plane, then a van pulled up between the hangar and the aircraft, obstructing most of Geoff's view.

Two men emerged from the van and pulled a figure out of the vehicle. They half-carried the person, who wore a hood and had hands and feet bound. A strong gust of wind blew off the man's head covering then and it landed twenty feet away from the van.

Even in the uncertain light, the hooded man looked like someone had beaten the shit out of him.

What the hell?

Geoff quick-drew his phone from a clip on his right hip and activated his cellphone's camera, holding down the camera trigger and taking one picture after another in rapid succession.

One of the men retrieved the hood from the ground and trotted back to the bound man. He pulled the hood over the bound man's head in a forceful manner.

Geoff continued to take pictures as the three men disappeared inside the plane. He zoomed in close enough to get a shot of the plane's tail number. Two men descended the airstairs and removed several bags from the van. They spoke loudly enough over the sound of the idling jet engines for Geoff to make out both voices. As soon as they opened their mouths, he knew they weren't speaking English. His first guess was Russian, although he didn't recognize one accent over another, truth be told.

His heart raced as he stood frozen.

Should I call the cops?

Immobilized by fear, he could do nothing but watch.

Two minutes later the van pulled away. The airstair rose and the jet turned toward the runway. Without stopping, it roared down the tarmac and disappeared into the pitch-dark sky.

Chapter 5
Vienna, Virginia

Eli Payne's thick knuckles struck precisely three times on the red door. He knocked hard—like cops should, he sometimes said. If the occupants weren't coming to the door on three, he believed, they weren't coming on five or six.

"There's a doorbell, you know," Stone said.

"I don't like them," Payne said. His eyes narrowed and lips pursed as he stared at his ad hoc probie partner du jour. "I prefer the feel of wood against my skin."

"Of course you do," she said and deliberately rolled her eyes.

A few seconds later the door opened only a few inches, the little brass security chain still attached. An older woman glared at them through the slim gap between the door and its frame.

Payne reached for his gold badge and creds in a leather folder and held it up to the door slot where the woman could see it at eye height.

"FBI agents, ma'am. Are you Rose Lewis?" His inflection sounded official, like he already knew her answer.

"Yes," came the reply. "That picture from your college yearbook?"

Payne's expression had indeed changed over the years since

he joined the Bureau, but his credential photo still held a passable resemblance.

He ignored her dig but dialed back the harshness in his voice.

"FBI, ma'am. You called about a missing person?"

The door closed with no response and then sound of metal sliding against metal as the security chain was released. The door opened revealing a short, older woman. Rose Lewis had an elegant look about her but had a pale complexion, like she didn't get out much, and she wore her snow-white hair pulled back in a tight dance bun. Rose wore a tan-colored floral-print dress that flowed to her ankles and a pair of red shoes, like Dorothy wore in Oz.

"I'm Special Agent Eli Payne," he said and gestured toward Stone. "This is Agent Katherine Stone. May we come in and ask you a few questions about your report?"

"Of course," said Rose, and she opened the door fully.

Rose led Payne and Stone through a dated but tastefully decorated foyer and into the living room. The room contained two taupe-colored couches with a glass coffee table between them. A fireplace with an ornate oak mantle and a large oil painting of El Capitan was in one corner of the room, while floor-to-ceiling bookshelves lined the wall behind one of the couches.

The shelves held not only books but photos and dozens of trinkets in various sizes. Several curio cabinets dotted the room filled with random items, mostly small but surely collectible except for the pile of obsolete Beanie Babies in a glass cabinet. Payne noticed the little details, and a story formed in his mind about Rose's life.

Rose Lewis noticed Payne noticing her stuff.

"My husband, Charlie, traveled extensively for work. He brought me back a little something each time he returned home," said Rose as she watched Payne scan the room. "He was thoughtful that way."

"I see," Payne said. "Is he away now?"

A sad look formed on Rose's face. "No. He passed many years ago. Cancer."

"I'm sorry for your loss," Payne said.

As quickly as the look came, it dissipated. "So am I."

Rose waved Payne and Stone to the couch on her right while she took a large, overstuffed wing chair. "Would you care for something to drink?" she asked.

"Thank you, but we're fine," Payne said.

"Let me know if you change your mind."

"We will." Payne jumped to the chase. "Now, can you tell us why you think your neighbor, Mr. Webb, has gone missing?"

"He didn't show up for our morning coffee."

Payne looked at Stone and she shrugged her shoulders in response.

"And that's unusual how?" Payne asked.

Rose said, "Ralph always comes over in the morning, seven days a week, unless he's traveling."

"Any chance he took a trip without you knowing?"

"None. Ralph was supposed to leave later this morning for a day trip and was coming back tonight. Plus, there's an upcoming trip overseas in a few weeks, one of those G-some-number meetings the president attends."

Payne couldn't hide his smirk at the G-some-number comment. "I'll be honest with you, Ms. Lewis, we don't normally assume someone is missing if they happen to skip a morning coffee. A missing child, I could see. But as for a grown adult, there are too many variables. The person really must be gone for more than a few hours before we accept they may be missing. Unless, of course, there is some evidence of them disappearing or an eyewitness to an abduction. Are either of those the case?"

"Well, no, but I'm sure he's gone. He assured me he'd be here today. And his car is gone, too."

Payne let out a discreet sigh. He needed to switch up the line of questioning.

"Sounds like you know his schedule pretty well."

"Of course. After all, I feed Ralph's cat while he's out of town."

"Can you describe your relationship with Mr. Webb?" asked Stone.

Payne turned and gave her a slight glare. They had agreed before they exited the car—he would do all the talking.

Like Payne, Stone occasionally had trouble following the rules.

"Well, Katherine, it's nothing romantic, if that's what you're implying," Rose said as her voice raised an octave.

"It's Kat, please."

Rose continued. "Lookie, dear, I have grandchildren your age. Ralph is almost thirty years younger than I am, and our relationship is purely platonic. He became a trusted friend over the past two years but nothing more. Ever since he saved me, he comes over at six-thirty a.m. sharp for coffee seven days a week before he heads to work."

"Saved you?" asked Payne.

"Yes. Ralph stopped two young men from attacking me one night while I was on a walk. I used to walk all the time in the neighborhood. Sadly, times aren't what they used to be."

"What happened?"

"Ralph came around the corner just as one of the men grabbed me. He moved like lightning—with just one punch, he laid that fella out cold. The others, well, they ran off when their friend hit the ground. Ralph let them go and focused on me."

Payne nodded sympathetically. "Sounds like he was your hero that night."

"He was."

"And when did Ralph tell you he worked at the White House?"

Payne made notes on a small black notepad as Rose spoke.

"About a year ago. I asked about his frequent travel, and Ralph admitted where he worked. Up until then, he'd talked in vague terms about a job that required him to be on the road."

"Why did he tell you he worked for the White House?"

"Not sure. I didn't gather his work was so secret. He's just a private man. Maybe I finally earned his trust. In almost four years of living across the street from him, I've rarely known him to have visitors. He has no family to speak of. It's only he and his cat."

"And what does he do at the White House?"

"He works for the president."

"Can you be more specific?" Payne asked.

Rose grew silent for a moment. "No, I can't," she finally said. "He never shared any details. It's private stuff. I don't ask, and he doesn't tell. I respect Ralph's privacy. And frankly, it's none of my business."

"It's fairly common for friends to discuss what they do at work," Kat kicked in. "Isn't that what friends do?"

"I guess so," Lewis admitted, "but his job isn't typical."

"But he told you he works directly for the president? He said those words?" Payne said.

"Yes."

"He's part of the presidential staff?"

"No."

"Then, is he a Secret Service agent?"

Rose frowned. "I know he protects the president, but that is all. Look, I've told you what I know, Agent Payne."

He scribbled a few more lines on his notepad before he looked up. "So, Ralph doesn't show up, and you call us first because he works for the White House. Correct?"

"Yes."

"Why not call the local police department?"

"I may be old, Mr. Payne, but I'm no dummy. I know how things work. The FBI is the premier organization for finding missing people, after the Marshals Service, I suppose, though they're about fugitives. Ralph's a missing federal government employee. You're a federal agency. It's simple."

"I appreciate the compliment, Rose, truly, but the FBI works closely with local law enforcement in these types of matters as well."

"Yes, I understand that, but based on what Ralph does for a living, I felt calling the FBI first was prudent."

"Fair enough. Back to the timeline. What happened after Ralph didn't show up this morning?"

"I went to his townhouse across the street to see if he was all right. Make sure nothing happened to him."

"You have a key?"

"Of course. I told you I feed his cat, Italia, when he's out of town."

"His cat is named Italia?" asked Stone.

"Yes. Ralph said he got her on a trip to Rome last year. A gift from the Pope."

Payne's eyebrows raised. "And you believed him?"

"Ralph is not a man to tell tall tales, Agent Payne. His word is his bond, he always says. But there's more than that."

Payne looked at her. His eyes narrowed, and his brow furrowed. "How so?"

"Things were out of place."

"What do you mean out of place?"

"Books stacked on the floor, papers were lying on the couch. Even the rug in his living room was rolled up."

"Maybe Ralph had to go out of town suddenly, and he was looking for something before he left?"

Rose shook her head back and forth as Payne spoke.

"I don't think so. I've never seen anything out of place at his home. Ralph's what you might call anal-retentive about his stuff. And if his schedule had changed, he would have told me."

Payne didn't want to get hung up on the condition of the man's house.

"Did you think to call the White House directly, if that's where he works?" he asked.

"No."

"Maybe they could have confirmed he left town earlier than expected for work?"

Rose said nothing in response.

Payne realized arguing with her would get them nowhere.

"You don't happen to have a photo of Ralph by chance, do you?"

"Sure, I do," said Rose as her expression changed to a smile. "Let me go grab it from the other room. Ralph wasn't keen on taking pictures, but I asked for one from time to time." She left the room and returned a moment later, clutching a four-by-six color print. "Here you go."

Payne looked at the image carefully. The man didn't look familiar. He knew a few people who worked at the White House, but not many. "Good-looking guy."

Rose blushed. "He reminds me of my Charlie when he was younger."

"Thanks for the photo. I'll get it back to you as soon as I can."

"I'd appreciate that."

Payne looked over his notes and thought for a moment. "Ms. Lewis, I know you said Ralph is private and doesn't discuss what he does at the White House, but did you notice anything different about him lately? Has he acted out of sorts, not like himself?"

Rose lowered her eyes but remained silent. Payne could see her eyes flutter back and forth.

After a long pause, Rose said, "Well, he has been a little distant recently."

"Since when?"

"The past few weeks."

"Anything in particular that stands out?"

"He made comments about what I should do if anything happened to him. That made me nervous."

"And was that out of character?"

"Highly. He's never said anything like before."

"And?"

"He asked if I would take care of Italia," Lewis said.

"That's it?"

"It's the only thing I can think of, yes."

"Do you think he knew he might be in danger?" Stone asked.

"I don't know. We weren't *that* close." Rose's hands fidgeted in her lap. She really was concerned. "Please find him, Agent Payne."

"We'll do our best, Ms. Lewis," Payne said.

The conversation carried on for several more minutes. Payne and Stone thanked Rose Lewis for her time and assured her they would be in touch soon. The last thing Payne did was give her his card and told her to call anytime if she thought of something else that might help.

As Payne and Stone left the house and walked toward the car, he couldn't shake a feeling that someone had eyes on him. Payne paused right in the middle of the road, the hair on the back of his neck standing up. He scanned the street in a grid pattern, looking for anything out of the ordinary. Nothing stood out and the neighborhood appeared quiet.

His senses told him otherwise.

Something was off.

Stone took several steps past him, then came to a stop. She

turned back. "What is it?"

"Nothing," he said after a few seconds. "Just a feeling."

"Good or bad?"

"I'm not quite sure."

They continued to Payne's G-car, and he scanned the block once more standing next to the car door.

"What about Rose? Is she bat-shit crazy, or is this Ralph Webb guy missing?" Stone asked as she climbed into the car.

Payne dropped into the driver's seat, buckled up and started the car. As he pulled away, he shook his head with a frown.

"I think *she* believes he's missing," Payne said. "She seemed sincere in her answers, but I do think she is holding out on us."

"How so?" Stone asked, reaching for her seat belt.

"Just her body language when she told us about him asking her to keep the cat."

"What about it?"

"There's something she didn't tell us."

"Thoughts on what it is?"

Payne shook his head. "Not yet."

"What's next?"

He smirked. "We get an introduction from downtown, and we head to the White House."

Stone side-eyed him. "Seriously?"

"Yes. We can't discount her story out-of-hand. I need to see if this Ralph Webb exists before we put out a want on a guy who just as easily might have gone fishing in the Virginia mountains."

"And you're going to march up to the front door of the White House?"

"Well, not the front door, no. More like the side door."

"You know what I meant. Why go there?"

"No reason to beat around the bush. We go to the source and see what we can find out."

Payne fumbled for his old-school flip phone to call FBI Head-quarters and the White House Liaison Office. He preferred burners because he was paranoid, though he categorized it as merely cautious. Paid for them out of his own pocket, too, so that he wasn't required to turn in any receipts or phone records without a court order.

Stone didn't respond to the comment but instead handed him the photo Rose Lewis had provided. "Something is wrong with this picture."

Payne stopped in mid-dial and closed the phone.

"How so?"

"The man in this photo. He isn't a Ralph."

"Huh?"

"His name isn't Ralph, I'm telling you. He doesn't look like a Ralph to me."

Payne's cheeks moved toward his eyes. The motion caused his pronounced crow's feet to stand out as he squinted. "And what does a person with the name Ralph look like, exactly?"

Stone pointed at the photo with a red-tipped index finger. "Not this."

Payne rolled his eyes. "Whatever."

"You don't think people can look like their names?"

"Never really thought about it, I guess," Payne said.

"What if I introduced myself as Jasmine when we met earlier today?"

Payne let out a chuckle. "Well, I'd say you were either a stripper or your parents were Disney freaks."

She rolled her eyes. "I think you just made my point."

"Or I gave you a not-too-subtle ribbing."

Stone ignored the statement. "Look, I'm telling you it isn't his real name," she said, pulling her out phone. "This is one of those inscrutable natural talents women have that men don't, like knowing when you're lying, or being friends with men without needing to sleep with them."

Payne just smiled but Stone reached for her iPhone Xs Max. It stood in sharp contrast to Payne's 1990s technology. "Who are you calling, your parents?" Payne smirked.

"No, smartass. I'm confirming if Ralph Webb even owns the townhouse across the street. I'll have Jessie back at the office run the property info down. And while he's at it, I'll have him see if Mr. Webb owns a vehicle and get its info."

"Who's Jessie?"

"Jessie James works on the second floor. He's the guy to contact if I need any data from other agencies, places like the DMV."

"You're saying we have a guy named Jessie James at the office?"

"Yes."

"Do we have a William H. Bonney who works our bank robbery cases as well?"

"Who's that?"

"You serious?"

"I am."

"Billy the Kid. Ever heard of him?"

Stone looked thoughtful for a moment. "Didn't Emilio Estevez play him in that 1980s movie *Young Guns*?"

"You've seen that movie?"

"Sure, my Dad liked watching it when I was a kid."

Payne shook his head. "Who said to go to Jessie?"

"My first day on the job, I was given a list of resources by the special agent who taught the new-recruit Indoc class."

"Huh, imagine that."

"I take it you didn't get a list when you started?"

"Not as I recall," Payne said.

"And what do you do when you need something?"

Payne half-smiled. "I yell, really loud."

"At?"

"Everyone. Until someone gets off their ass and gets me what I need."

"You must be a hell of a first date. I guess that's why no one likes you."

"Sweet. My charm offensive is working."

Payne flipped open his phone to call the liaison office and get their White House introduction.

A man sat slumped down in the car at the end of the street. His ball cap pulled low. He sat up after Payne pulled away and dialed a number.

"What," said the voice who answered.

"We may have a problem."

"What type of problem?"

"The old woman."

"The neighbor?"

"Yes."

"What about her?"

"She called the feds."

"Old news. We are aware of that already."

"They just left her house."

"So?"

"The front room windows were open. I used the directional microphone and was able to catch some of their conversations."

"What did she say?"

"The old woman knew something was wrong inside the house. That we went through his stuff."

"We don't need any complications."

"I understand. What do you want me to do?"

A pause occurred before the man responded. "Sit tight. Keep

an eye on her. I'll make some calls."

"I need to get back into his house. We didn't find it yet."

"Negative, too much heat right now, and certainly not in the daytime. We have to wait until things die down."

"And in the meantime?"

"Observe and report. When that changes, I'll let you know."

"There's another thing."

"Yes?"

"The two FBI agents are headed for the White House."

"What's your point?"

"Shouldn't we warn somebody?"

"No. That's not our problem either. It's his problem."

Chapter 6
The White House
Washington, DC

President Charles Steele sank into his favorite Chesterfield leather chair and let out a deep sigh as his body relaxed. He reached up with his left hand and rubbed his temples. His right hand held a tumbler of Woodford Reserve, the amber liquid drowning quarter-sized ice balls. Steele loosened the red tie he'd had on since seven that morning. He placed his feet on the walnut desk and leaned back.

The chair had been a gift from Queen Elizabeth II when she'd visited the previous fall. Six months before her trip to the United States, the president had traveled to England and was a guest in Buckingham Palace. He'd loved the ornate furniture and spent many hours touring the palace with his protective detail and a royal tour guide.

During his stay, he'd taken an interest in one of the queen's antique chairs, commenting on it several times. After the visit, the queen had commissioned an exact replica made for the president, which he'd accepted during her state visit to the White House.

His day had started at five-thirty a.m., as it had every day since he'd taken the oath of office. The full presidential entourage had left Joint Base Andrews at eleven a.m. for a few mid-term election campaign stops and arrived back at the White House around six p.m. In the Oval Office, the president had signed paperwork and reviewed three executive orders before a late dinner with his wife in the residential dining room, then the president retreated to the private study adjoining the Oval after dinner.

Steele appreciated comfort and an element of normalcy, and his private study offered him both things. When he closed the door to his sanctuary, everybody in the building knew to leave him alone. A Secret Service man stood silently outside the polished oak door to ensure it.

Tonight, President Steele made the mistake of leaving the door cracked. Not wide open, but not fully closed.

The president had two files on his desk. The top one was a red folder containing an intel report brought in earlier from the Secretary of Defense. The one on the bottom was jet black, and nobody—not even the senior members of the president's staff—touched it. With his family name embossed on the top in bold golden letters, the contents were for the president's eyes only.

Although the information inside the black folder gnawed at him, he decided to open the red file. The president leaned back in the chair and stretched his arms back over his head. A distinct cracking sound filled the room as his back popped. His back had done that since he'd played football at Boston.

A knock on the door startled him. "Yes?" the president said in an irritated tone. His feet came off the desk as the door slipped inward and he instantly regretted his irked response. His staff had tough jobs and sought only to serve him and their nation, and they didn't need extra attitude from their boss.

President Steele's chief of staff, Jacob Sterns, poked his head inside. "Sorry to intrude, Mr. President, but the door was ajar."

"Yes, well, I meant to close that damn thing."

"My apologies, sir."

"I'm sure it's important, Jake. What's up?"

Sterns cleared his throat. "I have an update for you, sir."

"Regarding?"

"It's about Danny, sir."

President Steele's scowl softened. "Is he out of surgery?"

"The hospital called. Well, I should say the surgeon himself called."

"And?"

"He's alive. The doctor is not sure how he made it through the surgery, but the initial post-op scans appear promising."

"Permanent damage?"

"Too early to tell, but if he lives he'll never walk again. According to the doctor, the slug missed the left carotid artery by only a few millimeters."

"Meaning?"

"He's one lucky son of a bitch, Mr. President."

"Will he recover?"

"No way to know for sure right now, sir. He's on a ventilator and in a medically induced coma. The doctor said he had a ten percent chance of surviving the surgery based on the head trauma he sustained."

"The other wounds? The ones to his back?"

"Amazingly, those bullets did no damage to his internal organs but the one just shattered his spine."

The president nodded and smiled grimly. "The Secret Service attracts a unique breed, don't they?"

"I agree. The best of the best, Mr. President."

"Danny's a fighter. If anyone can beat this, he can."

"You're right, sir."

"Was the witness to the attack able to provide anything useful?"

"Not much. Too far away, really." Sterns crossed his arms over his crisply pressed suit. Jake Sterns was a fastidious dresser and rarely sat or crossed his arms in meetings because he abhorred wrinkles in his clothes. "She believed the shooter was female, but the dress and physical description apply to most joggers running along the Potomac, male or female. The eyewitness said the shooter jumped into a waiting van and fled the scene. DC Metro found the van torched in Southeast near the Navy Yard a few hours ago."

Sterns lingered even though the president said nothing. One doesn't depart until excused. Finally, the awkward moment passed.

"Is that all?" asked the president.

"No, sir. "

"What is it?"

"I need to talk with you about the Body Man, Mr. President."

"Has he been found?" the president asked, unease evident in his tone.

"No," came the reply. "And we're concerned that he goes missing, and then someone tries to murder his apprentice on the same day—within hours of each other. I know you have concerns about both incidents."

The president frowned. Questions about how he felt irritated him. He exhaled a deep breath. "Yes, of course I'm troubled," he said, as if the answer was obvious.

"Secret Service believes they must be related," Sterns said.

"Yes, I don't believe in coincidences either," the president said, "but we must have more facts before drawing any conclusions."

"Have you spoken with Dave Kline?"

"Not since earlier today from Air Force One, but I can assure you the director of the Secret Service is taking today's events very seriously, as he should."

"And in the meantime, is he appointing someone to take the Body Man's place?"

"I think that's a little premature, don't you?"

"We need a Body Man, Mr. President. You need one."

The president's eyes visibly rolled. "'Need' may be a stretch, Jacob."

Sterns bristled at the president's cool remark. "Well, I'd feel better if you had one."

"No president had a Body Man before Kennedy," the president said with an annoyed look. *And I'm no JFK*, he thought.

"And all of them have had one since, sir."

The president turned his head away and looked at the wall where a painting of John D. Rockefeller hung. He admired leadership figures from many realms.

"Well, let's do our jobs and let David and his team do theirs. Goodnight, Jacob. Don't work too late. Get home to Amy and the kids."

"Thank you, Mr. President. Enjoy the rest of your night." Sterns nodded, turned and left, careful to pull the door fully closed on his way out by making sure he heard the distinct click of the latch.

Just as the door shut, Steele's private phone line rang. He looked at the number in Caller ID with no change in expression.

Then the President of the United States opened the black folder on his desk and reached for the phone.

Chapter 7
Washington, DC

It was supposed to be an easy hit. Even a gangbanger from the streets could have pulled it off—*especially* a gangbanger. They should have just gotten one of those.

The handler had vouched for her, even going as far as claiming she was the best female assassin in the world. However, shooting Danny Frazier hadn't been enough. He needed to die, and he wasn't dead.

The man growled audibly, his frustration growing stronger as each second passed. His hands curled into balls, and he struck the table several times in anger. Finally, after he'd collected his thoughts and compartmentalized his emotions, he reached into the drawer and pulled out a new burner phone.

The call recipient answered on the second ring.

"You've got a problem," said the man, not even waiting for the person to speak.

"I have a problem, or we have a problem?"

"The asset fucked up. Now you have a problem."

"What are you talking about?"

"The mark is still alive."

Silence ensued for almost ten seconds before the reply.

"That's not possible. He took two slugs in his back and one in his skull at point-blank range. Nobody survives that."

"Well, I guess Danny Frazier is a tough bastard."

"How?"

"I don't know how he fucking survived, but he's still sucking air, albeit through a plastic tube."

"And what do you want me to do about it?"

"Where is she?"

"Who?"

"Merci. The best female assassin in the world, according to you, though I think she will lose a few rank points after this screwup. Is she still in the States?"

"You know better than to use actual names on cell calls. The NSA can—"

"I don't give a flying fuck about the NSA or their PRISM capabilities. And besides, I'm on a burner."

"That is irrelevant; it doesn't—"

The angry man cut him off. "What I care about is the job being done and done right. So, answer my damn question."

"No, she is not still in the States. She boarded a flight out of Dulles several hours ago."

"Why?"

"She was given another assignment."

"By whom?"

"Himself."

"You spoke with him personally?"

"No. But she did."

"He didn't inform me."

"Is he in the habit of excluding you?"

The angry man ignored the question. "Well, clearly he chose her for another task before he knew of her failure."

"What do you want me to do about it? What's done is done."

"She needs to be neutralized."

"That's out of the question."

"And how do you know she won't fail at the next task?"

"She won't."

"And if you're wrong?"

"I'll put two slugs between her eyes myself."

The angry man considered the statement. "Fine. For now, she lives. But ..." His voice lingered without finishing the thought.

"But what?"

"We still have the apprentice to deal with."

"We?"

The angry man paused. "Well, no. You."

"Where is he?"

"George Washington University Hospital."

"And what do you want me to do about it?"

"Finish the fuckin' job."

"What's Frazier's condition?" Rollings asked.

"Bad. He's in a medically induced coma."

"Sounds like he's pretty well taken care of."

"If he has breath in his lungs, he's a threat to us." The angry man paused and added, "All of us."

"I thought he hadn't spoken with the Body Man?"

"We can't be sure what Danny knows, so just go finish the damn job."

"Is he guarded?"

The angry man snorted. "Does McDonald's have golden arches? The Secret Service isn't too keen on one of their agents getting gunned down in cold blood."

"Getting to Danny alone on the running trail was straightforward. Killing him now won't be."

"Then it should have done right the first time, and we wouldn't be having this conversation, would we?"

"This will take some planning."

"Jesus, you have a firm grasp of the obvious. If he wakes up and starts talking, the morgue will be accepting additional guests. You're smart enough to realize who at least one of them will be."

"Look, I'll get to him, all right? But I'll need to be creative."

"And fast."

"I get it. I won't fail you."

"That's the spirit. See, you catch on fast."

With that, the line went dead.

Several minutes of silence passed as Marcus Rollings held the phone in his hand.

Shit.

He picked up a clean burner phone and made a call across the pond. He didn't wait for the man who answered to say anything.

"What time does her plane land?" Rollings asked.

"Three hours," said the man on the other end.

"And where is she staying?"

"One of the safe houses in the countryside. Her new target is currently in Reims."

"I need to speak with her as soon as possible. Tell her to call in when she gets a secure line."

"We both know she marches to her own drum."

"Trust me, I know that better than most. But I still need to pass along time-sensitive information."

"I'll have her call you as soon as she checks in."

Rollings clicked off the line and fired up his laptop. Within a few minutes he had a detailed map showing the layout of the George Washington University Hospital.

It was going to be a late night, and it started right now. He flicked on a music file on the laptop to play Colin James wailing *Just Came Back (To Say Goodbye).*

Chapter 8
At 36,000 feet AGL

A steady whine from the engines and the heavily accented voices of his captors filled the Body Man's head once the plane took off. Thirty minutes had passed since they'd shoved him in the seat—at least that's what his internal clock told him. He'd learned the arcane time accounting method from a Danish fighter pilot, a man so skilled and reliable that he was trusted to fly his nation's royal family.

With his head covered by a hood, his sense of hearing had become more acute. If he moved his head far enough back, the bottom part of the hood expanded to reveal his waist, part of his legs, and his hands. Using his limited peripheral vision, he saw the flexicuffs his captors had used to bind his hands.

The thick black plastic restraints looked like standard-issue double restraints with pull loops, the kind used by police forces and military units around the world. Simple yet efficient, they were easily purchased on countless websites for a few dollars apiece. A thin zip tie ran through the thick plastic and under the seat, keeping his hands from moving more than six inches or so in any direction.

If only I had a piece of Kevlar cord to cut through them.

But he didn't.

The cabin sounds changed, and the voices trailed off, moving away until only the engine noise resonated in his ears. A distinct click sound indicated a door closing.

He had only seen the outline of the plane briefly on the tarmac as his hood blew off but felt certain his captors were using a Bombardier Challenger 350 to abduct him. A jet enthusiast, he knew the configuration of most private planes, especially the larger ones with military versions. As a Secret Service agent, he had the added perk of flying on many airplanes in the US government fleet.

If I could only break free from these restraints and block the galley door somehow, I might have a chance to breach the cockpit and take control of the aircraft. Maybe force it to land somewhere and make a play for my freedom.

But first, before he could act on his impulse, the Body Man needed his hands free.

He leaned slightly forward and pulled his flexed biceps toward his chest like he was doing an imaginary barbell curl, and using all his strength, strained and applied maximum pressure to the flexicuffs and the thin zip tie that connected them to the seat. He let out a muffled grunt, and the sudden *pop* sound as plastic snapped let him know the thinner zip tie had broken. His restrained hands hit hard against his chest, and he stayed still, listened intently, wondering if anyone had heard the noise.

With his hands able to move, he reached up and pulled off the hood. It took several seconds for his eyes to adjust to the cabin lighting, but once they'd focused, he looked around for anything useful to remove the restraints. His eyes zeroed in on a piece of metal that protruded from under the leather seat facing his.

Reaching down he used the exposed metal to saw at the plastic cuffs. The process was slow and arduous, but within minutes he had both hands free. He stood and suddenly froze. Two rows forward, a bald head cleared the top of a seat.

How did he not hear me?

With slow, measured steps he approached the seated man and without giving him time to react, got his thickly muscled arms wrapped around the man's neck. The Body Man performed a perfect carotid restraint, also known in bar fights as a sleeper hold. The bald man slumped over unconscious within seconds.

He quickly scanned the rest of the cabin and found no one. His eyes darted back and forth as he looked for something, anything he could use to block the rear door leading to the galley, where he believed the other bad actors must be.

The fold-out executive table caught his eye. He moved toward it and, reaching underneath, found a release switch. The table came off its pedestal, and he moved to the aft of the plane. Two high-backed flight attendant jump seats rested directly against the rear bulkhead on either side of the aft galley door. The Body Man figured he could slide the table between the seats and the wall, wedging the door in a closed position and trapping any other of his captors.

Once the galley door was secured, he would need to breach the closed cockpit door and somehow take command of the aircraft. That door might well be easier. Since the pilots probably needed to be available to the kidnappers, the Body Man thought the door to the flight deck might be unlocked. He didn't intend to fool around taking chances.

He picked up the table and pushed it down between the seats and the galley bulkhead. Confident it was secure, he turned and headed down the aisle toward the closed cockpit door. Behind him, he immediately heard someone trying to open the jammed galley door to no avail.

He knew firsthand that private planes didn't have hardened

flight deck doors like commercial airliners. The cockpit doors on the major carriers can withstand an enormous amount of pressure, but that isn't the case with small jets.

Eight feet from the cockpit door he lowered his right arm and turned his body slightly, leading with the thickest part of his shoulder. Running at the bulkhead, the Body Man slammed into the door with his full body mass. The door gave way with a loud splintering sound as the door swung to one side and his body powered into the narrow cockpit.

On the right, the co-pilot instantly reached down to his black map case and pulled a Smith & Wesson .40-caliber pistol, bringing it up to the Body Man's chest. The co-pilot was fast, but his skills paled in comparison to the Body Man's abilities. Before the co-pilot could depress the trigger, the Body Man grabbed the gun and in one lightning-fast motion spun the weapon around in the man's hands and trained it on him instead.

The co-pilot's eyes grew wide with surprise.

The Body Man didn't hesitate. Rage coursed through his body, like a rush of adrenaline.

He placed his fingertip on the trigger, angled the weapon hard against the co-pilot's chest in case the rounds went sideways—after all, they were in a pressurized airplane in flight—and pulled twice in rapid succession. The slugs slammed through the man's chest, the rear bulkhead, and the first three rows of seats, and two crimson spots spread over the co-pilot's pressed white shirt just left of his black tie. The Body Man watched as the life departed the copilot's eyes. It was over in seconds.

Momentarily deaf from the gunshots, he spun toward the pilot, who had been stunned by the fast action he'd just witnessed.

But he recovered quickly.

The Body Man suddenly felt the floor drop out from beneath him as his body pitched up toward the ceiling of the flight deck.

For seconds he was weightless, like the feeling of freefall when he used to skydive in his early twenties.

As he smacked hard against the lightly padded aluminum fuselage, he saw the pilot had pushed the yoke to the instrument panel, nosing the aircraft over into a steep dive.

If the pilot's goal was to throw the Body Man for a loop, he'd succeeded. But he didn't know the Body Man was intensely trained to work best under the most extreme circumstances.

The pilot had thought throwing him into the ceiling would knock him out, but by the time the pilot pulled back to level out the plane, the Body Man landed fully conscious on his feet and wrapped his left arm around the pilot's neck, pressing the cold barrel of the pistol firmly against the pilot's temple.

With gun pressed against flesh, the Body Man started a slow squeeze with the arm around the pilot's dark neck.

"Do you speak English?" the Body Man demanded. The pilot nodded affirmatively as best he could with a thick arm lodged under his chin.

"Say the words," the Body Man commanded.

"I speak English," the pilot croaked.

"Your asshole buddies are stuck in the galley and no cavalry is coming to rescue you. "You will put this bird on the ground right *now*," he yelled, still partially deaf from the gunshots in close quarters. His voice sounded harsh, gravelly. "Because if I have to kill you, it won't end well for any of us. Autopilot. Do it."

The pilot gave a strained head nod and pushed a button that lit up green on both sides, then took his right hand from the control wheel. At the same time, his left hand slowly reached down into the pocket hanging on the side of the seat where he removed a Gerber StrongArm serrated fixed-blade knife, keeping it low.

The Body Man continued to apply pressure but turned to check his six when he thought he heard a sound that might have been the other guys breaking down the galley door. The pilot saw the head movement and with his left hand swung the blade wildly toward the Body Man's exposed neck. He missed his intended target and punctured the top of a bicep, pushing the knife into flesh and twisting.

The Body Man cried out and his head snapped back toward the pilot. He screamed in pain as he pulled back his arm. His natural reflex was to deliver a vicious blow to the side of the pilot's head with the gun butt—because if he shot the pilot, like he wanted to, the rest of the flight would last only as long as the fuel.

The tan blade handle grossly protruded from his arm. It waggled back and forth before his wide, shocked eyes, mocking him and his inattention. He never got the chance to strike back.

A black aluminum Maglite ML300L flashlight—heavy and four D-cells long—crashed the top of his head with the force of a major-leaguer's Louisville Slugger. There was instant blackness and the ringing in his ears faded.

Two burly escapees from the galley dragged the Body Man's unconscious form out of the cockpit, then secured him, ankles and wrists, to a different seat with four sets of chrome handcuffs. They yanked out the knife protruding from his arm and wrapped the bleeding wound.

Then the biggest of the Body Man's captors took the seat facing him, holding the knife that still dropped blood onto the dark brown carpeting of the aircraft.

Chapter 9
Washington, DC

Payne could see Stone glaring at him as he pulled off Interstate 66 onto the E Street Expressway.

"What?" he asked.

"Are you going to share your plan with me, or are we walking up to the White House unannounced?"

"Relax. I know what I'm doing."

Stone shot him a glance that made it clear she wasn't convinced. "And that is?"

"I'm going where leads take us."

"Straight to the front door of the White House?"

"Nope, still the side door. But it's the People's House, right? So, it's our *casa* too. Plus, our White House Liaison Office got us an appointment to see Senior Aide Whoever, so we're expected."

"Uh-huh." Stone pursed her lips.

"Look, if this Webb guy worked for the Department of Motor Vehicles, we'd head to the DMV. If he worked at Domino's, we'd go there, eat a shitty pizza, and spend the rest of the day on the crapper. But this Webb guy reportedly works at 1600 Pennsylvania Avenue, so that's where we go. It's simple, really."

"You sure they'll even let us on the property?"

"I'm sure. But there's only one way to find out."

"You'd better not derail my career before it starts, Payne."

He smiled and made an exaggerated wink. "Trust me. I know what I'm doing."

"An ex-boyfriend tried that line on me once. That's why he's my ex now."

"You're funny, Stone." Payne threw her a sideways glance. "And I'm not surprised you're single."

"Guess it takes a ballbuster to know one," she said.

As he took the turn onto 15th Street NW, the entrance to the White House grounds on E Street NW was on the left. His body tensed as he pulled in behind a silver Mercedes with DC plates.

The man at the checkpoint waved him forward when the Mercedes moved on. "Can I help you, sir?"

Payne displayed his FBI credentials, as did Stone.

The man's eyes narrowed as he scrutinized both badges.

"Special Agents Eli Payne and Katherine Stone. We have an appointment with Mark Hancock?"

"Hold tight for a minute, Agent Payne." The agent turned, entered the small guard house and picked up a phone while tapping on a computer keyboard. He turned back several times and eyed Payne and Stone as he spoke into the receiver.

A minute later he returned and handed the credentials back. "You're confirmed, sir."

He handed Payne two oversize blue plastic cards attached to beaded chains. The center of the blue card had a large white V, for Visitor, and on a white field under the blue was the word ESCORTED in fire-engine red with a black bar code.

"Put these on for me such that they are visible at all times." He pointed forward. "Pull up there and take your first right, then park in any open space on the left-hand side. An agent will meet you at your vehicle and escort you to your next stop."

Payne nodded and did as instructed.

"Well, made it past the front gate," Payne said as he pulled forward.

"Guess you piqued their curiosity," replied Stone.

"We'll see what it does beyond that."

An imposing man dressed in a navy-blue suit with a white curly wire leading from his collar to his ear was at the side of the car within seconds of Payne putting the car in park.

Payne stepped out and the large man extended his hand. "Mr. Hancock is called away. I'm Brandon Walker, Special Agent, White House Detail."

"Special Agent Eli Payne, FBI, and this is my colleague Agent Katherine Stone."

Walker shook their hands. The first thing Payne noticed was the man had a grip that could crush barbecue charcoal into industrial diamonds. Next, he observed the man's stare. It was penetrating and not overtly friendly.

"Please follow me," Walker said.

Payne and Stone followed a step behind the towering figure. As they approached the building from the east, Payne recalled taking the White House tour as a teenager, back when it was easy to get tickets, way pre-9/11 and before the world and Washington security changed forever.

Times are different now, and not really for the better, Payne thought.

He hesitated as they crossed the threshold to the east entrance. Memories of her raced through his mind. He hadn't expected this reaction, not after so much time had passed. Always good at compartmentalizing, Payne had believed the feelings were locked away where they belonged.

They weren't.

Stone noticed the hesitation. "You good, bud?"

"Yeah," Payne said. "Just thinking."

"For a change, huh? I saw the steam." But she smiled.

As Payne and Stone stepped inside the building, they found four large men with serious expressions and physical builds similar to Agent Walker's. A metal detector blocked the way forward and an X-ray machine stood to its right.

"I'll need you both to surrender your weapons," Walker said.

"You got it, boss." Without hesitation Payne removed a Glock 22 from his belt holster, then pulled up his pant leg and unstrapped a Walther PK380. He dropped them into a gray plastic bin, and Stone did the same with her Bureau-issued Glock 23.

Once through security, and with the V-for-Visitor passes prominently displayed, Payne and Stone were led by Agent Walker down the Center Hall and past the North Hall, where they took a right and entered the Secret Service offices. Guiding them through several rooms, he turned into a conference room and closed the door behind them.

He pointed to two chairs. "Please," he said as he gestured to the chairs.

Payne and Stone took their seats as instructed and Walker took a chair opposite them and facing the conference room door

"You're working a missing-person case," Walker said without preamble. His face didn't forecast any hint of interest.

"We are," Payne said.

"And you believe the person in question may work in the White House for the Secret Service?"

"That's correct."

"What's his or her name?"

"Ralph Webb."

Barely a second passed before he responded. "No one by that name works here."

"You sure?"

"You'll understand that I know all my people here every hour of every day, Agent Payne, and I can assure you there is no Ralph Webb at the White House. Maybe he's over at Treasury or assigned somewhere else? It's a big government. Lots of federal agents around."

Payne looked at Stone. She raised her eyebrows and nodded subtly.

Payne said, "We have some reason to believe the name is a fake. The missing guy's elderly neighbor who made the missing-person call might have been provided an alias to protect his identity."

"Or the neighbor is mistaken," he countered.

"Of course, we're considering that too."

Walker asked, "Any chance you have a photograph of your guy? It would help."

Payne removed the photo Rose Lewis provided from his pocket and slid it across the table.

Agent Walker leaned over and looked down at the picture without touching it, his eyes blinking faster than before.

Is he afraid he'll leave fingerprints for me? Payne thought and watched the reaction on his face. "Have you ever seen that man?"

"Never." Agent Walker looked up and to the right.

Payne noticed the tell. As did Stone. As the polygraph examiner would say, *deception indicated.*

"You're sure?"

"Positive. I take it this is your Mr. Webb?"

"It is," Payne said.

"Let me run the name through our database," Walker said. Like I suggested, maybe this Ralph Webb works at another location. I'll be right back."

Agent Walker left the room and closed the door.

"Not often you find yourself in the White House," Stone said.

"And piss off the Secret Service at the same time," replied Payne. "Man, and I thought the FBI was full of dilettantes."

"He did look mad, didn't he?"

"More like he didn't want to soil his hands cooperating with a 'lesser agency.' These Secret Service guys are wired pretty tight—and the White House detail is the tightest of them all. Trust me, they don't like it when the Bureau shows up on the property."

"A little fed rivalry?"

"Something like that." Payne rolled his eyes.

The conference room door opened three minutes later, and Agent Walker stepped inside. He didn't sit.

"Well, I hate that you had to drive all the way down here, but there's no Ralph Webb in our system." He stepped toward the door. "So, if there's nothing else …"

That was quick, thought Payne.

Stone didn't move.

"He doesn't work for me or at the White House in any capacity. I can assure you of that."

Payne retrieved the picture and stood up. "I appreciate your time, Agent Walker. Sorry if you feel we wasted it."

"Merely doing your job, Agent Payne. Trust me, I get it. And I hope this Ralph Webb turns up safe and sound really soon."

"As do I." Payne paused at the door. "Oh, one more question."

"What?" There was no mistaking the perturbed *What now?* tone from Agent Walker.

"You don't have any missing agents, do you?"

"Of course not. All my people are accounted for."

"Okay," Payne said. "That's what I thought. Thanks again."

Mila Hall stepped out of the Palm Room and entered the

Center Hall on her way to the Secret Service offices on the ground floor for a venue assessment meeting. She was late, and Mila Hall hated being late. Several steps into the Center Hall, her body jerked to a stop as she saw the distinct profile of a familiar man taking a left-hand turn and walking in the opposite direction. Even though it had happened in a split second, she had no doubt who she'd seen.

What is he doing here?

Her heart rate amplified, and the muscles in her shoulders constricted as she watched him walk side by side down the Center Hall with a woman she didn't recognize. They took a sharp left at the end of the corridor and disappeared.

Once he was out of sight Mila quickened her pace and entered the small waiting area in the Secret Service office suite.

"Sandy," she asked the woman who sat behind the reception desk, "who were the man and woman who just left?"

"Two FBI agents," responded Sandy.

"What were they here for?"

"They met with Agent Walker."

"What was it about?" Hall asked, a touch of concern in her voice.

Sandy silently tilted her head and shrugged. *Who knows?*

Hall turned and looked at her watch. Her meeting was about to start.

I wonder how much Payne knows?

Once Payne and Stone were inside the car with the doors closed, he started the engine and they looked at each other.

"He lied to us," Stone said. "On top of being a total asshole."

"I agree on both counts."

"You could see it in his eyes."

"Yeah, as soon as he saw that picture. But did you notice he didn't claim to recognize the name?" asked Payne.

"Yes, I picked up on that."

"Interesting." Payne stroked his chin.

"Rumor around the office is that you're a pretty well-connected guy," Stone said. "Know people in almost every agency."

"True."

"But no Secret Service contacts?"

"I had one, once." Payne didn't elaborate.

"And?" Stone pressed.

Payne frowned. "It didn't thrive."

"You piss the guy off with your world-class charm?" she asked with a faint smile.

Payne raised his eyebrows. "I never said it was a he, did I?"

"Ah, the plot thickens. What's next then, Casanova?"

"We need to get inside Mr. Webb's townhouse. Or whatever the hell his name is." Payne looked at his watch. "I'd prefer first thing in the morning since it'll be dark by the time we get there. I would rather work a scene in the daylight with a rested set of eyes."

Stone smirked. "And the fact that the kick-off is in less than an hour?"

"Never crossed my mind," Payne said with a wry grin.

"You lie as well as Agent Walker."

They rode in silence for a minute before Stone's cellphone rang.

Payne only heard one side of the brief conversation.

"Sounds like you got an update?"

"Yes, that was Jessie," Stone said. "He ran the property records, and the townhouse is registered under the name—wait for it—Ralph Webb. He bought it about four years ago along with a 1996 silver-in-color Nissan Maxima four-door acquired about the same time. Nissan's registered to the same name at the townhouse address."

Payne nodded. "Good work."

"It's still not his real name. No matter what the property records or DMV might say. So, to me, this suggests a level of throw-weight that enables, pardon the expression, 'genuine false documents.' He had to have genuine-issue but fake docs to buy the townhouse and register the car in the fake identity."

"I agree."

Stone was feeling a little smug that Payne agreed with her investigative assumptions. "Plan of attack tomorrow?" she asked.

"We need to confirm whether he's really missing or not. And figuring out his real identity would be a good start as well."

"Sounds pretty straightforward, right?"

"Not exactly. Things that seem easy often take the longest time."

"Guess I have a lot to learn."

"It never stops, Stone. Once you think you've got it all figured out, something invariably helps pull the rug out from under you."

"You are so cynical," Stone said.

"I prefer to be thought of as a pragmatist."

Stone smiled. "Okay then—*really* cynical."

Chapter 10
The Gulf of Mexico

The jet's tires screeched when rubber met concrete and a shudder through the fuselage jostled the Body Man awake.

He tried to move, but his captors had restrained his upper body and legs after the incident in the cockpit. He didn't know how long he'd been out. Slumped to one side, he fought a wave of nausea. His head felt like Lars Ulrich had used his skull to drum a Metallica power song in an endless loop. Swallowing hard, he pushed down the urge to vomit and forced himself upright. His arm throbbed from the knife wound, and he wondered which hurt worse, his head or arm.

He went with the head.

With the hood again keeping him in relative darkness, he cocked his head slightly and listened. Several voices spoke in his vicinity, but their muted tones prevented him from making out specific words. The voices grew louder as someone approached and he made out a few words from at least two men. They both spoke English but with heavy accents that sounded Eastern European.

Russian maybe? One of the Baltic States?

One of his captors cut the restraint that kept his feet bound together. It felt good to move his feet back and forth independent of each other and regain some circulation in them. The freedom of movement was short-lived though, as one of the captors jerked him upwards.

His feet didn't touch the floor as the two men carried him sideways down the narrow aisle of the plane. His knees hit the seats as they hauled him toward the front. At the top of the airstairs, the unmistakable thumping sound of rotor wash filled his ears.

From a plane to a chopper.

Once inside the helo his captors restrained him once again. Within seconds the helicopter ascended rapidly, and his ears popped from the pressure change. The sound of the rotors meant he couldn't make out any voices. The only noise he heard was the rhythmic beat of the helicopter.

With nothing else to do he started to do the Danish time count in his head. Time slowed to a snail's pace as the chopper moved toward the unknown. Fortunately, his years in the Secret Service had taught him invaluable skills, the primary one being patience.

As they descended and finally touched down, he calculated they had traveled for roughly ten minutes.

The door to the left slid open, and he immediately recognized the smell wafting past his nose. Having grown up in Kill Devil Hills on the Outer Banks of North Carolina, he knew the unmistakable scent from miles away.

Saltwater, with a petroleum topspin.

The Body Man had lived the salt life for much of his adolescence. He missed the ocean. He rarely saw it now that he lived in Washington. Kayak trips in the Chesapeake Bay with friends from the Secret Service weren't the same as his childhood ocean adventures, although there was more beer.

Now outside, his senses were on the redline. When his captors dropped down from the helicopter, a metallic clanging sound from one of their boots caught his attention.

He felt the moisture against his exposed skin and breathed the salt air through his hood in deep gasps. A gust of wind caused by the rotors sprayed him with a fine mist of water and he felt the ground shift slightly under his feet. The shudder was subtle, but he noticed the tremor.

Wait. *Are we on a boat on the ocean?*

His mind reeled as he immediately thought about the Ark.

In the early 2000s, during the height of the war on terror, the Bush administration turned a former cargo ship into an off-the-books mobile prison. Known as a black site, clandestine agencies conducted extreme rendition activities on the ship far from the media or anyone else. With a name like the Ark, someone in the administration either had a wicked sense of humor or took the Bible way too literally.

It can't be, he thought. *The Ark's been shut down for almost a decade.*

Plus, he knew black sites no longer existed. The last president had seen to that. A not-too-subtle dig at the CIA, which he'd despised. Publicly the president praised the Agency, while privately he attempted to gut their clandestine services. Still, rumors persisted, and some believed black sites still existed with no ties to the United States government.

The Body Man didn't have time to dwell on the idea as his captors had him off the ground and moving forward. He heard the metallic sound with each step.

Then they stopped. One of the men grabbed his ankles and forcefully separated them slightly. He felt cool steel on his skin, then heard the unmistakable sound of leg cuffs tightening around his ankles. His hands remained handcuffed behind his back.

One of the men shoved him forward. He stumbled slightly but maintained his balance and shuffled along as fast as he could, considering the restraints.

A firm grip grabbed his shoulders and stopped him with a jostle. The sound of an electronic buzzer and the release of a lock followed by the screech of steel sliding on steel indicated a door of some sort had opened. The same firm hand squeezed his shoulder and directed him forward. They passed through two more electronic doors before coming to a stop.

A raspy voice before him said, "Prisoner's name?"

"I'm not a priso—" he started to say.

A vicious punch to the side of his head mid-word dropped him to the ground. Not knowing he was about to get hammered had made it worse. He had no way to brace himself for the brutal impact. Lying on his back, he felt a trickle of liquid flow from his ear.

One of his captors grabbed him by his shirt and with two hands pulled him back to his feet.

"You don't speak unless spoken to. Do you get that, prisoner?" asked one of the men with the heavy Eastern European accent only inches from his bleeding and ringing ear.

Prisoner. There was the word again. What the hell? he thought.

Not interested in getting struck again, he said, "Got it."

The man to his right said in a thick accent, "Prisoner is known as the Body Man."

Fuck, he muttered under his breath. *Did he say what I thought he said?*

"We've been expecting this prisoner. He's late."

"We are delayed," said the man in broken English. "Just sign him in and take off our hands."

"Patience," cautioned the man with the raspy voice. "The Sanctum has rules for these types of transfers. Rules everyone adheres to."

A few minutes of silence followed. Finally, the raspy-voiced man said, "Everything appears in order."

Another buzzing sound as a door opened down the hallway to the Body Man's right. He could make out multiple footfalls as two people approached.

"These men will take possession of the prisoner. You can leave now."

One of his captors gave him a parting punch in the kidney. He doubled over, the pain intense.

"Fuck you, 'Body Man,'" said the voice with a venomous tone. "That was for Boris, my friend you killed on the plane."

A moment later, two men led him down a long hallway and through one more secured door into a room. They sat him on a hard, metallic chair in front of a table. The guard unlocked the handcuffs, which released his hands from behind his back. He rolled his wrists around, grateful for the sudden relief from his bonds, but he didn't get a chance to enjoy the freedom long as both wrists were pulled in front of his body and handcuffed to a large steel ring connected to the top of the table. Then he did the same with the leg cuffs, affixing them to a ring welded to the floor under the table.

From the frying pan to the fire, he thought.

The guard removed the hood once the Body Man was secured, then left, locking the door behind him. His eyes involuntarily squinted at the bright light from a fixture hanging above the stainless-steel table, and the Body Man sat in silence while he adjusted to his surroundings.

When he could finally see more clearly, he looked around the stark room. Everything in the room, which only consisted of a table and two chairs facing each other, was metal.

He tried to shift his weight and move the chair, but it didn't budge. With his hands bound, he tried to move the table without luck, since everything appeared bolted in place. The space contained a door to his left and mirrored glass on the wall across from him. He figured it was a two-way mirror. The walls were barren, painted a gunmetal gray color.

Ten minutes passed. He stared at the mirror and wondered how many people watched him from the other side. Like an animal on display.

He looked at his reflection, and it confirmed what he suspected—he looked like crap. Dried blood covered much of his face, caked up around his nose and ears. But he didn't care about his appearance.

The door buzzed and opened.

In walked a man dressed in khaki pants with a blue golf shirt and brown loafers. The Body Man stared at him as he moved toward the table. He looked to be about five-eleven and probably about one hundred and seventy-five pounds. The man walked with a slight limp on the right leg. He wore black round-rimmed glasses and had brown hair parted from right to left. His hair was graying around the temples, and the Body Man guessed the man was likely in his early sixties. His face appeared expressionless as he stared back.

The man took a seat in the chair across, his back to the mirror. In his hand was a thick manila folder. He removed the contents and placed the papers down on the table to his right.

"Greetings, prisoner," he said in a flat tone as he looked directly into the Body Man's eyes.

"I have a name."

"That's right, and here in this facility your name is prisoner."

The Body Man paused for a moment. He'd spent enough training time with his CIA counterparts at Camp Peary, also known as The Farm, and he knew what to expect. He considered his words before he replied. "And what do I call you?"

"You may call me 'Sir.'"

"I take it you know who I am, Sir?"

"Yes, I do, prisoner."

"Then you know who I work for?"

Sir smiled and rapped his knuckles on the file. "I know who you worked for, prisoner, past tense. I know more about you than you realize."

"I was taken against my will. I have rights as an American citizen."

"Wards of the Sanctum no longer have rights."

That was the second time he'd heard that word since he'd entered the facility.

What in the hell is the Sanctum?

"I don't know what you're talking about, sir. And what is the Sanctum?"

Sir didn't respond.

"Where am I?"

Again, the question returned only silence.

"What do you want from me?"

Finally, after about a minute without response, Sir said, "Those are all relevant questions for you, I'm sure. But I'm not here to answer your questions. You're here to answer mine."

With his mouth open slightly the Body Man's tongue reached back to his missing molar.

Sir saw the movement and smirked.

"Like a good soldier, willing to die instead of revealing what he knows. I respect your dedication to seek death over compromise."

"I'll never talk. You should know that."

The man leaned in closer. "That's what they all say. Eventually, they talk. Every man has his breaking point."

The Body Man stared back in defiance. His squinted and revealed crow's feet around his eyes deeper than Clint Eastwood's in any Dirty Harry movie.

"Not me," he replied.

"I heard about the incident on the plane."

No response.

"Why did you shoot him?" asked Sir.

"He tried to kill me, and I objected."

"You felt killing him was justified?"

His eyes narrowed, his gaze piercing. "The self-preservation instinct is a bear."

"You like to operate in a black and white world, don't you, prisoner?"

"No, I live in the gray area. I exist in the space between both right and wrong."

Sir nodded. "Well, you've had a long day, and by the look on your face, you've been roughed up quite a bit. My men will escort you to a room, and you will get some rest, prisoner. We'll start fresh after you've had a chance to recover some strength and ponder your future."

The Body Man said nothing. The door buzzed and two men entered. They removed his restraints from the hooks on the table and floor and pulled him out of the chair.

"Until we speak again, prisoner," Sir said. He grinned warmly. "Get some rest. You will need it."

The Body Man stared back at him with an icy glare.

Ever since his captors had stuffed him in his car and he'd realized the suicide capsule was gone, the Body Man's mind had never stopped calculating probabilities and ways of escape. As the two guards pushed him into his cell after his first date with Sir, he saw a possibility. Whether it was the best chance or not didn't matter. He knew that to survive, he must first escape.

Once back in his metal room, the guard closest to him unfastened the leg shackles and started to reach for his wrist cuffs, but the Body Man twisted his body and landed a vicious roundhouse kick to the sternum of the guard behind him near the door. The sound of a heavy foot meeting bone echoed a cringe-worthy cracking sound in the small space as the blow took the man's breath away and his breastbone cracked.

Startled, the guard who still held the Body Man's wrist drew his other hand back to strike. The motion was too late as the guard's legs were swept out from under him and he fell face down to the concrete floor.

The Body Man was on the prostrate guard in an instant. With his hands still bound by the cuffs, he climbed atop the man's back and slid the cold steel under the man's face until the chain touched the warm flesh of his neck. He pulled his bound hands toward him with enough pressure to crush the guard's windpipe.

He would have gone for the handcuff key if two guards hadn't arrived.

The electric jolt from a Sabre contact taser turned his body rigid as 200,000 volts surged through his body. He convulsed and fell forward, landing on top of the guard he'd just killed.

Dropping the taser, the guard removed a baton from his belt loop and delivered powerful blows to the Body Man's stunned body.

Chapter 11
Palo Alto, California

Jase Marshall looked down at his watch. For once he was early. Not a common feat for a man who struggled with being on time every day of his life. Fortunately, he'd chosen a profession that didn't concern itself with punctuality.

As a programmer for Apple, Jase found the work rewarding financially while dull intellectually. Most days, life felt like an extra in the movie *Groundhog Day*.

Nothing ever changed.

Jase wrote code for the newest iOS mobile software updates Monday through Friday. Weekends were a blur, and a new week arrived way too fast. His life was, in a word, boring. But everything changed when a fellow programmer introduced him to the dark web. The more he learned about the Internet not seen through standard search engines, the more the hidden world fascinated him.

He entered chat rooms and met enigmatic people, willingly immersing himself in a hidden culture experienced by few "lusers"—a tech insider's term for an unsophisticated Internet user. Then late one night he stumbled upon a person who went by the screen name Mammon. Their interaction started innocently enough until one day the mysterious person made a request. Jase thought it was a joke at first, but soon wondered if maybe Mammon was a fed trying to entrap him.

The request was highly illegal and even frightened him at first. But before long the thought of pulling it off made him feel alive in some sick, twisted way. Butterflies flooded his stomach, and the hair on his neck stood up as Mammon discussed specifics a few weeks later, offering assurances he was no fed. The promise of a large sum of money followed, but Jase didn't accept the job for the money.

He did it for the thrill. He did it to feel alive, and maybe to assert a level of technical mastery that he didn't feel was acknowledged by his workplace superiors.

It took him almost a month working from home, yet somehow the government never knew he'd cracked into one of their most secure servers. The thrill of success overwhelmed any feeling of guilt he encountered as he downloaded the documents and schematics on Mammon's wish list, leaving behind no hint of his presence.

Jase half expected helmeted, heavily armed men in black outfits to rappel through his bedroom window when he downloaded the last file, but nothing happened. Only the sound of his air purifier and the whirring cooling fan of his hand-built PC broke the silence of the room.

For a few hours, he felt on top of the world. When he reached out to Mammon to announce his success, he received an immediate large down payment deposit of Bitcoin and a set of specific instructions.

That had been forty-eight hours earlier.

Jase felt nervous, more than when he'd stolen the actual data. His eyes darted from one face to another as he looked down the road and into the rear view mirror.

Too late for second thoughts.

He reached over and cranked the air conditioning on his Tesla Model S to its highest setting. The icy cold air chilled his body.

He was on Alma Street, one block from Stanford University. Jase nervously tapped the steering wheel to the beat of AC/DC's *Shoot to Thrill* playing through Bose speakers. The sudden rap on the passenger window startled him. Jase's eyes darted to his right, and he saw a figure hunched over wearing a dark brown hoodie. The person wore dark pants with a gray satchel hung over his shoulder exactly as Mammon had described.

Jase unlocked the doors and turned off the music. His heart pounded in deep pulses and felt as if it would burst from his chest. The stranger climbed in and pointed forward.

"Drive," he said.

"I need to confirm who you are first."

The man smoothly pulled a gun from the wide front pocket of his hoodie. He cocked back the exposed hammer and pointed it at Jase's neck. The weapon's cold steel pressed against his throat and made it harder to breathe. The man held it there for several seconds.

"I'm Mark Zuckerberg," the hooded man said as he stuffed the gun back under his clothes. "Drive the damn car."

"Absolutely—where to?" Jase asked, gulping hard.

"Drive. I'll tell you when to turn."

They drove in silence for forty minutes except for the occasional instruction to make a turn. They finally pulled off Highway 9 into Castle Rock State Park and the man indicated where to pull to the side of the road at an empty scenic overlook. Dusk had arrived and the sun was disappearing into the waters of the Pacific.

Once Jase had the car turned off, they sat for a minute in dead silence. The car got stuffy without air conditioning and his heart raced. He tugged his shirt collar away from his neck and beads of sweat formed on his brow.

None of this was going like he thought it would.

"Get out," the man said, cracking his door open a few inches and placing his right foot on the ground. "Over there," and he pointed to an outcropping of rocks.

"I'm okay here," said Jase as he tapped his leather seat.

"We will conclude our business out there," said the man forcefully.

Jase's gut feeling said to stay in the car, but the mystery man seemed like no one you wanted to disobey.

The man in the hoodie climbed out of the Tesla and led the way, seemingly unconcerned that his back was to Jase, who reluctantly followed at a slower pace.

As they neared the edge of the steep drop-off and its knee-high barrier, the man in the hoodie turned. "You got the thumb drive?"

"Yes."

"Let me see it."

"I want my money first."

The man's eyes squinted, and displeasure grew on his face.

Jase said, "Mammon said I get paid, and then I give you the drive. A deal is a deal." It took all the courage Jase had to utter the words.

The man in the hoodie grunted but said nothing. He walked past Jase, away from the edge of the drop-off, and stopped. Pulling out his smartphone he opened an app and typed a few characters before showing it to Jase, who initially took a step back and got closer to the edge.

"The transfer is complete."

Jase looked skeptical.

"Check your account," said the man. "I'll wait."

Jase took out his phone and went to the website of the offshore bank account he'd set up a few weeks before. He confirmed the substantial balance of his fee was all there.

A few clicks later he had texted a short resignation littered with profanities to his boss at Apple.

"You good now?" asked the man in the brown hoodie.

"Yes," said Jase.

"Give me the drive."

"It's encrypted."

"It'd better be. Your instructions were unambiguous."

Jase handed over the blue plastic thumb drive and the man in the brown hoodie pulled a Microsoft Surface Pro 7 tablet from his gray satchel. Inserting the stick into the tablet, he keyed in the prearranged eighteen-digit encryption key.

Curiosity got the best of Jase. "Are you Mammon?" he asked.

The man in the hoodie looked up from the tablet's screen. His eyes bore into Jase's soul.

"No."

"But you work for him?"

"I'm here," came the reply. "That's all you need to know." The man looked back at the screen and perused the documents from the thumb drive. Satisfied that everything on the list was included, he nodded his head. "It's all here."

"I told Mammon it would be," said Jase.

"And he appreciates your attention to detail."

The man in the hoodie reached back into his satchel and removed a Walther PPQ M2 with a suppressor. It was a different weapon than he'd pulled on Jase inside the Tesla.

"Hey, *wait-wait-wait*—" Before Jase could finish the statement, two suppressed muzzle flashes exploded from the end of the gun, illuminating the twilight.

Both 9mm bullets found their target between Jase's eyes and

exited the back of his skull, flying out into oblivion in the gorge. His instantly limp body crumpled and fell over the short barrier of the overlook, bouncing down and landing hard among the rocks two hundred feet below.

The man used the edge of his combat boot to scrape a few skull and brain bits over the side of the rocky ledge. It wasn't a perfect clean-up, but it was close enough for government work. And any small pieces of flesh and bone remaining would be long consumed by animals even before Jase's corpse had fully decomposed.

His mangled body wouldn't be found for months, and after a fall like that, the head trauma alone would camouflage the gunshot wounds on what was left.

The man in the brown hoodie could make out an outline of the motionless body barely visible below, scrunched into a crevice between large boulders where it might need years to be found. Satisfied Jase was dead, he stuffed the gun back in his bag and walked back toward the Tesla.

He was still wiping down the seat and door handle when another vehicle pulled into the scenic overlook, right on time.

He climbed into the passenger seat as the driver of the car nodded but said nothing. The instructions were clear. Drive and don't speak.

The vehicle sped away from the scene and a minute later took Highway 9 headed east. Once the car reached Highway 35, the man in the brown hoodie placed a call.

"I've got it," he said.

"You sure it's all there?" asked the voice on the other end.

"Yes. We have everything."

"Good. There's a jet waiting for you at Palo Alto. Hurry up. I'm needed back east, and you've got another job."

Chapter 12
Vienna, Virginia

A small stream of drool ran down the tinted glass, pooling on the rubber seal lining the window frame. The sudden ringing of the cellphone startled the driver from his momentary slumber. The phone display read 3:33 a.m.

The driver swiped his finger to the right and answered the call.

"Hello," he said in a groggy voice. He rolled his neck back and forth until it cracked multiple times.

"Are you both asleep?" came the stern tone, like a father scolding a child who disobeyed him one too many times.

"No, of course not. We've been taking shifts." He lied with ease as he threw a hard elbow at the man to his right curled up in the passenger seat and snoring loudly.

A loud grunt was followed by an audible, "What the hell?" The passenger stirred.

The driver ignored the outburst and continued talking to the man on the phone. "She fell asleep around 10:00 p.m. The streets have been quiet. A bunch of middle-aged people with grown kids and retirees live around here."

"Well, it's time to get to work."

"Where we headed?"

"Inside his townhouse."

"But I thought with all the heat we had to lay low?"

"Change of plans. You need to get in there and find it before dawn."

"Clean or dirty?"

"Dirty is fine, but don't wake the neighbors. It may be your last chance before the feds show up. No excuses this time, and if the heat shows up, you're on your own."

He ignored the comment. "But when the feds arrive, they'll know someone tossed it."

"That's not our concern. Find the damn thing. No excuses."

"Roger that."

"Damn, that hurt," Don Flynn said as he held his left ribcage.

"Boss says it's time to work, and I had to wake your fat ass up," said Ryan Polk.

"Next time shake my shoulders or something. You don't need to be a dick."

"Stop whining. Grab the two duffel bags from the trunk and get inside. Dawn is in a few hours, and we need to wrap up by sunrise."

Two minutes later Polk stood before the thick oak front door painted forest green. He used the same snap gun as earlier and within fifteen seconds had the tumbler lock disengaged. Once inside he carefully closed the door and re-engaged the lock.

Both men slipped on LED headlamps to keep their hands free.

"I'll take the main floor. You start upstairs," Polk said, handing Flynn one of the duffel bags. "Keep the house lights off and the blinds closed. We don't need to attract any unwanted attention."

"Got it."

Once Flynn headed for the stairs, Polk started his search in the living room. Earlier he had checked behind all the paintings and photographs, finding nothing. "Dirty" meant he could ransack the place without any repercussions. Polk removed a claw hammer from the bag and started wrenching several of the bookshelves away from the walls. He checked the walls and punctured the drywall in several places.

Nothing.

Next, he started tapping on the floor in a grid pattern, listening for any empty or hollow spots. By the sounds upstairs, Flynn must've been doing the same. Using the hammer, Polk pulled up dozens of hardwood floor pieces.

Still nothing.

After thirty minutes, the only thing he'd found was a cat under the couch. But even that was short lived as the feline quickly retreated to another room after giving him a distinct hiss. Polk wrapped up the search in the living room and moved to the kitchen and pantry. He knew from years of experience that crafty people hid important items in the most obscure spots.

He removed every drawer, moved the appliances, and even popped off tiles from the backsplash. An hour later, frustration set in as he hadn't located any secret compartment or hiding place.

Flynn's frantic call from upstairs over their two-way radio interrupted his train of thought.

"Get up here. I think I found something in the master," Flynn said in a staticky voice.

Polk made his way upstairs two steps at a time.

He entered the master bedroom and found Flynn against a large mahogany bookshelf.

Beside the bookshelf, the large room contained a cherry-colored king-sized sleigh bed, matching armoire, and a long six-drawer dresser. Thick ivory carpet covered the floor, which was pulled up in several places.

"What is it?" asked Polk.

"Worked my way through the upstairs and found jack shit. After starting in his room, I came across this bookshelf."

"What about it?"

"Tried to pry it from the wall with no luck. I cleared all the shelves and looked for mounting screws but couldn't find any. Then I found this. Check it out."

Flynn crouched low to the ground on the left side of the bookshelf and showed Polk the hidden pivot hinge concealed where the ivory carpet met the baseboard.

"I felt something metal when I rubbed my hands through the carpet. When I pulled it back and saw the hinge, I figured I'd better call you."

"Smart move."

"You think if we both use the big crowbars, we can pop it open?"

Polk shook his head. "No need. Give me a minute. There must be a release somewhere. This isn't a shitty do-it-yourself cabinet from that IKEA hellhole. Someone crafted this bookshelf by hand. He had to have a talented carpenter custom make this thing. It must have cost a ton."

He started low and worked his way up the right side until he found it. A small indent no bigger than a postage stamp that felt different from the rest of the smooth wood. Pushing the spot hard with his index finger, he heard the distinct click sound as the mechanism keeping the shelf aligned to the wall disengaged.

Polk grabbed one of the middle shelves and gave a firm tug. The door swung open, and a rush of pressurized air passed into the bedroom.

Polk stepped inside and found a light switch on the right side of the entryway. He flipped the switch and illuminated the room.

The space was narrow, no more than five feet wide, but the length appeared to be the entire size of the master bedroom, some twenty feet long.

Polk looked back at Flynn and frowned. "Didn't I tell you to check the measurements of all the rooms?"

"Yeah, and I did," said Flynn with a bewildered look.

Polk pulled up the house schematic from his iPad.

You want something done right, you do the damn thing yourself.

The master bedroom showed twenty-five by twenty on the diagram. He stepped out of the hidden room and removed his laser distance measuring tool from his back pocket. Within ten seconds he had his numbers. Twenty by twenty. He showed Flynn the readings.

"Well, asshole. If you did what I said instead of lying to me, we'd have found this hidden room an hour ago."

Flynn's upper lip curled into a snarl. "Well, we damned sure found it *now*, didn't we?"

Polk knew to argue the point made no sense. He shook his head and walked back into the secret room straight out of Edgar Allan Poe. As he looked to the right, he noticed one whole wall was lined with pegboard and hooks holding various firearms: semi-automatic rifles, some with suppressors; two sniper rifles; shotguns; and handguns. Boxes of ammunition of varying calibers lined the opposite wall.

"Jesus," said Flynn as he stepped in behind Polk and glanced to his right. "Is this dude a Secret Service agent, or a prepper?"

"Don't touch the bang-bangs," Polk said and pointed to the opposite end of the room. "That's not what we came for, after all."

At the end of the narrow space, a black safe built into the wall about four feet off the ground beckoned with a digital keypad.

Flynn smiled. "Pay dirt."

Polk asked, "Can you open it?"

Flynn walked to the far side of the room and examined the safe. "No problem. It's pretty run of the mill. This model costs around two grand. Might be rated for burglary and fire, but anyone that knows their way around a safe can crack it quickly with minimal tools."

"How long?" Polk asked.

"Ten minutes, max. Let me grab my gear."

"Hurry up."

Eight minutes later the safe door yawned opened.

The top shelf held stacks of documents and a lot of cash still in bank bundle bands. The middle shelf held a 9mm Glock 19 Gen 5 MOS pistol, two mags, and more papers, while the bottom contained only a thick manila envelope.

Polk grabbed the envelope and slid the contents out.

He smiled.

"We got it."

"Are we done?"

"Put that stuff he gave us into the safe with the other papers, then let's clear out before we overstay our welcome and the heat shows up."

"Understood."

"On the way out, we need to grab his laptop and printer from the downstairs office."

"I'm on it."

Polk left the safe door open, turned, and started to walk away.

"Whoa, hold on," Flynn said, and grabbed Polk's shoulder. "What about the cash, man? There's got to be a hundred grand in Benjamins on that shelf. Maybe more."

Polk frowned. "You know the rules. Leave it. We take what we came for, nothing more. Don't be greedy."

"Boss don't need to know." Flynn raised his hands in frustration. "It's literally found money, man. I got obligations."

"Shove your obligations. I'll *know*," Polk said. "And to be honest, that means he will know, too. Shut your damn mouth and collect our gear. We're outta here in five. And push the door closed on your way out."

Chapter 13
Vienna, Virginia

Payne met Stone at seven-thirty a.m. sharp in the WFO employee parking lot.

As she climbed into the vehicle, he had a shit-eating smile plastered all over his face. "You saw the score last night, right?" asked Payne.

Stone shook her head. "Good morning, Payne. I slept great last night. Thanks for asking. How about you?"

He ignored her snarky response. "Five touchdowns by the GOAT. Count them—*five*. It was a hell of a game, Stone. Sure you didn't watch any of it?"

"No, Payne, I was too busy staying up late watching the Lifetime network, eating bonbons, and braiding my girlfriend's hair."

"Girl, you missed it. There was one pass that … wait, did you say 'girlfriend?'" His eyes opened wide enough to almost pop out of their sockets. "Seriously?"

Stone rolled her eyes. "Sure, *that* gets your attention. Guys are all the same."

"I mean—" Payne tried to backpedal. "I didn't know you were a lesbian. That's cool and all. Like, really cool, actually."

"Uhh," Stone said as she exhaled a drawn-out breath and

smacked him across the chest with the back of her hand. "I'm not a damned lesbian, you moron. I was trying to stop your stupid story about the football game."

"Jeez, now I'm bummed."

"And ... it worked," she said and rolled her eyes. She glanced down at the floorboard and only the paperback novels remained. The wrappers and papers were all gone. "I see you cleaned up the car. Or the cleaning fairy visited you."

"Took your insult to heart. Figured I'd better straighten out my ride a little bit."

"You tell Wes about what we found yesterday?"

"No, not yet. I rarely bring the squad supervisor into the loop until I have something a little more concrete to go on."

"But what else do you need?"

Payne smiled at her paternally. "You tell me what we have."

Stone paused and considered the question. "Well, the lady who lives across the street from Ralph Webb says he is missing."

"Which we can't prove as of yet," interjected Payne.

"We go to the White House and a Secret Service agent recognized his photo but lied about him working at the White House."

"Possibly lied, again we can't prove that. It's hearsay."

"You're right, it sounds thin."

Payne said, "No. It doesn't sound thin, it is thin. We have no corroborating evidence. Only a nosy neighbor who may or may not know that the man across the street is missing. And a Secret Service agent who told us he didn't recognize the man in the picture and said no one by that name works at the White House."

"But you believed Rose yesterday and agreed Agent Walker lied to us."

"Absolutely, but that was my gut talking. It isn't admissible in court. We need evidence to make this into a full-blown investigation. Pure supposition doesn't cut it with the Bureau."

"What type of evidence are you hoping to find?"

"Something that confirms he worked at the White House, for starters. Plus, proof that he's missing."

"And you hope to find it at his place?"

"Yes. Mr. Webb—well, whatever his name is—must have left something behind that indicated where he worked."

"But how do we get into his place?"

Payne removed a piece of paper from his black notebook resting on the front seat of the car. "With this."

"How the hell did you get a warrant? You just agreed the evidence was thin. Well, actually, you said there wasn't any."

Payne smiled. "I have a few connections. Made a few calls at half time and pulled a few strings."

"Even though we don't know what we will find?"

"Yeah."

Stone didn't press the issue. "Okay, we have a warrant, but how do we get in? You gonna pop the lock?"

Payne winked. "We don't need to since we know someone with a key, don't we?"

Rose Lewis. "Well, yes, I guess we do. You're smarter than I thought, Payne."

His eyelashes fluttered comically. "I guess I should take that as a compliment."

She smiled and looked away quickly to conceal her amused grin. "And for the record, I do like guys."

Payne smirked and fluttered his eyelashes again.

"Normal guys. Not pervs," she added.

His smirk turned into a low, guttural laugh.

As his car came to a stop in front of Rose's house, Payne's cellphone buzzed. The new-text icon showed on his phone's display. The first thing he noticed was the text displayed the caller's phone number, meaning he didn't have the contact in his address book. Not unheard of, but also not common. Most texts he received were from friends or colleagues, though there was still no practical defense from a computer autodialing random numbers to tell you someone wanted to talk to you about your expiring extended auto warranty.

He touched the item and opened the message, and a bewildered expression formed on his face.

Stone watched his face change. "What does it say?"

Payne turned the screen so she could see it and said, "What the hell does this mean?"

> *Payne, don't stop. You must find the Body Man.*

"What the heck is a body man?" Stone said. "Who sent it?"

"No name on the Caller ID. It's just a number. The area code is 202, so it came from a DC number."

"'The Body Man' is a strange term. Is it a case you worked?"

Payne shook his head. "Not that I recall. Never heard that phrase before."

"Text them back."

Payne nodded. *Who is this?* he typed. He waited a few seconds, but the reply wasn't an answer to the question.

> FIND HIM, *Payne. You must recover the Body Man.*

Payne typed back a few more texts without any responses.

"Can you call your buddy Jessie? See if he can backtrace who the number belongs to?"

"Sure," Stone said. She placed a quick call. The call lasted no more than a minute. "Jessie's running late, he'll be at the office in an hour and he'll run the number for us then."

Payne looked out the windshield and toward the townhouse.

"Time to get to work."

Rose wore a simple yellow dress with her hair pulled back.

Her deeply wrinkled face displayed a warm smile as she opened the door for Payne and Stone.

"Good to see you both so soon. Do you have news about Ralph?"

Payne smiled back but shook his head. "Still gathering info but nothing concrete."

"Did you visit the White House?"

"We did."

"And let me guess. Whoever you spoke with said they didn't know him and claimed Ralph didn't work there, correct?"

As much as Payne liked Rose Lewis, he wasn't going to let her drag him down into a rabbit hole of consecutive questions that were not her business.

"Ma'am," Payne said patiently, "we aren't at liberty to disclose how an FBI investigation is conducted."

"It must be an alias," said Rose as she gently stroked her cheek. "Don't you think? His name?"

The statement surprised Payne. "Why do you think he used a fake name?"

"It makes sense," she said and shook her head. "I'm not surprised."

"Would that bother you?" Payne watched intently for her reaction. "If he gave you a fake name?"

Rose shook her head forcefully. "Not at all. Ralph had to protect his identity. I understood that. Did you show them the picture?"

"Yes."

"And?"

"The federal agent we spoke with claimed to not recognize the man in the photo, although Stone and I believe he was being less than forthright."

"Figures," said Rose. "They're circling the wagons."

Payne didn't expect this response but had to admit Rose was correct. "How so?" he asked, playing dumb.

Her voice, though frail, gained strength, and she became animated. "Government agencies don't like others to get in their business. I learned that from my husband, Charlie. After all, he was an Agency man his whole life. You get my drift?"

"Loud and clear."

"The Agency always hated when other government entities, as in the FBI or anyone else, stuck their noses where they didn't belong. I'm sure that is the case with the Secret Service. If Ralph is missing, you can bet a pretty penny they want to find him themselves and not have an FBI agent track him down."

Payne rubbed his chin. Her theory had merit. "Pretty astute observation, Rose," he said.

Her face lit up. "You pick up a few things when you're married to a spy for most of your adult life, Agent Payne."

"No doubt."

"Well, I'm sure you didn't come by just to tell me you've not found anything yet. So, what do you need?" Lewis asked.

"We would like to get a look inside Ralph's townhouse. Have a look around. I was able to get a warrant. It's limited in scope, but hopefully a cursory walk through of Ralph's house will uncover some evidence that he is actually missing."

"You'd like my key?"

"Yes, please. If it's not too much trouble."

Rose turned and disappeared into the kitchen. A minute later she returned. "Here you go." She handed Payne the key ring. "Do you mind feeding the cat when you go over there? I haven't been today. The food is in the pantry off the kitchen."

Payne looked at Stone with a slightly annoyed expression on his face. He hated cats and was certain he was allergic to them, but he also wasn't sure the allergies weren't just sympathetic because he hated cats in the first place.

Stone read his expression. "We would be glad to feed Italia, Rose," she said, nudging Payne with her elbow.

"Thank you, dear," said Rose.

"We'll bring the key back once we're done," Payne said.

As the door closed and they turned to leave, Stone gave Payne an icy glare. "Older women like cats, you know?"

"I'm not an elderly woman, in case you didn't notice."

"Yes, but you want something from her, meaning you play nice."

"What? I know how to play nice."

"Your facial expressions didn't convey that."

"But I don't like—"

Stone cut him off. "The point is not whether you like cats or not. You may be a good investigator, but I'm good at reading people. Like it or not, we're working together on this and we need to be on the same page. Trust me. A woman's intuition is more powerful than a man's bullheadedness."

Payne decided to stop before he dug too deep of a hole.

"I got it."

"Good. Now, let's see go what Mr. Webb may be hiding," Stone said as she playfully smacked his shoulder.

Chapter 14
Port of Los Angeles
Los Angeles, California

The tropical turquoise Chevy El Camino came to a stop alongside South Seaside Drive as Peter Casha reached inside his Italian leather jacket. He unsnapped a safety strap and removed the .45-caliber Kimber 1911 hanging from his Galco vertical shoulder holster.

Casha stared at the spartan engraving on the grip of the heavy pistol and rubbed the faded image in a circular motion with his thumb. He ejected the magazine, confirmed it was fully loaded, and slammed it back into the grip. With his left hand, he racked the slide, chambering a Barnes TAC-XPD hollow-point bullet. Casha didn't expect to use the weapon, but one can't be too careful.

Few people knew that Peter Casha wasn't his true identity, but the alias served him well. When he'd started in the game after high school, he'd learned that the fewer people knew about you— the real you—the better. Only his family and close friends knew his real name, and he intended it to stay that way.

He rolled down his window and waited. With the temperature hovering around fifty-eight degrees, the cool breeze felt refreshing. Five minutes later, a black cargo van approached from the opposite side of the road.

Casha looked at his Tag Heuer watch, a birthday present to himself a few years ago. With an hour and fifteen minutes before the cargo ship arrived, he still had plenty of time.

As the van pulled alongside, the driver eyed him suspiciously.

The driver's side window went down and the man said, "Get in." The van's side door slid open with a screeching sound as bent, worn metal scraped against metal.

Casha's muscles clenched but he grabbed the large green canvas duffel bag from the passenger seat, slung the thick strap over his broad shoulder, and climbed out of the car. He entered the van and sat in silence in the middle row. Beside the driver, another man sat in the passenger seat but said nothing.

The van weaved its way through several abandoned parking lots at the port. A couple of minutes later, the driver pulled onto Earl Street and stopped in front of a large white warehouse. All three men exited the van and headed into a side door of the building.

They walked in silence down a long, narrow hall. Several fluorescent lights that lined the hallway flickered, giving every-thing a greenish cast. The whole vibe was straight out of a horror movie. They arrived at the second-to-last door and the van driver gestured for Casha and the other man to enter.

Casha stepped into the room and looked from one side to the other. He'd already figured the best route out of the building if the meeting went south, and he clutched the green duffel bag tightly. There was a lot of money in it and, even though he could handle himself, he would rather things go according to the plan.

The sparse room had a linoleum-covered floor, wood-paneled walls, and looked like someone had designed it in the 1970s. It reeked of mold, and several ceiling panels had dark splotches indicating a permanent water leak. With little in the way of office furniture, the room contained two metal folding tables pushed together and eight folding chairs. In the corner, an old water cooler sat dusty and empty, its plastic water jug missing. A large whiteboard hung on the wall opposite the table. That was it.

Casha took a seat and placed the duffel bag on the ground near his feet. The other men stood next to the door.

"You going to sit?" Casha asked.

"No," replied the driver of the van. "We'll wait right here."

"Suit yourself."

Several minutes passed and the two men scrolled cellphones pulled from their pockets to pass the time.

Casha sat in silence. He watched the two men, studied their body language, and listened to their occasional banter. For their parts, they ignored his stares. Ten minutes later sounds echoed down the hall indicating more than one person had entered the warehouse.

Casha watched as five men shuffled into the room. They all appeared tired. Another long night on the graveyard shift at the docks will do that to anyone. Each of them looked unhappy to be there.

That was all about to change.

"Take a seat," said Casha to the men congregating near the door.

The men looked at the van driver, who nodded.

"You heard him."

Casha looked across the table to the van driver, Hector Fuentes, who had been his main point of contact for the past several weeks. "How we looking?"

"Everything's on time and on budget," Fuentes said.

"When did the eight containers arrive?"

"The semis pulled in from Rancho Bernardo about zero-two."

"Heavily guarded?"

Fuentes nodded. "Big time, *ese*. General Atomics don't fuck around, and they never let the containers out of their sight. They inspect the ship after it's loaded and wait on the dock until it sails before they leave."

"And you're sure everything is in place to make the switch?"

Another head nod in the affirmative. "Juan and Pablo know what to do." Fuentes looked at two of the men at the table.

The two men who must be Juan and Pablo both acknowledged. "Si, *padrone*."

"I'd like you to go over the plan with me one more time. I want to make sure we all hear it together," Casha said. "We only have one shot at this, and it can't fail."

A distressed look formed on Fuentes' face.

"If that's what you want."

"It is."

Fuentes laid out the plan for almost thirty minutes.

Pleased with the attention to detail, Casha said, "I'll need an overwatch position."

"I already have a spot picked out for you."

"Good. Now, for the real reason you're all here."

Casha reached deep into the green duffel bag and removed stacks of currency held together with mustard-colored straps. Each bound stack contained one hundred bills displaying the face of Benjamin Franklin. He lined them up on the metal table, individual stacks of fifty thousand dollars each.

With the money arranged, he couldn't help but notice the approving smiles from each man. Casha suspected the local liquor stores and jiggle joints would see an influx of crisp, new C-notes in the coming weeks. He pulled out two additional bound stacks of money equaling twenty thousand dollars and placed them on the far right stack, then looked over to Fuentes.

"This stack is for you." Casha pushed the pile away from the others.

Fuentes shook his head back and forth. "We agreed on an

equal share."

"Let's say you are first among equals. My employer decided you deserve extra for your extraordinary efforts."

"That's not necessary. An equal share is all I want."

Casha's eyes narrowed. "Not my decision, not yours. This is not up for discussion."

Fuentes frowned, knowing full well additional money might well put a target on his back with the other men.

Casha knew this too. The overpayment was intentional. It was all his idea, in fact, not his employer's. Money divides, and he wanted to keep the men on edge. If they had some animosity toward Fuentes, it would only work in Casha's favor. He grabbed brown paper bags from his duffel and placed them on the table.

"Come and get it," Casha said, and he tapped the large stacks of money.

Unlike when they'd first shuffled in, the men practically stumbled all over each other as they approached pay dirt. Everyone but Fuentes. He stayed back and let the others get their money before he retrieved his own. Once the men had collected their cash and stuffed it into the brown bags, they sat back down. Several of the men pulled out the bound stacks of bills with enormous grins and flipped through them quickly, making the sound of a fan.

Casha said, "You are being paid handsomely due to the sensitive nature of what we are doing here." He reached into his jacket, pulled out the .45-caliber Kimber, and rested his hand on the table. The barrel pointed straight ahead toward Fuentes. "My employer expects your silence." Casha paused. "Or should I say, demands it." He looked at each man one by one as he spoke the words. "There are only a few of you. If word leaks out, it won't be hard to figure out who squealed."

As he talked, he tapped the end of the barrel on the metal table one time after another, progressively getting louder with each strike. "And if *one* of you talks, *all* of you pay the penalty."

The expression on each man's face changed, including Fuentes. A tangible fear chilled the room.

"But I have nothing to worry about, do I?" Casha slid the Kimber back into his shoulder holster. "You will all perform your tasks and keep your mouths shut. Right?"

All seven heads nodded in unison.

"Perfect. Exactly what I expected." Casha looked at his watch. The time had arrived. "Time to earn your pay, gentlemen."

Chapter 15
Vienna, Virginia

Payne unlocked and pushed open the dark green oak door to Ralph Webb's residence as his right hand reached down to his holstered Glock. His fingers curled around the polymer grip.

"You know something I don't?" asked Stone. Slightly alarmed, she automatically mimicked Payne's move.

Payne shrugged. "Many things, but this is force of habit when I walk into the unknown."

As they stepped into the townhouse, the telltale signs that someone had ransacked the place were impossible to miss.

Stone pulled her Glock 23 and pointed it straight ahead.

Payne already had his gun out and raised.

"Maybe your habits aren't all that bad," she said in a whisper.

Payne raised his finger to his lips.

She leaned in close. "Backup?"

Payne didn't speak but shook his head. No. With hand gestures he indicated they needed to clear the house. Staying near each other, they started on the lower level and moved room by room in a slow, methodical process.

All the rooms were in disarray, and it took five minutes to clear the entire lower level. Next, they crept upstairs and followed the same process. As they made their way through the spare bedroom and closet, Payne called out, "Clear."

They both had perspiration on their faces.

"You ever cleared a house before?" asked Payne.

Stone shook her head. "Only what we did during NATs in Quantico."

Payne holstered his weapon. "Well, considering you aren't that long out of New Agent Training, you did a pretty damn good job, especially for your first time."

Stone smirked and followed his lead by putting her gun away as well. "Thanks, I guess. Where do we begin to look for evidence?"

He gave the area a quick once over. "Since we're already upstairs, let's start right here."

Even though they cleared the house, Payne's senses were on high alert not knowing if whoever ransacked the place might come back.

"Don't let your guard down," he said to Stone, "and be ready to draw your weapon if you hear any noises." He smiled in apology. "Sorry, Stone. Parental caution. You know this stuff."

"But we're alone," she said with a perplexed look forming on her face.

"Seem to be at the moment, yes."

"Do you think whoever did this is coming back? It doesn't look like they missed much."

"Don't know, but if they do, I want to make sure they are the ones who have the bad day and not us."

"Want to call for backup now?"

Payne's gaze narrowed and he spoke with a confident tone. "No. We got this for now. I'm not really a backup kind of guy."

Stone ignored his snark. "Well, they tossed this place good."

"Agreed. But did they do it before or after Ralph went missing?" She shrugged as her cellphone rang.

"It's Jessie," she said, and walked out of the room. She returned a minute later.

"What did he say about the number?" asked Payne even before she'd ended the call.

"There was no name on the account. Whoever texted you bought a prepaid phone from the 7-Eleven on Wisconsin Ave in Bethesda."

"No way to track them? They probably used a credit card to pay for it."

"Sorry, but according to what Jessie found, it was a cash transaction. One of these phones you buy, go online, and add more minutes if you want. The phone has only been used to send those two text messages. That's it."

"So, it's a burner phone?"

"Yes."

"Well, that got us nowhere."

"Maybe whoever sent the text will use it again."

"Guess we'll see. For now, back to work."

The search began in the spare bedroom, which was empty. Only hangers in the closet and dust bunnies in the corner.

They moved to what they thought served as the master bedroom. Besides a king-sized bed with its mattress thrown upside-down and a dresser whose empty drawers had been pulled onto the floor, the bedroom contained little else. Opening each drawer in the nightstands, they found no personal effects.

"It feels sterile in here," Stone said.

"Agreed. He might not be missing—he might have moved out." Payne spread his hands. "I mean, I'd take more of my stuff, but that's just me."

Attached to the bedroom was a full bath that was completely empty besides a hand towel and soap in a glass dish on the sink.

Stone said, "Guess this guy qualifies as a minimalist."

Payne nodded. "If he does work for the Secret Service, I doubt he's home much. And without any family, he probably doesn't have many visitors."

The bedroom included a large walk-in closet much larger than you find in most bedrooms. Stone stepped inside first and observed the meticulously organized clothes that lined the wooden shelves on both sides. Clearly, Webb used this as changing room of sorts. Over a dozen pair of properly shined dress shoes, sneakers, and hiking boots lined the left side of the closet, while the right side was full of clothes.

Meticulously folded T-shirts of various colors were on one shelf, and dress shirts, pants, and more than a dozen suits on cherry-colored hangers hung from a rod above. A grouping of flower-printed Hawaiian-style shirts to the far right of the suits caught her attention.

"Not what I might have expected," she said and pointed to the Hawaiian shirts.

Payne grinned. "Guess he thinks he's an '80s television star living in Oahu. All he needs is a Ferrari 308 and a dark blue ball cap with a white olde English D."

"And that mustache! Tom Selleck was hot, man," Stone said.

Payne shrugged. "Guy certainly did have a good 'stache and definitely a kick-ass car."

Stone exited the closet and walked down the hall to the guest bedroom. Payne was right on her heels but paused her at the threshold. He reached around and stretched out his arm in front of her as Stone looked down at his forearm, mere inches from her breasts.

"Umm, hello? You're violating my personal space, bucko," she said with her eyebrows arched.

Payne realized how close his outstretched arm was to where

it probably shouldn't have been. "Sorry," he said as he pulled his arm back from in front of her. "But hold up."

"What is it, footprints? We've been in here."

Payne nodded. "But not over there," he said and pointed toward the large mahogany bookshelf on the far wall.

"It's a shelf. Big whoop."

"Not the shelf. Look at the impressions on the carpet."

"What impressions?"

Payne walked over to the spot in front of the shelf and used the toe of his show to trace a subtle half-moon impression in the carpet. "These. This bookshelf pivots out from the wall."

Stone grabbed the shelf and gave it a firm tug. It didn't budge. "Looks pretty solid."

"There has to be a release somewhere." Payne ran his hand up the side of the shelf and found the spot thirty seconds later. He pressed it and it returned a soft but audible click.

Stone gave the shelf another tug and this time it pivoted open into the room. She looked at Payne with surprise evident on his face. "Well done, mister. Good eyes."

"Yeah, I'm more than just a set of hands," he quipped.

"Is that how you sweet talk all your female partners?" she said with a laugh. "And is that before or after you reach for their boobs?"

Payne's laughed. "Well, only chicks who like football."

"Mark me safe, then."

Payne pulled out a tactical LED flashlight and aimed it at the dark interior behind the bookshelf. "Ladies first," he said, and he shined the light into the darkened space.

"Well, how gallant of you." Stone stepped into the hidden room and found the light switch to the right of the opening.

She looked to her right, while Payne glanced to the left. Dull gleams reflected from what they found.

"Whoa—that's a friggin shit-ton of guns," Stone said as she saw the arsenal that lined the wall. "I'm impressed."

Many assault-style rifles were stacked individually in vertical racks; Stone figured at least one or more of them probably had a setting for fully automatic fire.

Several were mounted with suppressors and advanced optics. A dozen or more handguns rested on pegs. A large cache of boxed ammunition filled the shelves beneath.

"It is … a lot," Payne said. But his gaze was focused on something left of the doorway.

Stone followed Payne's stare toward the left. "Ooh, a safe."

"And it's open." Payne's eyes narrowed at the safe door swung completely to the side.

"That's not normal. At least, it wouldn't be in my house," Stone said, then shrugged. "If I had a wall safe."

"No, it isn't normal. Someone either cracked it, or our buddy Ralph left in a hurry." Payne shined his light on the outer safe door. There were no obvious blast or tool marks.

"Nobody hiding something leaves a safe wide open." She gestured to the rack. "Or leaves all these weapons behind, either."

"Agreed."

"But did whoever ransacked the house find what they wanted?"

Payne shook his head. "Dunno. Safe doesn't appear to be empty, either. Let's see what they left behind."

He aimed the flashlight into the unlighted safe. Close enough to observe the contents, they saw what sat on the top shelf.

"Who leaves stacks of cash in an open safe?" Stone asked.

"Someone not interested in money," replied Payne.

"Some backup now?" Stone asked.

"I'm thinkin' about it," Payne said.

G oogle stores data in exabytes—a thousand petabytes, or a billion gigabytes—and while much of the data is harmless, any data in the wrong hands has the potential to be used for nefarious purposes.

Marcus Rollings knew firsthand that information is power and expertly used it as leverage any chance he got. Over twenty-four hours in several stints, he'd downloaded a tremendous amount of data about the George Washington University Hospital. To formulate a plan, he'd needed information, raw data. Rollings had even paid a hacker to crack the hospital's servers so he'd know which ICU room held Danny Frazier. He'd studied the floor plans and compiled intel until he'd felt certain he could navigate the hospital better than most workers.

But it wasn't enough.

He needed something no floor plan or diagram could provide.

Rollings left his apartment in Adams Morgan and drove eleven minutes to downtown Washington. He walked into an apartment on K Street as a white male in his early thirties, and less than twenty minutes later emerged dramatically different. Gone was his close-cropped hair, light complexion, and narrow nose. Instead, the man who approached the McPherson Square Metro station had bronzed skin, wavy hair, and a slightly over-sized nose that propped up thick-framed black glasses.

As he boarded the Blue Line train, a heavyset man brushed against him right on schedule, deftly depositing a hospital badge into the left front pocket of his scrubs. When the train left the station, he removed the ID from his pocket and attached it to his left collar tab by the holder's alligator clip. The patient care tech-nician badge for the ICU would withstand even the most thorough examination, although Rollings didn't plan to be questioned.

Two stations later the train braked smoothly to a stop. As he exited at the Foggy Bottom-GWU station, he turned left and took the escalator to the street level.

When Rollings walked through the sprawling hospital's front door, he pressed the left side of the thick black glasses near the front of the frames, activating a video recorder. The images were automatically sent to the cellphone in his pocket and uploaded to a secure server.

He moved his head from side to side in a natural motion, care-ful not to attract any unwanted attention. He walked with a confident step as he made his way to the bank of elevators. Before he arrived, he recognized three Secret Service agents scattered around the lobby, marked their positions, and stepped onto the waiting elevator.

"What floor, sir?" asked the small Hispanic boy, no more than six, who stood by the control panel. He wore blue jeans and a car-toonish Iron Man T-shirt. His wide smile revealed the distinct scar from a cleft lip.

Rollings looked down. "Five, please," he said, giving the boy a wink and large grin.

"Thanks for helping everyone who comes in here," said the boy as he looked up at the badge hanging from Rollings' scrubs.

"I'm here to help," he said.

The doors opened on the fifth floor, and he stepped off the elevator. The police and Secret Service presence was unmistakable, in numbers heavier than he'd expected.

Two agents stopped him as he proceeded down the hall. After inspecting his hospital badge, both agents let him pass.

His pace slowed as he approached room 306, where two Secret Service agents stood on either side of the door. They both eyed him suspiciously as he walked past though neither man stopped him. Out of the corner of his eye, Rollings stole a glance through the glass door. In less than the fraction of a second it took to pass, he observed a person lying in bed. Tubes and wires seemed to protrude from every part of his body, and three nurses scurried around the room.

Rollings smiled. *Danny Frazier.*

His shoulders tensed as he continued down the hall and made his way down the stairs that led to the fourth floor. He focused on his escape route, which wasn't complicated, but it was precise. Fifteen minutes later he exited the front of the hospital and took the Blue Line downtown.

An hour later and back in his apartment, he looked at his watch. *Why hadn't she called?* Then the phone on his desk rang.

"Why the hell did you wait so long to call?" Rollings asked with a flustered tone.

"Excuse me?" asked the distinctly male voice.

It wasn't the person Rollings had expected. "Sorry," he said. "Wrong person."

"Is everything all right there?"

"Yes."

"The FBI agents are going through the townhouse right now."

"I thought you said the FBI wasn't our problem?"

"They're not," said the other man, *"per se."*

Rollings hated word games. "Meaning?"

"They'll find the planted evidence and hopefully chase their tails," the man on the phone said. He paused. "But ..."

"But what?" Rollings asked.

"It would be in our best interest if we slowed them down a little bit."

"How so?"

"You know ..." The man's voice trailed off.

"Like put a fucking hit on them? Are you insane? Do you know how much of a spotlight it would shine on the case?"

"No, not a hit. Do you think I'm some damn fool or something? Nothing like that. I'm talking about a traffic accident, something to startle the two agents looking into his disappearance. Like a good martini, I want them shaken. But it needs to look like an accident."

Rollings dialed back the annoyance in his voice. It didn't do to disrespect the man on the phone. "And how should I facilitate that? I'm stretched pretty thin right now."

"I'm sure you know someone who can orchestrate a motor vehicle incident."

Rollings stayed quiet for a moment while his mind raced. Finally, he said, "I might know someone I can get in a pinch."

"Perfect. Again, it doesn't need to be serious. Just give them a distraction to slow down their investigation."

"Understood."

"And no matter what, whoever you call, they cannot get caught."

Rollings had played the game long enough to know this wasn't a request. "Trust me—I'll take care of it."

The line clicked off and left Rollings with only his thoughts. *Where is she?*

Chapter 17
Vienna, Virginia

Payne took pictures of the safe from various angles with his phone. Next, he handed Stone a pair of latex gloves. "The tech guys may be able to get prints off whatever is in here, so we'll glove up. You take what's on the top shelf. I've got the middle."

"Copy," Stone said. "By the way, do you think it's odd that the bottom shelf is empty?"

"Not sure. Maybe whoever left the safe open only cleared out that shelf. Or it's always been empty. There's no way for us to know." Payne reached in and grabbed the gun, two mags, and a stack of documents. "We can sort through the contents on the dresser."

Stone removed everything from the top shelf and followed him into the bedroom and lay everything she collected out on top of the large dresser.

Payne ignored her and examined the handgun he removed from the safe with great interest.

"What are you doing?"

"Checking this out." Payne raised the weapon. "It's a thing of beauty."

"Why would he have a gun in a safe? I mean, he had a whole

wall of guns. What's the big deal with this one?"

Payne shook his head. "You aren't a gun person, I take it."

"Hardly. It's a tool. Nothing more, nothing less."

"Jesus. First you don't like football, now not impressed with guns. Do you hate dogs, too? What do you like?"

Stone smirked, clicked her tongue, and winked.

"Forget I asked. You'll probably say either crocheting or being a dominatrix."

"Maybe I do both," she said with another wink, this one from the other eye, "at the same time."

Payne raised his hands. "I don't want to know."

"So, tell me, Mr. Gun Nerd. What's the big deal about this piece? Looks to be a 1911 model, right?"

"Well, I'll give you credit for that at least." Payne removed the mag and checked the chamber. Sure, the weapon wasn't loaded, he held out the gun. "Here. Take this."

Stone accepted the weapon, surprised by the light weight and perfect balance in the palm of her hand.

"This magnificent piece of craftsmanship," continued Payne, "is called an SVI Tiki-T."

"Say what?" she asked as she examined the weapon.

"It's a high-end, custom-made weapon handcrafted in the great state of Texas by men who are not only gunsmiths, but patriots. They create works of art."

"And ... it fires bullets?"

Payne frowned. "Yes, it also happens to fire bullets."

Stone rotated the gun and looked at it with fresh eyes. "How much would this set you back?"

"They start at around $4,500, but that's only for the base model. Something like this, created from billet titanium, probably goes upwards of eight grand."

"You're saying this thing is the price of a used Honda Civic?"

"Yeah."

"How the hell does a Secret Service agent afford one?"

Payne shook his head. "Great question. Canny investing? Old family money? Damned if I know. I might a hazard a guess once we figure out where he got that much dough." He pointed to the stack of currency in front of her. "How much is that?"

Stone flipped through the neatly bundled stacks and let out a long whistle. "One hundred and forty thousand large."

"That's a lot of money." Payne examined the papers he'd collected. Most looked to be tax statements and insurance documents.

Then he found it.

He rubbed his chin. "Well, this is interesting."

"What is it?"

"A numbered Swiss bank account. It was opened at Lombard Odier, one of the oldest private Swiss banks."

"Let me guess. You're an expert in Swiss banks?"

Payne chuckled. "Well, expert, small-e. I took some international business classes in college and had a banking internship in Switzerland during my last year."

"Well, aren't you full of surprises."

Payne turned and his gaze swept the secret room full of secrets. "We're a small but distinguished group."

"He also has passports, too—lots of them." Stone held up the stack she'd found between some of the papers.

"How many?" asked Payne.

"Ten."

"What countries?"

"Britain, France, Spain, Germany. Several others."

"Any from the US?"

Stone nodded. "Just one." She held up the blue passport and handed it to Payne. "Name says Nick Jordan. It's the same guy in all the photos even though he wears a disguise in several of them and some of the names are different."

Payne grabbed the US passport and leafed through it. "Pretty sure this backs up your hunch the Ralph Webb name is a fake."

"Agreed. But which one is his real name?"

"I'd go with Nick Jordan. At least for now."

"Who the hell is this guy? Is he Jason Bourne or something?"

"Nah, but maybe he's Matt Damon."

She rolled her eyes. "Funny."

Payne looked down at the papers and flipped to the next one.

Stone's tone caused his head to snap back up. "Holy *shit*," she bellowed.

"What is it?"

Held between her fingers was an ID badge slightly larger than a credit card. Payne could only see the backside, which was stark white but obviously the back side of a common access card routinely used throughout the military and US government.

"Let me see it."

It was a White House ID showing the same face as on the passports. Printed below the picture was NICK JORDAN. The color code of the badge confirmed Nick worked for the Secret Service. Payne knew the badges well and immediately realized it was legit.

Stone said, "Looks like Rose was onto something after all."

Payne nodded. "Agreed. It proves Brandon Walker lied to us."

"That's not a shocker, but what do we do next?"

Payne pointed to her cellphone sticking up out of her front trousers pocket. "Take pictures of it all. Every passport, each page, plus all the cash bundles and the weapons. If you can find serial numbers on the guns, get photos of all that too. Get digital proof of everything we've found."

"But we have to turn all this in as evidence."

"And we will. After I brief Wes, the next call will be for an Evidence Response Team. But before I place either call you need to realize the shit is about to hit the fan. Big time."

"How so?"

"We have some pretty damning evidence of a Secret Service agent with loads of cash, numerous passports, special weapons, and bank accounts that he likely shouldn't have. God only knows what else is going on here—or who else may be involved."

"And?"

"If he's crooked, the old Potomac two-step will shift into high gear."

Stone's eyes narrowed uncertainly. "What does that mean?"

"Jeez, have you not seen the movie *A Clear and Present Danger*?"

"No, it was before my time."

"Did you at least read the book by Tom Clancy?"

"Um, no. My Dad probably has, though. He has all of Clancy's books," Stone said. She crossed her arms. "Old guys read Clancy."

Payne ignored the clear dig at his age. "What it means is people with real power may try to bury this investigation or side-track it into something it isn't. Especially if it drags any political types into it."

"By 'people with power,' are you saying the White House?"

"Possibly. I'm not sure yet."

"So, what do we do now?"

"Take the pictures, catalog the evidence. Figure out our next moves."

Stone took over two hundred photos of various objects and Payne counted over a dozen bank statements for various accounts worldwide, which he phone-scanned to PDFs. Some were in the name Nick Jordan, but most were not. After Stone finished taking her photos, Payne took her phone and uploaded everything via VPN to an encrypted server.

"What are you doing?" Stone asked.

"Covering our asses."

"From what?"

Payne looked toward the double windows on the far wall. For several seconds he was lost in his thoughts. Finally, he responded. "I'm not sure yet but covering it anyway. Is CYA no longer taught in FBI 101?"

"You sure that's legal? Sending those pics wherever you did?"

"Is what legal?" Payne smirked. He handed back her cellphone.

"This," she insisted, waving her phone in his face.

"I have no idea what you're talking about."

A thorough examination of the house revealed little else. While downstairs Payne pointed out that the study used for a home office looked as if equipment was missing. He showed Stone the empty stand next to the computer desk. "Printer is missing."

"How do you know he had one?"

"Cables are still there, but they aren't connected to anything. Also, I think he probably had a laptop as well, based on the mouse pad and other cables."

"So, who took them? The same folks that ransacked the place?"

"Maybe."

Finally, they ended up in the garage. The Nissan Maxima registered to Ralph Webb wasn't there. Payne pulled out his phone.

"Who are you calling?" asked Stone.

"I'm putting out a BOLO for his car."

"You think whoever took him may still have it?"

"Possibly."

"You realize he could have left on his own, right?"

"Of course, but if he did, I don't imagine he'd have left the cash and passports and a safe hanging wide open. Look around the house. Does a guy who lives this way strike you as someone careless enough to leave town in a rush and leave damning evidence behind? And did he trash his own house to throw off whoever came looking for him?"

"Doubtful, but you never know."

"Highly unlikely, based on my experience. Nick Jordan is probably in a lot of trouble right now. And that's if he's still alive."

Stone's eyes narrowed as she glared at Payne. "And here I thought you were taking me across town to meet an old lady with dementia."

"Welcome officially to the Bureau. Few things are ever as they seem at first glance."

Chapter 18
Reims, France

The lifting sound of soft music filled the festive *Bar La Rotonde* within *Domaine Les Crayères*. A luxurious hotel located inside a grand chateau in Reims, France, *Les Crayères* attracted an affluent crowd accustomed to the finer things without regard for cost.

Merci De Atta sauntered into the bar, an elegant series of adjoining rooms decorated with British accents. Four large oil paintings with regal figures adorned the wall facing the glass-enclosed sunroom. A half-dozen rounded tables had chairs upholstered in soft, aromatic leather and soft jazz music added to the ambiance.

Most eyes in the room, regardless of their sexual orientation, focused on the stunning woman as she made her way into the lively space.

The black skin-tight cocktail dress with plunging neckline hugged her curves and accentuated her partially exposed breasts. Merci knew how to draw attention when the need arose, yet she could blend into any crowd just as easily.

These were skills she'd worked hard to hone, and they served her well. A chameleon by trade, Merci integrated seamlessly into any environment depending on the role she needed to play.

Out of the corner of her eye, she singled out one man eying her. His lust was evident.

Merci knew the look well. A sly smile formed at the corner of her mouth as she contemplated what was likely to happen next. Without warning, the woman to his left smacked his chest loud enough to elicit a grunt and muttered several harsh words in French. His eyes quickly darted away from Merci and then snuck back to her.

Merci turned toward the opulent bar in the center of the room. It looked like something out of a James Bond film and so did many of the patrons. Fine leather stools lined the sweeping curves of the antique bar made of rich mahogany milled in the Amazon circa 1900. Only the second seat to the left remained open. A sign before it read *Réservé.*

She smiled at the bartender, who subtly nodded.

As Merci sat, the bartender removed the Reserved sign. The hundred-Euro note she'd slipped into his pants pocket an hour before had made her job a little easier. The fact that her hand had wandered aggressively for a few minutes in his pocket had sealed the deal.

Experience had taught her all too well. Men are so easily manipulated.

"*Un pinot noir,*" she said to the bartender. He was appropriately dressed in a white shirt with black bow tie. He winked and returned a minute later with an expensive glass of red wine for which he charged only the house red rate.

To her left was a tall man with black-and-gray-speckled hair. He looked in her direction when the bartender placed the glass of wine in front of her. His eyes purposely lingered on her ample chest before he looked up, making eye contact. He wanted her to know she was seen—and appreciated.

Merci enjoyed being seen and appreciated. She gave him a warm smile and rubbed the top of the wine glass in a counterclockwise manner with her index finger. She spun the liquid around in the glass before she inhaled the aroma of the wine. Then she took an exploratory sip.

"Well, how do you do, *mademoiselle?*" asked the man, extending his hand. "James Fowler, at your service." He bent and gently kissed the top of her hand, inhaling the perfume applied there for just this purpose.

"Very well, *monsieur*. I'm Merci, *s'il vous plait*—yes, my actual name. And how are you?"

He allowed that he was much better since Merci had taken her seat at the bar. For several minutes they engaged in small talk. He made her laugh, a bubbly sound, which caused him to take a greater interest in her. He continued to provide witty comments, and with each laugh he inched closer. They both finished their drinks at the same time.

"And what do you do?" Fowler asked as the bartender brought them both another round.

A enticing, devilish grin formed at the corner of Merci's lips. She brushed a finger along the contour of her cheek. "Oh, a little bit of this, a little bit of that," as she waved her other hand in the air. "Mainly, I travel and enjoy the finer things in life—a *Jacqueline* of all trades, mistress of but a few. Et toi?"

"I'm in the banking business," Fowler said with a practiced air of gravity.

"Really?" she said with feigned interest. "Do you manage a bank?"

He chuckled slightly. "Oh, no, my dear—I *own* them."

"'Them'? More than one?"

"Yes, my business is global."

"How *interesting*. And how is your business holding up in these uncertain times?"

That was all he needed to hear. A gorgeous young woman had caught his eye and took an interest in his line of work. He could blather on *ad nauseum* about banking minutia, and he did, all the while the drinks flowed. As the alcohol in his system increased, his defenses, not high to start with, waned by the glass.

Merci had previously arranged with the cooperative bartender that her drink after the first one would be plain grape juice, very slightly watered to color-match the real pinot. It tasted horrible but the charade was maintained.

After an hour, Merci and her new gentlemen friend moved away from the bar to a red velvet couch in the adjacent sunroom. Merci had no trouble keeping the discussion on him. Their conversation remained jovial, and he asked her occasional questions to seem interested in her, but he mainly discussed himself.

With his ego stroked and his drinks kicking in supplemental courage, Fowler edged closer and coolly rubbed a soft knee that was exposed by the provocative thigh-high slit in the dress when Merci had crossed her long legs. Slowly, casually, he moved his hand toward her upper thigh.

The time was now.

Merci pulled a room key from her purse. "Care to join me upstairs?" she asked as her tongue brushed against the top of her upper lip.

And the hook was set. "I thought you'd never ask, my dear."

"I should warn you, my room is on the smallish side," she said.

Fowler removed his key. "Mine is not—it's quite large. I have the largest one you'll find in the castle."

Merci winked. "We're still talking only about your room, aren't we?"

"Guess you're about to find out."

Five minutes later they were in his room. His hands examined her every curve and she did nothing to slow things down. As he unfastened his belt and unzipped his pants, she said she needed to freshen up. He protested, but she insisted.

She won. Merci always won.

She disappeared into the bathroom and pushed the door closed with her six-inch heel.

Coming out several minutes later, she wore only a black bra and matching thong-style panties. She asked if he wanted a nightcap. He nodded and pointed toward the wet bar. The black thong left nothing to the imagination as she moved away from the bed. The bra was intentionally too small, and it overflowed perilously.

As she walked toward the bar, Fowler said, "You know by now what I like."

Merci nodded and swayed her hips, sure his gaze watched each step.

How in the hell is this guy still standing? She'd plied him with so many drinks she'd lost count. And still he threw them down like they were little more than water on the rocks.

She returned with two glasses and handed him the one from her right hand.

He downed the glass of single malt Scotch in one gulp and turned his attention back to her.

Seconds later, the thick glass fell from his hand and shattered hard on the hand-scraped hardwood floor, sending shards in every direction.

Fowler's body turned rigid and his eyes fixated on the half-naked woman before him. Her warm smile turned sinister as she reached out and pushed him backward.

The bed caught his stiff body and he lay there in a paralyzed state. He attempted to talk, but no words formed.

Merci walked to her purse and removed three devices. She took the first one and digitally scanned each hand print. Next, she straddled him and brought the other device up to his face. A look of fear haunted his eyes as his gaze darted around the room looking for help that wasn't there.

"This won't hurt a bit," she said in a reassuring tone.

With the device two inches from his retina, she captured a digital image of his right eye, then the left. All scans completed, she climbed off him and moved to the far side of the bed, connecting the device to the tablet. Within thirty seconds she had uploaded the images to their destination.

The stiffness in the man's body turned into pain as he felt his internal organs burn.

Merci could see the suffering in his eyes. With her job completed, there was no reason to extend the man's agony.

She was an assassin, not a sadist.

She removed a glass vial from her purse and raised it above his gaping mouth, and said, "There, there, it's almost done. Thank you for a most wonderful evening, James."

Merci leaned in close to his ear. Her voice dripped with sarcasm as she turned the vial horizontal. The viscous fluid dripped into his open mouth. "You-know-who says he'll see you in hell, but you are going first to get a good table."

Fowler's eyes grew big. As the thick droplets touched his tongue, the pain radiating inside his body exploded in a fury of fire that started in his mouth. Like a match to gasoline, the fire spread in an instant throughout his body before the agonizing pain gave way to a cold shudder. Finally, the darkness came for him and only silence remained.

Merci located his briefcase and poured out its contents on the bed next to his still warm corpse. She found the key in less than a minute and stuffed it inside her purse.

Merci walked to her car ten minutes later. Before she opened the door, she made a single call. "It's done," she said to the man who answered the call. "I sent the biometric markings."

"That's great, but you have a problem."

"What kind of problem?" she asked. "I literally just left his room."

"The issue is not with him."

"Then what?"

"Make your way to the safe house. Marcus needs to talk to you immediately."

"I know. He's been trying to reach me since yesterday. You told him I was finishing this other job, right?" Merci's voice changed, and she spoke the last few words in a harsh tone.

"Look, don't shoot the messenger. I told him, but he kept calling. Said you had to check in ASAP. He sounds pretty pissed."

"Yeah, well, he can get in line," Merci said. "I'll call back in thirty minutes."

The call ended as Merci took a deep breath. She let it out slowly before starting the engine of the Audi A6.

Shit. Guess I can't delay this any longer. What the hell is going on?

Chapter 19
The Gulf of Mexico

Nick Jordan closed his eyes. All he wanted was sleep. The person everyone referred to as the Body Man ached from head to toe from his most recent beating.

As his head dipped, the sandman's comforting touch pulled him closer to slumber until Sir's heavy fist crashed down on the stainless-steel table, jostling him awake. After Jordan's assault on the guards, Sir had let him stay unconscious for forty-five minutes before they dragged him back to the interrogation room.

Sir had questioned him for almost four hours straight. He'd been relentless, like a used-car salesman behind on his quota and desperate to close a deal.

"One more time, prisoner. Who else knows?"

Jordan shook his head back and forth. "I've told you. Nobody else knows."

"And I think you're lying." Sir paused. He tapped a finger in a rhythmic tone, then opened the large folder before him and pulled out a single sheet from the stack of neatly organized papers. "Maybe we have the wrong person after all. Maybe we should talk to Danny Frazier instead."

Jordan didn't flinch. In fact, he watched Sir's movements and contemplated what the file must hold. *It can't be much. Mainly blank pages. After all, if they had solid intel, they wouldn't need me alive.*

He stayed stoically quiet.

"Nothing, huh?" asked Sir.

Jordan stared back at him but said nothing.

"And if we grab Danny Frazier, what will he say?"

"Cut the bullshit," he said. "You already have Danny."

"Do I?"

"Yes, and you're probably beating him senseless in the next room." Sir scoffed.

"We don't handle things like that here."

"Pardon me if I don't believe you." Jordan raised his bound hands as high as they would go until the chain securing his handcuffs to an eyebolt in the table made a metallic clinking sound. "Your goons sure did a number on me."

"You had that coming after you attacked them."

"Excuse me for trying to fucking escape," Jordan said.

Sir ignored the statement. "If I did have Danny, what would I learn from him?" he asked.

"Danny doesn't know anything, You're wasting your time."

"I have strong evidence that says otherwise," said Sir as he tapped his index finger once more on the thick file before him.

"Then you don't need anything from me."

"Oh, but I *do* need you. We have plenty of questions that need answers. Answers that I don't believe Danny has."

"The Sanctum, or whatever the hell bullshit name you call yourselves, probably already killed Danny."

Sir's body visibly tensed. His right hand balled into a fist, and he slowly tapped it against the table. He took a deep breath and opened his hand, placing it on the cool surface of the metal table. "And why would we kill him?" asked Sir.

"Maybe because you're psychopaths."

Sir's fist once again clenched. This time he didn't release his fingers into an open position. "I can assure you Danny is very much alive."

Jordan didn't believe a word. "Danny may be alive, or he may be dead rotting in some ditch somewhere. Either way, I don't give a shit."

"I think you do care. You were Danny's mentor."

"Look, I'm sure you have interrogated all kinds of people before. But you've not had many people like me. I know how this works. You know how this works. We both know you can't use Danny as leverage. Either you have him, or you don't. He's either alive or dead. But either way, it won't change what I'll tell you, which is jack shit. You'll have to step up your game and move me on to the next level of interrogative methods if you want me to squeal like a pig."

"As in?"

"Got any electric drills?" Jordan paused as his eyes narrowed. "How about pliers?"

"I do, in fact."

"Sounds like fun, but you and I both know those enhanced interrogation methods don't work either. I'll talk, but you won't know what's real versus what's incoherent babble from a lunatic writhing in agony."

"Is that so?"

"That being the case, I'll offer you a concession."

"And what would that be?"

Jordan managed a bloody half-smile. "Put a bullet in my head right now and we can both get some rest." He leaned forward and tapped his forehead with his raised index finger. "Or give me back my cyanide capsule and I'll end it myself."

"Not afraid to die, are you, prisoner?" A wry grin creased Sir's face. "Are you a hero? Or just stupid?"

Jordan didn't reply.

"Far be it for me to cut your heroic journey short," Sir said. "And I'd never want to help a man take the easy way out." He stood and paced the room stopping next to his captive. "I do think we've hit a little snag here, but I'll grant your wish."

Jordan smirked, victorious. "Yippee ki yay, mutha—"

It was a short victory celebration. Sir cut him off mid-*Die Hard* phrase by delivering a brutal punch to the bridge of Nick's nose, sending his head lolling backward.

Lights out.

Two guards dragged Jordan's unconscious body out of the room and down the hall, a steady stream of blood from his nose leaving a crimson streak behind them.

Sir paced the interrogation room. Adrenaline rushed through his veins. His hand hurt like hell and started to swell.

This fucking guy, he seethed in anger.

A tall, poised woman with mocha skin stepped into the room. "I thought you avoided violence?"

Sir shook his head from side to side. "He pissed me the fuck off. Nick Jordan is too smart for his own damn good. And besides, he didn't give me much choice. We need actionable intel, and we need it now."

"He flustered you. I've never seen someone get under your skin that quickly."

"I can't keep going around and around with him. I've got to take it to the next level."

The woman tapped her wrist and the watch that hung loosely from her smooth skin. "Time to use the chemicals?"

"I think so. It will take time to decipher fact from fiction after we inject him, but at this point it's our best option."

"Then we'd better get a move on it."

"Get the Chemist up to room three."

"What should he bring?"

"Everything."

Chapter 20
Washington, DC

Payne felt a skull-splitting headache hammering in the back of his head as he and Stone left Vienna. The acute migraine slowly followed the contour of his skull and made its way behind his left eye socket. He popped three Advil and washed them down with a sugar-free Red Bull, hoping the chemical combo would do the trick.

He looked over at Stone in the seat next to him.

"I was serious earlier. You did a good job clearing the house," he said.

"Well, can't say you were too shabby yourself. You learn to clear rooms at the academy?"

He looked taken back. "No, the Army."

"Yeah?"

"Yeah. Eight years."

"SEALs? CAG?"

"Why does everyone ask me that?" he said, rolling his eyes.

Stone punched his arm playfully. "Well, I mean, look at you. Your physique, the way you walk and talk. Plus, I heard you think you're a badass."

Payne frowned. "Jesus, number one, I said 'Army,' and SEALs

are squids. Navy. And not every guy who served was in an elite unit. Hollywood and thriller novels have given people a warped view of modern soldiers." The expression turned into a slight smirk. "But sure, I can be a badass."

"Who were you with?"

"Third Ranger Battalion, Fort Benning, Georgia—when we weren't deployed," he said, and swerved to the next lane and back to avoid a slower moving car.

"Well, then you were part of special operations. Rangers are pretty badass."

A subtle grin formed at the corner of his lips. "Ehh, yeah, mostly true, and we had our moments, but I was mainly a door kicker. I never went on to Delta."

"Why not?"

"I got out."

"Because?"

Payne exhaled. "I blew my knee out on a training exercise. Nothing glamorous. Took a bad landing off the tower on parachute sustainment training—not even a real jump. Shit happens sometimes when you train, and this time it happened to me. I decided during the recovery from ACL surgery that maybe I needed to rethink my career goals."

"And?"

"Chose not to re-enlist. Life in the sandbox can be hell on earth, and I needed a change of pace. Used the GI bill and went back to finish college. Applied to the Bureau the year I graduated and never regretted it."

"And another layer is revealed."

"I'm not that complicated."

Stone frowned. "Everyone's complicated."

Payne ignored the comment and focused on the road.

He headed east on Interstate 66 and followed his usual pedal-to-the-floor driving pattern, darting into the left lane. Stone ignored his speed and talked about what they'd found at the townhouse, while up ahead, a car in the fast lane drove much too slowly for Payne's taste. This prompted him to move into the middle lane.

In the rearview mirror, he saw something that made his muscles tense. A green Chevy Tahoe barreled down the left lane at a high rate of speed. Stone kept talking, but Payne didn't hear a word of it. The Tahoe drove erratically, the driver having a difficult time keeping the oversized vehicle in its lane. Payne's fingers gripped the steering wheel tight enough to cause the tips to turn white. When the Tahoe closed within thirty feet, Payne saw the driver's face. He looked Hispanic, with a thick black goatee and a bandanna covering his head.

Sure, it was a stereotype, but Payne thought he looked like a gangbanger. Not an uncommon sight in the DC metro area.

As the Tahoe pulled parallel with his car, Payne's entire body was on high alert and he rested his right hand on his firearm. The driver suddenly jerked into his lane. Instinct kicked in, and Payne's brain processed several commands faster than he could even articulate. Out of his peripheral vision, Payne saw the minivan in the lane to his right. Cutting the wheel hard toward the minivan wasn't an option. He only had one choice. His foot came off the gas pedal and applied maximum pressure to the brakes, which caused the anti-lock brakes to chatter and the car's nose to dive slightly, decelerating out of danger just as the Tahoe crossed the broken white line.

Payne knew a sideswipe at that speed might prove fatal—and it certainly would cause a spectacular crash.

Stone was thrown forward against her locked shoulder belt and she had just enough time to utter, "What the fu—"

Payne's relief didn't last as the Tahoe continued past his front bumper, missing by mere inches, and darted toward the slow lane. The Tahoe slammed into the side of the minivan with a loud crunching sound as sheet metal crumpled sheet metal, followed by the high-pitch screech of rubber on pavement.

Everything happened so fast, but oddly enough it felt like slow motion in Payne's mind. He watched the minivan as it flew off the side of the road and slammed against the concrete barrier lining the interstate. In the split second of the crash, Payne saw the frantic face of the woman driving the minivan. Then he noticed a car seat facing backward in the second row of seats.

Rage overtook Payne as the driver of the Tahoe recovered from the erratic swerve, straightened out his vehicle, and sped forward. Every fiber of Payne's being wanted to slam his foot onto the gas pedal and chase down the Tahoe. He could envision himself beating the shit out of the gangbanger with his bare knuckles. But as he watched the minivan slide up the concrete barrier and tip over, it slammed into a green power box and flipped several times.

Three words flashed in his mind.

Mother.

Child.

Help.

Without a second thought he jerked the wheel hard to the right and pushed the brake pedal to the floor as hard as possible.

Stone braced her hands on the dashboard as the car came to a halt. Without a word, Payne engaged the emergency lights in the grill and taillights and opened the door even before he fully slammed the gear shift into park. Stone was still unbuckling as Payne sprinted to the smoking minivan. The unmistakable smell of gasoline wafted through the air and his heart raced. His eyes darted around the severely damaged vehicle as he looked for proof of life.

The van sat right side up. Payne approached it and yanked

hard at the driver's side door with Stone on his heels. After several intense tugs, the door gave way and opened.

"Free the mother," he yelled as he reached for the handle on the side of the van. Payne pulled at the sliding door, but the force of the collision had jammed it shut. He gripped the handle with both hands and pulled the door along the track with all his strength, and the door ground open. Once it was open enough to lean in, he grabbed at the car seat and looked inside. A child, no older than three months, wailed uncontrollably.

Screaming is *good*, thought Payne. *The baby is alive.*

Payne reached for the seat harness holding the child, but it wouldn't release no matter how hard he pushed the red button. He didn't know how the hell to work the latch, but he pulled out his pocketknife and cut the seatbelt with one cut to the top belt and another to the lap belt, freeing the car seat.

He looked around the rest of the van and saw no other passengers, so he dropped the knife and pulled the baby seat out with both hands.

Stone already had the mother out. She was in hysterics, yelling, "My baby! My baby!" over and over.

"*Run!*" Payne shouted as he neared Stone and the mother.

Stone grabbed the woman by the arm and yanked her away from the vehicle and Payne sprinted off with the baby seat cradled in his arms.

They ran full speed for sixty feet before a deafening roar and a concussive blast knocked them to the ground when the minivan exploded.

Three hours later, Payne and Stone sat in the conference room at their FBI field office. They had recounted the harrowing crash tale more than once and finally got around to briefing the missing-person case.

The conference room table displayed the evidence found at Nick Jordan's townhouse, meticulously collected by the evidence response team. Payne's eyes focused on one thing, his precision glance laser sharp.

Two of the four assistant special agents in charge assigned to the WFO sat across from them at the table. The SAC was traveling overseas, or he too would have been in the thick of the discussions. Payne's squad supervisor, Wes Russell, was there with his normal eat-shit-and-die scowl plastered over his face.

Payne started from the beginning and relayed the events of the past twenty-four hours. With all the passports and money found, the evidence suggested not only did the White House have a missing agent, but it had a dirty one as well—one they knew about and weren't owning up to.

"I want you and Stone to catalog and enter all the evidence you've collected," said Mitch Bauman, the senior assistant SAC present, after Payne wrapped up his explanation of what occurred. "ERT will catalog and enter what it collected to avoid lengthening the chain of custody."

"But that will take hours," Payne protested. "We need to be out there looking for Nick Jordan, not buried in the evidence room up to our eyeballs in paperwork."

"Look." Russell stepped up to the ASAC their defense. "Payne and Stone had one hell of a morning, and we have others who can process the evidence. I need them out there to shake the trees and see what falls out. That is, if they feel up to it."

Payne looked at Stone, and they both nodded.

"We're good," Payne said.

"Stay away from the White House," Bauman said, pointing an index finger at them.

He was the most political of the bosses in the field office and usually the one most concerned with covering his own ass, especially when the SAC was on travel and he was left in charge. Bauman took two steps forward until he encroached on Payne's space close enough to feel his breath.

"You know, I've never been crazy about you, Payne. You're sloppy, undisciplined, and you think you walk on water because you ate some snakes in the Army." Payne remained stonefaced. "You impress only your mother and the waitresses at Hooters. You screw this up, and you'll be a fingerprint technician the rest of your short and unsatisfactory career."

Payne eyed him warily but didn't protest. Bauman had a well-deserved reputation of being a dick. In fact, Payne might have told him that to his face on more than one occasion. A likely reason, even with all his experience, that Payne still held a non-supervisory level role in the office.

Swallowing his pride, Payne replied simply. "Understood."

They hadn't exactly agreed. It was more like a truce.

In the spirit of solidarity with her partner, Stone piped up and said, "What about me?"

Bauman looked at her like she was a bug. "You're probationary. Let that be your guide."

Everyone in the conference room moved toward the door but Payne, who stepped toward the conference-room table. With one quick motion he scooped up Nick Jordan's White House ID badge in his right hand, the evidence bag and all, slicker than a Las Vegas pickpocket. Like a magician, he slid it into the front pocket of his khaki pants.

But Stone saw his move and raised her eyebrows behind the back of the exiting bosses.

Payne winked and raised an index finger to his pursed lips. *Shhh …*

Two hours later, after cataloging and entering the table full of Nick Jordan's stuff, Payne and Stone were walking toward the bank of elevators.

Squad boss Wes Russell jogged up behind them. "Hold up, Payne," he said.

"Yeah, what's up?"

"Listen, I need you to tread lightly out there, okay?"

"Meaning what, exactly?"

"You know what I mean. We both have been doing this long enough to know how DC works. If Bauman calls the Secret Service, things are going to escalate quickly."

"I'm just following the evidence, boss man."

Russell frowned. "I know, and I'm telling you if we have an FBI agent running around investigating a missing Secret Service agent without any inter-agency cooperation, all hell is gonna break loose."

"I don't think the hell breaking loose can be stopped, based on what we found in that townhouse," Payne said.

"You're probably right, but watch your back anyway."

"I'm more worried about my front. 'Cause I think I see what's coming."

Russell put his hand on Payne's shoulder. For all the back and forth, they really were friends. Russell squeezed his shoulder. "You sure you're okay, bud? The whole thing with the minivan could have damn near killed you."

"Yeah, we're fine."

"And you're sure it was simply a random accident?"

"Can't be positive, but yeah. I think so. What else would it be? Stone and I were merely at the wrong place, wrong time."

"Well, for that young mother and her child, you were the right person at the perfect time." Wes let go of Payne's shoulder as the elevator door made a *ding* sound.

"Guess so," Payne said as the elevator door opened and he and

Stone stepped inside. Russell held the elevator door open.

"Eli, I wasn't going to say anything because you know what these approval chains are like, but you should know your buddy Bauman is putting you both in for the Medal of Valor for that minivan save." He pulled his hand away when the elevator alarm buzzed and the doors slid closed. The last thing Payne and Stone saw was Russell giving them a congratulatory thumbs up.

When the doors closed and Stone and Payne were alone, she turned toward him. "Well, no kidding, huh?"

"I guess that's worth a few promotion points for you, rook," Payne said. "Good for you."

But a fire raged in her eyes. "Why did you take it?"

Payne played coy. "Take what?"

"Don't give me your bullshit. You know what. Jordan's White House ID badge. It's the most damning evidence we have."

"And?"

"You stole it. Evidence that's supposed to be logged and placed in a secure location."

"I didn't steal a damned thing. I retained it for legitimate investigative purposes. We'll bring it back."

"But *why* did you take it?"

"I need to show it to someone."

"Who?"

Payne raised his index finger and shook it back and forth. "Not yet, rook. I need to work out a few more details before I share."

"But they'll know you took it."

"Who? Me?"

"Are you trying to get fired—or even worse, get me fired?"

"Don't worry about it, Stone. I know what I'm doing."

"You're asking me to trust you without providing me with all the facts." Stone's eyes narrowed. She wasn't about to back down and Payne could see it.

He considered her words as they stepped off the elevator and made their way to the lobby. "You know what? Fair enough, I owe you a response. I'm pretty sure I know who can give me a straight answer regarding Nick Jordan if I show them the badge."

"And who is that?"

"Someone on the inside."

"The White House?"

"Yes."

Stone sighed. "I hope you know what you're doing."

"Me? I hope I do, too."

As they reached the car, Stone's cellphone rang. Payne climbed in while Stone stayed outside.

When she got in, Payne looked at her with an inquisitive stare. "What do you have?"

"We got a hit on our BOLO."

"They found the car already?" Payne asked, reaching for his seat belt.

"Yes."

"Where?"

"Days Inn Manassas right off exit 47 on I-66. The manager reported it this morning. You know where that is?"

"Yes, I know the area. I'm surprised it got reported so quickly," Payne said

"Manager said they make all guests register their cars due to vehicle break-ins. She found a Nissan Maxima in the back of the parking lot that didn't show up on any guests' registration."

"A proactive hotel manager. I'm impressed."

"Lots of people are good at their jobs, Payne."

"Yeah, well, plenty suck at them, too."

"And you normally interact with the latter?"

"Occupational hazard, I guess. Is the car still at the Days Inn parking lot, or did it get impounded?"

"Still there. Police told the manager they would send a roll-back, but it may be a while."

Payne started the car and pulled onto Third Street. "We can make it there in about forty minutes if we scoot," he said after looking at his watch.

"Should I call Prince William County and tell them to hold off on the tow?"

Payne shook his head. "Won't do any good. Manassas is an independent city. The county has no jurisdiction there. You'll need to call the Manassas PD. Ask for Sergeant Gervais."

"Friend of yours?"

Payne smiled. "We play against each other in a fantasy football league."

Stone sighed. "You're hopeless."

Chapter 21
Port of Los Angeles

Peter Casha's place high atop the Port afforded him an excellent vantage point. The wind blew hard from the west, gathering moisture from the Pacific, and each gust cut through the sky, sending shivers down his spine. His flimsy windbreaker did little to stifle the unusual chill.

Casha raised Leica Trinovid HD binoculars and watched the loading process. From his position, it looked like organized chaos as over a dozen cranes moved shipping containers of various sizes and colors through the morning sky like *Cirque du Soleil* acrobats performing complex maneuvers under the big top.

For all the activity going on, he only cared about eight containers belonging to General Atomics. Casha watched as the containers were offloaded from the semis and stacked next to the port side of the cargo ship, forming a pyramid shape. At eight feet wide, eight and a half feet tall, and forty feet long, the stack rose almost twenty-six feet into the air.

General Atomics security personnel hovered close to the containers, but Hector Fuentes had assured him the decoy containers were identical. Still, he had his doubts, and if the guards discovered the switch, the whole operation would fail.

Fuentes' voice sounded from Casha's two-way radio. "They're starting to move the containers."

"We still a go?" Casha asked.

"We're fine. My guys have everything under control."

Two cranes worked in unison to move the eight containers two at a time while other cranes continued moving containers onto the ship.

Casha watched as a helpless bystander while Fuentes' men orchestrated the movements.

The plan wasn't complicated, but a shell-game switch of ten-thousand-pound metal containers right in front of security personnel required deliberate and calculated movements. Fuentes' men had built up containers on the port side of the ship, obstructing the view from the dock.

The General Atomics security team could only see what Fuentes' men revealed.

Two at a time, the crane operators moved the containers over the stack on the port side, but instead of lowering them on the cargo ship bound for Italy, the cranes moved past the starboard side of the ship and instead lowered the containers to another smaller container ship docked on its right.

Within fifteen minutes all eight containers were off the dock and safely on the adjoining ship.

Next, the dock foreman, one of Fuentes' men, gave the General Atomics men the all clear signal, indicating they could board the ship and inspect the eight containers.

Casha watched the events play out, pleased with the progress.

His cellphone rang. "Yes."

"Give me an update."

Casha said, "The eight containers have been loaded successfully on the ship."

"And the security personnel?"

"Looks like they bought it."

"Are they still there?"

"Yes, they are inspecting the cargo ship bound for Italy now."

There was a pause on the line.

"Good."

"Is there anything else?" Casha asked, sensing that checking up wasn't the only reason for the call.

Another pause.

"Yes, one more thing."

"What?"

"It's about Hector and his men."

"Okay." Casha thought he knew what was coming.

"Have they been paid?"

"Of course."

"Good, but we need to make a slight change."

"And what would that be?"

"You need to kill all of them after the container ship departs."

Casha didn't think he heard right. "Say again?"

"Kill them all and do it today. Ditch the bodies at sea. No evidence can be left behind."

Rage welled up from deep within, but he fought the urge to let it overtake him. He took a deep breath. "What changed?"

"The boss decided the risk was too great that one of them would talk."

"What the hell? Is he getting paranoid or something?"

"Getting?"

"I'm pretty sure I put the fear of God in them. They're solid."

"And I'm pretty sure he didn't ask for your opinion."

Casha said nothing.

"Look," said the other man. "I know eliminating them wasn't part of the original plan, but as we both know, plans go to hell all the time. Trust me, this isn't how I would proceed if I was the shot-caller."

"I see."

"Boss said you could keep their take as a bonus for the extra hassle."

"You know it's not about the money."

"I know."

Casha was only slightly upset about the order, but he was a good soldier. "It takes time to plan a hit on seven guys. And I don't like last-minute surprises."

"You got this?"

Casha hesitated. "I'll be fine."

"You sure?"

"I said I'll be fine."

"There's something else."

"What?"

"Marcus, or should I say Merci, screwed up."

"Jesus," Casha said. "How so?"

"Danny Frazier is still alive."

"She didn't shoot him?"

"No, she did. But the bastard lived."

"That will complicate things."

"Yes, it will."

"What's that mean for us?"

"Not sure yet."

"Does he expect me to finish the job?"

"No, it's all on Marcus."

"I see."

"Look, he's here. I gotta go. The jet will be waiting for you at the Santa Monica Airport when it's done."

Before Casha could reply, the line went dead. He concentrated on the General Atomics personnel as they climbed down from the container ship, satisfied with what they'd found on board. At least that part of the plan had come together. His mind went into over-drive as he started to consider how best to eliminate Fuentes and his men. It was going to be a hell of a long day.

The shit show had officially begun.

Chapter 22
Midtown Manhattan
New York City

Joe Lagano massaged the bridge of his nose with his index finger and thumb. The anxiety of the past several weeks had started to show in small, subtle ways as dark circles formed under his piercing blue eyes.

He looked out from the twenty-sixth floor of his Fifth Avenue office toward Central Park. From his vantage point, people looked like ants scurrying across the streets and yellow cabs zipped down Fifth Avenue in a never-ending rat race, minus the cheese at the end of the maze.

His door suddenly flung open as Charles Steele Junior entered his office like a wave crashing into a rocky bluff. It was Junior's second incursion in the past few minutes. He wasn't the easiest person to be around. In fact, he was a boisterous asshole, according to most people who knew him. It hadn't helped when, at thirty-six, he'd become president of the privately owned family conglomerate and then acquired the title of CEO after his father divested himself of the business to go into politics.

His ego was larger than the Fifth Avenue office tower, and when Junior walked into a room, he wanted all eyes on him. With an undergraduate degree from Princeton and an MBA from

Wharton, his credentials were comparable to other CEOs within the industry. But those who knew him best recognized his flaws. He tended to delegate too often, and digging into the details wasn't his specialty.

"JoJo, where we at with the shipment?" Junior asked, sounding annoyed.

Lagano had picked up the nickname as a kid from those closest to him. A term of endearment when it came from family and friends, he loathed hearing it from Junior. Junior knew this, which was why he said it loud and often.

"I just talked to Peter. The containers will be headed out to sea within minutes."

"Good, and the other thing?"

"It'll be done."

"Peter's cool with it?"

"He'll do what you said."

"That's what I want to hear." Junior took a seat on the brown leather sofa against the far wall and sunk into the plush cushions. As he placed both feet on the cherry-colored coffee table, he leaned back with arms outstretched above his head until his right shoulder popped. "The pieces are falling into place."

Lagano nodded but didn't reply.

"Do you have the zip drive?" asked Junior as he fished his iPhone out of his pocket and responded to an incoming text.

Lagano slid open the top drawer of the desk. There, sitting next to the .45-caliber Kimber 1911 with the Spartan engraving on the grip, sat the tiny thumb drive FedEx had delivered overnight from Casha.

"Yes," he said. He removed it from the drawer and tossed it to his boss.

Junior turned it over in his fingers several times. A mischievous grin crept over his face.

"What does the rest of the day hold for us?" Lagano asked.

"I've got dinner reservations at Per Se."

"Just you?"

A look came over Junior. "Of course not. I'm bringing a lady friend."

"The one from the magazine?"

"Which one?" asked Junior in a braggart way.

"The one you said could suck-start a leaf blower."

A devious smile crept over Junior's face. "Yes, that's the one. She is quite impressive. Especially when her legs wrap around me and … well, you can imagine the rest."

"A quiet night in the city after dinner?"

Junior shook his head. "No, I'll need to head back to DC. Wheels up by nine."

"Only you?"

"Since when do I fly alone?" asked Junior, an incredulous look covered his face. "I need you with me."

"I'd say you have a pretty good security detail. You'll be fine without me."

Junior pursed his lips. "No, I don't need you for my security this time, JoJo."

"Then why?"

"I've got someone I need to meet."

Lagano knew where this was going. "And you can't be seen with them?"

"Precisely."

"So, I'll go in your place?"

"You catch on fast."

"I'll need to run by my apartment and pack some clothes."

"Nonsense, I'll send one of my people by your place."

"Fine."

"Anything else I need to know?"

"The FBI is starting to ask questions."

Junior turned his head from side to side, clenched his left hand into a fist, and slammed it onto the tabletop. "We're close, JoJo. Real close. The company needs this deal to go through and we can't afford to have some assholes in the FBI or any other agency to interfere."

"Not sure we can prevent that."

A fire burned within Junior's eyes, some of it fueled by the consecutive energy drinks he compulsively powered down all day long. "I disagree. Like my father always told me when I was growing up, 'Where there's a will, there's a way.' I'm willing it, so you gotta find a way."

He stood up fast and huffed out of the office, leaving Joe Lagano alone with his thoughts.

Chapter 23
The Oval Office
The White House

President Steele watched as the last reporters were herded by aides from the Oval Office.

The forced smile he reluctantly wore the past hour melted away and turned into a scowl. While some presidents enjoyed a love-hate relationship with the press, he simply loathed them. Based on the coverage he'd received since taking the oath, the feeling appeared mutual.

The president had the Oval to himself for a few precious minutes. A rare treat since his time was accounted for down to the minute most days. He leaned back in his leather chair and looked up at the ornate ceiling. A golden presidential seal, a decorative touch he'd added, stared back down at him.

The chair creaked and groaned as he tipped it back farther.

He relished such rare moments of silence until the voice of Dolores, his secretary, came through the speakerphone.

"Mr. President," she said.

Charles rubbed his temples for the briefest of moments before he sat up. "Yes, Dolores."

"Sorry to disturb you, sir, but the director of the Secret Service would like a word."

The president sighed audibly. "Send him in."

David Kline strode into the room with long, measured steps. He wore a dark suit, white shirt, red tie, and black wingtip shoes. His salt-and-pepper hair parted on the left side and deep wrinkles on his forehead betrayed his real age. He'd become the director five years before, and the stress of the job had made him look much older than his fifty-five years.

The president didn't stand up and instead motioned to a chair to the side of the desk.

"Thank you for taking the time to meet with me, Mr. President," Kline said.

"Of course. I hope you come bearing some good news."

"Well, sir, I do have an update on Danny."

"I'm listening," said the president.

"I got back from a visit to the University Hospital. Danny appears to be improving."

"He regained consciousness?"

"No, Mr. President. But the doctor said his brain swelling has gone down faster than they expected, which is a good sign."

"Glad to hear it, David. Any update on his prognosis?"

"No, Mr. President."

President Steele paused to appreciate this modestly good news. "How about the search for Nick? Anything to report?"

Kline shook his head. "I've got six of my best people on it, sir. But so far but he's simply gone."

"That's disconcerting," said the president.

"His townhouse appeared to have been ransacked."

"By whom?"

"We don't know, sir."

"Stay on it."

"There's something else, sir."

"Yes?"

"You mentioned yesterday you wanted this close to the vest and kept internal as best we can."

"I did."

"Well, the FBI is involved."

"I've heard that already. Something about a nosy neighbor across the street got the Washington Field Office involved and she reported him missing."

"Yes, but there's more now."

"Go on."

"The FBI agent looking into the missing person call came by here yesterday evening."

"Really? And what did he want to know?"

"Wanted to know if the missing person worked at the White House."

"And what did your people tell him?"

Kline said, "They kept to the script, sir."

"But that wasn't good enough?"

"No, sir. I've got a contact at the Bureau, and supposedly they found something in his townhouse that traces Nick back to the White House."

"What?"

"Not sure yet."

"You know my stance, David. This is our house. And I don't like anyone shitting on our carpet."

"I know, sir."

"Can we push back, delay the Bureau in any way while your team looks for him?" asked the president.

"We'll try, of course."

"Do they know about Danny as well?"

"Not that I'm aware of, sir. We kept the incident under wraps. Even DC Metro doesn't know."

"Good. Now, regarding Nick, how about you make some calls

over to the Hoover and see if you can get them to back down."

"Now that it is an open case, I'm not sure I can do that, sir. Moreover, a request like that would ruffle feathers over there and cause additional suspicions. Such a request would be leaked to the media within the hour."

The president leaned back in his chair, swiveled it around and looked out to the south lawn. I hate this fucking job. He thought for a moment more before turning to face the director.

"Look, I don't want you and your people getting in any hot water over this. Cooperate if you must, but I'll make a few off-the-record calls and see if I can get the Bureau to keep its nose out of our business."

"Whatever you feel is best, sir."

The president didn't hear the last few words. He'd already moved on.

The director of the Secret Service saw his time had expired. He stood up and said, "Thank you for seeing me, Mr. President. As soon as I have any updates, I'll be sure to pass them along."

"Yes, please, David. No matter what time it is, I want to know what you find."

"Of course, sir."

The Director Kline walked out of the room, and the president was left alone. He pushed the intercom button on his phone.

"Yes, Mr. President," Dolores said.

"What's the rest of my schedule look like?"

"You have a meeting with the Secretary of Energy in twenty minutes, but that is all you have on the books, sir. Nothing planned for this evening besides dinner with the First Lady."

"Okay, reschedule the meeting with the secretary for next available, and if he balks, let him meet with the vice president. I need to make a few calls and get freshened up for dinner."

"Of course, Mr. President."

Chapter 24
Manassas, Virginia

Payne came within a few inches of the car he'd cut off as he darted into the fast lane on Interstate 66 headed west. The driver of the car laid on the horn in response to the aggressive move. Payne wanted to raise his middle finger in the air but thought better of it.

"You did see that guy, right?" asked Stone from the passenger seat as she grabbed the door handle with a death grip.

"Yeah, so what?"

"You cut him off."

"And your point is?"

"That's kind of an asshole thing to do."

Payne took his eyes from the road long enough to glare at Stone. "Do you have a point?"

"Sadly, no. Evidently, that the man wasn't driving up to your lofty standard doesn't excuse your driving skills, or lack thereof."

"I drive just fine, thank you."

"Hello? We almost died earlier today."

"That wasn't my fault. Hell, if I hadn't reacted the way I did, we would have been splattered all over the interstate."

"Sure, we would have," Stone said as she rolled her eyes.

"And besides," continued Payne, "we're in a hurry. I don't want the car impounded before we get to the hotel."

"And that gives you the right to drive like a maniac?"

"Would it make you feel better if I turned on my lights and sirens?"

"I have a feeling you don't roll that way."

"Correct. I feel like a douche when I hit the lights."

Stone shook her head. "You've got a real way with the English language, Payne."

"Thanks," Payne said as he cocked his head and gave her an exaggerated wink.

"It's not a compliment."

"Oh, I know."

Two exits later Payne swerved from the fast lane over to the off-ramp to catch Exit 47. He took a left onto Sudley Road and the first right into the Days Inn Manassas parking lot. Payne knew the area well and pulled into a spot near check-in, put the car in park, and approached the lobby with Stone on his heels.

The hotel manager who'd reported the car stood at the front desk. A middle-aged African American female wearing tan slacks and a red hotel logo blouse, her hair was pulled back into a taut bun. She had an inviting smile as the two agents approached the chest-high counter. After Payne and Stone showed their badges and explained the situation, she called one of her people to man the desk.

The manager led them behind the hotel to the back corner of the parking lot, right near a Storage Sense building. The silver Nissan Maxima sat by itself, backed into the space, with no cars nearby.

Stone and the manager stayed near the front of the vehicle as Payne circled it, looking for anything out of place.

"Anyone try and open it?" asked Payne.

The manager shook her head. "Not that I am aware of, no."

"Have you been here the whole time?" asked Stone.

"All day, honey," she said, "and my dogs is barkin'."

Payne smirked at the comment and, surveying the area, looked back at the hotel. He noticed a surveillance camera on the corner of the roof. It looked to be pointed in their direction. He gestured that way.

"Does that camera on the roof work?"

"Sure does, sugar. We've had some theft issues over the years, and even though we aren't liable for anything in the lot, our guests wouldn't take too kindly to us saying, 'Yes, we have a camera, but no, it doesn't work.'"

"You reuse the tapes?"

"It's all digital but we keep the data for about six months."

"Can you get us a copy of the video from the past forty-eight hours?"

"Well, of course I can. You want it right now?"

"Why, yes, please," Payne said. "That would be wonderful." He looked at Stone. "Do you mind going inside with her and getting it?" Payne fished a thumb drive from his pocket and tossed it to Stone.

"I'm on it," Stone said. "What are you going to do?"

"Observe the vehicle." He said with a wink.

Once Stone and the hotel manager left for the office, Payne went back to his car and moved it next to the Maxima. He retrieved a thin piece of notched metal from his trunk and approached the driver's side window. Sliding the long steel into the gap between the door frame and the glass, he shimmied it around until he heard the tell-tale click.

With the door open, he spent five minutes thoroughly examining the front and rear seats. He looked under the seats, pulled back the floor mats, checked out the center console and glove box.

Nothing. The vehicle was clean. Too clean.

Stone walked up alone as he climbed out of the front seat and closed the door.

"You get it?" asked Payne.

"Yes," Stone said as she held up the thumb drive holding the parking lot video.

"Find anything on there?"

"Dunno yet. We didn't review the footage, just copied the last forty-eight onto the drive for us to review later. How 'bout you?"

"Not yet. The interior is spotless. Didn't find any evidence of foul play. I was about to check the trunk." He reached down to the left side of the driver's seat and pulled up the trunk release lever.

"So, you're saying Nick Jordan knows how to maintain a car unlike …" She cleared her throat theatrically. "… some other agent I know?"

"Real funny, Stone. We both know I'm not anal retentive like other agents."

Stone smirked. "Well, *that's* funny. I take it the vehicle was unlocked?" She looked down at the two-foot-long lock-out tool street police use to unlock cars.

"You don't tell me your investigative techniques and I won't tell you mine."

"Don't ask, don't tell?"

Payne winked. "Something like that."

They walked around to the back of the car and Payne lifted the decklid. The trunk was empty. No decomposing body of Nick Jordan stuffed inside. Payne had a hunch it would be empty.

Then he saw it.

The carpet in the trunk was a dark gray, but there was a spot about the size of a grapefruit toward the left rear wheel well that looked darker and wet. Payne shined the flashlight on the spot, his intense gaze focused on what he saw.

"What is it?" asked Stone.

"Not sure yet."

Payne reached down and rubbed his index finger into the matted wet spot. The tip of his finger came away dull crimson.

"Is that what I think it is?" Stone asked.

"Let's see. I have something that's more reliable than a test kit."

Payne went back to his G-car and rooted around the messy contents. He pulled out an unlabeled white plastic spray bottle with a red top, then returned to the Maxima.

"So, what's that?" Stone asked.

"Oxy spray. You know, like laundry stain remover?"

"Oh, so now you're tellin' me you do laundry, huh? Alert the media," Stone poked.

He leaned into the Maxima's trunk and doused the dark spot with several hard pumps of the clear spray.

"What the hell are you doing?" Stone cried. "You're destroying evidence!"

The stain Payne sprayed bubbled up forcefully into a white foam. The fluid was blood.

Payne stood with his hands on his hips and watched the foam subside.

"I'm not looking for evidence. I'm looking for proof."

Chapter 25
Reims, France

Steaming hot water streamed down Merci's lower back. It followed the curvature of her shapely bottom and fell to the marble shower floor before disappearing down the drain. The water helped ease her strained muscles while washing away the scent of her latest mark. Using a loofah, she scrubbed at the greasy residue left on her skin by his touch.

She dried off and pulled on a pair of brand-new silk pajamas she'd bought earlier in the day. She didn't bother with underwear or a bra. The *au naturel* look fit her and the smooth fabric against bare breasts felt sublime. Her wet hair left dark marks that looked like blood along the collar of the red silk top.

Merci knew Marcus Rollings would be irate that she'd waited this long to return his call. But she did things her way and gave exactly zero fucks what he thought, as he well knew. She bowed to no man. Not unless they came at her with a metric ton of money. Even then, she often turned down high-paying jobs because she could.

Merci never tried to dispel the criticism of men. She believed it added to her mystique in a world dominated by men who more times than not proved themselves to be incompetent assholes.

Unzipping her travel bag, she removed one of her half-dozen new burner phones and dialed the number only used between themselves.

Because it was Rollings, she'd take a little bit of his grief, because she still liked him, and he paid extremely well. But anyone else could go straight to hell.

The phone rang several times. Merci knew he was making her wait on purpose before he picked up.

"It's me," she said.

"Where the fuck have you been? I've been trying to reach you for over twenty-four hours." The anger was unmistakable.

"I told you I had another job. It took longer than expected."

"We both know that's bullshit—none of your jobs ever take longer than you expect. You blew me off, wanted to make me wait. You get off on that type of shit *and I fucking hate that*."

"Please, you know all too well what gets me off. But don't start with me. I'm not in the mood. I finished the job, and I called. What's got your boxers in a bunch?"

"Danny Frazier."

The name startled Merci. "What about him?"

"You failed."

"I what?"

"You screwed up the hit in DC."

"There is no chance of this. I killed him as I was paid to do."

"No, you didn't—he survived."-

Merci's stomach balled up and it felt like she'd done crunches non-stop until her midsection ached, and her chest tightened.

"That isn't possible," she said. Her voice went up an octave, the surprise evident in her tone. "I shot him point-blank in the back of his head."

"*Look!*" Rollings yelled. "I saw Danny Frazier in the hospital bed with my own eyes. He's fucking *alive*, dammit."

Merci felt a mild wave of nausea rise. This was a reputation killer, and no one was a harsher critic of her than herself. "So, you want a make-good? A refund, or a warranty claim?"

Rollings said, "Yeah, hilarious. Now I've been tasked with cleaning up this clusterfuck you've left behind."

"But I—"

Rollings cut her off. "He wanted me to kill you for the failure, but I managed to save your narrow ass. At least for now."

Merci's first inclination was to run. She felt confident she could disappear in any number of places around the world, though she favored the south of France. Africa, Chile, Thailand— she had numerous contingency plans if or when the need ever arose. But something else gnawed at her and kept her from hanging up the phone, grabbing her go bag, and falling off the face of the earth.

Personal failure.

Shocked and unsure of what to say, it took her a moment before she collected herself and fired back in typical Merci style. "I'd like to see those bastards try and get me."

"Christ, don't start your 'I'm indestructible' shit with me. You're aware I know your shortcomings. And you know as well as anybody that anyone can be gotten to, at any time."

Fight or flight was getting stronger.

"Do I have to bug out?" She had adequate financial reserves to live comfortably in the *Côte d'Azur* for a very long time.

Rollings grunted. "Don't bother. They'll find you if they want to." He sounded sure about that.

"Don't be so sure. I can vanish if need be."

"I can't let you do that," he said with finality, like it had already been discussed by others and decided it was an untenable option for her. "Anyway, they'll take it all out on me if you're gone, so don't fuckin' do it."

She ignored the statement. "What do they want from me?"

"Restitution."

"They want the money back? There you go. A refund, then."

"No. This has less to do with money. They want us to make it whole."

Merci laughed. "Okay—warranty claim. I'm a professional. I'm good for it either way."

"Get back here ASAP."

Merci snorted. "Why? So they can kill me there? Pass. If I fucked up, fine. I'm good for fixing it to their satisfaction. But I'm not coming back to face a firing squad."

"Look, if we fix this, our problem goes away," Rollings said.

This was something new for her. She needed to make things right. Not for them. Screw them.

For herself.

"Okay, I'll come back," she said.

"When?"

Merci looked at her watch. "I should be able to get the night flight out of Charles de Gaulle this evening."

"Good. Together, we will take out Mr. Frazier."

"In the hospital." Her skepticism was plain.

"Yes."

"Is he not heavily guarded?"

"Of course, he is."

"But you have a plan?"

Rollings disconnected the call.

She closed her eyes and slid out of the silk pajamas. A full-length mirror hung on the wall, and she examined her flawless, naked body in the reflection. A smile came to her face as her eyes closed. She needed a momentary distraction to calm her down and returned to bed.

With her eyes closed and her mind submerged in darkness, Merci drifted into a fitful doze. The faces of people she'd killed over the years flipped through her head like a pack of playing cards shuffled through an electronic deck. A few women, many men.

All of them dead because of her. *Except one.*

Danny Frazier's card flipped to the top of the deck. His dead face came alive as his eyes went round, his gaping mouth widened, and he said, "Boo!" Her eyes sprang open.

I'm already too old for this shit, Merci thought, and reached for her cellphone to call Air France for a Business Class seat, since this clearly was a business trip.

The flight had a three-and-a-half-hour layover at JFK, long enough to slip over to the spa in Terminal Five for a massage before reboarding to Dulles International.

Chapter 26
Manassas, Virginia

Eli Payne thought best on his feet.

He wasn't much of a runner since his ACL blowout. His right knee would ache something fierce if he ran for more than a half mile. Oddly enough, walks didn't bother him. He could walk for hours without any repercussions. Sometimes after a long day he'd hit the pavement with his mind focused on a stubborn case he couldn't crack. Often it was a way to clear his head.

He'd once worked a missing-person case where someone had abducted a four-year-old girl from her home in the dead of night. For forty-eight hours, the FBI conducted a massive search around the DC metro area for the child. Payne had found the little girl's body less than a mile from the family home, sexually assaulted and skull crushed. Payne shook visibly when he broke the savage news to her devastated parents.

The case had shattered him.

Like law enforcement types sometimes will, Payne often wondered if he could take a life in the line of duty. He'd done it numerous times while in a war zone, but that was different.

After he'd notified the family and ensured they had other family members to help with the next steps, he returned home.

He couldn't sleep. A rage had engulfed him, something he'd never felt during all the investigations he'd participated in during his career. That night he power-walked until his body could barely tolerate another step.

Payne had found a modicum of peace by the time he'd slumped onto his couch in his sweat-soaked suit, even as a deep laceration rent his soul.

The horrific events of that case and finding the little girl's broken body had never left his memory. At the same time, he'd confirmed his answer about whether he could take a life. The girl's killer was never found, and Payne envisioned that one day he'd be privileged to exact justice on the human garbage who had plucked such a dear angel from the face of the earth.

Payne had walked around the Nissan Maxima close to thirty times.

Stone had had enough. "*Payne,*" she said, exasperated. "Fercrissakes, are you ever going to stop circling the damned car?"

He paused, a curious look on his face. "I'm thinking," he said.

"Yeah, I know. Some people stand still when they think. You should try it out sometime."

"I don't work that way."

"Hello, Captain Obvious."

Somehow the exchange triggered something in his brain and a light bulb finally went off. "I need a map."

Stone reached into her pocket and pulled out her iPhone. She opened the Google Maps app and handed it to Payne.

He pushed her hand away and marched past her.

"What the hell?" she asked as he disappeared inside his G-car.

It took a minute, but he found it in the glovebox.

"Got it," he said, and walked to the hood of the Maxima to unfold the paper map. Stone looked dumbfounded.

"What the hell is that?"

"A map, Miss Smarty Pants."

"And I've got one on my phone that works fine. Better, actually. Shows all the Waffle Houses and gun stores."

"Not like this one," Payne said as he tapped the map with his index finger. "Gas station classic. Almost collectible."

"That thing is for dinosaurs—I can't believe they still make them." Then she laughed. "I can't believe you can read that small type, either."

"The map on your iPhone sucks. The screen is teeny-tiny. I can't see anything on that, either."

"Maybe it's because you're old," Stone said with a wide grin forming on her face.

"Bite me."

"You really need to take the Bureau's new sexual harassment online tutorial."

"That's pretty funny, Miss Age Discrimination. We'll take it together." Payne fully opened the map and smoothed it out with both hands. It measured three feet by four feet and blanketed most of the car's hood. "Now, let's make a hypothesis."

"You *make* a pie," Stone said. "You *form* a hypothesis."

"You know you're a probie, right? Now, I'm working off the premise Nick Jordan was forced against his will out of his residence in Vienna, placed into his car's trunk, and driven to this location, where he likely was transferred to another vehicle. I believe it was his blood we found in the trunk, proposing his reluctance to cooperate with his relocation."

"I agree. But is he alive?"

"Well, that's one question, but I think he was alive when he came out of the trunk. There's not enough blood in there to suggest he's dead."

"And did they take him out here in the parking lot? And, if so, what did they do with him?"

Payne looked up and around the parking lot. "Doubtful. Even in the dead of night, there's no cover in this location. You'd have to be pretty stupid to remove a body, alive or dead."

"Then you think the car was dropped here after the fact?"

"Yes."

"Why here?"

"Not sure. The proximity to Interstate 66 makes me lean toward it being a matter of convenience."

"Okay, but where's Nick?"

Payne looked back at the map. "Let's assume he was brought within ten miles of this spot where we found the car." He took a pen and drew a circle around the area that he believed included a ten-mile radius.

"And what makes you say that?"

Payne shrugged. "A hunch based on the other cases I've worked over the years. It's unlikely they brought him somewhere and drove the car terribly far to dump it."

"Speaking of that, isn't this a lousy place to ditch a car?"

"Part of me says yes, but with little to go by, it's really hard to say. Lots of cars in and out of here every day. Maybe the kidnappers thought it wouldn't be discovered for a while since it's a heavily used parking lot. Who knows?"

"Okay, let's go down your rabbit hole," Stone said. "Ten-mile radius—what's around here? Strip malls, small businesses, lots of residential neighborhoods. So, where is he?"

"Well, he could be anywhere, but I'm pretty sure if he was abducted, it was not to bring him to Manassas."

"You're saying this location was a springboard for taking him somewhere else?"

Payne nodded. "Yes."

"Then why not drive him there in the car?"

He pointed to the map and tapped his finger repeatedly on one spot. "Good question. Maybe wherever they want to take him is not within a reasonable driving distance. There's not much here besides what you already mentioned, except for the Manassas Regional Airport."

"An airport. Really."

"Yes, it's not that far away, only—" Payne squinted at his gas station classic map.

"Six and a half miles," Stone said, holding up her phone and touch-tapping the screen. "My Google Maps serves a purpose after all. Man, you put the 'special' in Special Agent, don'tcha?"

"Smartass," Payne said.

"But how likely is it someone brought him out here to take him away by plane? That would be awfully difficult."

"It would be easier than you think. Taking him against his will through Reagan or Dulles would be an impossibility, even via the business terminal. But using a small regional airport like Manassas would be easy if you knew what you were doing and timed it right. Lots of private planes there, some fairly large."

"Enlighten me," Stone said.

"A couple charter airline companies use Manassas, and there are plenty of private jets there."

"Guess we're headed to the airport?"

"We are unless you have a better idea."

Stone shook her head. "Lead on, Obi-Wan," Stone said as she headed for the car.

"Are you going to help me fold up my map?" asked Payne.

"No can do, gramps. I've got mine right here," as she held up her phone.

"Ballbuster," he muttered.

"I heard that," Stone said.

"You were supposed to," Payne said.

Chapter 27
The Gulf of Mexico

Sir brought the Marlboro up to his lips and took a deep drag. He closed his eyes and strained his head back as the warm smoke filled his lungs. His neck cracked as he swiveled it from side to side. Exhaling the smoke, he contemplated the tranquil water below.

He didn't care for life on the platform. The Sanctum led him all around the world, and rarely did he find the assignments in desirable locations. The pay made up for the lousy locations, and he told himself only working six months a year was a sweet gig.

The two cigarettes in less than five minutes had achieved the intended goal and helped calm his nerves.

This Nick Jordan was a hard nut to crack.

During his career, he'd experienced a variety of people who'd passed through his interrogation rooms. The big strong ones, men built like tanks, often were the easiest ones to break.

Physically, they could withstand discomfort, but mentally they were weak—and life is ninety percent mental. Beat someone mentally, and they crack like an egg on the edge of a countertop.

The Chemist had injected Jordan with the second round of engineered truth serum. The first round had proved an absolute waste of time. Nick had grown angry but revealed nothing. The drugs hadn't worked, but the Chemist had assured Sir the second dose would achieve better results.

Holding the metal rail tightly with his right hand, he took one last drag and flicked the cigarette into the dark waters below. He watched as it descended almost eighty feet before landing in the water. Behind him, the door creaked open.

Evelyn Rhimes pulled her coat tight and walked over. "It's chilly out here," she said.

"I needed some fresh air."

A gust of wind pulled at her jacket, exposing her skin to the cool air. "We need to chat inside."

Sir nodded.

Rhimes opened the door and he followed her inside. A coat rack stood to the left of the door, and they both hung up their coats before they proceeded to the right, where two couches faced each other.

She pointed to one of the plush leather couches. "Take a seat."

Sir obliged. "What's up?"

She didn't say anything at first. Her dark brown eyes narrowed as she stared at him.

"You unhappy with my interrogation techniques?" asked Sir, breaking the silence.

"No, you know what you're doing."

"Then what is it?"

"I got a phone call."

"From?"

"You know," Rhimes said.

"What did he want?"

"You read the report about what they took from the townhouse, right?"

"Yes."

"Their IT analyst cracked into his laptop and determined Nick printed four copies."

"And they retrieved one of them from the safe," said Sir, finishing her thought.

"That's correct."

"So, I need to determine what he did with the other three."

Rhimes nodded. "They want answers ASAP."

"We both know cracking into a person's mind can't be rushed without a combat tomahawk. Not if you want solid intel."

She said, "Of course, but this is a valuable client, one who can greatly benefit the Sanctum due to his ..." She paused. "Contacts."

"You could attend a session and see if you can get him to talk."

"Use my feminine charms?" Rhimes asked.

Sir smirked. "Something like that."

"No, I'm content staying behind the mirror on this one."

"You think he'll recognize you?"

"I can say without a doubt I've never met the man before he arrived."

Sir glanced at his watch. It was almost time. "The chemical cocktail should be kicking in any minute." Time to go to work.

"Earn your pay," she said.

"Don't I always?"

"So far," she said with a perceptible frown.

Nick Jordan stared at the mirror across from where he sat. He felt a shiver run up his spine, then back down. The cold chill appeared to pulsate through his body. And he was weakening, but still lucid.

It's the drugs, he told himself. *They're trying to overtake me.*

His body shivered uncontrollably. It wasn't an *I'm cold* shiver; it was a get-this-out-of-me shake from the tips of his toes all the way up to the crown of his head.

Fight it, Nick, he told himself. *Damn it, you can't give in.*

He tried to go back to his bedrock, what made him tick. *Ignore everything else and focus your attention on why you get up every morning.* It wasn't to earn a paycheck, not to make a living. His existence mattered, and he performed a role few knew existed or understood.

"I protect the office," he said out loud, but a little slurry. He said it once. After a few seconds passed, he repeated the statement.

He knew what Sir wanted. It had to be the reason they'd taken him. The one thing he couldn't reveal. Jordan placed the memory at the bottom of a large chasm within his mind, then he opened the flood gates of memories and emotions and let them run down into the void to fill it until the thought of what he buried was lost to time and space.

Chapter 28
Situation Room
The White House

FBI Director Kendall Ludington pushed back his chair and stood as the National Security Council meeting finished. He pulled his navy-blue suit jacket taut to his body and buttoned it as he turned to leave. An invitation to the NSC was rare for him. Ever since 2005, when the director of national intelligence position came into existence, the DNI got a seat at the NSC, essentially dropping the FBI director down a notch.

With the DNI out of the country, Director Ludington had attended the meeting today. He'd normally pass, if possible, since he and President Steele didn't see eye to eye on much.

Relieved when the meeting ended, the director reached the door as the president's boisterous voice called out from behind.

"*Ken ...*"

Ludington turned around and, in the process, curled his lips back into a neutral expression. "Yes, Mr. President."

"May I have a word with you?"

"Of course, sir."

Ludington walked back to the chair he'd vacated and pulled it away from the table.

"No, not here. Let's go somewhere more discreet."

More discreet than the Situation Room? he thought.

The director pushed the chair back toward the mahogany table. "As you wish, Mr. President."

President Steele and a covey of Secret Service agents breezed past him. "Follow me," he said without looking back.

Ludington took long strides to keep up with the president who, considering his size, walked at a brisk pace. After a quick left and then right, they approached a door with wood paneling made to blend in with the rest of the hallway. A Secret Service agent opened the hidden door, revealing an elevator.

The FBI director stepped inside with the president and two Secret Service agents. The elevator had cherrywood walls and dark brown carpet. The control panel to the left of the doors only had two buttons with letters in bold, U and D. One of the agents pushed the lower button.

The president looked at Ludington. "Wondering where we are going?"

"Yes, Mr. President."

"You're in for a treat—you get to see the DUCC today."

Ludington looked surprised. "I thought the Deep Underground Command Center was a myth?"

The president let out a laugh of sorts. "As did I until my second day on the job."

"It's real?" asked the director.

"You'll see," the president said. "Your ears are about to pop."

Seemingly on cue the pressure built up in Ludington's ears as if he'd dived into a deep pool. He involuntarily yawned, which caused the tension to release.

The elevator stopped without a shudder.

"End of the line," said the president as the doors slid open, revealing a lobby of sorts with no chairs or furniture.

Along the wall were three biometric stations stacked vertically: a hand scanner, a microphone, and a retinal scanner. The president approached the stations and placed his hand on the scanner and his eye to the retinal scanner while he said in a booming voice, "I am the great and powerful Oz," into the microphone.

Two seconds later, a smooth whoosh sound came from the wall as a four-foot-thick vault door slowly swung opened. Turning toward the director of the FBI, Steele said, "See? I have a sense of humor. I'm not the asshole the media likes to play me up as."

Surprised by the candor, Ludington wasn't sure he believed the latter part of the statement. He paused for a pregnant moment before speaking.

"Of course, you aren't, sir."

The president winked. "Not until I need to be. It can be something of a job requirement."

It took almost ten seconds for the door to fully open. Once inside, President Steele led Ludington down several long hallways that had numerous doorways lining each passageway. The bunker system appeared quite extensive and was only sparsely staffed by a handful of maintainers. At the end of the wide hallway, the president pushed open a door. The Secret Service agents didn't follow them inside.

Ludington was completely alone with the president. Not an experience one encountered much with the leader of the free world—and never down here in one of the most secret places on the planet.

The president took a seat at the desk. "Well, what do you think?"

"It's quite impressive. How far underground are we?"

"Let's just say far enough to keep both of us out of harm's way in case of a nuclear strike," said Steele before he added, "And then some."

"I see. Expecting company, are we, sir?"

The president laughed. "Not today, Ken. Please, have a seat," said the president as he gestured to the chair in front of his desk. "I rarely have visitors down here."

"You come often?"

"As much as possible, which is not often enough. I find it relaxing. It's the one place I can truly get away from everyone and be alone with my thoughts. The residence is private enough, but I still get interrupted from time to time. Down here, it's different. Only a couple people outside of essential personnel have access to this bunker, very few people can follow me down here. The first lady doesn't even have access," he said with a smirk and wink.

"Bet that goes over well," Ludington said.

The president ignored the comment. "I've got an office, bathroom with shower, bedroom, and even a wet bar and lounge down here with a big TV and cable. It's like a home away from home when I need space." For the next ten minutes, the president discussed the building of the bunker, which had taken place under a previous administration. After an awkward pause, he transitioned to why he'd invited the director to the bunker.

"If you're unaware of the investigation, I'm sure you will be soon enough."

"Which investigation is that, Mr. President?"

"We have a missing Secret Service agent."

The director sat up a little straighter in his seat. "Sir? Missing how long?"

Indeed, Ludington had not been so informed. He instantly resolved to discipline whomever had left him out of the loop.

The president's eyes narrowed, but he didn't respond.

"Missing as in flew the coop, or missing as in abducted?" Director Ludington asked.

"We don't know, but there's some evidence of the latter."

"And you brought me down here to tell me this why?"

"I thought we could discuss a delicate situation about which maybe you were already aware."

"Well, I wasn't," said the director. "Whichever field office is handling it must not have enough for it to rise to HQ level yet."

"The FBI headquarters received the initial call about this missing person. It was bingoed to the Washington Field Office for action."

The director was now seething inside, though the turmoil didn't show outwardly. "And this call came in from ...?" He let the word drag out as he said it in a questioning tone.

"An elderly neighbor friend. She lives across the street."

"Again, sir, I'm wondering why you brought me down here to tell me this when a simple phone call would have sufficed. I would have had ready access to resources and could probably provide you with a more informed update."

Ludington made to reach for his cellphone to get some fast answers.

"You're kidding, right?" the president said with a half-smile. "Not down here."

Ludington saw there were no service bars. Suddenly the tightly enclosed space seemed to be airless and choking him, even though small waving blue ribbons attached to the tan HVAC vent verified fresh air was still being provided.

Steele stood and paced around the desk. Several times he stopped and tapped his foot on the soft carpeted floor. He decided it was time to turn up the persuasion.

"Ken, we've known each other for a while, and I consider you a close friend and a trusted counselor."

What a load of crap that is, Ludington thought.

"I brought you down here because I wanted to talk man-to-man... and I thought the Bureau could provide some professional courtesy."

"To whom exactly, sir?"

"The Secret Service, as well as the White House."

"The White ... wait—is he on your detail?"

"Not personal protection, *per se*, but yes. He is on the White House team, so the Secret Service has their own people looking into their missing agent."

Ludington bristled. "And now that the FBI has an active investigation, you'd like my people to do what? Pitch in, or stand down?"

"Well, perhaps just slow down. Play second chair on this one. This is a Secret Service matter and they want it handled in house."

The director shook his head left and right.

"You know I can't do that, Mr. President. Once an investigation has begun, I can't tell my people to stop."

"But you can offer supervisory oversight such that—"

Ludington cut him off but dialed back his tone as to not come across as confrontational.

"Are you trying to hinder the investigation, Mr. President?"

The president raised his hands defensively and shook his head. "Of course not. I'm simply asking on behalf of the Secret Service for some additional time to let them find their agent without outside interference."

"'Interference?' I thought we were all on the same team. And besides, if a federal agent has been abducted, it would be a federal criminal case."

The president knew he had a strained relationship with the FBI director, and the trifling attempt to butter him up had failed miserably. It didn't help that Steele had threatened to fire the director on more than one occasion. Once on television.

"Nevertheless," Steele said, "I think the Secret Service should run point on this."

Ludington didn't back down. "Why wouldn't you want us to

work together?"

"I don't intend for the Bureau excluded—in fact, I've instructed the Secret Service to coordinate with your office directly for whatever backstop they need. But I believe they know their man and are best equipped to find him."

"With all due respect, Mr. President, the FBI is the premier investigative agency in the world. I have nothing but respect for the Secret Service and Director Kline, but his staff is not on par with my people when it comes to investigative horsepower. The FBI employs the best of the best. If anyone can find their agent, it's us."

"Look, Ken. I concede your point and I'm not denigrating you or your fine people. However, I feel strongly that the Secret Service needs to take the lead here. I understand your qualms and agree the FBI can't discard its investigation now that it's begun. But we have to work together on this thing." The president paused. "There may be national security implications, and I need you in your chair until the end of your term, at least ..."

There it is, Ludington thought with a frown. *The threat to shit-can me if I don't play ball.*

"But you'd like us to back off," Ludington said dully. His gaze turned up to the air vent and the happily waving blue ribbons that verified no one was suffocating here today.

Except possibly Ludington's career.

Steele jammed his hands in his pockets. "Yes. Or at least slow things down to let the Secret Service get a handhold on this thing."

The director put his head in his hands and rubbed his temples. It took him several seconds before he raised his head.

"What's the agent's name? The one who is missing."

"That's isn't relevant to our discussion," the president said.

"Of *course* it is," Ludington said more sharply than he

intended. "I might know him."

"You don't," said the president in a curt tone.

"Is he on your protective detail?"

"Adjacent."

"You know him well?"

"Very much so," said the president.

That snapped it off for Ludington. *Screw this. I support and defend the Constitution, not this political dipshit.*

"Then, Mr. President, I highly encourage you to let my team do its job and take the lead on this so we can get your man back ASAP. I'd be happy to assign anyone Director Kline requests to work alongside my team in a good-faith effort of inter-agency cooperation."

President Steele was taken aback by this change in attitude. He thought he had co-opted Ludington into the bag, but the FBI director had made a handbrake turn away from cooperation.

"And I highly suggest that you give the Secret Service a little more time to find him," Steele said.

Ludington laid the trap. "Just so we're clear, suggest? Or order, Mr. President?"

"I'm suggesting, in the most direct way possible."

After a few moments, Steele looked down at his Omega watch and stood up abruptly. "You know, Ken, I've got to head topside for a meeting."

"I don't want to make you late, sir," said the director as he stood. An uncomfortable silence filled the space.

"You and the exceptional folks that work for you will, of course, do the right thing—the correct thing."

"Yes, sir, we will." Ludington smiled. "As always."

The president exited the office. and walked down the hallway without looking back, leaving the FBI director alone with a Secret Service minder outside the door.

Ten minutes later the director had been escorted from the DUCC and to the north portico and his vehicle. His security held the heavy door open, and he climbed into a black up-armored Suburban built by GM Defense. It left the White House grounds followed by his war wagon and additional heavy security.

"Where to, sir?" asked his driver, a man with a severe crew cut and dark suit. He looked like an NFL linebacker, except he carried a badge and a large firearm.

"Is it too early to hit up a bar?"

"We both know it's five o'clock somewhere, Mr. Director."

"Don't tempt me, Will. Maybe next time. Back to headquarters, please."

"Yes, sir."

As the Suburban turned out of the White House complex, the director placed a secure call. His assistant answered on the first ring.

"Favor to ask, Annie."

"What do you need, sir?"

"Go into SENTINEL and find out if we have an open case involving a missing Secret Service agent."

"Can you hold?"

"Sure."

Two minutes later Annie came back on the line.

"We do, sir."

"Subject's name on the file?"

"There are two names listed. Ralph Webb and Nick Jordan."

The president had been right after all. Neither name rang a bell with the director. "Who's working the case?"

"The investigation is being handled out of the WFO. Special Agent Eli Payne is lead on it. He's working with Probationary Agent Katherine Stone."

Ken smiled when he heard the name. "Payne, huh? Well, I'll be damned."

"Sir?" asked Annie.

"Oh, it's nothing. Please send me the SENTINEL link and have a copy of the file print-out on my desk when I get back? ETA is about twelve minutes."

Ludington could hear her keyboard clicking in the background. "Of course, sir. I'm printing it off now."

"Thanks, Annie. Oh, one more thing."

"Yes?"

"I need a cell number for Eli Payne."

Peter Casha finished lunch at Sushi Roku on Ocean Avenue, wiped his mouth with a napkin, and looked around. This was still one of the best places to eat in Santa Monica, probably in all of California.

The waitress, a cute blond with pigtails and legs that went on forever, approached and placed his bill on the round table. She gave him a warm smile, and her sideways glance as she moved past him lasted a little longer than expected.

Yeah, still got it, he thought.

He dropped a crisp, new C-note into the leather bill folder—a great tip on a forty-dollar lunch—stood up and walked outside.

The sun beat down on his face and a strong breeze from the ocean brought the smell of saltwater to his nostrils.

His phone vibrated.

"Yeah, what's up?" he asked.

"Where are you?"

"Santa Monica."

"It's windy. I can't hear shit," said the caller.

Casha saw a coffee shop to his left. "Hold tight." He stepped inside and picked a seat in the far corner away from any prying ears. He made sure to have his back to the wall where he could see the two points of entry. "All right, I'm inside. It should be better now," Casha said.

"Much better."

"So, what is it?"

"Do you have a plan worked out?"

"Yes," Casha said. "I'm meeting Hector Fuentes and the others at four in Marina del Rey."

"What did you get for a boat?"

"A Lagoon 400 S2."

"Is that big enough?"

"It's plenty big for what I have planned."

"And that is?"

"Doing what he told me to do."

"How?"

"Never mind that," Casha said. "I'll give you details when I see you later. Tell him I'll be feeding the fishes soon enough."

"What did you tell Hector?"

"That I had another job for him and his team." Casha flicked a smidge of lint from his pants.

"And he agreed?"

"Not at first. He was skeptical. I had to triple his money."

"Smart move."

"He wanted it in advance."

"You fronted it?"

"Yeah, I roll heavy."

"Well, I hope you don't roll stupid. The boss will recoup all your costs. I suppose you know that."

"I have a question," Casha said.

"Sure."

"I'm not worried about him paying me back, but what about him double-crossing me?"

"Bro, seriously. You think I would let that happen?"

"He turned on Hector. He might want to cut off other loose ends at the same time."

"Hector was expendable, but you're irreplaceable. You should know that by now."

"Everyone is replaceable, bro." Casha knew this first-hand.

"Not you. Besides, I got your six."

"You better. Because if he makes a play on me, I'll come after him with everything I have. I don't give a shit how powerful his family has become."

"Finish the job and catch the flight back. We'll be celebrating with a Tito's and lemonade tomorrow night. My treat."

"Well, if your cheap-ass is buying, that's a special occasion. I'm in."

Casha clicked the end button and stashed the phone back in his front left pocket.

The barista behind the counter had been eying him for a few minutes, but not the way the waitress at Sushi Roku had. This was more of a *you-sure-as-hell-better-buy-something* look. He stood up, walked over to the counter, and ordered a classic vanilla latte, two extra shots, no whip.

It was only a modest blow to his ego when she snubbed his attempts at small talk.

Chapter 30
Manassas, Virginia

Payne turned onto Sudley Road and checked his mirrors. He felt paranoid, though; the minivan crash incident from earlier was still crowding his mind.

But everything looked clear.

The drive to the Manassas Regional Airport would only take about twelve minutes if he hit the lights right. A half mile down the road, he was stopped for the traffic light as it turned red. His brow furrowed, and he felt a knot form in the pit of his stomach as he thought of Rose Lewis. He'd learned to go with his gut, and rarely did it let him down.

He looked over at Stone, who noticed.

"What?" she asked.

"I'm getting one of my feelings."

"And what would that be?"

"That I need to do something."

"There's a gas station on the next corner if you need to use the little boy's room."

"No, smartass, not that kind of feeling."

"Then what?"

"It's about Rose."

"What about her?"

"I feel like we need to check on her."

"Right now?"

He paused and then said, "Yes."

"That's kind of hard to do when we are out here in Manassas."

"I know."

"We can swing by her place later tonight on the way back to the office."

Payne nodded but didn't agree. "Or …" He didn't finish his thought and instead grabbed his phone from the center console.

Wes Russell answered on the third ring.

"Hey, numb nuts," Payne said, turning on the speakerphone.

"Hello to you. You know I sign your evals, right?" Russell said.

"And not a day goes by that you don't remind me."

"You were born with the correct surname."

"So I've been told," Payne said with a chuckle.

"What did you learn in Manassas? Is it Jordan's car?" Russell asked. He was unconvinced a Secret Service agent was missing.

"Yes, it's his car, and we found blood in the trunk."

"Where are you now?"

"Headed to the Manassas Regional Airport."

"Why?"

Payne said, "We're following up a hunch."

"I don't typically like your hunches. They tend to be expensive for the government."

"Line of duty, boss. But how often are they wrong?"

"Rarely," Russell admitted. "Did you call me to ask permission for something?"

"No, it's something else."

"I'm all ears."

"Can you to run by the townhouses where Nick Jordan lives?"

"Why?" Russell asked. "I thought the ERT recovered all the

evidence?" An annoyed tone had crept into his voice.

"It's not that. I need someone to check on Rose Lewis across the street."

"The one who reported him missing?"

"Correct."

"Why?

"A feeling. I just need someone to check in on her."

"Look, Payne. This is the FBI, not some check-on-the-Geritol-granny wellness check service."

"Wes, I wouldn't ask if it wasn't important."

"What's wrong with her?"

"Nothing. At least not that I know of."

"But you want us to do a drop-by and make sure she is okay?"

"Yes, please. You got anyone handy right now?"

"I guess I could do it. I'm lightly tasked this morning. And what do I get out of this?"

Payne thought for a second. He knew several things Russell was fond of. "An ice-cold Mountain Dew, light ice."

"Let me get this straight. You want me to drive to Vienna, and all I'll get is one lousy Mountain Dew? That's bullshit, and you know it. Maybe for a six-pack, and I'd consider it."

"A six-pack? Have you lost your mind?"

"You throw in a pack of Marlboro Reds and you may have yourself a deal."

"I'll upgrade your Dew to a two-liter, but I'm not buying you cancer sticks. If you don't give them up one day, those things are going to put you in an early grave and I won't have time to train up a new supervisor."

"Man, I've already expended my nine lives, and the good Lord has seen fit to double me up. And besides, I'll take death by nicotine over lead poisoning any day."

"I won't be a part of putting you in an early grave, not by nicotine or bullet."

"Yeah, yeah, yeah. Well, it's a Dew and a pack of smokes or you can check on granny on your own."

"Fine. They're your lungs."

"Might be an hour before I make it over there," Russell said.

"So we have a deal, jarhead?"

"That's Gunny Jarhead to you, slug," Russell said. He unconsciously rubbed the globe-and-anchor USMC tattoo on his upper left arm. "And yes, we have a deal."

"Once a Marine, always a Marine, huh?"

"*Ooorah,*" Russell said, "and don't you forget it, dogface."

Chapter 31
Dulles International Airport (IAD)

Merci De Atta cleared US Customs at John F. Kennedy International Airport in record time. It didn't hurt that the line moved at a brisk pace and appeared to be half the normal size. Also, she'd ended up in a line managed by a young agent. With dark hair and a chiseled physique, he looked like he'd spent a lot of time in the gym when not trapped behind Plexiglas looking at passports.

The young man sat up straighter when she stepped forward with her passport. The three open buttons on her blouse and the way she managed to bend forward to display her ample cleavage didn't hurt, either. After a few perfunctory questions, he'd let her pass with a warm smile, which she reciprocated.

"Welcome home, ma'am," he said with a big smile, and slid the passport back to her with an entry stamp. She smiled back and departed.

Men are so easy.

She walked over to Terminal Five and got a vigorous massage from a large, muscular woman with golden blonde pigtails who may have been an escapee from a Norwegian prison camp. After some post-massage recovery with a latte, Merci made her DC connection and flew into Dulles.

On the ground and deplaned at last in far suburban Washington, she clutched her lone carry-on bag and walked past a large floor-to-ceiling sign that read, "Welcome to the UNITED STATES OF AMERICA and the COMMONWEALTH OF VIRGINIA."

Two minutes later she exited the Arrivals terminal and saw the black SUV with heavily tinted windows at the curb. Merci climbed into the front passenger seat. The driver didn't speak but put the vehicle into Drive and departed the airport.

After a few minutes of silence, they had merged onto 267, which was still called the Dulles Access Road for fourteen miles, all the way to Olney Park. Finally, Merci could stand the lack of conversation no more.

"How nice of you to pick me up," said Merci .

Marcus Rollings took a few seconds to answer, then muttered, "Flight was okay?"

"What are we, some old married couple who talks about their boring-ass day?"

"No—*Kramer*," Marcus said, an obvious reference to the long-running TV comedy *Seinfeld*, one of their favorite shows to watch together. Before she could reply he added, "'It's *prison*, Jerry—*prison*.'"

Merci laughed her feminine laugh. Men found it very sexy. That included Rollings.

They drove in silence for five more minutes before she turned to him. "You've got a plan to take out Danny Frazier, huh?"

"I do."

"How many people do we have?"

"Only you and me."

Merci frowned. "Do you have a death wish? Because I do not."

"No. There's a heavy Secret Service footprint all over the George Washington University Hospital, but my plan is straightforward. I don't foresee any issues."

"Evac, if things go south?"

"All worked out. I've made a few visits to the hospital over the past twenty-four hours and placed some items we may need in strategic locations. When we get back to my place, I'll go over the specifics with you."

Merci leaned over and grabbed his right thigh, giving it a firm squeeze and suggestive rub. "Back to your place, huh? Isn't that a little forward? What kind of gal do you think I am?"

Her playfulness threw him off. Even though they'd had a romantic relationship in the past, it had ended a few years back.

Rollings grabbed her hand and pulled it away from his leg. "I know what kind of gal you are very well," he said with a sly grin. "I think we learned our lesson in Paris, didn't we?"

"How so?" she asked, her voice taking on a sultry tone.

"You're screwing with me, right?" He shot her a glance.

"Remind me of Paris?" asked Merci as she threw her head back.

Rollings decided to play along. "That time we posed as husband and wife in Vincennes and were supposed to take out the older couple."

"Oh, yes. Right-right-right. Paris. In the wine cellar. We got caught in a compromising position."

"Yeah, that's right. Buck-naked, weapons in plain sight on top of our scattered clothes, and no way to reach them before Mr. Jenkins hit the silent alarm."

"Guess I should be grateful you have a good arm."

"My good *aim* is what saved us."

"I must say I've never seen a man struck in the head with a bottle of cabernet sauvignon from twenty feet," said Merci with a slight laugh. "And you didn't even break the bottle."

Rollings laughed as the full memory returned. It had turned

out to be one hell of a night. Incredible sex, violence, and a lot of alcohol. A perfect combo.

"Nope," he said, "I picked it up off the cellar floor and we drank every last drop. Then we went upstairs, capped the missus, and finished what we started."

Merci pulled her shirt away from her heaving bosom several times in a rapid motion. "Jesus, Marcus. You're getting me all hot and bothered over here."

"Good times," Rollings said.

"And that was the last time?"

"Sure was."

"How far away is your place?" asked Merci.

"About ten minutes. But we have a stop first."

Her body tensed and she crossed her arms. "Where?"

"The hospital."

"Recce?"

"Yes. I want you to see the layout with your own eyes."

"Disguises?"

"In the back."

Merci was getting aggravated. "Is this a good idea, considering how many times you've already been there?"

"No worries. Each time I've gone my appearance has been dramatically different. Plus, I have several different outfits for you, so we're good."

"After we take out Frazier, how can you be sure we won't be double crossed?"

"To be honest, I can't. That's our business risk."

"You got an insurance policy? Something you can dangle out there to keep us safe?"

Rollings smiled. "... and I hope I won't need to use it."

"Seriously? You won't tell me?" She smiled, half amused, half amazed.

"You got your secrets, I've got mine."

Merci shook her head. "And they say I'm a tease."

He huffed. "Oh, trust me, you are."

Chapter 32
Fairfax, Virginia

Ryan Polk tapped his index finger and thumb on the steering wheel to the rhythmic beat as *With or Without You* by U2 came on the radio. Within a minute, he was whisper-singing along with the chorus, grateful no one could hear his voice, off-key even at a whisper. Someone had once told him surveillance work consisted of ninety-eight percent sitting around bored off your ass while the other two percent might contain a little excitement.

Keyword being *might*.

The two percent seemed like a stretch tonight as he looked around the parking lot of the Wegmans on Monument Drive. He let out an elongated breath.

God, I'm bored.

His cellphone rang. "Yeessss ..." he said in a drawn-out manner.

"Where are you?" asked the caller.

"Wegmans."

"Weg-what?"

"It's a grocery store, hoss."

"Why are you at a grocery store? You should be watching her."

"We are. She went out, and we followed her into town."

"Well, I'm about to throw you a curveball."

"Ten-four. Whatcha got?"

"Do you still have those FBI jackets and badges?"

"Yep, in the trunk. Why?"

"I need you to talk with Rose Lewis. Give her a few minutes to put away her groceries, and then you and Don pay her a visit."

"Like shoot the shit with her?"

"No, you idiot, I want you to question her. We need intel."

Polk tried to keep the annoyance from his voice. "What are we going get from her that the real FBI agents didn't find out?"

"We confirmed from the printer and laptop you guys retrieved he printed off four copies of the docs. You recovered one from the safe, but we need to know what happened to the other three."

"And you think she knows where they are?"

"That's what I need for you to find out."

"And if she won't talk?"

"Be persuasive. Firm. Tell her it's a matter of national security. Explain that you work with Agent Payne and, based on evidence he recovered, additional questions arose. Ask her about the documents. See what she knows but keep it low key."

"And if she doesn't know anything?"

"Thank her for her time and leave, Sherlock."

"We can handle that. No problem."

"If I had more resources, I'd lean on them, but right now, you two are all I have."

"Won't let you down, boss."

"You'd better not."

The line clicked off.

Polk smiled from ear to ear.

Ten minutes later Rose emerged, and a few feet behind her walked Don Flynn.

Flynn climbed into the car and shook his head. "Man, that old lady can shop till she drops."

"You get me the burnt peanuts like I asked?"

"Yeah, I got your shitty peanuts. You owe me five dollars and thirty-eight cents for this test-tube snack."

Polk gave him a sideways glance. "For candied peanuts?"

"Tell me about it," Flynn said.

Polk told him about the call.

Flynn's eyes lit up.

They climbed out of the car wearing FBI raid jackets.

"Remember, play it cool," Polk said.

"As a cucumber," Flynn agreed.

When they reached the top of the steps, Polk gave the red door a rap.

After a minute of silence, an elderly sounding voice said, "Who is it?"

"FBI, ma'am. May we have a word with you?" He spoke with an air of authority.

The door cracked open and Rose looked out. Polk and Flynn both flashed the fake creds and badges in official-looking black folders, which were good enough for her to open the door.

She stepped out of the house onto the covered porch.

"Where are Agents Payne and Stone?"

"They are tied up on the case elsewhere," Polk said. "Special Agent Flynn here and I were asked to help them gather additional evidence."

Lewis appeared hesitant. "How can I help? I gave them a full statement already. What else do they need from me?"

"We appreciate your participation, ma'am, but we have some follow-up questions based on some evidence we've uncovered. Do you mind if we come in and talk for just a few minutes?"

Lewis' eyes darted back and forth between the two men.

Something about them seemed off. Her insides tightened and she felt an uneasiness when she looked into their eyes. She took a tentative step back and started to close the door. "I have Special Agent Payne's card. Let me call him first."

For a lady her age, she moved fast and almost had the door closed before Flynn shot his leg out like a switchblade and the force of his kick caused the worn latch to pop, thrusting the door inward. It struck her squarely on the left side of her body, the force knocking her to the floor.

Without a thought of the consequences, Flynn pushed through the door and straddled her on the floor, covering her mouth with one meaty hand and grabbing her throat with the other.

Polk hadn't expected this violence.

"What the hell are you doing?"

He followed Flynn inside the door and pushed the door closed with his foot, peering through a peephole to see if anyone had been watching.

An expression of unconditional terror covered Lewis' face as her body tried to ball up in a fetal position. Flynn's weight held her frail body firmly to the floor and he glared at her with dark eyes and an almost lifeless expression. Satisfied Lewis wasn't going anywhere, he looked over his shoulder and responded to Polk.

"What was I supposed to do? She was going to call Payne."

"So you jumped her?"

Flynn gritted his teeth. "I did what I did."

"And what do you think we should do now?"

"Get the info the boss needs."

"But he was clear. Don't touch her."

"Well, he isn't here now, is he?"

Polk's expression turned to rage, and the color of his skin went from café au lait to beat red in seconds.

"Dude, you really fucked up this time."

"No, I didn't. She will tell us what we need to know." Flynn looked back down to Lewis. "Won't you?"

Her heart raced as Rose Lewis nodded her head and said, "Uh-huh," in a muffled, frail voice.

Chapter 33
Pacific Ocean off Catalina Island

A brilliant reddish hue stretched from the horizon and engulfed the late afternoon sky in majestic splendor. Peter Casha stood at the helm. He piloted the forty-foot cruising catamaran with the confidence of a man comfortable on the open sea.

They'd left Marina del Rey twenty minutes before the sun dove for the horizon. Neither man had said a word since the boat left the dock.

"Pretty sunset," Casha said then, staring ahead.

Hector Fuentes looked to the crimson sky. "Yes, I suppose it's nice."

"Spend much time on the ocean?" Casha asked.

"Me? No, I grew up in Mexico City. We were very poor without a pot to piss in. On the rare occasion I saw the ocean, we couldn't afford to go out on a boat. You?"

Casha knew Fuentes would be dead shortly, and he'd be the one to usher him into eternity. Something in his brain said *Fuck* it, and he violated a cardinal rule—never reveal more than you must. The philosophy had served him well in life, and for the first time he could remember, he answered a stranger's question honestly. Except for those closest to him, he lied for a living. He lied so often, the truth was tangled within a web of stories and false-hoods.

Whatever I tell him will go to the bottom of the sea anyway, Casha thought. *And since dead men tell no tales, my words will perish with him.*

"I spent a lot of time on the ocean as a young man. The salt life is in my blood," he said.

"You from California?"

"No. Long Island."

Fuentes looked up. "A New Yorker? I have some people in the South Bronx myself." He smiled at a memory that he didn't share. "You don't have an accent."

Casha grunted. "It slips out when I'm home."

"Make it back often?"

"No."

Fuentes became quiet for a few minutes.

Neither man talked for minutes as the wind picked up enough to rock the catamaran.

"Can I ask you a question?" asked Fuentes as the breeze sub-sided.

"Sure, I guess," Casha said.

"Tell me what is in the containers?"

Casha looked over at Fuentes and smiled but didn't say anything.

Fuentes continued. "I get it. I'm the hired help. *Haz lo que te dicen, espalda mojada, y mantén tu maldita boca callada.*" Do as you're told, wetback, and keep your fucking mouth quiet.

"It's just … well, I'm just curious, to be honest with you," Fuentes said. "I'm out there every day and see a lot of crazy shit around the dock. I know General Atomics is a defense contractor, and I'm pretty sure the containers must have something to do with the military. Maybe weapons? Bombs? I know where the ship is headed, meaning whatever we gave them must be pretty serious."

"Good guess," Casha said. "You want to know?"

Fuentes nodded.

"What if I said I could tell you but then I'd have to kill you?"

"Then I am not that interested," Fuentes said with a nervous smile. His body tensed and he leaned away.

Casha laughed. It was the first time in a very long time. "I'm only playin' with you, man."

In specific detail, he explained to Fuentes what each container held.

Fuentes' eyes grew wide. "This is a pretty big deal, *ese*," he said, using the slang term for dude. "I mean, you're in this weapons transfer business pretty deep."

"Me?" Casha said. He scrunched his nose and pushed his lips together. "Not really. I'm a small cog in a well-oiled and much larger machine. I do what I'm told just like you and report to someone higher up the food chain. The folks with the real hard part are the ones dealing with the Body Man."

"Who's the Body Man?" asked Fuentes.

Casha looked off to the horizon, unsure how to answer that question. "Yeah, never mind. He's a nobody, a dead man walking. Anyway, it's complicated and not my problem. We need to get down to business and focus on the next phase."

"What we're doing in Catalina has to do with this weapons transfer?"

"Correct," lied Casha.

Fuentes grew quiet, but Casha's posture had straightened in his seat.

He looked down at his watch. The time had arrived. "You mind taking the helm for a few minutes?" Casha asked.

"Who me? I never steered a boat."

"It's not complicated, kind of like a car. Keep an eye on this dial and keep the wheel steady. I'll be back in a few minutes."

"Where you going?"

"Below, to hit the head."

"The head?"

"That's right, you don't know boat terminology. The bathroom. *Cuarto de baño.* I've got to go take a piss, Hector."

"Ahh, yes."

"I'll be back in a few."

Fuentes nodded and kept his eyes toward the horizon and occasionally studied the compass dial to keep the boat on course. They were so far out on the trackless ocean that there was no danger that he'd strike another vessel with the big catamaran, but Hector Fuentes took every assignment quite seriously.

After climbing from the aft cockpit, Casha made his way through the main salon. One level down Juan and Pablo were on the port side while Mateo, Jorge, Felipe, and Angel were on the starboard side, all resting. The men had pulled an all-nighter and they were exhausted.

Casha would take out the men on the starboard side first. He had stashed the suppressed Walther PPQ M2 inside a cabinet within the main salon before the others came on board. Casha retrieved the gun and checked to make sure a round was chambered and the safety disengaged. The magazine held fifteen rounds, and he grabbed the two extra mags stacked next to the gun and shoved one in each back pocket. This was plenty bullets for the job, although he hoped not to need them all.

It was all a numbers game, and he wanted to eliminate his threats as quickly as possible. He carefully descended the steps leading to the starboard suite.

Slow is smooth, smooth is fast.

He took the last few steps as quietly as possible and turned the door handle, the suppressed Walther raised to a ready-to-fire position.

Casha had expected to find the four men fast asleep, but instead, Mateo, Jorge, Felipe, and Angel sat around a small round table in the center of the cabin. A tall stack of cards teetered on the table, and each man held several of them. All eyes turned to Casha as he stepped into the room, the Walther extended from his body.

He didn't hesitate.

Felipe and Jorge sat closest to the door, and Casha drilled them each with a suppressed round exploding in their skulls, showering Mateo with blood, brain matter, and chunks of flesh.

Movies got it all wrong. When a character uses a suppressor in Hollywood, it sounds like a dull pop, and nobody hears the sound from a room away. In reality, while a suppressor helps to reduce noise, this bullet leaves the gun at over thirteen hundred feet per second. The sound is unmistakable and loud in an enclosed space.

The next bullet found Angel's temple and he crumpled to the ground, half of his skull hanging from the right side of his head by only the scalp. Mateo's face was still covered with Felipe's remains, so he didn't see the shot that tore through his skull and sent him on the split-second journey to join his friends in the afterlife.

Casha spun around, exited the cabin, and moved across the narrow passageway to the port side of the boat.

From the first shot, he'd started an internal countdown. He knew time worked against him and the more slowly he moved, the greater his danger.

Before Casha made it two steps, the door leading to Juan and Pablo's cabin jerked open. With the gun still raised, Casha fired twice and struck Pablo in the bridge of the nose and left cheek as

Juan pushed the barrel of a handgun around the man's falling body.

Clever boy, but not clever enough.

Casha put two more rounds in Pablo's lifeless chest, causing his body to jerk further back and Juan lost the cover afforded by his friend's body mass. He had the window he needed, and two more rounds left his Walther, eliminating Juan.

Casha heard movement from his left at the top of the stairs. With ten shots expended, he had five more in the mag, plus the spares.

Six men down, and only one to go.

Peter controlled his breathing to ensure the final shot would come from a steady hand. As he pulled himself up the stairs, the boat took a sudden sharp turn, enough for him to lose his balance. He gripped the railing, which kept him from falling off the stairs to the deck below.

What the hell is Hector doing?

Clearly, he'd heard the gunshots.

Casha made his way through the salon and turned the corner with his Walther up, but Fuentes wasn't at the helm.

He sensed Fuentes before he saw movement. Casha lunged to his right in time to avoid the two bullets that splintered the wood decking boards right near his foot. In one quick motion, he ejected the used mag and slammed a fresh one into the weapon to not need reloading in the middle of a gunfight.

Moving fast to the starboard side, he crept away from the stern and made his way forward. The nearly full moon provided enough light to illuminate the deck, leaving few places to hide.

A clanging sound to his rear caused him to turn. Casha's eye caught the glimmer of a shiny metal object as it bounced along the wooden decking. He recognized the distraction was his mistake just a second too late.

The first bullet pierced his shirt and grazed his flesh under the rib cage, missing bone by less than an inch. He wasn't as fortunate with the next round. A searing pain tore through his left shoulder as lead found bone and knocked him to the ground. Several more bullets sailed high past his head and struck the deck.

Casha rolled to his left and the pressure on his shoulder was excruciating. It was all he could do not to cry out and give away his position. With the window leading to the salon open, he rolled through it a fraction of a second before bullets punctured the spot where he'd lain. He landed inside the floor of the salon on his right side, sparing his left shoulder additional damage and more pain. His Walther never left his grip, and he raised the weapon from the floor.

Fuentes' leg passed by the window, but he moved slowly. With no chance for a kill shot, Casha squeezed off two rounds. The first shot grazed the shin while the second one struck in the middle of his left kneecap, turning it into a fractured, bloody mess.

Fuentes fell to the deck in searing pain, but he'd fallen forward out of the window space. Despite his own overwhelming pain, Casha gathered his strength and resolve. Using all his will, he ignored the desire to vomit and stood, making his way up the stairs to the main deck.

Fuentes heard Casha's stumbling climb and he scrambled up onto his one good knee. He teetered there for just a moment, deciding, before lunging off the deck into the dark ocean water.

Casha fired his last three shots at the darkened silhouette as it disappeared overboard and the boat motored slowly away from the spot. He climbed the steps up to the helm and pulled sharply back on the throttle to slow the boat, then spun the wheel to circle back and find Fuentes.

Casha's bullet wound streamed blood down his arm and it pooled on the polished teak deck. He grabbed a large duffel bag next to the helm and removed the first aid kit. He placed several large pieces of gauze on the wound and taped them in place, tearing the lengths of tape off with bared teeth. He knew it wouldn't hold for long, but he needed to apply pressure and slow the bleeding.

For twenty minutes he traversed the ocean in a loose grid pattern without luck as he looked for Fuentes. It was dark now. A crescent moon gave off some light, but scudding clouds obscured it for the most part. Using a handheld spotlight to cut through the darkness, he searched the sea without success. With a devastating bullet wound in his leg and a destroyed knee, Fuentes wasn't swimming anywhere far. He had either drowned or he'd been already consumed by the sharks known to patrol the Pacific between Los Angeles and Catalina Island.

Casha's shoulder thumped with pain that reverberated all the way down to his tingling fingertips.

The tape Casha had used to apply the gauze wasn't sticking to his skin because of all the blood loss. He removed the gauze and used his teeth to tear open the package of QuikClot and he poured it into the open wound, then re-wrapped the shoulder in fresh gauze. Next, he injected two syringes of morphine near the ball of his shoulder. The quick fix wouldn't last long, but given the distance to land, he had no good options.

It took a few minutes for the morphine to kick in, but when it did, he decided to ditch the boat. His initial plan involved weighting down the bodies and dumping them at sea, then returning to Marina del Rey with the boat. But with his left shoulder torn up, he knew there was no way he could lift the bodies and dispose of them, and explaining all the bullet holes and bloodstains would be challenging. He needed to implement Plan B.

Casha didn't like the idea of torching the boat, but he squinted at the GPS and saw he was twenty-six miles from the coast. He inspected the dinghy attached to the stern, a competent Highfield Ocean Master 390 rigid inflatable boat with a decent Honda outboard. After confirming its seaworthiness and fuel level, he used the powered winch to lower it into the calm water.

Then Casha went to the bow and spread the extra gasoline onboard for the RIB over the deck of the catamaran and down into the cabin. He hated to torch the gorgeous boat, but he had no other choice.

He stepped onto the small escape craft and untied the rope securing it to the catamaran. With a heavy sigh, Casha struck a match from a pack of matches advertising a truck driving school, igniting the entire pack, and tossing it onto the catamaran's wooden deck.

He pushed off, started the engine, and pointed the bow toward land. It seemed a long way off.

He glanced back over his bandaged shoulder only once, as the big boat became engulfed in flames. The orange and red inferno filled the horizon with a crimson glow, but the catamaran's death would attract no more attention out here than the dead men.

Fuentes had learned to swim as a child in a public pool near where he'd lived in Mexico City. Even though he had a certain level of comfort in the water, he'd never tried to see how long he could float in it. Given the events of the night, he was surprised how long he lasted with just one leg able to kick.

The pain in his knee subsided slightly. The makeshift tourniquet he'd fashioned out of his shirt sleeve helped to control the bleeding, but blood still oozed into the water. He hadn't learned about another round that had hit his upper back until he'd dived into the ocean, but the shot appeared to be through and through. It hurt like absolute hell, but he felt certain it hadn't hit anything vital. But it was also bleeding.

One of the times Casha had disappeared into the lower deck, Fuentes had swum over to the ship and removed a life ring from the port side. His arms and legs ached, and the relief provided by the ring had likely saved him from drowning.

As soon as he saw Casha begin pouring the gas, he knew what was going to happen.

Fuentes didn't consider himself overly religious, but as the flames on the boat grew higher, he prayed out loud that someone would see the dancing red silhouette and investigate.

He believed that if nobody came, he would die tonight. Either he'd drown, or something would start chewing on his dangling legs underwater and quickly finish him off.

The idea of being a main course wasn't his idea of a way to go.

Payne and Stone approached the last hangar on the list provided by the airport operations manager, a no-nonsense,
straitlaced guy named Phil Butler who seemed to have the personality of unbuttered toast. Butler wore a snappy, hand-tied bow
tie, something that struck Payne as being a bold choice. Butler
was reluctant to provide them any info until Payne mentioned
bringing in his entire team to do a forensic crime scene search.
Might take days, Payne mused.

Butler was more cooperative after that.

The hangar in question sat off by itself at the farthest point
from the main business terminal. Payne rubbed his temple as the
long day continued with no end in sight.

Stone said, "What happens if this last charter company isn't
any help? Where do we go from there?"

"Well, we have hours of surveillance footage to pore over, and
you can start going through it tonight," Payne said, before adding,
"you know—instead of painting your toenails." Payne took a big
sip of lukewarm coffee he'd bought from the airport terminal
vending machine. Saying it tasted like used motor oil defamed
used motor oil.

Stone gave him a dirty look. "Dump on the newbie, huh?"

"Stripes aren't given, they're earned."

"Good note. I haven't heard that one before." Stone just shook her head. Evidently no veteran FBI special agent remembered being new.

The banter stopped as they crossed the tarmac to the most remote hangar on the airfield, a large steel building that was dull white twenty years ago. The sign to the right of the hangar doors read "Dibaco Aviation." Between the sign and a large bay window was a gray door with a small placard with thick red letters that read *Employees Only.*

Payne turned the doorknob, surprised to find it unlocked, and entered. A series of offices lined the right side of the building and the hangar bay contained two small puddle-jumper airplanes. Along the back wall, several storage racks held airplane parts in various shapes and sizes. Two mechanics worked on the engine of the plane farthest to their left. Neither man looked up as they entered.

Payne heard a voice coming from the first office on the right. He approached and gave his loud cop knock on the hollow wood door. He entered without waiting for a response.

A man with red hair and a bushy *Duck Dynasty*-type beard put a finger in the air, indicating he needed a minute. Payne and Stone waited as the man finished the call.

"Can I help you with something?" asked the man as he placed the cellphone on the desk. He looked mildly annoyed that two people had entered his office without permission.

Payne flipped open his credential folder. "FBI, sir. Couple questions if you don't mind."

His expression changed as he saw the gold badge. "Whoa, feds. Don't see you people out here too often."

"Special Agent Eli Payne, and this is Special Agent Kat Stone."

"What can I do you for?"

"Were you here last Wednesday?"

"Sure was. I own the place, so I'm here most days unless I'm flying." He extended his hand. "Darby Caldwell."

Payne approached and shook the extended hand. "And what time did you arrive and leave, Mr. Caldwell?"

Caldwell pointed to two chairs in front of his desk. "Please, take a seat. Am I in some sort of trouble? Do I need a lawyer?"

"No, sir, it's nothing like that. Just asking some routine questions."

Caldwell pushed a few papers around his cluttered desk and flipped open his daily planner. "Let's see, Agent Payne … our first charter flight was seven a.m.," he paused and looked at the high ceiling, remembering. "Pretty sure I got in around six. Last flight arrived around eight p.m., and I left about twenty minutes later. DoorDash brought lunch from my Chinese place, so I was here all day."

"Did you see anything out of the ordinary?"

"Nothing that stands out," Caldwell said. "Pretty quiet day on Wednesday. Same old, same old, as far as I recall."

"And nothing odd happened that night?"

"Compared to what?" Caldwell chuckled amiably. "Again, not that I'm aware of. What's this all about?"

"We're investigating a missing-person case and have reason to believe our subject may have left via this airport," Payne said.

"Well, I'll help in any way I can. Do you think someone took your guy against their will?"

Payne nodded. "Possibly."

"Damn." He thought a moment. "I had survival and escape training in the Army—" Caldwell laughed. "—since color TV but before the internet. If your guy was taken without his consent, that's like being a prisoner of war. I didn't like that much. I 'spect your guy doesn't either."

"Any surveillance cameras on the premises?" asked Stone.

"I don't have any, but the airport does, here and there."

"Did any of your employees stay late Wednesday night?" asked Payne.

"No. I'm the last one here most nights. The other charter services close by the time I wrap up. But there is someone here real late most Wednesdays."

"Who is that?" asked Payne.

"I've got a cleaning lady here on Monday, Wednesday, and Saturday nights. She comes in late, around ten or so. And she's here for two to three hours."

"Can we get her contact info, please?"

"Sure. Her name is Ann Watson, but she didn't come this week. Had some nasty stomach bug that's been floating around."

Payne shook his head. "Sorry to hear that."

"Her husband Geoff came instead."

"Great. We'd love to speak with him."

"Ann called me in the morning Thursday and said she didn't make it. But I knew someone came because of the empty trash cans. Knew it must be Geoff because the toilets weren't as clean as normal. Men ain't as good when it comes to scrubbing the toilets. Ain't that right, Ms. Stone?"

"That's the truth," Stone said.

Caldwell's eyes lingered on her for a long beat, then he looked away from Stone and back to Payne. "Geoff works just a mile down the road at a masonry supply store if you want to have a word with him."

"I would appreciate that. Can I have the address?"

"Sure thing," Caldwell said. He jotted down the address from a page in his planner on the back of his business card and handed it over. "That's my info here on the card, if you need it."

Payne and Stone rose to leave, exchanged thank-yous and handshakes, and made to leave.

"Thanks for the cooperation, Mr. Caldwell," Stone said.

"Anytime, Ms. Stone," Caldwell replied.

As they walked away from the hangar, Payne looked over at Stone.

"Y'know, I think ol' Darby has a little thing for you," he said with a wide grin.

"Well, there's no faulting his taste," Stone said.

They pulled onto Prince William Parkway as Payne's personal cellphone started to vibrate. He forgot he'd turned the ringer off when they'd talked with Darby Caldwell.

The number came up blocked, but he answered it anyway.

"Eli Payne here," he said.

"Agent Payne, this is Annie Hertzell from the director's office."

Payne recognized the name but had never met the director's assistant. Uh oh, this cannot be good.

"Hello, Ms. Hertzell. What can I do for you today?"

"Please hold for the director."

"Of cour—"

Before he could finish speaking, the line had already gone to hold. Every few seconds an electronic tone would sound to confirm the line hadn't disconnected. Payne looked over at Stone. The expression on his face looked dire.

"What is it?"

He held his free hand over the microphone. "Director wants to speak with me."

"The director of what?"

"*The* director—of the entire FBI."

"Seriously?"

"Yeah."

"Shit. Do you think they know you took the White House badge?"

Payne looked thoughtful. "No, the director of the FBI does not know about, nor does he care about, the fact I borrowed a piece of evidence. Come on, Stone, get with the program."

"Then what does he want to talk with you about?"

"I think I'm about to find out."

The voice of the Kendall Ludington interrupted their back and forth. "Agent Payne, thanks for taking my call."

"Pleasure is mine, Director Ludington. How may I help you?"

"You're working the Ralph Webb-Nick Jordan case, right?"

"Yes, sir. I'm following up on a lead right now in Manassas. Is there a problem?" A long pause followed before the director responded.

"Well, I'm not sure. There might be an issue."

"Can you elaborate?"

"Not over the phone. Would you and Ms. Stone swing by my office after things wrap up in Manassas?"

"Of course, sir."

"You know where my office is, correct?"

"Everyone knows where your office is, sir."

"Good, I'll be here for a while. Call Annie when you're on your way."

The line clicked off before Payne could respond. He sat there for a few seconds and looked at the phone as he placed it back in his pocket.

"Soooooo ..." Stone said when it became clear Payne wasn't going to say anything.

"He wants to talk about this case."

"What about it?"

"He didn't say. But he wants us to come to his office."

"*Us*, as in both of us?"

"That's typically what 'us' means, Stone. Besides, he asked for you by name."

"Have you ended my career before it started, somehow?"

Payne shrugged. "Better I ended your career than your life."

"What's that supposed to mean?"

He cocked one eyebrow higher than the other.

"Didn't anyone tell you what happened to the last probationary agent they dumped on me?"

Before Stone could respond, he winked.

"Jerk," Stone said.

Chapter 35
Manassas, Virginia

Geoff Watson shifted his eyes back and forth as he sat across from Payne and Stone in the break room at Pelham Supply, his workplace. The plastic Costco folding table and metal folding chairs might've been cheap, but they were also very uncomfortable.

Payne and Stone had badged him and accepted offers of decent coffee. And Geoff Watson looked like a man hiding something.

"Is this about Wednesday night?" Watson asked. A bead of sweat had already formed on his brow and slowly trickled down the side of his face.

Bingo, Payne thought. Hiding something.

"It is, isn't it? Because of what I saw at the airport?"

Payne and Stone shot each other furtive glances.

"Probably," Payne said.

"Man, I knew I should have called the cops."

"Don't worry about that now, buddy," Payne said as he flipped open his black leather-bound notepad and clicked the top of his pen. Stone opened a dictation app on her phone and placed it on the table with the mic facing Watson.

"But am I in some sort of trouble for not reporting it?"

"No, you're not in trouble, but we would like to hear what you saw that night."

Watson sucked in a big gulp of air and slowly exhaled. "A plane landed at the Manassas Airport real late Wednesday night. I was cleaning the hangar and I saw a guy get loaded onto the plane before it took back off."

Payne frowned. "I'll give you a point for being succinct, but we need more. Can you be more specific? Walk me through everything you saw. Even the minutest detail may be of help in our investigation."

Watson spent about ten minutes telling them about why he was at Dibaco Aviation that night.

"I know you said your wife normally cleans and you fill in from time to time, but is it normal to have jets land that late?" asked Stone.

"I've never seen one, and my wife said it's pretty rare. She's there three nights a week. I think she knows what happens around here."

"Okay, the plane pulls in close to the hangar, and two suspicious guys descend the stairs?"

"Yes."

"What happened next?" asked Payne.

Watson described a cargo van and how two men led a hooded, bound man from the van to the plane. "Then his hood blew off."

"Did you get a good look at him?"

"I can do one better," Watson said eagerly. He was hoping his cooperation meant he wouldn't get in trouble. "I snapped some pics on my phone."

"Seriously?" Payne felt his pulse quicken.

Watson extracted his cellphone from a back pocket and opened the photo app. He scrolled through the photo gallery.

"I took pictures of more than just the hooded guy's face."

Watson found the clearest photo. The picture wasn't sharp in the poor lighting, and it had a little grainy blur to it, but he used his fingers to zoom in and turned the phone around for Payne and Stone to see.

"*That's him*," Stone said, the excitement in her voice impossible not to notice. Payne knew he shouldn't be surprised. Once again, his gut had proved to be right.

"Who is it?" Watson asked.

"The man we're looking for," Payne said.

"Can you tell us the rest of what you saw?" asked Stone.

"Where was I? Oh, that's right. I left off with the hood blowing off." Watson continued with what happened next. On occasion, he'd flip his phone around and show them pictures.

"Tell us more about the guys who went to the cargo van to retrieve the bags. You said they were talking and you could make out some of their conversations?"

"Well, I heard them speaking, but like I said, I couldn't make out what they said. Sorry, I should have clarified. It wasn't because I couldn't hear them—it was because I didn't understand the language they spoke."

"It wasn't English?" asked Payne.

"No. I'm not that good with foreign accents. I only speak English. Know a few Spanish words, but mainly just how to order two beers and say my friend will pay."

Payne smiled. "Can you venture any kind of guess as to their nationality? Maybe try to mimic what it sounded like?"

"Well…" Watson paused and pursed his lips. "If I had to guess I'd say they sounded Russian, at least what people from Russia talk like in the movies. I saw that Jason Bourne movie last night with the wife while we were lying in bed. My two guys sounded like that assassin who killed Jason's girlfriend on the bridge in India. You know, shot her instead of him. The vehicle goes off the bridge, and Bourne leaves her dead in the water. You know what movie I'm talking about?"

Payne nodded. "Pretty sure that's *The Bourne Supremacy*. Great flick."

"Yes, that's it. The guys had the same kind of accent."

"That helps a bunch," Stone said.

"And you got a picture of the jet's tail number, which is more valuable than you realize," Payne added.

"You sure I'm not in any trouble?"

Payne said, "No, of course not. You've been very helpful, Geoff." A pause, then, "But I am curious why you didn't tell anybody about this. Are hooded men hustled onto waiting jets by Russians a regular thing here?"

Watson thought the FBI man might have been making a joke, but he wasn't sure, so he didn't laugh. "Fair question, Agent Payne, but I didn't even tell my wife."

"Why not?" asked Payne.

"Well, when it was happening, I thought this can't really be happening to me. It seemed like one of those spy shows you see on Netflix."

"But you have the pictures. Clearly, it happened."

"I know. Trust me. When I got home, I could hardly sleep. Felt guilty at first for not calling the cops. Then I thought maybe these are real bad dudes who kidnapped this guy, and if I call the cops, it will come back to me, and my family will be in danger. Then I thought what if it's that thing the government does."

"What type of thing are you referring to?"

"You know that thing," Watson paused for a moment. "You know that R-word—removal? No, that's not the word."

"Rendition?" asked Stone.

"Yes, that's it—rendition. That thing the CIA does to people in the movies when they snatch them away in the middle of the night. Then they do things to them to get info."

A wry smile crossed Payne's face. "You thought maybe our own government grabbed this guy?

"Thought crossed my mind," Watson said.

"But you said they didn't speak English."

"Well, good point. Guess my wild conspiracy theory doesn't hold much water, does it?"

"Never mind that," Payne said. "What matters is what you've told us and especially what you've shown us. Agent Stone and I will need a copy of all the pictures." Payne pulled a bright yellow Post-It note from a pad on the table and scribbled on it. "Can you email all that to me right away?"

"I'm glad to help in any way I can," Watson said.

They talked for another ten minutes before Payne and Stone thanked Watson for his time and headed to Payne's car. Stone leaned against the passenger's side door and put her hands on top of the roof.

"What's next?" asked Stone.

"Back to DC and meet with the director. On the way, I need you to forward the pictures to my secure server and send a copy to the tech guys at the WFO so they can start analyzing them."

"That's it?"

"I need to make a few calls. Anytime a plane flies above eighteen thousand feet, they must file an IFR flight plan. We need to find out where that jet went."

"We can use the tail number to track the jet?"

"Hopefully, yes. They would have been in contact with air traffic control, and we should be able to figure out where the jet went."

"What if they didn't fly that high?"

Payne frowned. "One problem at a time."

Chapter 36
The Gulf of Mexico

Warm turquoise water gently lapped against the soles of Nick Jordan's feet as a blazing sun toasted his skin to a light layer of bronze.

Man, this feels good.

He lowered his hands from the beach chair into the coarse sand, and his fingers gently dug through hot granules. They slipped between each finger and some lodged under his nails.

A deep breath of salt air entered his lungs, and he exhaled slowly. The only sound was the waves crashing against the rocky beach.

Nick looked to his right and saw nothing besides the narrow strip of white sandy beach that went on as far as he could see. Large dunes lined one side of the beach, and beyond them, only blue skies were visible, dotted with an occasional palm tree. As he turned to his left, he found more of the same. He had the beach completely to himself, a little slice of heaven. It was as if he'd died and woke up in paradise.

This is so nice. If only there were a couple of bikini-clad women. Some eye candy splashing in the water. Then life would be perfect.

A set of hands grabbed his shoulders.

The sand and water disappeared. Gone were the beach, the blue skies, and the palm trees.

Jordan jerked his head up to find the unsympathetic face of Sir staring down at him.

"Well, welcome back, prisoner," said Sir. "I'm glad the Chemist finally found the right concoction."

Jordan balled his restrained hands into a fist, but he remained quiet.

"Interesting stories you shared about MOGUL."

That name—the Secret Service code name for the president. A quiet rage welled up from within him and he knew whatever drugs they'd given him must have caused him to crack. *No one can hold out forever,* he reminded himself. Only one question ran through his mind.

What the hell did I tell them?

Sir exited the interrogation room and walked down the hall. He needed a cigarette but all he had was a pack of those horrible French Gauloises Blondes, plus he thought he could use something stronger than nicotine. The bottle of Macallan 15 stuffed in his footlocker under his bed came to mind. Before he reached the northern staircase, Evelyn Rhimes' voice echoed down the narrow, dimly lit hallway.

"Where you headed?" she asked.

Sir turned around and raised the cigarette pack.

"Smoke. Care to join me?"

"No," she said in a curt tone. "Where are we with the Body Man?"

"The third round of drugs worked."

"And?"

"He's blabbering, which is good while also less good."

"How so?"

Sir shrugged his shoulders. "It's always a challenge to separate fact from fiction."

"Go on."

"I did get him to confirm he printed off four copies of the documents."

"You didn't prompt him?"

"No, he did it on his own, and since it backs up what they found on his laptop, I tend to think he's telling the truth."

"And what did he do with the other three copies?"

Sir paused. "He either gave them to Rose Lewis, the next-door neighbor, or Danny Frazier. Maybe both."

"Well, which one?"

"I think he's trying to protect Rose, but I have the feeling she didn't get anything. It's too obvious."

"So, Danny has them?"

"Yes and no."

"What the hell does that mean?" Rhimes scowled.

"Jordan's talked in circles, with elements of truth twisted among the lies. He is really good. He was trained by the best to withstand interrogation methods and it shows."

"We're being paid for answers, not excuses."

"I know."

She pressed him. "If he gave Frazier the documents, does he still have them? Were they missed at his apartment in DC?"

"Possibly, but I'm not sure. I need to get back in there and keep pumping him for answers. I really feel like we're getting closer."

"Skip your nicotine break and get back in there. Break him. I don't give a shit what's required. Just do it."

Sir's upper lip curled. "I will."

She turned and under her breath muttered, "You'd better."

Marcus Rollings and Merci De Atta walked into the front lobby of the hospital and went directly to the bank of elevators. Ten feet separated them, with Rollings leading the way. He spotted two Secret Service agents in the lobby and looked straight ahead to avoid unwanted eye contact.

Rollings, Merci and several people entered the elevator and he stood closest to the door, pushing the button for the fifth floor. After two stops, they arrived. Another person got off with them, turning right while he and Merci took a left.

Shift change was occurring as the doctors, nurses, and half the Secret Service agents swapped out. Rollings had purposely chosen this time when things naturally turned a little chaotic. The plan was simple enough. He would enter Frazier's room and administer the drugs intravenously through the IV port.

Just another med drop, right on schedule. No biggie.

Merci was his backup if things went south. Rollings knew she could handle herself against a Secret Service agent—or anyone else. He'd seen her put down men three times her size.

The drugs Rollings would inject into Frazier's bloodstream worked slowly. The deadly cocktail was designed to shut down vital organs over twenty to forty minutes. A thorough blood panel done during his autopsy would likely find the abnormal chemicals, but by that point, it wouldn't matter. Frazier would be dead, and he and Merci would be long gone.

The first step was to get past Danny Frazier's guards.

As they approached the ICU room, Rollings and Merci held up the hospital IDs hanging from neck lanyards. They knew no one would be admitted to Frazier's room without them, so they acted as if they'd shown IDs here dozens of times before.

A bad-tempered agent in a navy-blue suit took each badge and scanned their bar codes with a small device he'd removed from his suit jacket. The LCD screen turned green, and their photos and fake hospital information instantly popped up on the small screen with the word APPROVED.

The protocols satisfied, the agent took a deep, bored breath and said, "We need to pat you both down."

The female agent on the other side of the doorway stepped forward.

"Yep," said Rollings. He held aside a metal tray with the meds and syringe covered in a white cloth. The male searched Rollings and the female patted down Merci.

"Highlight of my day," Merci said as she winked at the agent. Her response garnered the slightest bit of an amused Tina Fey snort from the woman searching her.

After the searches ended, the agents moved aside and the assassins entered Frazier's room. Two more agents sat on either side of the bed near the headboard. They sat up straight and eyed them wearily.

"Meds time," Rollings said as he approached the bed.

Both agents remained quiet. The one on the left side gave a subtle head nod.

Merci stood to his left.

Rollings reached the footboard as his cellphone vibrated in his right front pocket. Only one person had the number. He pulled out the phone and didn't need to look at the display.

Why the hell is he calling now? This can't be good.

He considered ignoring the call but knew that wasn't an option. He'd wing it.

"I'm with another patient. Can this wait?" Rollings said into the phone. The voice on the other end said one word.

"Abort."

His stomach tensed. "What was that?"

"Abort. Now."

"Not possible."

"Did you already administer the meds?"

"No."

"Then don't give him the drug, damn it. And get the hell out of the hospital right now."

"Understood. On the way"

The line went dead and Rollings stuffed his phone back in his pocket. He pivoted close to the footboard and faced Merci, careful not to change his expression. He used a prearranged code phrase to let her know they needed to terminate the mission.

"Mr. Brown took a turn for the worse. We need to go ASAP."

"Okay," said Merci.

"And we need to be delicate since his family is in the room." That phrase instructed her they couldn't take a life as they fled.

"That should be interesting," she replied. She turned to the agents. "Thanks, fellas. See you next time." Rollings nodded but said nothing.

They turned and started for the door.

"Hold up."

The Secret Service agent sitting to Frazier's right was looking at Rollings. Like he'd seen him before.

"Yes, officer?" Rollings said as he turned back, careful to keep his tone even keeled, his expression friendly.

"I know you ..." said the agent. He slowly stood. The second agent was on full alert now too.

"Well, we've been taking care of Agent Frazier the past few days."

"No. That's not it. I saw you yesterday near the elevators, but you looked different. It's your eyes—"

Rollings saw the agent's eyes dart toward Merci.

Connected to the footboard was a white plastic clipboard dangling from a hook. It contained Danny Frazier's chart. Rollings didn't have time to think, only react. With one smooth motion, he grasped clipboard, pulled it from the hook, turned it horizontal, and whipped it through the air at the agent's head like a Frisbee.

Merci reacted in tandem. She spun around and lunged for the agent on the left side of Frazier's bed.

The agent on the right drew his gun and started to raise it as the clipboard struck him above the bridge of the nose with the corner of the hardened plastic. His left hand reached up to cover his face as a sharp pain spread across his eyes and momentarily made him unsteady. Rollings dropped his shoulder like a linebacker trying to drill a receiver and he hit the agent square in the solar plexus, sending him off the ground. The agent landed unconscious against the wall behind the hospital bed with a dull thud.

Merci had achieved her *sam dan*, or third-degree black belt, in Taekwon-do by the time she'd turned twenty. Her scissor kicks were vicious and served as her go-to move to immobilize threats. She moved through the air with the grace of a swan but the ferocity of a hawk. A kick struck the agent below his throat, rendering him unconscious immediately.

They both knew the agents outside would enter within seconds and they were ready.

The first agent pushed the door open and stepped inside but made a tactical error of not drawing his weapon. Rollings reached full stride and hit him with a closed-fist punch to the side of the head, causing the man to crumple like a rag doll onto the floor.

The second agent breached the door with her weapon drawn, ready to fire. Merci swept hard at her legs and cut them out from under her. She discharged her weapon, the deafening sound inside the small area causing a tremendous ringing in Rollings' and Merci's ears. The round sailed high over Merci's head and lodged in the ceiling and the back of the agent's head hit the floor with a loud *thump*, knocking her out cold.

Rollings and Merci knew they weren't out of the woods. As planned, they exited Danny Frazier's room in full sprints. She took a left and he took a right.

Merci screamed at the nurses' station as she fled. "Those Secret Service agents were fighting and one shot a gun! Get security up here stat!"

Merci ended up with the easier escape route. She encountered only one security officer before she reached the south stairwell and he was running flat-out toward Frazier's floor, right hand on a radio mic clipped to his shirt and calling out his location as he closed the distance.

He didn't stand a chance as she delivered a vicious throat punch and he fell to the floor, rolling back down the stairwell to crumple against the painted cinder block wall.

Two minutes later she arrived at the rendezvous point without further incident. She pulled off her hospital scrubs and tossed them into the trash compactor. The electric grinding of the compactor as it crushed the latest batch of trash caused her to turn around. In her head, she'd kept track of the time since she'd fled the chaotic room.

Where the hell is he?

They'd planned to meet at the rear of the building on the ground floor within five minutes of their escape. Seconds dragged on, and before long, the five minutes had expired. Her escape within sight, all she needed to do was run down the alley, take a right-hand turn, then a sharp left. She'd be at the Foggy Bottom-GWU Metro station in less than three minutes. From there she would blend in and disappear like a ghost.

Rollings had told her not to wait if he didn't make it. To go and not look back. But Merci didn't follow rules.

Marcus Rollings found himself trapped alone in the north stairwell. Within fifty feet of Danny's room—before Rollings had even left the floor—the quick-response Secret Service team on standby in the cafeteria had found him. And they were asking questions later.

The first bullet screamed past his head close enough for him to feel the air displaced next to his cheek. The round struck the wall before him and sent fragments of drywall into his eyes like a puff of smoke. There had been no *Stop or I'll shoot!* command first.

The lesson had been loud and clear: You endanger a Secret Service agent, you get hit back tenfold. With four agents down, there were still six more on the premises. Three had formed a protective bubble around Danny Frazier while the other three had gone on the hunt.

Rollings had pushed his strained muscles to the max and reached the far nurse's station. Pushing off with his right foot, he had plowed through the north-facing stairwell door to the left of the nurse's station, but not before his outstretched hand had grabbed a black stapler from the counter. As he cleared the door jamb, another bullet had hit inches from the door frame.

Man, these bastards don't give up.

He assumed the stairwell would afford him some measure of cover, but Rollings needed to make it down three more flights of stairs to his prepositioned Glock 19 on the second-floor landing. Finding a groove, he took the steps three at a time before pivoting at the landing between levels to catch the next series of steps.

After he'd hustled down two sets of stairs, he heard the agents descending from above. There was just enough time to dive into an alcove on the landing before a hail of bullets tore up the cinder block wall before him.

Rollings was trapped with only his wits and a black Swingline stapler. With his possible death looming, the only question left was if it would be best to dive for the next flight of steps and make good his escape—or die in the hail of bullets from the approaching agents.

Merci raced back up the stairwell and heard a torrent of bullets as she opened the glass box containing a fire hose mounted in the second-level stairwell. She reached behind the large, wrapped hose and wiggled free the hidden Glock 19. With the weapon cradled in her left hand, she took two steps at a time. On the way up, she racked the weapon to verify it was hot.

As she arrived at the top of the stairs between the second and third floors, she saw him. Rollings was huddled in the corner with a black object in his hand. They exchanged a series of hand signals.

He lowered three fingers, one at a time. When all three fingers were down, she watched him lunge from the sliver of wall that had provided him limited shelter. Armed with his black stapler, the darkened object appeared to be a gun. At the same time, Merci leaned out from the stairwell, exposing only her arm, and pointing the Glock toward the top of the stairs.

Merci emptied the magazine, spraying bullets all around the top of the stairs. She grabbed Rollings by the white lab coat, pulled him toward her and moved down the steps to the lower level. Fifteen seconds later they both sucked in fresh air as they emerged from the stairwell on the ground floor.

Without looking back, they ran flat-out down the alley toward the main road. Marcus shed the white lab coat and they tossed the discarded clothes and empty gun into a garbage can. With no fresh mag, the Glock was nothing more than an expensive paperweight.

With the coast clear, they emerged from the alley and, not wanting to raise suspicions, strolled arm in arm until reaching the relative safety of the Metro station several blocks away.

They took the Blue Line train and got off at the third stop, Metro Center. Before switching to the Red Line, Rollings retrieved a small duffel bag hidden in a trash can at the end of the platform, and in the restroom they quickly changed clothes and removed the facial disguises.

Next, they boarded another Red Line train for two stops and got off at Judiciary Square.

They still hadn't said a word since they'd left the hospital. After walking up the stairs and exiting at Fourth and D Streets, Rollings paused.

"Where we headed?" asked Merci.

He shook his head. "Damned if I know, but I need a drink. A stiff one."

"Now you're talking."

"Ever been to the Billy Goat Tavern?"

"Um, no," said Merci with raised eyebrows. "It sounds shady."

Rollings laughed out loud. "Worried about your reputation, are we?"

"A girl only has her reputation and her good looks."

"Not sure about the former, but as for the latter, you've got that in spades." Rollings gave her backside a good pat. "Pretty sure you'll fit right into this place."

Chapter 38
Santa Monica Municipal Airport (SMO)

Peter Casha climbed aboard the corporate Gulfstream G280 jet, both of its engines already hot and turning. Each halting step up the airstair caused a jolt to his injured shoulder, shooting pain down his arm like a steel pinball and across his upper torso. The morphine he'd injected on the boat no longer dulled the hurt from Fuentes' bullet.

At least *he's dead*, Casha thought.

The attractive flight attendant, Cindy, met him at the door and could tell from his ashen face he wasn't well. Casha normally remarked on her chestnut hair, the smell of her cocoa butter lotion, and her warm smile. She'd worked many of the flights his company arranged for him, and they'd often engaged in harmless flirting with each other.

Cindy asked him if he was all right, but when Casha only dropped heavily into a chair and didn't reply, she scooted to the flight deck and notified the pilot.

The pilot came out of the cockpit. "You okay, Mr. Casha?"

He looked up, a smirk that clearly masked pain formed in the corner of his mouth. "I've been better, Ted, thanks for asking ..." With his one good arm, he struggled to remove his golf shirt and reveal his thick gauze-wrapped shoulder. The white bandages revealed deep-red blood stains.

"Jesus—have you been stabbed?"

"No. Shot."

"We need to get you to a hospital immediately."

"No, not here. I need to get back to the city."

Ted shook his head in protest. "You're in no condition to fly across the country. It looks like you've lost a lot of blood."

Casha didn't want to get into a pissing match with the pilot, who he thought was a good guy just trying to do his job. But a GSW meant paperwork and a call to the police. That wasn't an option for him.

"Trust me, I'll survive. I need to clean out the wound, get some more morphine, and apply a fresh dressing on the shoulder. I'll be all right after a couple of drinks."

"Are you sure?" asked Ted. He didn't look convinced.

"Sadly, yes," Casha said. "Let's peel some paint and get me back east as quick as possible. We have people who can patch me up."

"If you say so, Mr. Casha." Ted shook his head. Cindy arrived with a comprehensive first aid kit, including morphine. "This hot rod can do Mach point-eight-five, and we're light to begin with even with a full fuel load. We can get you home in about four and a half hours." Ted patted Casha's leg. "Cindy will help you with clean dressings once we're airborne. Wheels up in five minutes."

"Okay Ted, that's good to go," Casha said.

He pulled up the short sleeve of his golf shirt for Cindy and she injected him with the pain killer. She helped him buckle his seat belt and then returned to her seat, buckling up for takeoff.

Once aloft, Cindy returned with three fingers of Tito's vodka straight up and he sipped it while she peeled off the blood-soaked gauze and cleaned the wound. Her gentle touch and reassuring voice helped calm his nerves.

"Hope you don't faint at the sight of blood." Casha said.

"You're in luck," Cindy said with a wide smile. "In a former lifetime I was an ER nurse and worked in a trauma bay. Plus, I'm the official paramedic on these flights, so you're in good hands if you don't need, like, a kidney transplant. Few things faze a girl like me."

"No kidding?"

"No kidding."

"Why leave that to fly assholes like me around in a fancy taxi-cab at all hours?"

Cindy laughed. "Well, for starters, the pay is a lot better for far fewer hours. And until right now, there wasn't any blood."

Cindy finished cleaning and dressing the wound while Casha finished the vodka. On top of the morphine, the pain had sub-sided, and he was starting to feel pretty good. Cindy helped him put on a fresh shirt that buttoned in the front so as not to require pulling a new golf shirt over the damaged shoulder. She made a fast exam of the second wound, which had stopped bleeding and seemed like it wasn't infected. She applied a fresh dressing and gave Casha more antibiotics.

"We have any more Tito's on board?" he asked.

"Of course. We always keep extra on hand when we know you are joining us. Up, on the rocks, or maybe mixed with some of that lemonade you like?"

Casha smiled from ear to ear. "I'm kinda in love with you right now," he said. Maybe it was the morphine kicking in. "Just the bottle will do perfectly, Cindy."

Cindy returned with it a minute later, opened it for him and set it on the tray. "Any thoughts about food?"

With his good arm, he raised the bottle level with his head. "A liquid dinner for me tonight."

"You got it, boss." Now that it looked like her client wasn't going to die in her hands, Cindy's voice had resumed its usual southern California perkiness.

"Oh, I do need one more thing."

"Of course. What is it?"

"I need a phone. Lost mine earlier."

Cindy returned with a new iPhone still in the packaging. She unwrapped it and inserted a custom SIM. "We keep a box of burner SIM cards on the plane. The battery is charged, and I'll dispose of it when you're done if you like?"

He thanked her and took a few long drags from the bottle. The liquid warmed his throat and spread through Casha's body as effectively as the morphine. He dialed the number from memory.

"Yeah?" said the uncertain voice.

"Joe, it's me."

"Bro, I didn't recognize the number. Plus, you sound different."

"New phone. Had a rough night."

"Where are you?"

"On the jet. We just took off from Santa Monica."

"What happened? I tried calling, but your phone went straight to voicemail each time."

"Hit a snag."

"Is the job done?" Lagano asked.

"Yes," Casha said.

"Then what's the snag?"

"It got complicated, and I got shot."

"Fuck. How bad is it?"

"Going to need to go under the knife. He got me good in my damn shoulder."

"Who did?"

"Hector."

"Tell me exactly what happened."

He spent the next twenty minutes telling Joe everything.

"Look," Joe said. "I'm in DC but I can make a few calls and get a team to meet you at Teterboro."

"Why are you in DC?"

"Junior wants me to meet with someone."

"Who?"

"The prince hisself."

"Are you going to deliver the flash drive to him?" asked Casha.

"No, not yet. At least not all of it."

"Where are you meeting him? The embassy?" Casha had wanted to be present for that.

"No, they want to meet somewhere public."

"Who's going to have your six?" Casha asked.

"I was thinking at first of asking you, but you're not up to it in your condition."

"True enough, but listen—the prince isn't to be trusted, Joe, under any conditions. You need more than the standard security detail if you're going to meet with him."

"Suggestions?"

"Is Marcus available?"

Lagano sighed. "He almost got his head blown off by the Secret Service at the hospital."

"Almost? He's okay, though?"

Joe laughed. "Yeah, he made it out alive because Merci saved his ass."

"What about Frazier? They get him?"

"No, the hit was called off at the last minute and their evac went all to shit."

"Called off? Why?"

"New info received from Jordan's interrogation."

"I thought they were afraid Frazier knew something and might talk if he regained consciousness."

"That was the case," Lagano said, "but now they believe Danny might be the only person that has the info needed."

"Jesus, this is getting complicated. I'm gonna tell the pilot to take me to DC instead. We can land at Manassas."

"But our doctor is in New York."

"Either get him to DC, or we can make other arrangements."

"What other arrangements?"

"The Sanctum has a med facility near Washington."

"But I thought you didn't trust them?" Lagano said.

"I don't, but they're a money-making business. If we pay them what they want, they'll come through with the services we need."

"You sure?"

"Yes. Get Marcus to go with you to meet the prince. What time is the meeting?"

Lagano paused to look at his watch. "In ninety minutes."

"Perfect. When that ends, you can meet me in Manassas at the airport. I'll feel better knowing I've got you to watch my six when the Sanctum patches me up."

"If you say so."

"Deal," Lagano said. "Let me make some calls."

"Cool," Casha said. "You go do your thing. I'm going to pass out for a while."

Chapter 39
Vienna, Virginia

Wes Russell pulled up in front of Nick Jordan's townhouse and rolled down the window of his anonymous-gray Ford Fusion government car. He grabbed a wooden strike-anywhere match from the center console, scraped it fast against the steering wheel causing a flame to dance off the end of the match, and lit the Marlboro Red.

The cigarette dangled from his lips like he was Humphrey Bogart. With his gaze fixed across the street, he sucked in several long drags as the bitter taste of match sulfur filled his mouth. Nothing looked out of place. Even though it was only seven at night, the street appeared empty.

He grabbed his cellphone and dialed Payne. The phone rang four times before it went to voicemail.

"Hey, Payne, it's me. I'm at Rose's house. The street appears quiet, and I'm about to head in. I expect the Dew and smokes on my desk when I get in tomorrow morning. Oh, and don't be such a dick to Stone. Later, dogface."

Russell hung up the phone and finished the last few puffs of cigarette. He knew he needed to quit smoking and he told his squad he would seriously consider stopping one day. Out of habit, he drew his Glock 19, checked the mag, and confirmed he had one in the pipe. With the weapon confirmed hot, he slid it back into his right hip holster and rolled up the window, climbed out of the car, and dropped the smoking butt on the asphalt.

He ground the last dying embers into a pulp with the heel of his brown shoe and crossed the street. As he reached the bottom step to Rose Lewis' porch, he absently tapped the Kevlar vest he wore under his short-sleeve shirt.

After four tours in Iraq, Russell knew firsthand all it takes is some jackass with a gun and a lucky shot to ruin a good day.

He took the nine steps three at a time and approached the red door. Before he raised his hand to knock, he reached into his front pocket and pulled out the sticky note to confirm the address. Left of the door affixed to the siding were the numbers 2207.

Good, right place.

Few things embarrassed him more than rolling up on the wrong house and flashing his creds to the wrong person. As Russell raised his left hand to knock on the solid door, his eyes glanced down. He noticed the slight gap between the door latch and the frame.

Something's not right.

His right hand reached down and withdrew the Glock while his left hand went from a balled fist to an open palm to apply slow pressure to the door.

Old people sometimes forget to close their doors all the way.

With little pressure, his palm pushed the door open. The hinges hadn't been greased in years, and they gave a not-too-subtle creaking sound as it swung open. With the Glock raised and level with his chin, Russell stepped into the house. His eyes darted back and forth as he looked for anything out of the ordinary.

Don Flynn stood over Rose and berated her with one question

after another, getting nowhere.

Ryan Polk, his partner, was getting sick of his shit. "Dude, she doesn't know anything."

With a shake of the head, Flynn said, "I don't believe her. The Body Man must have told her something."

"Stop using that reference in front of her," Polk said.

"What, 'the Body Man'?" Flynn scowled. "Whatever, dude."

Confused about what was going on, Rose Lewis looked back and forth as the two men bickered.

"Look, I told you, she obviously doesn't know anything," Polk insisted. "You don't think she'd have spilled by now? She's an old lady, not a fucking SEAL."

"And you know this how?" Flynn replied. But he was starting to believe it was true: The old woman probably didn't know squat. "Then what are we going to do with her?"

"You should have thought about that before you kicked in her door, asshole."

Flynn shrugged. "Man, I reacted; it's as simple as that."

"Bring her," said Polk. He exited the living room and walked toward the adjacent dining area.

"What are you going to do to me?" Lewis asked from the chair. The obvious panic evident in her thin voice gave Polk a dull ache in the pit of his stomach; she was so much like his own grand-mother.

Polk said to Flynn, "Gag her."

"This is for your own good," said Flynn, stuffing a white dish-rag from the kitchen into her mouth and placed a long piece of duct tape over it. She had stopped resisting. It did her no good.

Polk and Flynn walked into the kitchen and stood on either side of the island in the center of the room, facing one another. Polk nervously tapped on the glass cooktop embedded into the marble island with his index finger, thinking. Flynn said he just wanted to put a bullet in her head and call it a day, but Polk was trying to figure another way out of their clusterfuck.

"Look, I need to grab her some water," Polk said as he turned toward the kitchen sink.

Then Flynn's head snapped to the left. "You hear that?" he asked.

"Hear what?" Polk asked.

Flynn didn't wait for a response. The creaking sound from the front of the house had drawn his attention. He paused and raised a finger toward his partner. Silence returned and he listened for about twenty seconds before Flynn took three long strides and reached the galley-style door that separated the dining area from the kitchen.

Russell cleared the foyer, his gun raised, eyes scanning the room for threats. Once he turned the corner into the living room, he saw an elderly woman duct-taped to an overstuffed armchair.

Rose Lewis? Damn it. I should have called for backup.

It was too late now, and he knew it.

The old woman saw his movements and looked toward him. Her eyes grew wide, pleading for help. She didn't try to talk but swiveled her eyes several times in the direction of the kitchen. Russell raised his left hand and brought his extended index finger to his mouth, signaling she needed to stay quiet. She nodded, and he got within a few feet of her as the door to the adjoining dining room swung open.

Fifteen feet away, an armed man took a step into the room.

Russell shifted his weight, pivoted his arms, and had the man sighted in before his body fully cleared the doorway. The gun the man gripped in his right hand swung up.

With a firm voice, Russell said, "FBI! Drop your weapon!"

Then time slowed to a crawl.

Russell's mind flashed back to Mosul, where *hajjis* popped out of doors, windows, and cars parked on the roadside to spray and pray with vintage AK-47s. You name it, they hid behind it. Back then you didn't announce who you were. As a soldier, you engage a hostile threat without question.

The man continued to raise his gun in slo-mo.

Russell went on autopilot. The man with the gun posed an immediate threat, not only to himself but also the innocent woman taped to the chair. That was enough.

Two smooth trigger pulls sent two consecutive rounds from his Glock to the man with a gun. Both bullets struck the man in the forehead within an inch of each other. His head lurched back as the rear of his skull exploded. Blood and brain matter splattered all over the white ceiling and wall behind the mahogany buffet.

Before Russell had time to process what had occurred, another man emerged through the galley door.

Barely two steps behind his partner, Polk watched the back of Flynn's head explode like a fragmentation grenade and chunks of hair-covered skull and blood splatter over the wall and ceiling.

He froze.

Polk's eyes darted to the left, where a man with an FBI badge on his left hip stood in front of Rose Lewis. The FBI agent's gun moved from Flynn's lifeless body and was now pointed toward him. Polk turned his body, raised his gun to hip level and triggered two snapshot rounds.

Without any aim the first bullet missed the FBI man and passed to the left of Rose's head, slamming into the far wall of the living room. The second bullet somehow found its mark and struck the man in the upper left chest.

Before Polk's mind recognized the successful shot, he felt two very hard punches to his chest. The Kevlar vest was the only thing that saved his life. His left hand clutched at his chest while his legs gave way and he started to fall to the side. With his right hand still raised he squeezed off two more rounds, although he could tell from his angle of descent both bullets flew far to the left of his intended target.

Russell felt a sledgehammer hit his chest as Polk's shot struck his body armor. In the same split second, Russell instinctively reached for his chest and squeezed off two rounds from his Glock, deafening sounds in confined space. He didn't hear the ricochet as Polk's second round struck a thick antique bronze plaque hanging on the wall behind him.

A searing pain burned the back of his neck below the hairline and Wes Russell croaked two unintelligible words only he understood.

"Oh, shit …" he said aloud.

His left hand moved from the dime-sized hole over his vest to his throat, which suddenly felt on fire. The ricocheting bullet had penetrated from behind between Russell's sixth and seventh vertebrae, deflected slightly upward and exited his windpipe below his Adam's apple, causing an exit wound the size of a golf ball. Blood spewed from the wound and his legs buckled with his spinal artery punctured.

Russell's brain commanded his finger to pull the trigger again as he fell. Two final bullets spat from the barrel of the Glock and found their intended target as they struck the side of Polk's head.

Russell dropped to one knee, his body convulsed, and a steady fountain of blood sprayed from between the fingers clutching his throat. He dropped the Glock, and his right hand joined his left in gripping his throat. It was a natural reaction but unsuccessful in slowing the bleeding.

His last conscious thoughts flashed rapidly like a movie playing in fast forward. He saw Beth Ann's face, thought of the first time they spoke, and the sound of his children's laughter.

God, I'll miss them.

The light faded until only darkness remained.

Chapter 40
J. Edgar Hoover Building
Washington, DC

Payne and Stone stepped off the elevator, took a sharp right turn, and headed down the polished hallway toward the director's suite.

"You ever been up here before?" Stone walked next to him and kept his hurried pace.

"His office or this floor?"

"The director's office."

"Nope."

Arriving at the desk, Payne handed one of his cards to the director's assistant, Annie.

She took the card and looked up with a warm smile. "Go ahead inside, Agent Payne; the director has been awaiting your arrival. You as well, Agent Stone."

Payne knocked respectfully and the two agents stepped inside. The office smaller than he expected. A large cherry desk sat near the far wall, and several stacks of papers near a simple brass reading lamp adorned the desk. A small round table sat in the corner closest to the entrance with four chairs and two leather couches facing each other near the center of the room.

Lining the walls were shelves filled from floor to ceiling with books, plaques, framed photos of the director with politicians and famous people, and other keepsakes. Several pieces of artwork hung on the walls, the most vivid an epic five-foot-long oil painting of Monument Valley. A fireplace on the wall behind one of the couches crackled and hissed as a fire roared.

Director Ludington stood as Payne and Stone entered. He walked around the desk to meet them between the couches.

"Mr. Director, good to see you again. Have you met Probationary Agent Katherine Stone?"

Ludington had a firm grip and gave Payne's hand a solid shake. His eyes left Payne and looked at Stone, whose hand he shook as well. "Ah yes, a pleasure to meet you, Agent Stone. You go by Stone, correct?"

"That's right, sir."

"Hope Payne is treating you well?" asked the director as he shook her hand. "He's got a reputation of being slightly, umm, challenging at times," he said with a wink and warm smile.

Stone laughed. "He's been great, sir. Don't believe the bad things you may have heard. I take it you know each other?"

"Yes, we do. Payne didn't tell you?"

Stone jabbed her elbow into Payne's right rib, and he winced in discomfort. "No, he failed to mention that on our long drive here." Her piercing eyes revealed her displeasure.

"I was going to tell you," Payne said as he darted his gaze away from hers.

"Tell her how we met, Payne," Ludington said.

"Well, we played on the Bureau's softball team."

"The FBI has a softball team?" asked Stone.

"Several," said the director.

"And you played together?"

"Nooo," Payne drawled. "We were on opposite teams. The director has a C-level team but it's made up of all the big dogs."

The director let out a deep laugh; his voice inflection sounded like an old engine as it sputtered back to life. "We played against each other for the league championship three years ago."

"That was one hell of a game, sir," Payne said as a wide smile covered his face.

"And I still have the scar to prove it," said the director as he pulled back a tuft of hair, revealing a one-inch scar on his scalp.

"Yikes," Stone said. "You got that playing softball?"

"I got that from courtesy of Agent Payne here. It felt like I got hit by a freight train."

Stone looked at the director. "And you didn't fire him?"

The director laughed. "No. Actually, I almost promoted him about a year later."

"But?" Stone's eyebrows arched upward.

"That, Stone, is a story for another day." The director pointed to the couch closest to the fireplace. "Please make yourself comfortable. I want to discuss the Webb-Jordan case. I've read through the file but hope you have more to tell me after today."

"We have lots to share, sir," Payne said.

The director took a seat opposite them. "All right. My time is your time. Read me in."

It took Payne almost thirty minutes to lay it all out. He deferred to Stone several times, and between the two of them they left nothing out. The director interrupted numerous times with concise, pointed questions, like the federal prosecutor he'd once been.

A Coke-bottle-thick glass coffee table with an outer metal frame separated the two couches. When they'd first sat down, Payne had put his work cellphone face down on the table and made sure to set it on vibrate.

As Payne finished the update, the phone shook in quick pulses, sending short tremors through the table. He reached over and hit the side button of his phone, silencing the call. "Sorry about that, sir," Payne said, looking slightly embarrassed.

"Can I see the Jordan abduction images?" asked the director, who ignored the vibrating phone.

"Of course," Payne said as he handed over his tablet.

The director flipped through them one at a time and zoomed in using his thumb and index finger on the ones that might depict Nick Jordan most clearly.

"I mean, our guy looks like this guy in the photo, but it's hard to say with certainty."

"We're pretty sure it's him, sir," Payne said. "And I think this photographic evidence proves his abduction."

"So, where did these men with Russian accents take him?"

"Sir, I made a few calls on the drive here," Stone said. "We requested the flight plan and should have the details from the FAA within the hour."

"I have some contacts within the FAA. If anyone gives you a hard time, let me know. If you track where the plane went, maybe you'll find Jordan," said the director.

"Yes, sir, that's the plan," Payne said.

"Question is, why'd they abduct this Secret Service agent?"

"The White House won't even admit he works for them," Payne said.

Ludington rubbed his chin with his thumb in a slow, circular motion. "Yes. Well, speaking of that, I had an interesting conversation with the president at the White House today regarding this investigation. That's why I requested you come by my office."

Stone tapped Payne's foot under the table.

"How does the president know about this case?" asked Payne.

"The president called me into a private meeting—just the two of us, at that—and said he wanted to discuss an active FBI investigation looking into a missing Secret Service agent."

"Why does he care?" asked Stone.

"Well, number one, Jordan is on his security team. And number two, because he wants us to back off."

"What?" asked Stone.

"He didn't say as much directly. He's too canny a political operator for that. He didn't order it. He told me he wanted the Bureau to slow down. 'Take second chair' to the Secret Service is how he put it. He thinks they should be on point to locate their own guy."

Payne's cellphone vibrated again. He disliked bulky rubber safety cases, so the unprotected phone danced around the glass table. Payne looked perturbed as he leaned over and muted the incoming call once again.

"He asked you to back off an active investigation, sir?" asked Stone.

"More or less. I told him in no uncertain terms that he'd want the Bureau to take the lead on this—and we wanted to take it."

"What did he say?" asked Payne.

"He agreed, but suggested we still let the Secret Service find its guy. Said he's their man and they want to find him without any outside assistance."

"But that doesn't make any sense. Why wouldn't they want us involved?"

"He wouldn't even tell me the missing agent's name. I had Annie pull the file from SENTINEL when he made it known he knew you two were making inquiries on the case."

"They're hiding something," Stone said.

The director and Payne looked at Stone, and they both nodded.

"Seems so," Ludington said.

"The president wouldn't give me a name, but he did admit the agent was on his detail."

"Then I may be able to help," Payne said.

"How so?" asked the director.

"I have a, well, let's just say I have a contact on his detail."

"Can you approach him discreetly?"

"Maybe. But it's not a he."

"Uh oh. A friend or a 'special friend'?" A slight smirk formed at the corner of the director's mouth.

"Currently, she's neither."

"Well, that doesn't bode well."

"I think it'll be a decent start, though, sir. It's time I shake the tree hard and see what falls out," Payne said.

"But the president told us to back off the investigation," Stone said. She was fearing for her employment again.

The director cleared his throat. "Let's get one thing straight. The President of the United States does not call the shots here. The FBI is an autonomous agency and there's a reason my term of service is ten years. He might be my ultimate boss, but he has no authority to tell me how to run our investigations. If a federal agent is missing, it's the job of the FBI to find him."

"What do you want us to do, sir?" asked Payne.

"Your jobs," the director said. "For the record, I want you to continue your investigation as you would any other missing-person case. I want you to find this man and get him back safe and sound while following Bureau procedures. But, off the record..." The director paused, seemingly lost in his thoughts.

After almost half a minute of silence, Payne asked, "Sir? Off the record?"

Ludington reached into his pocket and removed two business cards, handing one to Payne and the other to Stone. "This is my personal cell. Very few people have it. You will reach out to me as needed. Off the record, you can have *carte blanche* access to whatever investigative tools and resources you need. I don't know what game President Steele is playing, but something isn't right. My intuition says he doesn't want his guy found. If he did, he wouldn't interfere. Or if he does want him found, he doesn't want us to be the ones to do so."

He paused and looked at his two agents teetering on the edge of astonishment. He gave them a hard stare.

"We on the same page?"

"Yes, sir, chapter and verse," Payne said. "Find him but don't get caught if we need to bend protocol."

Ludington smiled and offered a not-too-subtle wink.

Payne's cellphone started to vibrate for the third time.

"Someone really wants to talk to you, Payne," Ludington said. "Do you mind, sir?"

"No, of course not. Take it."

Just then Annie knocked twice on Ludington's door—it was her *I'm coming in right now* signal. She entered and hurried over to the director, handing him a single sheet of paper.

Payne flipped over the phone and recognized the number as the Washington Field Office. He answered in a gruff tone. "Where's the fire, Miller? I'm in a really important meeting."

Stone watched the blood from drain from Payne's face. When she turned to the director, the same face greeted her.

"When?" Payne said. After a brief pause, he replied, "I'm on my way." He tried to stand, but his legs appeared weak.

"What is it, Payne?" Stone demanded. "You look like you've seen a ghost."

Payne shook his head in disbelief. His mouth hung slightly open for a moment.

"Mr. Director, I'm sorry to have to tell you that my squad supervisor, Wes Russell, was just killed in a shootout. He was checking on a witness in this Jordan case at my request. She's the one who placed the missing-person call."

Ludington held up the sheet of paper.

"I know," he said. Ludington had been a street cop before his prosecutor days and then joining the FBI, and his PD had lost three officers in an ambush. The sickening nausea and despair that greeted the death of a warrior brother or sister never lessened.

And now an FBI agent. On his watch.

"Is Rose okay?" asked Stone, her voice cracking.

"She's being transported to the hospital, but she's alive. Sounds like she's pretty shaken up." Payne tried standing once more and this time made it to his feet. "I'm sorry, sir, but we really have to go."

Stone was already on her feet. Ludington also stood, anger burning plainly on his face.

"I'm coming, too. My security team will get us there faster," the director said.

Stone leaned forward and hugged Payne. She pulled him in close to her and let his head fall on her shoulder. "I'm so sorry, Eli."

Payne stared at the fireplace and watched the flames dance. His face hardened.

"It's all my fault."

Chapter 41
The Lincoln Memorial
Washington, DC

Joe Lagano told the driver to stop at the corner of Constitution Avenue and Henry Bacon Drive NW. The blacked-out Mercedes S560 pulled up to the curb and came to a quick stop. Joe climbed out of the passenger seat and told the driver to sit tight. Marcus Rollings and Merci De Atta emerged from the back seat and fell in behind as he walked down the sidewalk.

The pathway split. To the left was the Vietnam Veterans Memorial. Even at this late hour, it still had a handful of visitors.

Lagano also veered left. As they got close to the metal barricades surrounding the entrance to the Lincoln Memorial's circle drive, two olive-skinned men stepped from the shadows.

Both wore finely tailored Armani suits and Testoni Italian shoes. With dark hair and short, neatly trimmed mustaches, they could have passed for twins. The only distinguishing features were one man wore a red tie, the other a charcoal gray.

"Good evening, gentlemen," said the one with the red tie. He looked back and forth between Lagano and Rollings and eyed the latter suspiciously. He then looked at Merci. "And you as well, ma'am, of course."

Merci uttered the word *asshole* under her breath. She had

some deep-seated issues with men from Middle East countries, primarily due to their abhorrent treatment of women.

The man in the red tie either didn't hear her or chose not to respond.

"Where is he?" Lagano looked around with arms wide. "The prince?"

"He has arrived, but before we can escort you, I'll need to check the three of you for weapons."

Lagano immediately realized what he had on his right hip.

The man with the red tie approached Joe and pulled back his suit coat, exposing the hilt of the Omega dagger. The steel was a work of art designed by Half Face Blades, an outfit in San Diego founded by a former Navy SEAL. After checking Joe's pockets and running his hands up and down his legs and torso, the guard pointed to the weapon. "May I?"

"Of course." Joe nodded as he looked down at the hilt.

The man removed the elegant weapon from the sheath and examined the craftsmanship of the seven-inch-long knife. Above the trident on the hilt, an engraved Spartan with the words *Never Forget* were etched into the steel. The red tie man smiled.

"That is a fine blade, Mr. Lagano, but of course I cannot let you near the prince with it in your possession. Nothing personal, just protocol."

"I understand. No problem, as long as I get it back."

"You will. My associate here will hold onto it for safekeeping."

Next, the two men searched Rollings and Merci, who were unarmed.

"Follow me," said the man in the red tie.

A full moon hung low in the night sky and appeared to hover atop the Washington Monument at the other end of the reflecting pool, bathing the structure in a subtle glow.

Streetlamps illuminated the sidewalks and beams of light

shone upon the thirty-six fluted Doric columns of the memorial. A sharply dressed man stood on the fifty-eighth step, his gaze toward the painted sky dotted with stars.

The two guards led the way with Lagano, Rollings, and Merci following up the steps. The guard in the red tie leaned toward the shoulder of the man who pondered Lincoln's statue, his back to the reflecting pool. He whispered something into the sharply dressed man's ear.

Prince Abdul bin Salman was known to much of the world simply as ABS. He turned around slowly and looked down at the three visitors several steps below. Unlike his bodyguards, the prince did not wear a fancy Saville Row suit.

Instead, he wore a blue sport coat over a white, button-down, long-sleeve shirt with light-gray pants and black shoes with a matte finish. A Piaget Polo S watch adorned his wrist.

ABS turned around to face his American visitors.

"Please, my friends. Join me."

Lagano approached and extended his hand, "Your Highness, my name is Joe Lagano."

Prince Abdul took the extended hand and gave it a firm shake. "Please, no need to be formal here. You may call me Abdul."

Lagano said, "This is Marcus Rollings and Merci De Atta. They, um ..." He paused for a moment.

"... are here to keep you safe," ABS said, finishing the thought and the statement.

"Yes, something like that."

"Well, it's a pleasure to finally meet you, Joe. We've spoken several times, and I've enjoyed our conversations. Your boss is quite passionate about his business and appears eager to see our deal finalized."

"I agree," Lagano said.

The prince turned to his right and looked out over the reflecting pool and toward the Washington Memorial. The United States Capitol loomed large in the distance. ABS smiled in honest appreciation.

"I've traveled the world but can say without a doubt, the National Mall is without equal." He looked down at Lagano. "Don't you agree?"

Lagano nodded. "I read your bio, Abdul. A bachelor's from Columbia in New York City and a master's in international business from Georgetown here. You've spent a lot of time in two of our largest cities."

"And I have loved every minute of it." ABS smiled beatifically. The man looked like a oil painting. He waved his hand in the air at the city. "Growing up in the House of Saud affords one many privileges. One of them is an excellent education. We are encouraged—well, I should say required—to attend the most prestigious schools in the West. If you want to be the best, you have to learn from them, or so I've been told."

"And you took that education back home where you've recently been named the minister of commerce and investment," Lagano said.

"Yes. Crown Prince Salman, my cousin, has found favor in me. I like to think he saw my talent for business and decided to use it for the betterment of the kingdom. Our hope is this arrangement will benefit not only our regional interests but also prove a profitable venture for your organization."

"That's Junior's intent as well."

In a subtle motion, the prince pulled back his shirt sleeve and checked his watch. "It's late, and I'm sure you've had a long day in New York before coming. Should we proceed to business?"

"Yes, let's," Lagano said as he placed his arm behind his back. Rollings placed a seven-inch-wide tablet in his hand while Merci continued to watch the two guards with caution. Lagano brought his arm back around his body and handed the tablet to the prince.

"Here it is," he said, careful not to drop it. "You'll find everything you're looking for on the device."

ABS took the tablet. For several minutes he said nothing and merely scrolled through the data provided. Several times he pursed his lips and nodded slightly.

"Well, I am no engineer, but everything looks to be in order. I must admit, the crown prince will be happy when he can have the full schematics and not only this incomplete version."

"Show the crown prince what we've provided when you get back to Riyadh. Consider this a good-faith gift and a preview of what is to come once we conclude our business," Lagano said.

With a glance and a nod over his shoulder, Abdul indicated to the guard with the red tie to hand him a thick bundle of paper folded three times. "Here is a copy of the agreement with the Kingdom of Saudi Arabia for signature. Please have Junior and his legal team review the documents thoroughly and let me know if you find any discrepancies."

"Of course."

"The crown prince is eager for the shipping containers to arrive in Jeddah," ABS said.

"We have several people on the ship, the weaponry is secure, and we will continue to provide updates on its progress. Transporting them undetected via container ship was our best option."

"Agreed, but the slowness of the ocean crossing is very frustrating for us at present."

"We understand. Regrettably, there was no way to use air transport, but fortunately our port system has enough security lapses that we were able to procure safe passage with little risk of detection."

ABS nodded and snapped his fingers. The guard in the gray tie stepped forward and handed the knife to him.

"Do you mind if I look at this?"

Lagano nodded. "Not at all."

The prince looked over the weapon, careful to not brandish it in a flashy way and attract the attention of the National Park Service police, who monitored the memorial.

"Handcrafted?"

"Yes, only a few made."

"I'd love to get one like it."

"The designer is someone I know well; I'd be happy to make a few calls for you."

"I'll pay whatever he asks; money is not an issue." The prince checked the balance of the blade. Perfect. "Do you carry it with you often?"

"Always," Lagano said. "I'd be naked without it."

"Have you ever had to use it?"

Lagano smirked, the left side of his mouth curving upward. "Let's say it's steel teeth have tasted blood."

"I find knives fascinating. Too often men resort to the crudity of firearms. Effective, yes, but impersonal. But to use a blade such as this one against an opponent—that is the sign of a true warrior."

Lagano reached out with his right hand, and the prince placed the knife in his palm. The security men took a step forward but were stopped by the prince's gentle wave-off.

"I completely agree, Abdul."

Chapter 42
Inova Trauma Center
Falls Church, Virginia

Payne awoke with a start in a hard plastic chair. He looked around the drab hospital room, unsure at first where he was or how he'd gotten there in an out-of-context moment. His mind in a fog, his hands gripped the armrest hard enough that his fingers turned pale.

Then he saw her.

Rose Lewis lay sleeping in the hospital bed to his right.

The memories of why he was there flooded back like a torrential rain.

Payne looked at his watch; the display read twelve-fifteen a.m. He'd arrived at the hospital three hours before with Stone and FBI Director Ken Ludington. Stone had wanted to stay until Lewis woke up, but Payne insisted she go home and get some sleep. She hadn't liked the idea, but after several minutes she relented and left with the director and his security detail.

He and Stone had planned to meet at seven sharp to follow new leads.

After arriving at the hospital, Payne had called his friend Dony, a detective with the DC Metro Police Department. Payne knew his fair share of people on the job, but Dony possessed something you couldn't find in the phone book—connections. Payne had planned to meet him at Café Bonaparte in Georgetown at nine for breakfast. One good meal could pay dividends when trying to crack a case.

Now fully awake, a fresh feeling of guilt washed over him like a towering wave as he thought about Wes Russell lying on a metal slab four floors below in the morgue.

It was supposed to have been me.

An hour passed in silence before Rose stirred. Payne sat at the edge of his seat and cupped her hand in his. Her eyes opened and she looked over at Payne, a slight smile at the corner of her burgundy-colored lips.

"Hey, Rose. It's me, Eli Payne."

"Hello, Agent Payne." Rose glanced around the room, and a concerned look spread over her face. "Where am I?"

"You're at the Inova Trauma Center in Falls Church, and you're okay. The doctors are keeping an eye on you to make sure everything looks good, but you're in good shape for all the excitement. You had one hell of a night, didn't you, Rose?" Payne carefully laid his hand on hers.

"I had a visit from two men claiming to be FBI agents that worked with you. Clearly, they were impostors."

"That's right, Rose."

"Did one of them get away? I know the one named Don was shot by a man who entered claiming to be an FBI agent, but when he started to exchange gunfire with the other one, Ryan, I blacked out."

"Both the men who assaulted you died, as did the man I sent to check on you."

"Who was he?"

"My squad supervisor. His name was Wes."

Tears welled up and started to flow down Lewis' wrinkled

face. "I'm sorry for your loss, Agent Payne. His actions certainly saved my life."

"I believe you're right, Rose." Payne dipped his head in sorrow, but mourning would have to wait. "So, can you tell me what happened?"

"Of course. I remember everything they said and did from the moment they entered my house until the gunfire and I blacked out."

Payne fished his recorder out of his pocket. "If you don't mind, I'd like to record your statement."

"Of course. By all means, record away."

For the next hour plus, Lewis recounted the events inside her house with dramatic details. Payne stopped her when she started talking about the documents they wanted. "Go back a second, Rose. They called him what again?"

"The Body Man," said Rose. "The one named Don, the vulgar one, he referred to him the Body Man several times."

Payne felt the hair on the back of his neck stand up at the reference. He thought back to the mysterious text messages he'd received. "Are you sure he said it just like that?"

"Yes, I'm positive. Is it important?"

He patted her hand and nodded. "Yes. Right now, everything is important."

She continued. Payne interrupted her with questions from time to time and took copious notes.

Around three a.m. Lewis was getting fatigued again, so she and Payne wrapped up so she could get some rest. He stood and kissed her forehead, picked up his messenger bag of stuff and stepped out into the hallway.

Payne walked down the hospital corridor to the empty waiting room and took a seat in a threadbare armchair. He took his laptop out of the messenger bag and logged into the FBI server using his encrypted VPN access. Over the next forty-five minutes he added what Rose told him into SENTINEL, the Bureau's case-file database system. He was sure to include the term "the Body Man" in the notes and tag the file updates to Director Ludington who would want to know the missing Secret Service man's new title.

He logged off and stowed the laptop as sank deeper into the chair thinking about the Jordan case. Finally, he gave in to the sleep his body craved and nodded off.

At five-thirty a.m., the alarm on his smartphone went off and Payne struggled awake. He was groggy and the brief sleep hadn't been enough. Payne stood up, stretched his back, and walked down the hall to the nurse's station. He was on the prowl for a decent cup of coffee.

One of the nurses noticed his bloodshot eyes and grabbed him a cup of hot and black from the break room. Payne thanked her and headed back to the waiting room after a brief stop by Rose's room to confirm she was still asleep.

Back in the waiting room, he knew whom he needed to call. The minute he'd heard Rose say "the Body Man" in reference to Nick Jordan, only one name came to mind. It took all his strength to dial her number. Based on how they'd left things, he wasn't sure she'd be too excited to hear his voice.

Will she be up? He knew the answer to that question. *She's the only person who sleeps less than I do.*

Payne dialed a private number from memory and she picked up on the second ring.

"Yeah," said the voice he hadn't heard in almost eight months.

"Mila. It's Payne."

There was a slight pause. "Not the first voice I expected to hear today."

An awkward pause stretched while Payne waited to be hung

up on. It had been eight months since they'd last talked.

"I'm sure."

"How are you, Payne?" Secret Service Agent Mila Hall said.

"I'm good, thanks," Payne said. "It's been a while."

"I'll say."

"Sorry to call this early."

"No worries. You knew I'd be up at this hour—I've been up since zero-four-thirty working out. Is this business or monkey business?"

"Business. Might be life or death."

"I think I saw you in the White House the other day. This about that?"

"Maybe so, but we need to talk. Somewhere private."

"Is this something that could get me in trouble?" Hall asked.

"Let's say it needs to be off the record." There was a pause long enough that Payne almost asked if she was still there.

Then she decided.

"Meet me at the usual place in thirty minutes."

Payne looked down at his watch. "Roger that."

"Park a couple of blocks away and no funny electronics. You got that last part, right?"

"Thanks, Mila. I wouldn't ask if I had someone else I could go to. You're the only one who can help."

"Yeah, well. We'll see about that."

The line clicked off.

Peter Casha opened his eyes to see Joe Lagano standing at the foot of his bed. Casha looked around the space that was a standard hospital room. In addition to the white-tiled floor, beige walls, and an adjustable bed with vital-sign monitors to the right of the headboard, there was also the unmistakable aroma of a bleach-based cleaner.

He vaguely recalled the drive at one a.m. to the industrial park in Pentagon City, slightly southwest of downtown Washington. It was dark, and the featureless buildings lining the road looked like the backside of a strip mall.

Very few people knew that hidden within one of the structures off 15th Street South, the Sanctum operated a level-one trauma center, basically a hospital for hire utilized by those who's care required discretion.

The facility could handle any emergency—including open-heart surgery, reconstructive surgeries, or even an occasional craniotomy—with virtually no advance warning. The procedures were performed by staff and on-call surgeons, a Who's Who of world-renowned medical professionals largely free of political leanings who preferred to remain unidentified.

Unlike on television shows where off-the-book procedures for criminals are performed by drunken or defrocked doctors in filthy, rat-infested conditions, the Sanctum ran a professional facility so clean you could eat off the floor minutes after a surgery concluded.

The advanced capability all came down to one thing.

Money.

With enough of it anything could be purchased, including exceptional anonymous healthcare.

Casha tilted his head focused his eyes on his best friend.

"You good?" Joe Lagano asked.

Casha nodded his head and raised a thumb. "You can't hurt Superman, bro."

The shoulder throbbed where the bullet hole was bandaged, but it felt amazingly good. He couldn't feel more than a twinge from the repaired second wound. He knew whatever narcotics he'd been given masked the pain. He was also aware that in the next few days and weeks, he'd wean himself off the drugs. For now, the pain-free party would go on.

"Doc said we could leave whenever you're ready," Lagano said.

Casha smiled. "I'm ready to bounce. Never been a good patient, and I sure as hell don't want to stay in this damn hospital bed any longer than I have to."

The doctor walked into the room a minute later. "And you're up. How are you feeling, Mr. Casha?"

"Like a million bucks, doc. I'm heading straight to the golf course after I leave here."

"You let me know how that works out for you," said the doctor with a smirk. "I wanted to stop by before you left and let you know what I found in surgery."

"I'm all ears."

"The bullet struck one of the thickest areas of your shoulder."

"Was that a good thing?"

"Very much so. Any lower or higher and it would have shattered the bone. Then we would've had a real mess on our hands. You probably would've bled out long before you arrived here."

"So, I should thank the guy who shot me?"

"If that's how you want to word it, sure."

Casha said, "Well, I can't because he's not taking any calls."

The doctor ignored the comment. He'd heard such things in this facility before and continued employment, as well as personal safety, depended on his discretion.

"I removed the slug." He raised a small, clear plastic pill bottle and shook it. The bullet rattled like dice in a cup. "Here's a handsome parting gift." The doctor placed the container on the tray. "There's additional damage to the muscle around the shoulder, but you'll heal in time. I don't foresee any permanent damage."

"That's good news."

"Just one last thing before you leave."

A man stepped into the room pushing a small cart holding several electronic devices. He was desperately thin, with sparse, close-cropped hair and classic Coke-bottle glasses with black frames. He wore a white medical smock over dark pants, a white shirt, and a navy-blue tie. At a glance, he looked like a bean counter dressed like a doctor.

"I take it you want to get paid," Lagano said with a grin.

"The management rather insists," said the man with the navy-blue tie. "We want to provide service to you the next time it becomes necessary, sir. And as you know, all accounts must be paid upon the patient's discharge."

The man with the navy-blue tie held a digital tablet in his hands and switched between several screens with a rubber-tipped stylus, tapping several times. "That will be seventy-eight thousand dollars, please, gentlemen."

Lagano reached for his Halliburton briefcase at the foot of the bed, entered the six-digit rotary combination and pushed the silver button. The latches clicked open, and he took out three stacks of hundred-dollar bills and placed them on the table near the bed. From a fourth stack, he slipped off the bill strap and counted out thirty additional bills.

"Count it."

The accountant turned to his cart with a small machine no bigger than a toaster and he fed the stacks of bills into the device. It took only a few seconds for the bills to fan through the scanner and for a digital readout on the front of the machine to display the correct number.

"We're good," said the bean counter. "It's a pleasure to be of service to you both. Forgive the sentiment, gentlemen, but we hope we don't see you again."

Lagano and Casha laughed out loud. They didn't want to need the facility's emergency medical services again either.

"This concludes our business tonight," said the doctor with a subtle wink. "We're open just like 7-Eleven, gentlemen. We never close, on the off chance you need our services again."

Safely in a black Suburban headed down Interstate 385, Lagano drove toward the Jefferson Memorial.

"We're not going to Manassas?" asked Peter.

"No, Junior wants us to stay in the city tonight."

"Where?"

"You know his preference."

"The Hay-Adams?"

"That's right."

Casha changed the subject. He knew talks involving Junior sometimes didn't end well.

"How'd everything go with the royal dipshit?"

"Fine. No issues."

"Marcus had your six?"

"Yes, he and Merci kept me safe."

"How much longer before he's tapping that again?"

"He told me that ended a long time ago."

Casha raised his eyebrows.

"Marcus is a red-blooded man. Everything circles back around again, including old relationships if you have them nearby for long enough."

Chapter 44
The Diner
Washington, DC

Payne entered the front door and immediately found himself overwhelmed by déjà vu. Here he was once more, not just at any place, but *their* place. As he walked past the small receptionist stand, he read the sign attached to the front of the wooden podium that read WELCOME TO THE DINER – PLEASE SEAT YOURSELF.

Back when they were an item, The Diner, a twenty-four-hour restaurant on 18th Street, had served as their regular meet-up spot. With her unpredictable hours at the Secret Service and his at the Bureau, it became a constant in a relationship fraught with dysfunctionality.

As he walked past the twelve chrome barstools that lined the counter, he knew where to find her. Two people blocked his line of sight to the back of the restaurant but, when they moved, he saw where the high-backed, red-cushioned bench seats started to curve. Mila Hall chose the spot because her back would face neither the front nor the rear door. A creature of habit, she never sat where she didn't have a clear line of sight to all the exits.

As he strode toward her, he remembered how much of a pain in the ass it was going out to new restaurants with her. The hostesses always gave curious stares when his girlfriend would ask to check the layout before they were assigned a table.

Their eyes met, and Hall slid out of her seat in the booth and stood as Payne approached. Her straight, raven-colored hair was pulled back in a ponytail and hung low, about six inches above the curvature of her lower back. The black pantsuit hugged her toned legs, and she wore a long-sleeve white blouse with ivory buttons, the top two noticeably undone. The necklace that nestled in the top of her cleavage was in the shape of a heart. Payne recognized it as the one he'd given her the previous Christmas.

God, she looks fine, he thought.

Payne wasn't sure what to expect as he got close enough to smell the strawberry crème lotion she used daily.

Hall answered the question as she reached her arms around his broad shoulders and pulled him in for a firm hug. He felt her heartbeat against his chest as the embrace lingered.

Emotions and feelings washed over him like a blast of hot air.

She let go and she slid back behind the table. Payne took the wooden chair opposite her and turned it around, the back butting up against the tabletop.

"You look good," she said with an approving smile.

"As do you," Payne said, unable to hide the slight change in his voice.

She snapped her fingers. "Eight months went by pretty quick."

"Life moves at a fast pace, especially for people who've chosen our types of careers."

He didn't mean it as a knock but regretted saying it as soon as the words left his mouth. It was thoughtless, considering how things had ended. While lying in bed after a marathon session of lovemaking, Payne had done the unthinkable—he'd brought up marriage and kids. She had clammed up. It had taken her a while to open back up but when she did, everything felt different.

She'd explained to Payne that the Secret Service was her life, and marriage and kids didn't fit into the lifestyle. The rest of the night became a blur. They'd tried to work things out for about a month, but the magic had faded. In the end, she'd said she felt they would both be better off if they moved on. It had felt like a sucker punch and hurt like hell.

They hadn't spoken or seen each other since.

Hall asked, "Ever come by here and grab a bite, for old times' sake? Just to relive the vibe?"

"No. I don't have a reason to visit this part of town anymore."

She nodded. "Makes sense. I still come by for the apple pie."

"You mean for the whipped cream on top?"

"Yeah, that too." A smile formed at the corner of her lips.

A few seconds of awkward silence occurred. Not something typical when they were an item. Breaking the silence, a waitress came and took their orders.

"You said this was about a case?" she asked. She took a sip of coffee and stared at Payne over the steaming top of the cup.

"Yeah, it's pretty important."

"I'm listening."

"It's in regard to an investigation for a missing Secret Service agent." Payne watched as her body tensed. Even the muscles in her neck and jaw constricted.

"You don't say," Hall said through gritted teeth.

"Does the name Nick Jordan ring a bell?"

For as long as Payne had known her, she'd been a terrible liar. "Never heard of him," she said.

Payne pulled the White House ID for Nick Jordan out of his pocket and slid it across the table toward her with the picture and name right side up so she could see it. He leaned in closer.

"You and I both know that's bullshit. Jordan is on the presidential detail. You are on the presidential detail—you damned well do know him. I might not be member of Mensa, but I've drawn stronger conclusions from less evidence. That being the case, don't tell me you have no idea who he is."

Hall started to slide her body out of the booth. "I'd better go."

Payne reached out and grabbed her hands, coupling them in his own. "Look, Mila. I wouldn't come to you if there were another way. I'm here because the people who took Nick killed Wes."

She paused. "Say what?"

"He's dead, Mila. They killed him."

"Wes is dead? *Your* Wes?"

Payne nodded. "Last night. I asked him to check on a witness, a woman named Rose Lewis who lives across the street from Jordan. She had reported him missing and told me he worked for the Secret Service. I went to the White House, and Brandon Walker lied to my face, said he didn't have a clue who I was talking about."

"Brandon's an asshole. I could have told you that. Tell me what happened to Wes."

"Two men showed up at Rose's place last night impersonating FBI agents, said they were working on the case with me. Rose didn't buy it. She tried to call me, but they busted inside her house, tied her up, gagged her, and gave her a grilling. Wes came thirty minutes later and had a gunfight with the two scumbags. He killed them, but he took a slug to the neck and bled out before help arrived. Rose said the two men wanted to know what Jordan did with 'the documents.' Who he'd given them to?"

"What documents?" asked Mila.

"I don't know. That's what I'm trying to figure out."

Hall's eyes darted around the restaurant. "Did you leave your phone in the car?"

"I did."

"This conversation is off the record. As in, I'll deny it ever happened to my dying day and then I'll find you and hurt you. You understand that, right?"

"Yeah, I understand."

"I'm serious. I'll lose my job if anyone finds out we even spoke about this."

"About Nick Jordan?"

"Yes, about Nick."

"Then you do know him."

"Of course, I know him."

"Why all the secrecy?"

"We've all been told by the bosses to talk to no one, not even each other. But you know how it goes."

"Why would the senior brass not want you to talk with anyone?"

Hall swirled her coffee in the cup. "Because they are trying to find Nick themselves."

"So I heard, but they don't appear to be doing a bang-up job."

"Agreed. The whole thing is fishy. Something isn't adding up."

"You want to tell me what Nick does for the Secret Service?"

"What do you mean?"

"I was told personally by the director of the FBI, who was told by the president in a private one-on-one meeting, that Jordan wasn't on the presidential detail per se, but 'adjacent.' Something is not right here, and my gut says it starts with his real role with the Secret Service."

Hall shook her head. "Look, Eli, I want to help, really—but I can't say anything more."

"Can't or won't?"

"Can't."

"You want to tell me why he's called the Body Man?"

The stern expression she displayed faded as her lips moved back to a smirk. "So, you finally figured out I was the one who sent you the text."

Payne's brow furrowed. "What?"

"The Body Man texts. You figured out it came from me."

"Wait—*you* sent that text?"

"Yes. But if you didn't know then why are you here?"

"When Rose said the two men who assaulted her called him the Body Man, the first thing I thought of was I needed to talk with you. But if you sent the text, why didn't you use Nick's real name instead of saying the Body Man?"

"Over electronic communications? Really? Come on, man. I expect more from you. I sent the text from a burner phone I bought at a 7-Eleven in Bethesda. Figured you might start to ask questions and I hoped you could piece together that the Body Man was really Nick."

Payne paused and leaned in close. "No more games. I need you to read me in, Mila."

Her eyes darted around the room.

Payne knew the look. Like when a witness is about to reveal secrets but clams up and changes her mind at the last second. He was *this close* and couldn't lose her now. Payne lowered his voice and used a softer tone.

"Look, Mila, we go way back. I know somewhere inside you still trust me. Believe me when I tell you I need to know who Nick Jordan is and why somebody would want to kidnap him. We're trying to help him, fercrissakes! You texted me the Body Man reference for a reason. I suspect it's because you want Nick found and you realize the Secret Service is no closer to finding him now than the day he went missing. I'm the guy who can do it, but I need your help. Please, Mila." Payne's tone turned to a plea. "Please."

Mila's hard-as-steel exterior softened as her body relaxed.

"I do trust you, Payne. But..."

"But what?"

Chapter 45
The Diner
Washington, DC

Hall looked into Payne's eyes. The glare pierced deep. "I have a question," she said.

Payne looked back with an intensity of his own, but almost immediately he looked away. She always had a way of disarming him with a single glance, and she always won an argument. And if Payne had the upper hand in a debate, it only took one look from her, and he melted.

"Okay. What is it?" he asked.

"What is the primary job of the Secret Service??"

Payne's face contorted to a puzzled look as he pursed his lips and scrunched his brow. "Are you serious? Is this a Civics test?" he asked.

Hall frowned. "No, Elijah," she said in a stern tone. She only pulled out his given name when she grew irked. "Just answer the question since you want me to answer yours. Trust me, it's a relevant question."

He relented. "All right, I'll play. The Secret Service has many responsibilities, including investigating counterfeiting, forgeries, and other financial crimes. But the primary objective is to protect the President of the United States and various leaders within the government."

"Protect the president from outside threats, correct?"

"Umm, yeah," Payne said. "Everyone knows that."

"Well, the job of the Body Man is to protect something much more important than the physical body of the president."

"What's more important than his safety?"

"The Body Man is tasked with protecting the office of the presidency, which is more than one man's or, one day, one woman's well-being."

Payne's eyes narrowed. "Sorry, I don't follow."

Hall smiled. "You will," she said, adding, "I know you love history."

"I do."

"Well, it all started in 1963 during the last few months of the Kennedy administration. As most of the world knows, JFK was quite the ladies' man. The Secret Service spent almost as much effort trying to protect him from assassins as it did ushering women into the White House for the president's, umm, amusement, you could say."

"Yes, I've heard the stories of Marilyn Monroe."

"Please. Marilyn was only the tip of the iceberg because she was so famous. The director of the Secret Service at the time, James Joseph Rowley, and several key members of the White House leadership, were concerned about the president's off-duty behavior. They also realized the world was changing rapidly and the media's infatuation with the president was growing at an unmanageable pace. JFK was the first television president. His good looks and swagger were far more appealing than his legislative experience. It was only a matter of time before the president's private adventures became public fodder and someone raised legitimate concerns about what would happen to the office if the stories got out. Less important activity by some people has resulted in lost clearances and lost jobs. It was at that point the powers that be decided to create a new position we internally refer to as the Body Man."

Payne interrupted. "And this Body Man role keeps the president out of trouble?"

Mila shook her head. "It's much more complicated than that. Everything the President of the United States does matters. Everything he says or doesn't say, does or doesn't do, is consequential. So, if they can keep the president from doing something that will damage the presidency, they intervene if possible. But most of the time they step in after the president screws up. The Body Man's job is to clean up the mess and make it go away." Her gaze went to the traffic beyond the restaurant's window. "They have almost unlimited power and authority."

"The Body Man is a cleaner for the office of the presidency?"

"In some ways, yes."

A slight laugh slipped out of Payne. "Well, Clinton's Body Man really screwed the pooch."

Mila rolled her eyes. "You don't know the half of it. Poor Jacob. He really was a superb agent, but he never lived down the fact he let that goddamned blue dress leave the White House."

"So, he should have done what?"

"Let's just say the dress should have never left the grounds." Mila paused, "Or she shouldn't have."

Payne raised his eyebrows.

"That screwup," continued Mila, "ultimately led to Jacob's replacement."

"You mean firing?"

"Not exactly."

"What do you mean?"

"The Body Man is part of our team but not in the ways you think. They offer the role to an agent with ten to fifteen years of experience, but he or she has to fit a certain profile."

"What kind of profile?"

"For one, they need to be single with no kids and few extended family."

"Why is that?"

"Because of the ultra-sensitive nature of the role and because it's the last position they'll ever hold within the government."

Payne's gaze narrowed. "How so?"

"They must leave when their term comes to an end—as in leave the United States, for good. The government sets them up with a very generous severance package and they are relocated into unknown parts at the far end of the world forever. It's the ultimate retirement deal. They'll die one day, hopefully of old age, and the secrets they acquired on the job will die with them."

"What the hell? And people sign up for this bullshit on purpose?"

"Absolutely." A perturbed look spread over Hall's face "And this is no bullshit, Payne. It's an honor to be the Body Man. This person is the protector of the presidency. People compete for it."

"Can't say I see it that way." A growing frown on Payne's face grew more pronounced. When he'd walked into The Diner tonight, he had no idea the conversation with Hall would follow go this way. A dozen questions flew through his brain at once, but he settled with asking one. "How does it work exactly?"

"It's a two-person responsibility—there's always a Body Man and an apprentice. More like an understudy, because we can't count on nothing occurring while an apprentice is learning on the job. An understudy knows the job now and can step in seamlessly if needed. After all, one man can't be with the president 24/7, and when the Body Man's term ends, the understudy steps up into the role and a new understudy is appointed."

"And if you fuck up big enough, you get replaced?"

"Correct, but that's pretty rare. It's happened only twice."

"There are lots of stories floating around about President Steele within the alphabet agencies, and some aren't flattering."

"Some are probably true, most are nonsense. He's not overly difficult to protect. His business dealings raised some flags early on, but up until Nick's disappearance, nothing major occurred. But I must admit Danny's shooting on the same day has everyone freaked out."

"Who's Danny?"

"Danny Frazier was Nick's understudy."

"Never heard of him."

"Didn't his name come up in your investigation?"

"No. I told you, the White House is stonewalling us, and the president said nothing about Frazier to the director."

Hall didn't say anything.

Payne continued. "If the Body Man disappeared the same day his understudy was shot, I'd say this is a bigger problem than the Secret Service suspects."

"Agreed."

Payne took a deep breath and exhaled slowly, rubbing his temples. "Okay, my brain is starting to hurt. Back to how the Body Man cleans up the messes. Explain. What does he do exactly?"

"Whatever needs to be done."

"Are you trying to be intentionally vague?"

Hall leaned in closer. "Is English your native tongue? The Body Man is tasked with making problems for the office of the presidency go away using any means necessary."

"That sounds arbitrary and open for interpretation."

"It isn't, actually. That's exactly how it works. I'm not saying anything else, other than it's the Body Man's job to protect the office of the presidency at all costs."

Payne needed to press a different way. "How did you personally find out about the role?"

"I worked with Nick for several years before he became the Body Man. We were buddies. He started as the apprentice for training and became the understudy, but he took over the main role when the Body Man at the time took ill and had to step aside. Since I knew Nick pretty well, he filled me in on some specifics."

Payne said, "And I never heard a word about him when we were together."

"Dude, I know you understand need-to-know, right? And you didn't. I wasn't allowed to reveal to anyone what he told me. Even to you, the man I was sleeping with," she said with a crooked smile. "But really, what would I say? Our services keep secrets, right? But it's even more simple than that. Did you tell me how many calls you made? Trips to the head or the water cooler? It's just a thing, a part of my job. I know stuff. None of it concerned you."

"Let's take a step back," Payne said. "If Nick Jordan, the Body Man, is part of the Secret Service, he has to abide by your code of conduct."

She shook her head. "Well, he's not exactly a 'Secret Service agent' once he takes the position."

"What do you mean?"

"He reports to the director of the Secret Service, but technically he works independent of our rules."

It kind of made sense to Payne. "That's what President Steele meant when he told Director Ludington that Jordan was 'adjacent' to his detail. But someone has to tell him what to do."

"Not really. The directive is to protect the office of the presidency. How he achieves that is solely up to the Body Man's discretion."

"So, the Body Man can do whatever the hell he wants to cover up the president's acts without fear of reprisal?"

"For the most part, yes. He has code-word authority to access vast resources."

"What about prosecution? If the Body Man screws up and someone at the Justice Department gets wind of some illegal acts performed on behalf of the presidency?"

Hall sat back slightly in her chair. "Each new president signs a PPD reaffirming the role, its authority, and its protections."

"A what?"

"Presidential policy directive."

"Yeah, okay. I've heard of them."

"They're like an executive order except they can be kept secret from virtually everyone, including Congress. They have the same authority as an executive order but aren't public knowledge."

"And the PPD affirms the role but is vague on what it does?"

"Correct. The Body Man is also provided a blank presidential pardon. In theory, they can use it for any prosecution brought against them."

Payne shook his head in disbelief. "No way. The president can't sign a secret PPD saying someone can break the law whenever they want. I mean, hell—they'd be breaking the law to protect the person who signed the directive in the first place. That's nonsensical. And then a blank pardon, like a get-out-of-jail-free card? The Supreme Court would tear that thing to shreds, Mila. Give me a break."

Hall nodded her head. "You might be right, but it would never come to that."

His eyebrows raised. "Meaning?"

She looked into her coffee cup, now empty. "They'd adhere to one of the few ironclad rules the Body Man agrees to follow."

Payne raised a flat hand. "Hold up. Let me guess. The first rule of fight club is you do not talk about fight club?"

"Kinda sorta. But it's not about being quiet. Each Body Man

agrees to take their secrets with them to their grave."

"You're saying they agree to off themselves if it ever comes to that?"

"Precisely."

Payne back in his chair, flabbergasted. "I've worked in federal service for a long time, and this is the god*damne*dest thing I've ever heard of. You're making this all up, right?"

"You're so funny," Hall said with a small, pitying smile. "How is it you can't imagine not knowing all the super secrets on Earth? No, everything I told you is the God's honest truth."

"This is seriously fucked up. You get that, right?"

"I don't. It's government. It is what it is," Hall said.

"You know what the media would do if they got wind of this? This is like a deep-state conspiracy on crack. You're sitting here telling me the President of the United States can break any law on a whim. And a government employee who technically doesn't exist condones illegal acts and covers them up."

Mila remained quiet. "I'd spin it a different way, but I see your point," Hall admitted.

"Doesn't that bother you?" pressed Payne.

"I almost understand your trepidation about the role, but the country needs it. Absolute power might corrupt, but we don't elect Eagle Scouts." Hall laughed. "Wait, I guess sometimes we do. Point is, presidents are flawed yet charismatic men who knew how to do one thing better than anyone else."

"And what's that?"

"Make people they will never meet, nor much care about, vote for them. Even if it's all smoke and mirrors."

Payne rightly figured arguing that point would get them nowhere. "Well, we're still left with the primary questions: If someone abducted Jordan, what do they want from him? And is he already dead? I mean by his own doing."

"It's certainly possible, but if someone snatched Nick, in theory, they must have known who he was."

"And if they knew who he was, they would know about the directive to kill himself?"

Hall nodded. "In theory."

"And they'd prevent him from doing so."

"Bingo," Hall said. "Trust me, when I heard about the Body Man, I figured it was some lame-ass story from a fiction writer with way too much time on his or her hands. If he wasn't real, you couldn't make it up."

Payne sipped his coffee and it was cold, but he didn't want the interruption of signaling for a refill. "Okay, now that you've blown my mind making me think the Internet conspiracy wackos might be the sane ones, next question is who took Nick and why?"

"The list of who would want him is endless. Any foreign intelligence agency that learned about a person with that much raw intelligence would kill at the chance of snagging him and bleeding him dry."

"But I thought few people know about the role."

"Yes, that's true." Hall lifted her hands in frustration. "But this is DC, after all, and people talk. Some talk too much. Talk, and information sharing, is the currency of Washington." She stared at Payne for a couple of seconds as she said the last few words. "I do feel confident few people outside the Secret Service know the full breadth of the role. You're now part of a small circle. I trust you, Payne, and know you'll keep what I told you on a strictly need-to-know basis."

"I'll have to read in the director, Mila. There's no way I can hide from him what you've told me."

"I get that."

"Any chance the Russians know about the Body Man?"

The question surprised her. "Unknown. Why?"

"Because the men who kidnapped Nick and flew him out of Manassas on a private jet spoke Russian."

"Are you sure?"

"An eyewitness confirmed it."

Hall said, "I think you ahould fill me in on your investigation."

"You may be right," Payne said. "Here's what I know ..."

Chapter 46
The White House
Washington, DC

Charles D. Steele II, or "Junior," as everyone called him, strode up to the east security checkpoint of the White House. A stiff breeze blew from the west, and he pulled his overcoat closer to his body as a chill ran up his spine.

It pissed him off royally that he had to show a security badge to pass through the checkpoint like every other visitor. A nuisance he bemoaned to his father without any sympathy in return.

The uniformed Secret Service guard on duty, Willy Daley, blocked the entrance with his imposing six-foot-four, two-hundred-thirty-pound frame. He smiled as Junior approached. "Good morning, Mr. Steele. I didn't know you were back in DC."

"Hey, Willy. I got in last night for some meetings. How are you?" Junior came to a stop and presented his security badge and Daley made a notation on a computer in the guard shack. Notwithstanding the stature of the visitor, Daley scanned the badge per protocol anyway. Only after the digital display on his console read APPROVED did he step aside.

"I'm fine, sir, thanks." He handed the badge on a lanyard to Steele Junior. "No car this morning?"

"No. I decided to walk."

"Exercise will keep you young, Mr. Steele."

"I've heard that," Junior said as he nodded and started down the pathway that led to the east entrance. Seven minutes later, he was ushered into the Oval Office. His father sat motionless at the Resolute desk, reading papers arranged horizontally atop the desk, laid out from left to right.

The president glanced over the top of half-eye reading glasses teetering on the edge of his nose as his son entered, and he turned his attention back to the papers.

Patience wasn't one of Junior's virtues, but he knew the drill. He took a seat on one of the cream-colored, floral-patterned couches in the center of the room with the presidential seal embroidered on the rug.

Junior pulled out his phone and started to check email while he waited for his father, who was a notoriously slow reader.

After five minutes, the president finished, removed his reading glasses, and placed them on the right side of the desk. When his glasses touched the surface, he yelled out, "Dolores, clear my schedule for the next fifteen minutes and close the door, please."

"Yes, Mr. President." His secretary stepped in far enough to grab the door handle and close the door.

Charles Steele Sr. regarded his son but said nothing once the door clicked shut.

"Mr. President," Junior said as he placed his phone back in his pocket. Most children of presidents called their father Dad when they visited the White House, or anywhere else for that matter, but this wasn't the case for Junior. No, Charles Steele Sr. insisted his son call him Mr. President after the election. Steele Sr. was big on expecting respect, but short on extending it to his son.

"Anything new to report?"

"Not yet, Mr. President."

"*Really?*" Charles Sr. said as his tone rose sharply. His muscles tensed, and he started to yell at the top of his lungs as he stood up. "Then tell me why the Jack D. Fuck your guys killed an FBI *agent* last night in Vienna?"

The sudden outburst startled Junior. His father had a propensity for anger but rarely raised his voice.

Junior raised his hands in defense. "Hold up, Give me a chance. I can explain everything."

In a swift and violent motion, the president picked up one of the two small bronze busts shaped like Abraham Lincoln's head that served as bookends on the table behind his desk. The president had played baseball in his college days and still had quite the arm as he threw Lincoln's head across the room. It sailed several inches over Junior, who ducked down on the couch. The heavy object slammed against the door leading to the secretary's office and waiting area, striking hard enough to shake the door and leave a deep brown gash on its otherwise pristine white surface.

The bust lay on the floor for only seconds before three Secret Service agents burst into the Oval through two separate doors. Their faces appeared hardened, and their eyes scanned the room as they entered with hands on the butts of their service weapons.

The president raised his own hands outward and did his best to lower his enraged voice. "Stand down, guys. We're good. I lost my cool, that's all."

"You sure everything is all right, Mr. President?" Agent Chris Albanese looked back and forth between the president and Junior.

"Yes, yes, Chris, I'm fine. We're fine." His gaze shifted away from the agent and toward his son, "Right, Junior?"

"Of course, Mr. President," said Junior, who sat up from his slouched position. He adjusted his tie and straightened his suit coat, but his wide eyes screamed Save me.

Albanese looked warily at the president and then at Junior. "You good, Junior?"

"Fabulous," said Junior sarcastically, unable to hide the anxiety in his voice.

Chris raised his sleeve and spoke into a mic concealed at the end of his shirt. "MOGUL is fine. Repeat, no threat to MOGUL. Only a false alarm." As he said the last words, he started to back out of the room but looked back at the president. "We're just outside if you need us, sir."

"Thanks, Chris. I appreciate that. I'm good. We're good."

With the agents gone, the president looked back at Junior almost as if the incident had never occurred.

"You were saying?" he asked, his voice back to a calm tone.

Junior took a thick glass from the set on the table between the two couches and poured himself some water. He actually needed a Scotch, but that would have to wait. After several large gulps, he said, "Look, Mr. President, the guys were supposed to impersonate FBI agents and ask a few questions. That was all. We got some intel from the interrogator, and I decided to act on it."

"So, they busted into the neighbor's house and tied her up?"

"You're right, they fucked up."

"Who hired them?"

Junior lied. "Marcus Rollings."

"Why did he hire two pieces of shit that acted like rank amateurs? Do I have to do everything?"

"It was a mistake on his part."

"I'll say, and because of their careless actions, a senior FBI agent lost his life."

"The two men paid for that mistake with their own lives. The agent killed them both before he died protecting the neighbor."

"I don't fucking *care* about them." The president was getting spun up again.

Junior snorted. "And you're going to tell me you care about a damned FBI agent?"

"No, but I care about the magnifying glass it'll place over this case. I've been trying to get the FBI to back off, but you can sure as hell bet that won't happen now. Not with one of their men dead."

"Again, these guys went rogue. They were not to harm her."

"And left us holding the dripping bag of wet shit. Why not use someone reliable, like Casha?"

"Peter was still on the west coast at the time."

Steele Sr. put his hands on his hips and glared. "And then you had the incident at the hospital with Frazier."

"They made it out."

"They almost got caught by the Secret Service!"

"Hold up," said Junior as he raised his hand and voice. "You authorized the event, then pulled the plug at the last minute. Marcus followed his orders."

"Well, that bitch of his messed things up to start with."

"And you gave her another mission," countered Junior.

"That was before I knew Danny Frazier was still alive." The president started to pace circles around his desk, his standard practice when the incredible stress of this job weighed on him. He paused in front of the desk and glared at his son. "You've exposed us."

"Me?"

"Yes, *you*." He jabbed an index finger at his son.

"Whatever." Junior was recovering from his near-death experience with Lincoln's bust. "None of this can tie back to us."

"Who says?"

"The guys who died in Vienna were nobodies with no connection to our company or us."

"*My company*," said the president in a vitriolic tone.

Junior rolled his eyes. *It's only his company when it's successful and raking in the money.* Then, out of caution, Junior did look casually for the other Lincoln bookend.

"And what's this about Casha getting shot?"

"Who told you?"

"I spoke with Joe."

"Peter will live," said Junior. "We used one of the Sanctum's secure med facilities outside the city to patch him up this morning. He's at the Hay-Adams, resting."

"Should we be concerned with Casha being injured?" The president ran a hand through his hair. "Is he a weak link?"

Junior shook his head. "No, he's a strong one. Peter is a valuable asset. He oversaw the transfer of the containers and eliminated Hector Fuentes and his team. The evidence of their involvement is buried at sea."

"If you say so."

"I do say so. We're close, Mr. President. The deal will go through."

"This is your deal. You negotiated with the Saudis."

"You thought it was a good idea at the time. And, after all, everything I'm doing is to grow the business."

Charles Sr. changed the subject. "Updates from the Gulf?"

"Nick is talking. The drugs did the trick, and Nick confirmed he printed off additional copies. We believe he gave them to Danny Frazier."

"Believing isn't good enough, Junior. We need hard proof as to what he did with those copies. Simply killing Jordan and Frazier won't do. God knows if they've set up some way to release the evidence he collected once they're dead."

"I understand. We'll get to the bottom of this."

"Solutions going forward, not more excuses," the president warned.

Junior pivoted. "The other day I asked you about Merci."

"What about her?"

"Where did she go after the hit on Danny?"

"France."

Junior frowned. "Why?"

"Because someone needed to die."

"Who?"

"Not your concern. Someone powerful."

Junior considered the recent deaths he'd read about online. Then it dawned on him. "She killed James Fowler? I read he dropped dead in France, according to the front page of *The Wall Street Journal*. But I thought it was a heart attack?"

The president looked away for a moment before his eyes locked back onto his son. "Don't believe everything you read, Junior."

"Why Fowler?"

"For starters, he's one of our biggest competitors."

"And with him gone someone else will step into his role. It will only be a temporary blip, and I don't see Fowler's death helping the Steele global brand in the long run."

"You fail to see the bigger picture," the president said dismissively.

"Evidently. Please enlighten me."

"All in due time. Before Merci killed him, she retrieved his biometric signatures, specifically his fingerprints and retinal scans."

"For what purpose?"

"She and Marcus are on their way to New York this morning. James kept a personal safe deposit box at a bank in NYC, and I need them to retrieve the contents."

"His bank will change all the access codes upon his death, standard protocol. The biometrics are worth jack shit with him dead."

"At his bank they are, I agree."

"I don't follow."

"His bank will make changes, but the box is not in his bank. James was far too clever to hide something in plain sight."

"Then where is it?"

"*Our* bank."

"Which one?"

"Our flagship branch."

Junior thought about the setup at the branch. "We have biometric access to the top-level boxes at that location, and it's open 24/7. Our clients arrive and depart without interacting with bank personnel by using the biometric access area."

"Exactly."

"And we won't change that for some time upon a person's death," said Junior as the realization dawned on him.

"I know. I designed the protocols."

"What does James Fowler have in his box?"

"Dirty laundry. Lots of dirty laundry."

"On whom?"

The president extended arms out from his body. "Everybody—including me and the senior members of my administration."

"You didn't tell me about this file before."

"No. No, I didn't." The president's voice trailed off as a thought occurred to him.

Junior noticed the change in his body language. "What is it?"

"Casha. He was black ops, right?"

"More or less," Junior answered, wondering where this was leading.

"Any experience interrogating?"

"Of course."

"Send him down to the Gulf," the president ordered. "Instead of him sitting around with his dick in his hands, maybe he can extract useful intel from Jordan."

"You think he'll get something out of the Body Man that the interrogator hasn't?"

"Only one way to find out."

"And if Peter fails as well?"

"Maybe I'll get the military to blow up the entire platform. Destroy all the evidence in one swoop. We could claim drug runners used the platform as a smuggling distribution center. Heaven knows, it probably served that purpose before they took it over anyway."

"If you destroy the platform, you'll be starting a war with the Sanctum. Especially with the Chief."

"Fuck the Sanctum, and fuck the Chief."

"He's a powerful man. Plus, you know who he reports to."

"And who am I?" The president spewed out the words and shot Junior a look of disdain, including a snarled upper lip.

"You are the leader of the free world."

"Damn right, I am. And about the Chief, when you make a deal with the Devil, you'd better anticipate some heat."

Junior snorted.

"Which one of you was the Devil again?"

Chapter 47
Torrance, California

Hector Fuentes lay in the Harbor-UCLA Medical Center hospital bed. An IV ran from his arm to the clear plastic bag above the headboard, a steady drip of narcotics merging with his bloodstream in a timed release. His vital signs remained stable, and his broad chest moved up and down in a rhythmic motion.

He looked serene.

FBI Special Agent Darius Gabel stepped into the room through the open doorway without making a sound. A nurse stood next to the side of the bed, charting Fuentes' vitals on a tablet. The woman with shoulder-length auburn hair turned around and gasped as the shadowy figure entered her line of sight.

"Oh, you startled me." Autumn Salazar reached up to cover her mouth with her hand.

"Sorry, didn't mean to give you a scare." Gabel whispered with a warm smile. He displayed his creds. "I'm Special Agent Darius Gabel from the Los Angeles FBI field office. I was told a patient asked to speak with us about some urgent matter." He gestured to the still man in the bed. "Is this the man?"

The nurse smiled.

"Yes, Agent Gabel. My name is Autumn Salazar. He can't be

very helpful right now, I'm afraid. The patient has been in and out of consciousness since he was brought him in."

"You've been his nurse since he arrived?"

"That's right."

"And he asked you to call the FBI?" Gabel asked.

"Yes, earlier, when he was conscious."

"What can you tell me about him?"

"His name is Hector Fuentes."

"Who brought him in?"

"He was found floating in the Pacific between Santa Monica and Catalina by some fishing boat. The fire department medics who brought him in said the captain saw flames on the horizon but by the time he arrived, the boat had sunk. He found Hector bobbing around clinging to a life ring, barely conscious. The captain notified the Coast Guard, who transported him to the shore, and a city ambulance brought him here."

"Injuries?"

"Beside almost drowning, he was shot in the left knee. Another round struck his shin, and a third hit his upper back. The knee and shin are the concerns. They're shattered, frankly, and will need complex surgeries to repair them."

"What is his condition?"

"Hector is lucky to be alive. He was shark bait out in that water. I'm not sure why Jaws didn't snack on him."

"Understood. So, what did he say that would merit a call to the FBI?"

"A lot."

Darius pulled out a pad and pen, slowly tapping the point of the pen on the white notepad. "I'm listening."

Salazar recounted the bits and pieces of Fuentes' story while Special Agent Gabel asked questions from time to time.

"Did he say what was in the shipping containers they loaded

onto the cargo ship?"

"He said they were military-style weapons."

"So, was this some sort of arms sale?"

"I don't know if it was a sale. He made it sound more like a theft."

"Someone stole these weapons?"

"Yes."

"Did he say where the cargo ship was headed?"

"The Middle East."

"Which country?"

"He didn't say. I didn't ask for details. He did all the talking."

"Okay, go on."

She talked for another five minutes before he held up his hand.

Gabel knew he'd only gotten part of the story. He needed to talk with Fuentes. "Did he say what the other job was that this Peter Casha asked them to perform?"

"No, but something else he said was odd."

"And what was that?"

"He used the phrase the Body Man."

"The Body Man?"

"Yes."

"Those exact words?"

"Yes."

"In what context?"

"Not sure, but it struck me as strange. Like, maybe something you'd hear about the mob. I don't know, maybe it's because I saw the movie *Goodfellas* recently."

"A classic," Gabel said, nodding and smiling.

"Yes, well, the reference made me think of it. Strange, right?" She smiled broadly. She thought Gabel was cute and he didn't wear a wedding ring.

"Not the norm, for sure. But do you believe him?"

Salazar pondered the question before she replied. "Yes, I think so. He wasn't delirious or drugged up. He was in a buncha pain, but he was lucid. And, you know how you can hear a story from someone, and it just rings true? That's what this was."

Gabel shrugged. "Well, when he wakes up, I can come back and question him."

Gabel thanked her for the attention to detail. Before he left the room, he handed over his card and asked her to call him the moment Fuentes regained consciousness. "That's my personal cell number on there," he said as they shook hands. "In case you need it." He held Salazar's hand just an extra few seconds longer and gave it a light squeeze before letting go. "I hope to see you again."

Gabel drove back to the office on Wilshire Boulevard and sat down at his desk. By seven-twenty a.m., he'd opened a case file in SENTINEL and filled out the basics of what he knew, which wasn't much. As he clicked through filling in the information fields in the secure system, he thought about that Body Man reference— and when he typed those three words in the file they were recognized by the system and returned an open-case hit from the WFO in DC. A few clicks later, he pulled up the contact info for the agent of record and placed a call. It went straight to voicemail.

I hate leaving messages.

At the sound of the beep, Gabel said, "Payne, this is Special Agent Darius Gabel in the LA field office. When you get this, give me a callback, please? It's about your Nick Jordan case. The Coast Guard fished a guy out of the Pacific, and he started talking about a military weapons shipment headed to the Middle East and a ref to somebody called 'the Body Man'—and you have the only other reference in the system with that phrase. Might be a crazy coincidence, but let's talk, okay? Out here."

Payne and Stone arrived outside Café Bonaparte in George-town about twenty minutes early for the meeting with his friend Dony Harbaugh, a Metro PD detective. As they approached the café, two black-out Chevy Suburbans pulled up to the curb only a few feet to their left. The heavily tinted back passenger window slid down, and the director of the FBI called out, "Can I have a quick word with you two?"

"Of course, sir," Payne said as he walked toward the SUV.

A muscular man in a blue suit with a white coiled earpiece jumped from the front passenger seat and opened the heavy right rear door. Payne and Stone climbed into the back row of seats with the director in the second row.

"How did you know we'd be here?" Stone looked perplexed.

The director glared at her. "Stone, you know your cellphones are nothing more than glorified tracking devices. We followed you via the GPS chip. We track the movements of all of our agents around the clock."

Stone's mouth hung open. "You *follow* us?"

"Electronically. But yes, of course. Full video, too, when we decide to turn on your camera." Ludington noticed Stone's shocked response and the crimson flush rising in her cheeks. "Even when your phone is off."

Stone was frantically trying to remember where her phone was pointed last night when her new boyfriend was over.

The director smiled. "I'm kidding, Stone."

Payne let out a deep laugh and placed his reassuring hand on Stone's forearm. "Relax. I texted him last night about our meeting with Dony."

The director glanced at his watch. "Look, I have a conference call at nine, so we need to keep this brief. What updates do you have?"

"We heard back from the FAA," Stone said. Her face resumed normal coloration. "The plane landed at the Houma-Terrebonne Airport."

"Where's that?" asked the director.

"Louisiana."

"What's down there?" Ludington asked.

"Not much from what I know," Stone said. "It's right on the Gulf. A lot of fishing and petrochemicals."

"And what happened to the plane?"

"It stayed at the airport for two hours before it headed back north and landed in New York City," Stone said.

"You ran the tail number?"

"Yes, sir," Stone said. "It comes back to a shady LLC in the Bahamas."

"How am I not surprised," said the director. "What entity is it registered under?"

"That's where things get murky," Stone said. "We've still got people digging, but the LLC name is listed as J. Higgins Enterprises."

"A shell company?"

"Seems to be, yes, sir."

"It's a start. Who's down there checking out the airport in Houma and shaking the local trees to see what falls out?"

"No one yet. We only just got this intel a few hours ago," Payne said.

Ludington nodded, thinking. "Sounds to me like you need additional manpower."

"Well, it's only Stone and me at the moment."

"That's not good enough anymore. I'll mobilize a team to Louisiana ASAP and detail some HQ assets to coordinate everything here."

"Is this still—"

The director could tell where Payne was going. "Yes, this is still your case; the team will be notified that you are the special-agent-in-charge of this task force, and everyone reports to you. Think of it as a field promotion, and you get some much-needed assistance. I need you at full capacity for us to solve this thing. I'll have my HQ people report directly to you with a dotted line to me. That work for you?"

That did work for Payne, and he relaxed. Having an angel who was your biggest boss couldn't be a bad thing—unless he screwed up royally. Payne pledged not to do that.

"Yes, sir," Payne said. "Thank you."

"As I told you yesterday unofficially, you now officially have whatever resources you need. Just ask. Capeesh?"

"Understood, sir."

Ludington looked again at his favorite watch, an Omega Seamaster 300M on a NATO strap given to him by Daniel Craig at an exclusive DC premiere of *Spectre* in 2015. "All right, I gotta roll. Anything else you two need right now?"

Payne hesitated to say anything more, but to withhold what he learned from Mila Hall felt misguided. "There is something else, but it may take a bit to discuss."

"Give me the Cliffs Notes version, less than sixty seconds."

"Sir, have you ever heard of the Body Man?" As the words rolled off Payne's tongue, he recognized an instant change in Ludington's demeanor.

The director was quiet as he collected his thoughts. "I ... um, I have, yes. At least I've heard of the terminology."

"Roger that. Do you know what the role does?"

"Officially, no. But off the record, I've heard the rumors. People talk." Ludington's eyes widened just a bit. "Are you telling me Nick Jordan is *the Body Man*?"

"Yes, sir, I'm afraid so."

"You sure?"

"As much as I can be at the moment, yes."

"How do you even know about it?" the director demanded.

"I don't want to say at this point, but my source is very solid."

"This source, are they on the inside?"

"Yes, sir—*inside-inside*."

Ludington said, "Well, if your source is correct, this case is now infinitely more complicated. And it might explain why the White House is trying to keep us from participating in the search."

"I agree, sir."

The director shook his head. "Look, I've really got to go. But you need to find Nick Jordan, and I mean now. If he is the Body Man, it's a national security concern to have him abducted. Call my cell at noon. I've got a lunch appointment, but I'll be able to slip away for a few to get an update."

"Thanks for having our back on this, sir."

"Just watch your front, Payne," said the director, redirecting his eyes. "You too, Stone."

Chapter 49
New York City

The four-room apartment Marcus Rollings rented in DC was small by most people's standards. He'd splurged on a nice California King-size bed that took up most of his living room because it didn't fit in the bedroom, so he used the bedroom as his office.

After dropping Joe Lagano off at his hotel, Rollings and Merci De Atta made good use of the plush mattress for about an hour. Rollings might have believed things were over between them, but the harrowing events in the hospital had dredged up long-buried emotions and desires. The neighbors a floor below banged on their ceiling with a broomstick more than once to no avail.

After the marathon sex session ended, Rollings and Merci fell fast asleep within minutes. The cellphone alarm clock went off at four-twenty a.m., and they were out the door ten minutes later to catch the seven a.m. Delta shuttle from Reagan National to LaGuardia.

After the driver picked them up outside Arrivals in New York, Rollings had him stop at Lexington Brass for breakfast. As the hostess brought them to their table, he was pleased to see Scott, his usual waiter, working their section.

After a delicious breakfast consisting of *crème brûlée* French toast and Belgian waffles, Rollings and Merci climbed back in the car a few pounds heavier and headed toward their destination.

Rollings climbed out of the black Lincoln Town Car on Fifth Avenue and took in a deep breath of the rank city air while Merci slid out of the passenger seat and stood next to him. The street vendor on the corner hung a fresh batch of oversized pretzels, and the smell drifted to where they stood.

"Ahh, nothing like the smell of pretzels, piss, and body odor to start a big-city day," he said.

"I only smell pretzels," said Merci as she cocked her head toward the Pakistani vendor.

"After all these years, you're telling me I was wrong and you're a glass-half-full kind of gal?"

She reached out and grabbed his large hand, giving it a squeeze right at a pressure point.

"*Oww!*" he said as the pain radiated up his arm.

The feel of a ring on her finger gave him pause as she held his hand. Merci typically eschewed jewelry of any kind unless a job called for it. He looked down and saw the oversized ruby ring surrounded by tiny diamonds. Rollings wondered how he hadn't noticed it earlier. He knew the ring well since it was a gift from him for one of their jobs years prior.

"Wearing the ring, I see."

Merci looked at him with a devious smile. "I am."

"Expecting trouble?"

"A girl never knows what rascals she may bump into in the big city, does she?"

"No, indeed."

They walked together up to the imposing building on the corner of Fifth Avenue and 57th Street. Most New Yorkers simply referred to it as the First Bank of Steele. The location, the flagship branch, had been opened by Charles Steele Sr. four decades earlier, and it served as the crown jewel in his banking empire. The façade of the building constructed from mirrored glass and brass reflected the rays of sun that crept down the grand boulevards of Gotham.

A man with white gloves, a long black coat, and matching top hat opened the heavy brass doors for them as Rollings and Merci approached. Rollings nodded at the courtesy and the two of them entered the ornate lobby with a twenty-five-foot ceiling. The center of the room was littered with black leather couches and high-backed, white leather chairs while oversized elephant-ear plants dotting the area, forming an oval sitting area.

They walked past the lobby and turned left, where they entered a wide hallway lined with neo-Gothic artwork. The hall split, with the right side leading to a large vault containing safe deposit boxes from floor to ceiling. Marcus and Merci stayed to the left, and the hall continued for another seventy-five feet before it dead-ended at a plain steel door with a biometric hand scanner to the right of the entrance.

Already wearing the prefab glove containing James Fowler's scanned fingerprints, Rollings raised his hand and placed it palm down on the electronic reader. A beam of bright green light scanned from right to left and read the fingerprints. After a few seconds, a small LED light to the left of the door showed green and the door opened.

The next passageway was less than twenty feet long, with another steel door at the end. This time a small box to the right of the door contained an optical reader. Rollings had the contact lens with Fowler's eye scan in his right eye and aligned it to the retinal scanner, which recognized the data. The locking mechanism disengaged with a slight hiss and the door swung open.

They entered the expansive room. The hardwood floors were made of hickory, while the center of the room contained several long tables with high-backed, leather-upholstered chairs. Two of the three walls were lined with floor-to-ceiling cherry cabinets like those found in the locker room of a high-end country club, and the third wall contained small rooms the size of department-store dressing rooms. Red velvet curtains provided privacy for anyone who required discretion while examining their items.

Rollings examined the cabinets and saw numbers for each located in small black letters on the bottom left corner. Each individual compartment measured eighteen inches high and twenty-four inches wide. The door to his left said "No. 1" on the bottom, while the one closest to the small rooms read "No. 100."

Rollings approached cabinet No. 34. He opened the cherry door saw the shiny surface of the safe deposit box had no markings except for a single keyhole.

Marcus turned to Merci and extended a hand. "The key."

She looked into his eyes as the tip of her tongue came out and gently rubbed against her lower lip. "You mean this key?" asked Merci as she reached down between her breasts and slowly drew an inch-long bronze key from her bra.

"You're incorrigible," Rollings said with a lascivious grin.

Merci winked. "You've reawakened a lioness," she said, placing the key in his open palm.

He spun the key around in his fingers a few times and rolled his eyes, but did glance over to the curtained-off rooms. A thought crossed his mind as his eyes wandered to Merci's ample cleavage, but he pushed the tantalizing thought aside.

Merci followed his gaze and read his thoughts. "I'm game if you are, big boy."

Rollings smirked. "Tempting, but business before pleasure."

"Okay, Mr. Responsible. Your loss."

He looked her up and down and gave her a devilish grin. "I know."

Rollings inserted the key in the receptacle and turned it clock- wise. The sound of the lock disengaging made a distinct click as the door swung open. Marcus grabbed the thick metal panel and opened it all the way. The ambient light inside the safe deposit box illuminated four shelves inside. He saw a black over-the-shoulder bag crammed into the bottom shelf—the item the president had sent them to retrieve. The top shelf contained bound stacks of currency in various denominations from over a dozen countries. The middle two shelves held identical metal boxes, four inches high and twenty-two inches deep.

Merci slid out one of the metal boxes and flipped open the lid. Inside were hundreds of neatly folded white envelopes. They looked like wedding invitations without any addresses. Merci opened one of the envelopes. She let the contents slide into her open palm and her body gave a natural quiver.

A four-carat, pear-shaped diamond sparkled in the light as she rocked it back and forth in her hand.

She looked up at Rollings, her eyes wide and hopeful. "You think all of these envelopes contain diamonds?"

The big man shrugged. "S'pose so," Rollings said.

Merci checked several other envelopes and her heart rate rose with each new one.

"But why are they in envelopes?" Rollings asked. "Thought they'd be in suede bags with a nice ribbon tying them shut."

Merci let out an audible sigh. "You're cute but dumb. That's how they do it in Hollywood, dear, but this is real life. Only a dia- mond can cut a diamond. Anyone with a serious understanding of the industry would know you keep precious jewels separated for transport. Jamming them into one bag would damage them."

"If you say so."

"President Steele said to bring him the files, and the rest was ours if we wanted it," Merci said. She looked around the expansive room. "And I fuckin' want it."

She saw black cylindrical canvas bags measuring eight-by-eighteen inches hanging from pegs on the wall. She hurried over and grabbed one and brought it to the safe deposit box. Using both hands, she emptied the contents of the top three shelves into the bag as fast as possible.

"We could take this and disappear. Start fresh. There's enough here with the diamonds alone to set us up for multiple lifetimes."

"What about the contents in the document bag?" asked Marcus.

"Toss them," said Merci.

Rollings frowned. "Can't do that. I don't think the president would appreciate that."

"To hell with him. We don't owe him anything."

"I was hired to do a job, and I intend to complete it. Then and only then can we disappear."

"Always the Boy Scout, aren't you?"

"I was an Eagle Scout."

"Whatever. Pretty sure the Scouts might frown upon your career choice."

"And my choice in women."

She looked over her shoulder at him. "Well, at least you have one redeeming quality."

"Look, I told the president we would bring him the bag, and we are doing that. Then our obligations to him are over."

"Until he asks for something else—and trust me, he will."

"I'll say no."

"He's not used to people telling him that."

Rollings chuckled. "Tough."

Chapter 50
Washington, DC

Payne and Stone climbed out of the director's black SUV and walked to the front door of Café Bonaparte.

"After you." Payne opened the door and stood to the side.

"Wow! Who says chivalry is dead?" Stone curtsied and slipped past Payne into the restaurant.

"Oh, it's dead all right." A smile crept over his face as he bowed slightly at the waist. "Dead as a doornail."

"Sounds about right, Renaissance man."

Payne followed behind and gave her a good-natured poke between the shoulder blades with his index finger.

A few steps inside the café was Dony Harbaugh sitting at one of the back tables.

"There he is. Follow me." Payne led the way.

"What's up, G-man?" Harbaugh stood and gave his friend a firm handshake with a hard smack on the shoulder.

"Living the dream, Three-Six. How about you?" Payne said. He used Harbaugh's radio call sign like he always had.

"Wife and kiddos are good, and my caseload is quieter than normal. I really can't complain."

Stone cleared her throat in a not-too-subtle way and stood a step behind Payne.

Payne got the hint and moved aside. "Dony Harbaugh, MPD, meet Kat Stone, FBI."

Harbaugh extended his hand. "Pleased to meet you, Stone. You must have screwed up somewhere to get stuck with this idiot here."

Stone smiled. "My parents always told me anything doesn't kill you, it makes you stronger."

The waiter came by to take their drink orders as they reviewed menus.

Harbaugh smirked. "Stone, order as much food as possible. With G-man here paying, we don't walk outta here hungry. I plan on eating for two today." He gently patted his stomach.

Payne cut him off. "It already looks like you have been." He pointed to his friend's paunch. "Hitting up the Dunkin' every day, I see."

"Har-dee-har-har," Harbaugh said. "A tired cop joke—and coming from a fed, nonetheless."

"We eat cronuts since our palates are much more refined than those who walk the beat."

Harbaugh laughed, and the three of them engaged in small talk waiting for the waiter to return. Once they'd placed their order, the discussion turned serious.

"Since you didn't call me here to buy me a fancy breakfast and chew the fat, Payne, what's up with your case? What do you need?"

"I kept it intentionally vague when we spoke on the phone, but here's a little more backstory," Payne said.

He took the next ten minutes to give Harbaugh a high-level overview of what they'd discovered up to that morning. He said little about what Nick did with the Secret Service, and when Harbaugh asked for a physical description, Payne pulled out the picture from Rose.

"No ransom demands, presumably, as you didn't mention any." Harbaugh said.

"Nope. Nobody has stepped forward or said anything. If it weren't for Rose reporting him missing, the Bureau wouldn't be involved." He half-frowned. "Possibly nobody would be involved."

"How about motive? Why would someone want him?"

"I believe for the sensitive government info he's privy to," Payne said.

"And who do you suspect took him?"

"Not sure. Possibly some Russians, but no hard proof to corroborate that yet."

Harbaugh said, "Well, you were vague about his role. Is he on the investigative side or a protective detail?"

"Left that out intentionally. I can't read you in as to his actual duties. Let's say his eyes and ears are around lots of classified material all the time."

"And this sensitive information comes from the tippy top, I take it."

"Roger that."

"Then there are a lot of people who would like to know what's in his head," Harbaugh said.

"Yep, especially foreign governments. This is a matter of national security."

"Well, if that's the case, I think we're outside my wheelhouse."

"Not what I was hoping to hear," Payne said.

Harbaugh raised a hand. "Not to worry. I know a guy who specializes in this type of thing."

"I'm listening."

"He's eccentric, but this guy knows everything there is to know about international kidnapping, spycraft, toppling governments, you name it."

"Who does he work for?"

"A three-letter agency that starts with C and ends in I-A."

"What's the chance he would talk with us?"

Harbaugh snickered. "There's no chance at all ..."

Payne frowned.

"... unless he knows Dagger sent you."

"Who's 'Dagger'?" asked Payne.

Harbaugh rocked a thumb back at himself but didn't say anything.

"New nickname?"

"Not really, but it's what he calls me."

This was a story Payne had to hear. "Why?"

"I met him a few years back on a Metro investigation that turned into a full-blown international affair regarding a foreign embassy."

"The Qatar affair?" Payne asked.

"Oh, you know about that one, huh? We spent a lot of time together on that deal, and I told him one of my favorite spy movies as a kid was *Cloak and Dagger*."

"The old '80s movie?"

"The one and only."

"You are a dork. You know that, right?"

Harbaugh smiled. "And proud of it."

"What's this guy's name?"

"Zed."

"First or last?"

"That's all he goes by."

"How do I get in touch with this Zed?"

"You can't, but I can. Hold tight." Dony reached down toward the floor and hauled a black 5.11 Rush 72 backpack up to the empty seat next to him. Within a minute he had his laptop out and connected through a secure VPN via the free WiFi offered by the restaurant.

"We're in luck," Harbaugh said. "He's online."

Payne pulled his chair around the table to see the screen. "Zed, your super Secret Squirrel guy, uses Microsoft Lync?" The old Microsoft program for audio and video calls had been merged with Skype in 2015.

"Of course. What did you think? I'd send a carrier pigeon with a note written in invisible ink attached to its foot?"

"Two Dixie cups and a string, maybe."

Harbaugh and Zed exchanged more than a dozen instant messages. To the casual observer, it looked to be a random chat between friends, but for the two skilled professionals, it was a discussion with deeper meaning. Finally, Harbaugh typed his thanks and disconnected.

"All set. You'll meet him at the Denny's on the corner of State Highway 123 and Fairfax Boulevard."

"Denny's? Are you serious?" asked Payne.

"Yeah. He likes Denny's. You got a problem with that?"

"Will he want the All-American breakfast?" Stone joked

"More than likely," Harbaugh said, grinning.

"I've worked with enough spooks over the years." Payne let out a long sigh. "They do breed some weird ones at Langley."

"Keep in mind, he's hyper-paranoid about everything but mostly about people. Especially feds."

"But he's a fed."

"Yeah, sorta, but don't remind him of that little factoid," said Harbaugh, winking. "And whatever you do, don't bring anything electronic with you. He has a detector and he'll know. You spook him and he'll be back in the wind, and you'll be sitting there with your All-American breakfast getting cold."

"You sure he can help?"

"If someone took Nick Jordan, and especially if it were a foreign government or agency, Zed would be the only one who could help you find out who it was and where they took him."

"If you say so."

"Watch out for his tics, and please for the love of God, don't point them out."

Stone laughed. "Tics, huh? Really?"

Harbaugh nodded. "Yes, lots of them."

"Great, just great. Anything else I need to know?" asked Payne.

"Yes, he's big into conspiracies."

"Like, he believes in them?"

"Oh yeah—Roswell, the Kennedy assassination, even alternative 9/11 theories. The whole schmear."

"You're saying the CIA has a top-tier analyst who's a certified whack job?"

"No, I'm saying the CIA employs a brilliant analyst—a certifiable genius—who also believes in fringe theories about legitimate American events."

"And they let him have a Top Secret clearance?"

"Oh, higher than that, I think. Thing is, he's one of the few people I believe could really know background stories about these things, you know? You'll understand when you talk with him."

"Okay," Payne said. "We'll see him."

"Sometimes you've got to pass through the darkness to appreciate the light."

Payne rolled his eyes. "Whatever the hell that means."

Harbaugh chuckled. "As I said, you'll see. I gave him your cell. He'll ping you when he wants you to meet with him."

Payne shook his friend's hand and grabbed the check. He counted out a few bills for the three coffees and left a generous tip. "Next one is on you, cheapskate."

Harbaugh nodded. "The dollar menu at the golden arches it is, then!"

They got up to leave and Harbaugh shook Stone's hand.

"Nice to meet you, Stone. Keep my boy here safe, okay?"

"I'll do my best," she said.

Chapter 51
Washington, DC

Peter Casha listened to Junior's pitch, but he wasn't buying it. "Why would I have more luck than the interrogator already grilling Nick?"

"The president has faith in you," said Junior.

Casha frowned. "Wonderful. But I have a firm grasp of the obvious and you didn't answer my question."

"JoJo tells me you have interrogation experience, right?"

"Some, but I'm not a trained professional like the men employed by the Sanctum."

"Their results have been less than impressive. Especially considering how much money we've paid them."

"Look, Junior, I'm not the sharpest knife in the drawer, but I'm pretty sure me showing up down there isn't going to go over well." He rubbed his arm, still in a sling. "I'm still recovering from my last deal."

Junior's gaze narrowed. "I don't give a shit what they think, and neither does the president. We need to know what Nick Jordan did with the files. The Sanctum hasn't delivered, and we are out of time. Simple fact."

"Nobody likes it when the neighbor's dog comes and drops a

big shit in their front yard."

The comment provoked a smirk from Junior.

"Then make sure it's a small turd that doesn't smell terrible and keep it out of sight under a bush. Understood?"

"I don't get a say in this, do I?"

Junior snickered. "Did it seem like you did?"

Casha rubbed his shoulder. It was healing well but it wasn't perfect yet. "I did get shot, after all."

"You're a doer. Your president needs you, and he'll reward you accordingly for your loyalty. You're not going to say no to him, are you?"

Casha had no problem telling the president no, or anyone else for that matter. But Junior was right. No way could he sit around and do nothing. "Guess I can get back in the game."

"That's the spirit. I've already called the airport. The plane that brought you to DC from Cali is prepped and ready to take you to Louisiana."

Junior paused as if he were considering his next words carefully. "Do whatever you have to, but get us actionable intel. We must know what the Body Man did with those documents."

Casha nodded.

"Oh, and one more thing."

"Yes?"

Junior rose to leave. "When you get the information, I want Nick Jordan sleeping with the fishes in the Gulf. Give him a burial at sea—the bin Laden special."

Casha looked surprised." I thought the Sanctum was going to take care of that?"

"They've been such a disappointment to this point, the president feels Jordan needs to be neutralized by someone we can trust to get it done. If the Sanctum reneges on our deal, Jordan could be a massive liability if what he knows goes for sale to the highest bidder."

"Let me make sure I have this straight. Go down there, figure out what he hasn't told them, and then make sure he's dead before I leave?"

Junior nodded. "Bingo," he said, and left the apartment without another word.

Joe Lagano waited until Junior left before he said anything.

"You sure doing this is a good idea?"

"No," Casha replied, "but I'm not sure saying what I thought would have mattered."

"Valid point."

"Besides, Junior might be a fucking dick, but he's right. What am I going to do? Sit around and do nothing while I recoup?"

"You could binge-watch Netflix or a ton of porn."

"Not my style."

"I know, but you still need to rest the shoulder."

"It's not like I'm going down there to waterboard the son of a bitch or punch holes in his hands and feet with an electric drill. It won't be physical. Besides, if I have a cot, a hot shower, and some food, I'll be okay."

Lagano stood and looked out of the window that looked down on the parking lot. "Think you can get him to talk?"

"Guess I'll find out, won't I?"

Lagano nodded but said nothing.

"Hey, aren't you forgetting something?" Casha's look was serious.

A confused look spread over his friend's face. "What did I miss?"

A faux stern look was plastered across Casha's face. "You owe me a Tito's and lemonade. How the hell could you forget something like that?"

"We still got a few hours before lunch," Lagano said. But he walked toward the kitchen. He knew Casha always kept those very ingredients at hand. "A little early for a drink, isn't it?"

"The adage always rings true: It's five o'clock somewhere."

Chapter 52
Fairfax, Virginia

A few hours later, Payne's cellphone pinged with the tone assigned to unknown numbers. He looked at the Caller ID, but it only displayed SPOOKY. The text read, 33 MINUTES FROM NOW. THERE. FLOWERS FOR ALGERNON.

As they drove to the designated Denny's, Payne peppered Stone with questions about growing up. Small talk, mainly. Payne wouldn't admit it, but he enjoyed having Stone around. There was something unique about her, a perspective he'd rarely seen with new recruits. She was certainly attractive, but that wasn't the appeal. Payne had been with attractive women before, so he was proficient at looking beyond the surface.

Probationary agents straight out of Quantico universally had a puppy-dog determination, some might even call it an arrogance. After all, it takes a special breed to serve as an FBI special agent and rarely does one lack in confidence. Stone may have had the confidence common in others, but she also had a fire, deep down. A hunger that set her apart. It didn't hurt that she was sarcastic and occasionally funny as hell, qualities Payne not only understood but respected.

"Your folks call you Kat when you were a kid?" He looked

toward her as she stared out the passenger window oblivious to his gaze.

She turned her head in his direction. "No, it was Katherine until high school. We moved around a bit because my dad was military."

"Oh, yeah? What branch?"

A reluctant grin formed at the corner of her lips. "I was an Army brat."

"How did I not pick up on that before? Let me guess: Miss Popularity, head cheerleader and prom queen, top of the class, and never got in trouble."

Stone laughed. "Not quite. More like a loner, back-talker. Halfway decent grades, and only got suspended once."

"You got suspended? Bullshit. You're a Miss Goody Two-Shoes if I ever met one."

Stone shook her head. "Hardly. We were living down in Fay-etteville while Pops did a stint at Bragg. That year the kids at school started to call me Kat. Before long, that was turned into Kitty by some of the jocks."

Payne sensed where this was going.

"Yeah," Stone continued. "So, there I am in Home room one day and the captain of the football team, a real king douchebag, decides to start meowing at me. I quietly told him to buzz the fuck off and he ups the ante, calling out, 'Here, pussy, pussy, pussy.'"

"Ouch. Wrong move, douchebag." Payne shook his head.

"You got it. I snapped. I stood up with the biggest grin I could muster."

"And?"

"What do you think? I cold cocked that motherfucker into first period. Split his lip in two places and broke his nose. He ended up sprawled out on the floor with blood all over the place."

"You go, girl. It sounds like that little shit deserved exactly what he got."

"He did, but not everyone agreed. It turned out his Dad was on the school board."

"Oh, that's not good."

"Nope. They tried to expel me until Pops paid the principal a visit."

"Bet that guy got an earful."

"The principal was a woman."

"Equal opportunity butt-kicking."

Stone smiled warmly at the memory of her father coming to her rescue. He'd been her personal hero before this but became a God after.

"You could hear my Dad screaming at her in his loudest command voice from the other side of the high school. After some tense discussions, they settled on a three-day in-school suspension, on account of I did lay him out. The boy's family decided not to press assault charges after his father heard what he'd said to me—they thought it might harm his chances for re-election to the school board if his son's filthy taunts made the local news."

"You're like a freaking rock star, Stone." Payne jabbed her with his elbow. "Minus the groupies."

"Who says I don't have groupies?" Stone laughed.

Two minutes later Payne pulled into the Denny's in Falls Church. To the right of the restaurant a dilapidated 7-Eleven looked like it had seen better days. Big Bite hot dogs, Munchos, and orange Hostess cupcakes were a staple for Payne in his younger days, and his stomach turned over just thinking about it. As instructed, they shut their phones down cold and stowed them in the glovebox before exiting the G-car.

Stone let out a muffled *whoa* as she walked around the side of the car and looked toward the entrance.

"Wow, 'Back To The Future Four.' I haven't been in one of these places in years. I can't even recall the last time I had a Rooty, Tooty, Fresh 'n Fruity."

Payne grimaced. "That's IHOP, Hawking. Wrong commercial."

"You sure?"

"Uh, positive."

Stone cocked her head sideways. "Whatever. Wait, who's Hawking?"

"You serious?"

"Yes, why?"

"Jesus," Payne said, shaking his head. "I blame a public school education. Disregard."

"You think this Zed guy will show?" asked Stone.

"My guess is he's been here for a bit, watching to see who arrives and departs. And if Dony says he'll be here, then I believe he will be."

As they walked toward the door, Stone turned toward him and poked her finger into his chest. "By the way, don't make fun of Stephen Hawking again."

Payne laughed. "Oh, you got that dig?"

"I did. Stephen Hawking was freaking brilliant."

"Yeah, I tried reading A Brief History of Time once," Payne said.

"And?"

"It took me some time, and it was a brief read, as in I made it halfway through the first chapter before I gave up and watched the movie instead."

"And went back to what? A Vince Flynn novel?"

Payne put his hands together reverently and his gaze turned heavenward. "Do not disparage the master." He opened the glass doors and they stepped into the restaurant.

The hostess desk was empty. Instead of a worker, a hand-written sign on a white folded piece of paper taped to the counter read, "Pleaze Seat Yourself" in thick black letters.

"Figures," Payne said under his breath, unsure if the word please was jokingly misspelled on purpose or not.

"Well?" asked Stone. She stood close enough that her breath blew against the scruff of his neck. Payne liked it.

"I don't know what he looks like. Dony said he'd come to us."

Payne scanned the mostly empty restaurant. To his left, a mother with a tired expression and two well-mannered children sat in the booth closest to the front door.

Further down the row of high-backed booths and toward the back of the restaurant, a man with a long gray beard sipped at a cup of steaming coffee while his free hand twirled the end of his beard and twisted it around his finger. Payne thought the man looked edgy.

To his right, Payne saw the row was mostly empty except half-way down the aisle a FedEx worker dressed in the standard black-and-purple golf shirt appeared to be finishing his meal.

"Which one is Zed?"

"My money is on gray-bearded dude."

Stone nodded. "Mine, too. He looks psychotic. And the beard looks like it came right out of Central Casting."

Payne stepped to the right and walked down the aisle. Payne sat closest to the window and Stone took the aisle side of the narrow booth. At the end of the row, a sign hung from chains affixed to the ceiling panels that read RESTROOMS.

"Why are we sitting on this side if Zed is over there?" Stone said as she gestured toward the other side of the restaurant.

"Dony said he'd come to us. We'll wait for him. We're playing by his rules." He looked down at his watch. "Old graybeard will be over here in two minutes flat. Just wait and see."

The FedEx guy at the counter took his bill and stood, grabbing his bag and starting down the aisle, presumably for the restroom. Neither Payne nor Stone could suppress their surprised looks when he slid into the seat opposite them.

"Can we help you?" asked Stone, irritated.

"Pretty sure I'm the one here to help you," Zed said in a raspy voice. He reached into his bag and handed a small bouquet of fresh roses to Stone and turned to Payne, uttering the confirmation code phrase. "Flowers for Algernon."

Payne extended his hand to Zed, and they shook. He nodded at the charmed Stone. She looked at him over the elaborate flower arrangement and they shook hands with just the fingers.

"By the way, some professional advice? Neither of you should ever plan to work undercover. You might as well be wearing raid jackets with the letters 'FBI' stenciled across the back. You both scream FEDERAL OFFICER in twelve languages."

The man reached back into his bag and withdrew a device about the size of a Zippo cigarette lighter. He pressed and held a button for a moment and a green light was displayed. No electronic devices were detected.

"Zed?" Payne asked.

The FedEx man ignored the question. "One-word response, or I bail. Who sent you?"

"Dagger," replied Payne in an even tone.

Zed nodded. "I've been told you need to find someone."

"What's with the FedEx outfit?" asked Payne.

Zed leaned in closer, squinted his eyes, and stared at Payne. His right cheek twitched, followed by his eye rapidly blinking for several seconds. "It's called a disguise. You can Google it. Maybe try it sometime."

"Got it," Payne said as he took in the strange facial tics and remembered Harbaugh had told them to expect some tics.

"Back to my question. Who are you looking for?" asked Zed.

"A missing federal agent," Payne said.

"Which agency?"

"Secret Service."

Zed sat back and grew silent. The facial tics appeared to increase in intensity and length, and he replied with one word. "Interesting." Then he placed his left hand on the table and started to tap his fingers, beginning with his pinky and moving down to his index finger as if he were playing an imaginary piano. Each time, the movements became faster. "This missing agent have a name?"

For a moment, Payne considered not saying the real name.

Stone could see his hesitation and kicked his foot.

"The agent we're looking for is named Nick Jordan."

Zed started to make a clicking sound with his tongue against the roof of his mouth. "So ... the rumor is true?"

"What rumor is that?" asked Payne.

"The Body Man went AWOL."

"You've heard of the Body Man?"

"Of course," said Zed in a matter-of-fact tone, as if everyone knew. "You know I'm in the actual information business, right?"

"I was under the impression few people outside the Secret Service were aware of him."

"Dagger shared with you what I do for the Agency?"

"He did." Payne paused. "Somewhat." Payne looked down at the scarred Formica tabletop. "Well, not really, no."

Zed smiled and nodded. "It's my job to know things that I'm not supposed to know. If I didn't know them, I wouldn't be good at what I do."

Payne believed him.

Zed's eyes darted back and forth. His body slouched in the booth. "Is the man missing of his own accord, or was he taken?"

"The evidence leads us to believe he was abducted," Stone

said, "but the White House has stonewalled us, making it hard to get the facts."

Zed looked back and forth between Stone and Payne.

"Who took him?"

"Not sure yet, but we have an eyewitness who thinks the men who took him spoke Russian. They forced him onto a private jet at the Manassas Regional Airport in the middle of the night," Payne said.

"Destination?"

"Houma, Louisiana," Stone said.

Zed's eyes grew wide.

"*Houma*? No shit? Are you *sure* about that?"

"One hundred percent confirmed with the FAA," Stone chipped in. "The plane stayed in Houma for several hours before it flew back to New York City."

Zed said nothing for almost a minute and merely rubbed the bridge of his nose while he made a dull humming sound. "Are you familiar with black sites?" he finally asked.

Payne scrunched his nose. "Conceptually. You're referring to secret prisons, right?"

"Correct. Know much about them?"

"Very little. I know the last president got rid of them, which caused a lot of murmurings within the DOD and other agencies. From what I heard, it pissed off the Agency."

"It did for a time, yes, but we're a resilient bunch."

Stone's head cocked to one side. "Are you insinuating the practice is still alive and well?"

"Well, I can most assuredly tell you the changes instituted by that administration remain in place, and the United States government no longer runs any black sites."

"I have a hard time believing the practice ended," countered Payne. Zed's voice lowered just slightly in pitch and volume.

"Start paying attention to the precise meaning of words. Christ, I thought you'd be doing that already." He looked up at the water-stained ceiling tiles. "Listen to me carefully: We no longer control any black sites. Period. End of story."

"Then why bring them up?"

"The key word in what I said was we."

"Meaning?" asked Stone.

"If a person with an intimate knowledge of our presidential secrets has gone missing, we must assume someone took him."

Payne and Stone looked at each other, perplexed.

"I agree ..." Payne said, looking back at Zed.

"And they must be holding him somewhere. Plus, you said it's possible men who spoke Russian took him."

"That's our working theory, yes, but why did you bring up black sites?" Payne said.

"Because when the government took away the governmental option, the free market stepped in to fill the void. That's why I said we no longer maintain any sites. I didn't say black sites no longer exist."

"Then who runs the sites now?"

"For one, a syndicate out of Russia. They've placed facilities around the world to fill the vacuum created when we shut down our locations."

"When did they start to do this?"

"As soon as we got out of the business of secret prisons. This criminal syndicate goes by the name the Sanctum. They offer highly illegal services at a premium cost. It's a vicious organization that operates outside of any laws or jurisdictions."

"Russians engage in torture *for us*?"

"They employ a number of Americans, of course, plus a sprinkling of French, Germans, Brits. Folks from nations who need or simply want the services. Torture, interrogation, murder. Hell, they even run their own secret hospital facilities for people of ill repute who can't walk into a regular hospital with GSWs and the like."

Payne smirked. *Gunshot wounds.*

"Great. They rough people up, then they might make money fixing them up after the fact?"

"One astute observation," said Zed.

Payne was still connecting dots in his head. "And you think this group has Nick why?"

"Because the men spoke Russian. Plus, where they took him."

"Houma, Louisiana?"

"Correct."

"What's so special about Houma?" Stone asked.

"The Sanctum operates a facility in the Gulf on an old, decommissioned oil platform south of Houma."

"How do you know this?"

"Because the Agency sends people there from time to time."

There was a slight pause.

"Unofficially, of course," finished Zed.

"What the hell? You're saying the US government pays a Russian crime syndicate to torture and interrogate people?"

"Strange bedfellows, am I right?" Zed chuckled.

A strong wave of tics slowed him down for a few seconds. Now, both hands were on the table and started to drum rapidly as he continued to talk. "The Agency and others, even some at your illustrious Bureau, do what is needed at times to keep the populace safe from external threats. That includes paying for services of emergent need but sometimes questionable legality."

"Questionable? It's downright illegal."

"Don't be naïve, Special Agent Payne. It's a moral quandary at worst, depending on your perspective."

Payne didn't have the energy to get into an ethical argument and rightly figured he wouldn't get far with someone like Zed anyway.

"If what you're saying is true, how can we determine if this facility has Nick Jordan? I mean, who says the plane didn't stop in Houma and they moved him via another mode of transportation? If the Russians grabbed him, he could be in a gulag by now, and Putin could be torturing him for everything he knows. Hell, he could be in any number of countries—or in a condo at Del Boca Vista for all we know."

Zed smiled. It was the first time he'd cracked even the faintest of genuine smiles since he'd sat down.

"Seinfeld reference. I like it."

Payne wasn't sure what to say.

Zed continued. "True, he could be anywhere. As for how we can find out if the Sanctum has him, leave that to me. I have a hunch he's there since—pardon the expression—I'm constitutionally opposed to believing in coincidences and nobody has any real reason to go to that part of the country." Zed thought for a moment longer. "Or ocean, for that matter."

"I'm sure lots of people have reasons to visit Louisiana," Stone said.

Zed frowned. "Not likely. Have you even *been* to Louisiana?"

"Yes, I have, as a matter of fact," Stone said. "Mardi Gras is quite fun."

"Sure, if you want to drink, see boobs of every shape and size, and vomit in the street by the end of the night."

"I stayed fairly sober at Mardi Gras," Stone said, "and I kept the girls covered up that time, thank you very much."

Zed took a wanton look at Stone's chest. "A pity," he said. "What I'm telling you is that the primary reason a plane would leave Manassas, Virginia, in the dead of night and fly to Houma is not for crawfish etouffee."

Payne was getting antsy by the minute. "How long will you need?"

"Give me an hour, two at the most. I'll turn over some rocks and see what tries to slither away."

"And if you're right and the Sanctum has the Body Man?"

"What do you mean?"

"How do we get him out?"

"The Agency pays to use Sanctum facilities and its personnel, not break people out of them."

"Then what do you suggest?"

"The FBI is resourceful. You'll think of a way to get him out if we find he's being held in the facility."

Payne shook his head. "How do I get in touch with you?"

"I'll contact you directly. Don't need anything more than I have. If I do, well, I work for the CIA, not the county library."

"How will I know it's you?"

Zed's chest heaved slightly suppressing a giggle. "You'll know."

"Are you sure you don't want my business card?"

Zed put his hands out to rebuff the card Payne thrust in his direction. "Keep it," said Zed. "I dislike taking things from people's hands directly."

"Who are you, Tony Stark?" Payne said as he withdrew his hand and put the card back into his wallet.

Zed reached into his pocket and produced a long, thin piece of paper. "This is for you," he said as he stood up and walked toward the front door. He walked with a slight limp on his right side, exited the restaurant, and continued outside without turning around. He climbed into a clapped-out blue Datsun 510 riddled with car cancer, the kind of creeping corrosion you don't see on modern cars made with better materials. The engine fired up instantly though and it sounded like a lawn tractor as it pulled out of the parking lot. It disappeared down the road with a high-pitched automatic-transmission whine and clouds of blue oil smoke.

Payne smirked and looked down at the piece of paper. It was a receipt for an All-American breakfast. "Well, Dony called that one, didn't he?" Payne said as he handed the breakfast bill over to Stone.

"You expecting me to pay or something?"

"Yeah, we can go dutch. I paid for Dony's breakfast; you can pay for Zed's lunch."

Stone handed it back. "Man, please. Girls don't pay, boys pay. It's in the handbook."

A bewildered look spread over Payne's face. "It does? Wait, what handbook?"

"Mine." Stone grinned. She stood and walked out the front door.

Payne sat alone in the booth. A lone voice broke the silence as the gray-bearded man from the other side of the restaurant held a bill in the air and said, "You can pay for mine too while you're at it, mister." A crooked smile revealed blackened teeth and more than one that appeared missing.

With a shake of his head, a wide smile formed, and Payne retorted, "Bring it on over, Gandalf—I might as well."

Chapter 53
The Gulf of Mexico

Nick Jordan lay flat on his back and opened his eyes. A dense fog was trying to lift from his mind as he awakened from a heavily drugged slumber.

His gaze settled on a spot above his cot no larger than a half-dollar coin that appeared discolored compared to the rest of the ceiling. His mind homed in on abnormalities, a necessary skill for a man in his line of work. He couldn't be sure how long his captors had kept him drugged, but for the first time in recent memory he felt like he might be coming out of it.

He sat up slowly and looked around the sights of his cell. It reminded him of his status—a prisoner.

Jordan was unrestrained as well. He raised sore arms and rubbed his temples in a circular motion. *How long have they held me?* He couldn't be sure. His initial thought was several days, but deep down he knew it could've been much longer.

The uncertainty of not knowing what he'd told Sir nagged at him. Memories flooded back like waves pounding the rock face of a towering cliff. He remembered resisting. He had even concocted all manner of disinformation to confuse Sir and muddy the waters. But had it been enough? Thankfully, he didn't know the specific banks where Danny Frazier had hidden the documents, but had he told Sir they were in a safe deposit box? He couldn't be sure.

The sound of the electronic door lock disengaging made his head snap to the right. His eyes fixed on it as it started to swing open. Two large men who could have been NFL linebackers entered the room. They said nothing but approached Jordan with a set of shackles.

Binding his hands and ankles, the two men yanked Jordan to his feet, ushered him out of the room and down the hall. They passed through two secured doors that required outside intervention to buzz them through before they arrived back at the interrogation room. It was the same room they'd brought Jordan to every day that he could remember.

Sir sat at the familiar stainless-steel table but didn't look up as the large men fastened Jordan to the table and floor. Satisfied that the Body Man was going nowhere, the men left him alone in the dim room with Sir.

The routine questions started, but after a few words, another thing out of place caught Jordan's eye. The item protruded from inside the thick file under Sir's folded hands.

The tip of a Skilcraft number-two wooden pencil protruded from the center of the file, stuffed between several sheets of paper. As Sir spoke, Jordan formulated a plan in his head.

The questioning dragged on, with Sir asking questions and rephrasing the same question time and again while Jordan did his best to evade and deflect, but never giving Sir what he wanted.

After ninety minutes of conversation that got them nowhere, Jordan made his move. Even though they had secured his hands to the table, he still had about eight inches of play in his chain, and he lunged for the file.

Sir reacted fast and pulled the file from Jordan's strong grasp though he held the corner of the thick stack of papers and yanked hard. The ensuing struggle caused the thick manila folder to spill open, dumping its contents over the table and the floor. Sir's attention turned away from Jordan and toward the scattered pages long enough for the prisoner to grab the pencil that had landed on the table within his grasp. Once secured, he kept it hidden in the palm of his hand.

Sir looked up. "What the hell was that about, prisoner?"

"I wanted to see my file," Jordan said in a defiant tone.

Sir's face turned red and his hands visibly shook in anger. "The contents of this file are none of your damned business. Are we clear?"

Jordan answered, "As a bell."

Jordan knew the mirror had to be a two-way type, and he wondered if others watched his movements. As Sir reached down to pick up more of the papers, Jordan carefully used the index finger from his opposite hand to slide the pencil down past his elbow and slowly work it toward his torso. Carefully he finagled the pencil toward his body before he hid it in the waistband of his pants, which resembled scrubs used by hospital staff.

No one burst into the room to relive him of the pencil, so the observation room with the two-way mirror had been empty.

After the file was reconstructed, the interrogation continued for another forty-five minutes. When Sir had enough, the same large guards came back to the room, unfastened Jordan's binds, and ushered him to his room. Fortunately for Jordan, neither man patted him down before they left the interrogation room or after he returned to his cell.

Now alone, Jordan hid his newfound tool in the far corner of the bed between the mattress and the wall. The tip was dull, but he'd figured a way to grind both ends of the pencil sharp enough to serve as a deadly weapon.

Sitting on the edge of the bed, Jordan knew he had to find an opportunity to escape or make one. Personal survival wasn't the only reason why he needed to set himself free. The information in the files he'd given Danny Frazier and what was stored in his mind needed to see the light of day.

At any cost.

Payne and Stone said nothing as they drove from Denny's back to the Washington Field Office. The pain and anger at Wes Russell's killing was still fresh and disturbing. It served well the silence in the car.

Traffic was light—something abnormal in DC. Then a deep sound disturbed the silence when Payne's stomach growled loud enough for Stone to turn and stare.

"Is someone hungry?" she asked.

Payne patted his abdomen. "Clearly, I'm half starving to death."

Stone rolled her eyes. "Should we stop? You're not going to get any less hungry, and since you're already ornery, I'd rather limit my exposure to your crankiness."

Payne frowned. "It's just shocking to me that you're still single."

"Ditto," she retorted. "Where we going to eat?"

"I need some pizza."

"Need is a stretch, but I can go for a slice or two."

They pulled in at the nameless local hole-in-the-wall pizza joint near their office. The only sign had weathered neon block letters over a faded red metal arrow that pointed down to the door. The sign wasn't lighting up the "A" anymore, so the sign only read PIZZ. Each letter illuminated by itself, then the word flashed three times and went dark, and the sequence starting over again. More than one wandering drunk from the bar next door had seen the sign and come in to take a leak on the floor in front of the cash register.

The agents favored a "buy local" practice, and this store had fed them many nights beyond closing time when big cases had kept agents in the office to all hours.

Payne called Ken Ludington with an update at noon as he waited for the order. He promised to call the FBI director again when they heard back from Zed.

Payne barely got two bites into his pepperoni and jalapeño pizza before his cellphone vibrated. A text message read, *Are you in your office?*

The number on his Caller ID read 999-999-9999.

Zed.

No. Close though, he typed. *Grabbing pizza nearby. Want some?*

The phone vibrated a second later. *Meet me @ the WW2 Memorial in 20 mins. 2 slices for me.*

Payne sent back a single thumbs-up emoji.

"That was fast," he said.

"Zed?"

"Yeah. And he's hungry."

They circled the memorial on foot twice, dodging a fair number of visitors enjoying the National Mall amid a sunny day. Stone carried a short cardboard box with six individual pie-slice-shaped boxes, each holding a wide slice of pizz.

Stone saw him first. "There." She nodded her head toward the far end of the fountain.

"Where?"

"Under the Connecticut pillar. Yellow shirt, green hat," Stone said, and then laughed. "Wearing the Ray-Bans."

Payne squinted, but it didn't help. "How can you see that far? People look like blobs from this far away."

"Younger eyes. What can I say?"

"Yeah, rub it in, why don't you?"

"I will," she replied over her shoulder as she started around the pool and fountain.

Zed looked past them as they approached. He fidgeted as he bounced on the balls of his feet.

"Come alone?"

"Yeah," Payne said. "I mean, plus Stone and the pizza." He shook the cardboard box and the individual boxes of pizza slid around.

"Good. Sit with me." They walked behind the concrete memorial and sat in the grass under some trees. Zed looked into the box and grabbed the top slice. He seemed less twitchy than earlier.

"It's trite but I'll say the words: What I'm about to tell you didn't come from me. Got it?" He popped the lid on the pizza slice and inhaled the aroma before pulling it from the container and attacking it.

"Got what?" Payne said the classic reply as a wry smile formed at the corner of his lips.

"Catching on faster than most feds, Agent Payne. Fantastic."

Zed held a cellphone in his right hand. With his left finger, he swiped across the screen, and immediately Payne's cellphone buzzed.

Payne looked at the message, which included several photos. "Is this what I think ..." But he didn't get to finish the thought.

"That first photo was taken as they processed Nick Jordan at the Sanctum's facility in the Gulf of Mexico. The images came from their in-house security system."

"And how the hell did you get them?"

Zed shrugged his shoulders but didn't speak.

Payne examined the photos. Stone moved close enough that he could smell her perfume, a subtle scent of lilac and strawberries. She leaned on his broad shoulder and Payne found her proximity distracting.

"The diagram is of the entire facility? Schematics are accurate?"

"They are."

"And it's up to date?"

"The facility is not that old. The Sanctum moves around quite often, and they've only been in that location a short time. Complacency doesn't serve anyone well in their line of work."

"Why do they use an oil platform? That's a long helicopter ride and an even longer boat ride."

"The real question you should ask is why not? There may be thousands of abandoned structures in the Gulf, and they are almost impossible for agencies like the Bureau of Safety and the Environmental Enforcement to keep tabs on them. Old, abandoned platforms have been used for illicit activities for decades. Most often by drug runners and sex traffickers, but now the Sanctum uses them as well."

"Sex traffickers? Are you serious? The drug runners don't surprise me, but I had no clue the sex industry utilized structures in the Gulf."

"Absolutely. It's a brave new world, man. The traffickers come to the Gulf via Mexico and Central American countries, and they have sorting facilities on abandoned platforms. Then the best talent is sent to Atlanta."

Stone said, "I've read some of the official briefs the Bureau puts out. Atlanta is a hotbed of the sex-trade industry for the East

Coast." She looked at Payne. "Maybe you should read your email from time to time. Lots of interesting factoids are sent out all the time."

Payne ignored the dig. "Oil platforms run by crime syndicates—they're major cities used as sex-trafficking hubs. What are we? Some bass-ackward third-world nation?"

"Quite the opposite. We are the land of the free and home of the brave," said Zed. "Meaning the brave criminal elements realize they have free rein to do whatever they want as long as they bribe the right person and manipulate our loopholes. Power is the money, money is the power."

Payne was hung up on the platforms. "And our federal agencies know about these activities on the platforms?"

"I'm not saying the United States is complicit, but we certainly turn a blind eye to them, yes."

Payne shook his head. "Why?"

"It's complicated. Lots of them are in international waters—and believe it or not, under international law, deep-water oil rigs are treated like ships, not real estate."

"That's bullshit."

Zed didn't disagree, but he had the intelligence background to understand the principles.

"Corruption has always been a part of life and of governments, and it always will be. Those who believe in justice have to work hard to save a ship with far more holes than buckets."

Payne shook his head but didn't reply.

"Regarding the platform operated by the Sanctum ..." Zed motioned to the images on Payne's smartphone. "Everything you should need is right there. Including lat and long coordinates."

"Look, Zed. Don't take this the wrong way because we're grateful, but why are you helping us? Certainly, you're taking a risk by talking to us and then taking more chances by sharing this intel. I want to know why."

"Guess you think because of what I do for a living I have no conscience?"

"I didn't say that," Payne said.

Zed's tics started anew as he flicked his thumb and index finger together in rapid succession. "I'm a smart guy, see? Okay, I'm a literal genius. I'd be a card-carrying member of Mensa if they could keep up with me. I'm smart enough to know our government uses my intellect for unethical means. I could have gone to the private sector and made more money than I could have dreamed of, but instead, I decided to serve a higher calling."

Zed's face got serious.

"I think this guy you're looking for, this Nick Jordan, the Body Man, is doing something similar. Protecting not one man but the office of the presidency is a noble calling. Covering up a leader's indiscretions to spare the country pain and disgrace is admirable, if morally ambiguous."

Zed closed the lid of his empty pizza slice box and traded it for a full one. "Man, I'm tellin' ya. If there was no such thing as pizza, I'd have to invent it." He took a smaller bite and chewed thoughtfully. "I'm not sure why the Sanctum has him or who ratted him out, but it bothers me to the core that he's in this predicament. It might sound corny, but helping with this is the right thing to do. Sometimes my analytical skills are used to steal fortunes, or even take a life, and this time maybe they can help save one." Zed paused and took a slow, measured breath. "Does that make sense?"

Payne nodded. "It makes perfect sense to me."

"Same," Stone said.

Zed rose to leave. "Oh, and by the way, to answer your question before you ask it, platforms like that need to be resupplied. Think about that."

Before Payne or Stone could respond, he reached into the box for a carry-out slice and walked away.

No goodbye, no good luck, no kiss my butt. Just gone.

Payne said *Thank you* at his back but couldn't be sure if Zed had heard him. With a shrug of the shoulders, he looked over at Stone, and she gave him the look.

"What?" he asked.

"Next?" asked Stone.

Payne took a deep breath from his nose and exhaled it slowly out his mouth. He tossed empty pizza slice boxes and sauce-stained napkins back into the cardboard box.

Rising, he said, "Follow me."

Chapter 55
Washington, DC

Payne's feet felt like lead weights as he walked to the car. The director's admin had called and conveyed the order to report to headquarters for a debrief ASAP, but the long days and sleepless nights were starting to take a toll on Payne's body. The stress of the investigation demanded an immense amount of energy, and he needed to regroup and get some time soon to rest and properly grieve Wes Russell.

He looked at Stone as they walked the gravel path. "This is a hard job, Stone. Mentally, physically, and even emotionally. I hope you don't plan to have a family while you're in the FBI."

"Well, that's random as hell." Stone stopped along the pathway, raised a hand to her hip and stared at Payne.

He stopped. "I just want you to know what you've signed up for. Especially if you decide to make a career out it."

"I'm a graduate of the FBI Academy, Eli. Got the framed certificate from Quantico and everything. I'm still getting my feet wet, and I don't know if I'll go career-status until I'm in it for a while. But if I want to have a relationship or get married or have kids—with or without a man—I'll damned well do that."

"That's smart, Stone. And take it from me, the job is hell on a relationship. No set schedule, lots of time away. It's pretty hard to maintain any semblance of anything normal with a spouse or, God forbid, kids."

"Is that why you're single?" They started walking again.

"Maybe. Probably. Well, that and my bubbly personality." A wide grin formed on his face.

"Is that what killed the relationship with the Secret Service agent?" Stone looked over at him. "Your job was too hard?"

"Kind of, but so was hers." He grew quiet for a moment before he continued. "You can get by sometimes when one partner has a stressful job, but when both do, it becomes critical mass. Plus, I think fate stepped in."

"Fate's a bullshit excuse people throw out there to ignore the true issues that doom a relationship," Stone said with a forceful tone.

Payne was taken aback by the ferocity of her response.

"Let me ask you," continued Stone. "Do you still love her?"

"That's sort of personal."

"You started this conversation, mister," Stone said, "not me."

"Valid point," Payne said as he grew quiet. An entire minute passed before he replied, "Honestly, Stone, yes, I do."

"Then maybe it's meant to work out after all?"

"Doubt it."

"Why do you say that? Is she with someone else?"

"Not that I know of. Like me, she's married to the job."

"Maybe you should give it another shot," Stone said gently.

Payne frowned. "It ended badly."

"Jesus, Payne. Lots of relationships end badly. What are you, fifteen?"

"Hey, watch it! Most guys are fifteen, at least in their heads."

"Granted. But that doesn't mean it has to end for good. Relationships are hard, especially the really good ones, and God forbid if there's a penis involved. Those things fuck up everything they come in contact with. Literally." She jabbed him in the side as she uttered the dig.

Payne let out a guttural laugh. "Point made. And by the way, you might be more of a mess than me, Stone."

"Is she hot, by the way?"

"*Pffft*—of course," Payne said as he pursed his lips.

Stone laughed. "Then get back on that pony and take her for another ride around the ring, moron."

He shook his head. "You're not like most women, Stone."

"Yes, I know. I'm God's gift to the female race," she said and rolled her eyes.

His eyes narrowed.

"That's sarcasm, Payne. False bravado."

"I'll miss our banter when this case is over."

"Believe it or not, I will as well. You're starting to grow on me."

They arrived at his G-car and climbed in. Payne's cellphone buzzed, and he fished the phone from his pants pocket. The display in the corner of the screen indicated he had four voicemails.

Payne handed the phone to Stone, and he pulled out of the parking space. "Play these messages for me while I drive?"

"Sure, can do." Stone said.

She played the messages. On the second message, she smacked Payne on his right arm, which caused him to jerk the wheel slightly right.

"What gives? I'm trying to drive over here."

"Payne, you've got to hear this."

"Put it on speaker."

Stone replayed the message. When it finished, she asked, "Do you know this Special Agent Gabel?"

"Never heard of him."

"What do you want to do?"

"I need to call him back. Mind dialing his number for me? Put it on speaker?"

Stone gave him a crooked glance. "Sure, as long as you don't start thinking I'm your secretary or any such nonsense."

Payne smirked. "Nah, this is one of those partnerships deals."

The phone rang two times before a baritone voice answered. "Special Agent Gabel."

"Darius, it's Eli Payne from the Washington Field Office."

"Payne, yes. Thanks for getting back to me."

"Your message said you got a hit in SENTINEL on the words 'Body Man,' and you saw it referenced in my case file? We didn't see it here 'cause we've been out and about all day."

"Sure did. Pretty unique phrase, and I wondered if this guy they fished out of the Pacific last night might have something to do with your active missing-person case."

"Can you tell me more about this person you spoke with?"

"I haven't talked with him yet. I'm on my way back to the hospital now. His name is Hector Fuentes, and he was in rough shape when they brought him in. The nurse spoke with him last night and he asked to speak to the FBI when they got him stabilized. Something about military arms to the Middle East, and then he said something about 'the Body Man.'"

"Tell you what. I'm less than ten minutes out from headquarters and I'm about to walk into an important meeting. I could be a while but call me when you're in the room with Hector. I'll see if I can step out and be on the phone."

"Works for me. I'm about thirty minutes from the hospital."

"Thanks, I'll talk with you soon." As the call ended, he glanced over at Stone and gave her the Spock look, with one eyebrow arched higher than the other.

Payne and Stone tag-teamed the conversation with the FBI

director and three assistants and deputies. Tension filled the air as they got into the specifics, including the Zed connection and his detailed if brief info dump. The lines on the director's face became more pronounced as the story unfolded.

Payne finished with the call and information he'd just gotten from the Gabel connection in LA.

When Payne pulled up the oil platform diagrams on his smartphone, the director held a hand up in the air.

"Stop. We're moving this into the Strategic Information and Operations Center." Ludington walked over to his desk and pressed an intercom button on his desk phone. "Annie, please call down to the SIOC and tell them we're moving our meeting in there. We'll be there in the next few minutes. You know which room I want." He disconnected and turned back to Payne and Stone, who sat on the edge of the couch. "We're about to see if what this Zed says is legit intel or utter dogshit."

"I believe Zed," Stone said.

"So do I," Payne replied.

The director shook his head. "You're probably both right. I guarantee after what the last president did to restrict our intelligence-gathering competences, someone stepped in to fill the void. I didn't want to tip my hat earlier, but I'm familiar with the Sanctum. They are a massive international crime ring. I wasn't aware of any facilities stateside or in the Gulf, but their reach is far, and their grip is tight."

"What will happen if we confirm what Zed told us?" asked Stone.

The director considered her question. "Well, then the real fun stuff begins, Agent Stone. And you're about to be the first probationary agent to step foot into a lion's den."

Chapter 56
J Edgar Hoover Building
Washington, DC

Payne stared at the four oversized 8k hi-def screens lining the far wall of SIOC Operations Room One. His eyes narrowed as real-time intel flashed across the screens in a dizzying array of text and imagery.

Located on the fifth floor of the Hoover headquarters building, the space serves as a crisis management hub where global events are monitored, and operational initiatives are created. Each of many screens measuring four feet high and six feet wide, with less than an inch gap between the corners of the four biggest ones. It almost looks like an IMAX screen from the rear of the room.

The bottom left image held Payne's attention as it showed a satellite upload from the Gulf of Mexico. The other three screens displayed various images uploaded from Payne's case file, along with the oil platform diagrams and wire frames sent from his cellphone.

The feed showed live, real-time images above PIKE 84, an oil platform located in the Gulf of Mexico exactly at the coordinates provided by Zed. From space, the warm Gulf waters appeared still, the platform a stoic figure alone in a vast expanse of blue.

According to analysts from the Bureau of Ocean Energy Management and its sister agency, the Bureau of Safety and Environmental Enforcement, the platform had been mothballed eighteen months ago.

However, like many other abandoned platforms, its official fate hadn't been determined and the structure remained intact, albeit officially abandoned. While the BSEE was supposed to periodically inspect decommissioned platforms, the backlog and lack of resources made a physical inspection of many platforms virtually impossible.

Payne absorbed the constant activity inside the operations center and processed the sights and sounds. To his right sat the director in the center seat of a crescent-shaped wood and glass table that sat five. High-backed leather chairs sat spaced beside the table, and the room contained four identical tables all facing the wall of HDR screens.

The tone of the room had changed twenty minutes earlier when the director walked in and told everyone to lock it down. The room commander—at least, he'd been in command until Ken Ludington showed up—ordered the space locked. With a push of a single button, an electronic lock secured the only door to the room and a red light in the passageway lit up, reading ROOM IN USE – DO NOT ENTER.

Payne watched the director lob instructions at various staff members who scurried around the room in response. An unmistakable sharpness was present in the man's eyes as he absorbed data flickering from numerous sources simultaneously.

"What have the eyes in the skies revealed?" asked the director. "Do we know how many people are on the platform?"

"We have orbital and atmospheric assets in hand," replied a senior analyst, "but we need thermal images from the drone to be sure. We've been compiling images from satellites making passes over the platform."

"I thought you had images from NASA's WorldView satellite?"

"We did—do—and they show at least two people outside the structure on the seventh level. But we can't be sure; the satellite was only in range for a few minutes before it moved on."

"How long until we get thermal images and real-time video?" Ludington asked.

One of the other analysts with a phone placed to his ear cocked his head toward the director. "I'm on with Joint Reserve Base New Orleans. They're fitting the drone with a thermal imaging camera. It should be airborne within fifteen minutes."

"That's the best they can do?"

"We're lucky they even had one, sir. The Gray Eagle was only on base as a training tool, and they hadn't expected to use it for the purpose we requested. If you hadn't gotten on the horn, we would be tasking a bird from much farther away."

The director looked around the wealth of talent that filled the room and watched the several live and replayed satellite feeds of PIKE 84. "So tell me, ladies and gentlemen—is this it? Do we have the right spot?"

Micah Richardson, one of the senior analysts, spoke first. "Based on the intel we've collected, whoever is running the place didn't set up a vacation spot. The drone images will fill in some gaps, but I agree with the assessment that this platform is being used for illicit activity. We can't be sure yet what they are doing on the platform, but it's abundantly clear that they aren't supposed to be there."

The director stayed silent for several minutes.

"What are you thinking, sir?" asked Payne.

Ludington rubbed his chin and looked away from Payne and toward the image of the platform on the far-left screen. "Think it's time to call Quantico and get the Hostage Rescue Team ready for a trip to the Gulf."

"How long do they need?" asked Payne.

"They can be ready to deploy globally in four hours. I'll tell them they have two. I want a tactical operations center set up in Houma by dinner time."

Payne's phone started to vibrate. He looked down at the number and the area code showed a 310 number.

"This is that call I need to take, sir."

"Yes, of course," the director said. "Take it. I'll get the ball rolling with HRT and coordinate the trip to the Gulf."

Payne answered the call but covered the microphone with his hand. "Sir, Stone and I request to go with the HRT team."

The director smiled. "I wouldn't dare leave you here and miss out on all the action."

Payne gave the thumbs up and removed his hand from the microphone.

"This is Eli Payne."

Chapter 57
The Oval Office
The White House

President Steele shook hands with the Speaker of the House as she left the Oval Office, all smiles for the official photos snapped for the record. He noticed her wide smile twist into a menacing frown before she even made it past the doorway.

Dolores peeked in the doorway seconds after the speaker left. "Sorry to interrupt, Mr. President."

"Yes?"

"Director Kline is here. He has some urgent news regarding Agent Frazier."

The president's posture stiffened, and his heart rate increased. *Will this ever be over?* "All right. Please send him in."

Dolores stepped aside of the doorway and Secret Service Director David Kline strode in.

"Is this a good update, David, or a bad one?" asked the president as he gestured to the leather chair positioned in front of his desk.

Kline took his seat as instructed, taking in a deep breath before he spoke. "It's good news, sir."

"About time. Go on," said the president.

"The hospital called to inform us Danny is conscious."

President Steele appeared startled. "He's awake?"

"Yes."

"Talking?"

"Not yet. He's still intubated and heavily sedated."

"But he's aware of his surroundings?"

"It appears so. In and out, mostly out. But he's made requests for water and so on from nurses. He scratched a few things on a pad, but they're illegible."

Steele dropped into his chair and felt the room start to spin. Kline continued to relay what the doctors said about Frazier's condition and prognosis as the president's mind went into overdrive.

When Kline finished his update, the president said, "I want to see him."

Kline looked surprised and hesitant. "You want to ... see Danny, sir?"

"Correct."

"I guess we could arrange a visit. When?"

"Right away. Now, if he's awake," President Steele demanded. "I want to spend a few minutes with him."

"I didn't realize you two were that close?" The director eyed the president with a perplexed look on his face.

"He's an American hero, David. I've been worried sick about him ever since he was shot and want to see him with my own eyes and offer him my support."

"It will take some time to secure the floor and configure your motorcade route for this time of day, Mr. President."

"Bullshit," said the president with a firm tone.

The director appeared taken back by the outburst. Although the president was known for his temper and foul mouth, the director hadn't expected it at that moment.

"Pardon me, sir?"

"What did I say that was unclear? The floor is already secured by Secret Service agents, and we don't need to go full entourage. Send me with the same manpower you use on Saturday nights for poker at Al's house in Georgetown." Steele rarely missed a poker night at his college friend's home, but he'd started to miss more of them lately.

"That's different, sir."

The president rose from his seat and leaned his large body toward the director. "This is different too," Steele said coldly. "I'm not asking you if I can go, David. I'm telling you I'm going. You have your job because you're resourceful, so make the arrangements. I want to be on my way to the hospital in or before thirty minutes."

Before Kline could respond, Steele turned back to his desk, picked up a telephone and pressed a button. "Dolores, ask the motor pool to bring around my Corvette, please. The new blue one. Yes, North Portico will be fine."

Director Kline swallowed hard.

"I'm rolling into DC traffic in twenty minutes, Dave—with you or without you."

Kline nodded. "Yes, Mr. President. I'll tell the team we're traveling light today."

"See? That wasn't hard," said the president, who dismissed the director with a wave of his hand.

Once the director left, the president again lifted the receiver on his phone. "Dolores, get me a secure line. And disregard the Vette."

At the Plaza Hotel in midtown Manhattan, Marcus Rollings looked down at the Caller ID of the vibrating phone dancing atop the nightstand.

He looked away from the phone and toward Merci as she crept

toward him on all fours from the far corner of the large bed.

"You better not answer that *damned phone*," she said, her upper lip snarled as she uttered the last two words.

Rollings traced her voluptuous body with grateful eyes and then they rotated back to the vibrating phone.

"Got to. It's him." Rollings clicked the green *Accept* button. "Yes, sir."

"Where are you?" the president asked.

"Still in Manhattan, Mr. President."

"And did you retrieve the file already?"

"Yes, sir."

"Is Merci with you?"

"She's here."

"Having fun with her at the Plaza?"

"Wait—what?" asked Marcus, unable to mask the shocked tone in his voice.

"Marcus, I'm the President of the United States. Kind of hard to keep secrets from me."

"We're together at the moment, yes," Rollings said.

"Good. All I care about is the file. Did you look at it?"

"Absolutely not."

"Keep it that way. There was money or other stuff in the box?"

"There was. The box included …"

The president cut him off. "I don't give a shit what else was in there. It's all yours. I only want the file."

"Understood, sir, of course. Thank you, sir," Rollings said.

"And by the way, our buddy Danny Frazier woke up."

Rollings felt like Mike Tyson had slammed him with an uppercut. "Is he talking?"

"Not yet, but that will likely change soon. I'm on my way to the hospital to have a word with him."

"Regarding?"

"I'm going to get the location of the three remaining files. I need you back in DC tomorrow afternoon with your file. Both of you."

"Yes, sir, understood."

"Junior sent Casha down to the Gulf. He'll have a few words with Nick Jordan."

"And after we deliver the file to you?" asked Marcus.

"Your services will no longer be needed. You'll be free to go."

"No strings attached."

"None whatsoever."

"Thank you, Mr. President. We'll see you tomorrow."

The line went dead. Rollings tossed the phone back on the nightstand. "Where were we?"

Merci's arm cut through the air like a scythe through switch-grass and swatted his arm away while her free hand knocked him back against the headboard with a loud thump.

The action startled him. "What the—"

Merci was on him in an instant.

"It's my turn to show you some tricks."

Chapter 58
Houma, Louisiana

Peter Casha's shoulder throbbed hard with each bump and jostle on the two-hour flight. The 100mg Tramadol capsules and two shots of Gentleman Jack had worked some to dull the pain, but he was comfortable being uncomfortable and, at the end of the day, he knew he'd survive this.

His eyes closed as the compounding stress of the week surrendered to opioids and alcohol, and he slept. Thirty-four minutes later an abrupt jerk startled him as the aircraft's wheels touched down at sleepy South Lafourche Airport, the public airfield closest to the Gulf of Mexico.

The aircraft taxied to Galliano Airbase to refuel and disgorge its passenger. Casha stepped off the plane exhausted despite the cat nap. The Cajun heat and stifling humidity assaulted him like a Turkish steam bath. His clothes now clung to him like a second skin, irritating his wound that started to itch as he walked across the tarmac to a waiting helicopter painted bright yellow.

A five-seat Robinson R66 turbine engine spooled up as he approached, and the rotors began turning. Casha carried only a small duffel bag with essentials, including changes of clothes, although he hoped to complete the task before him in less than twenty-four hours. Two men greeted him at the left rear door of the helo. Casha noticed the R66's skids were equipped with emergency floats against an unscheduled water landing, but he smiled. If the helicopter was forced to land in the Gulf, it was unlikely the floats or the high-visibility yellow paint would save anyone.

One man took his bag to stow in the chopper and the other leaned in closely and spoke into his ear loud enough to compensate for the rotor wash and turbine whine. Casha nodded his head in response and climbed in. A few minutes later, the helicopter lifted off and made a smooth ascent into the air, turning toward the Gulf.

FBI Special Agent Fred Simmons watched the man with his left arm in a sling climb out of the Gulfstream G280 and proceed to the waiting helo.

He had concealed himself behind a large steel door while the rest of his team were setting up equipment in an empty hangar they'd turned into a de facto tactical operations center. They'd arrived around seven that morning and he dispatched two of his men to the marina in Port Fourchon as the others established the command post.

Through his powerful Nikon binoculars, Simmons watched the way the man walked and tried to memorize his facial features. The mystery man climbed into the bright yellow helicopter as Simmons made a call.

"Rich, it's Freddy."

"Hey, Uncle Freddy," said Rich Knappick, an FBI aviation analyst back at headquarters. "What can I do you for?"

"I need you to contact the FAA and track a helicopter."

"You still at the Houma airport?"

"Yeah, close. South Lafourche. Tail number is N as in November, two, zero, four, C as in Charlie, T as in tango."

"Solid copy. November-two-zero-four-charlie-tango?"

"Aye-firm. The helicopter will be headed south over the Gulf."

"I'm on it. We'll track and provide a flight path ASAP."

"Thanks, Rich. Let me know where it lands."

"Will do."

Next, Fred called the SIOC at FBI headquarters in DC. His great friend and partner in crime, a woman he'd worked with for almost twenty years, picked up the call.

"SIOC, Sanders," a female voice announced. She pronounced it *SY-OCK*.

"Kathy, it's Freddy."

"Hey, mister," said Kathy Sanders, "What's shakin' in the land of skeeters and gators?"

"Need a knife to cut this humidity. Maybe a chainsaw."

"I bet."

"A Gulfstream landed at the public airport in South Lafourche. Can you look up registry info for me on that?"

"Sure thing. Go ahead with the tail number."

"N as in November, one, nine, zero, N as in November, B as in bravo."

"Copy November-one-nine-zero-november-bravo, correct?"

"Affirmative."

"I'll ring you back when I've got something, hon."

"Appreciate it, Kath. Pull me a comprehensive flight history as well."

"Will do."

"Is the rest of the team on their way?"

"Yes, they left Quantico for Andrews about an hour ago. The director is even joining the HRT."

"No way—really?"

"You bet, and when the big dog joins in—"

Freddy cut her off and finished the statement. "—forget the bark and fear the bite."

Chapter 59
President's Private Study
The White House

President Steele leaned back in his chair. Large bags had formed under his eyes over the past few days, and he rubbed his temple in a slow, methodical fashion, trying to ease the stress from his overworked mind.

The study door swung open fast and startled the president from his reverie. Steele looked up to see his son restrained in the doorway and struggling against three large Secret Service agents. Behind them hovered Dolores, a frantic look on her face.

"I'm sorry, Mr. President! I'm so sorry, I told him you were busy and he rushed right by me ..."

Junior said, "We have to talk!"

Steele's face hardened and he waved off the protective detail. "It's all right guys, he's okay. Dolores, no calls, please."

"Yes, Mr. President!" Dolores said, on the verge of tears. The Secret Service agents released their holds on Junior and the younger Steele smoothed his hands down a three-thousand-dollar suit. "I told you, dumbasses," he spat at the agents as they withdrew, and Dolores closed the tall door.

"What the *hell* do you think you're doing?" the president shouted. "What *exactly*."

Junior replied, "I didn't hear back from you. How did the visit go with Danny?"

The president was angry, and he did nothing to hide it. "You're not planning on sleeping in the Lincoln bedroom, are you?"

Junior knew he wasn't welcome in the official residence. His father had made that clear soon after he'd moved in. "Of course not. I have my normal suite down the road."

"Perfect."

"The visit?" pressed Junior.

The president's mouth puckered. Slowly, he moved his head from one side to another. "Not as I hoped."

"Was he conscious?"

"Yes, for a few minutes."

"Did he talk?"

"No. He's still intubated."

"But he knew you were there?"

"Yes. I could see the recognition in his eyes. I asked how he felt and if he knew who I was. He nodded his head. One of the nurses gave him a notepad and pen, but what he wrote was illegible, gibberish really. Nothing more than a series of lines and dots." Steele frowned. "He's on lots of pain killers. He's probably all scrambled inside his head from the gunshot wound anyway."

"What did his doctor say?"

"There's a team of doctors now, and they're being vague. The consensus is that after a brain trauma, surviving patients will sometimes have to learn to speak and write all over again."

"'Surviving.' Possibly in doubt," Junior said. "Anything else?"

"They might remove the trach tube later tonight. If so, I've left clear orders that I want to be the first one to talk with him."

"Won't the Secret Service want to question him first?"

"Of course, but they work for me, don't they? I've made it clear that it would be better if I tell Danny about Nick's abduction.

Director Kline is on board with my decision."

"What if Nick already told Frazier the truth, or if he looked at the documents Nick gave him?"

"I'll improvise."

"Meaning?"

"Just what I said. I'll roll up my sleeves and do what is needed."

"You normally have others do your dirty work." Junior saw the grimace form on the corner of his father's mouth as he added, "Mr. President."

"You'd be surprised what a man is capable of when the fate of his presidency rests in the hands of others less capable."

Junior changed the subject. "Casha arrived at the facility."

Steele looked up. "When will he see Nick?"

"In the morning."

"If he fails at cracking him, well, let's say the circle of who knows what you've done is too big. In that case, I think it would be best to thin the numbers."

"What I've done?" Junior exclaimed, the intensity in his voice rising an octave.

"We're not having this discussion again, Junior," said the president as he raised his open hand and closed it fast into a fist.

Junior seethed. Through gritted teeth, he said, "And how do you suggest I 'thin the numbers,' as you put it?"

"However you see fit, but I don't want to know or be involved, anymore. There's already enough blowback on me."

Junior crossed his arms defensively. He wasn't entirely sure he'd be immune to any of the president's "thinning" program, son or no son. "Cleaning up a mess can get expensive and bloody. Depending on who I involve, they might not appreciate retribution on fellow operators."

Charles Steele glared at his only son. "Everyone has a price. After all, how do you think I got elected?"

Payne peered out the window at what looked like a snow-white down comforter covering the horizon contrasting with the deep blue sky above. He'd never been on a private jet, and the taxpayers' Gulfstream G550 served as one hell of a first time.

The director walked down the aisle past his seat and slowed up long enough to give Payne a nod.

A full contingent of Hostage Rescue Team operators from Quantico were following in two trailing planes. While special ops typically work in small numbers, the HRT works by the philosophy of safety in numbers. Formed in 1983, the elite group had come about due to the 1972 Olympic Games, when eleven Israeli athlete hostages were murdered by Black September Palestinian terrorists. The FBI vowed not to allow a similar incident to occur during the 1984 games held in Los Angeles and so created the HRT in response.

Payne was lost in thought as Stone walked down the aisle and stopped. He didn't notice her until she cleared her throat and snapped her fingers several times. Finally, he looked away from the window.

"Jeez, you zoning out or what, Payne?"

"Sorry. A lot on my mind."

"You don't say."

She went to sit next to him, where a book occupied the empty seat. She picked it up, and a broad smile spread over her face. "*The Escape Artist*, huh? You trying to find a way to ditch me?"

He raised his eyebrows but didn't respond.

Stone continued, "You and your novels. Always have a book within arm's reach, don't you?"

"I can't help the fact I'm educated," he paused before he continued. "Besides, most of the time the make-believe world is a hell of a lot more interesting than reality."

"Testy, testy," she said, emphasizing her T's and Y's.

"What do you need, Stone?"

"I got a call when you were on with Darius."

"Yeah? Who was it?"

"WFO. The tech guys were able to use facial recognition software and matched two of the guys from the photos we got at the Manassas airport manhandling Nick with the footage we retrieved from the Days Inn."

"Cool, guess we now have proof the same guys who dumped the car were at the airport with Nick?"

"That's correct. The match was ninety-five percent certain."

"I'll take those stats," Payne said.

"You going to tell me how your call went?" Stone asked. "As soon as you got back into the operations room, everything went nuts. I know you spoke briefly with the director about the call, but he had me working on other tasks and I never got the skinny."

Payne rubbed his eyes. "Oh, where to start."

"From the beginning. We've got some time before we land in Houma."

He recounted the conversation until Stone cut in.

"And you spoke with Hector Fuentes?" she asked.

"Yes, but only after I gave him immunity."

"Immunity? From what?"

"He was engaged in activities that may or may not have something to do with Nick Jordan."

"So why did he use the phrase 'the Body Man?'"

"Hector works at the Port of Los Angeles. A man named Peter Casha hired Hector and six other men to transfer shipping containers delivered by General Atomics from a ship bound for one of our bases in Italy to another ship. Hector and his men were paid to switch the containers."

"And where was this other ship headed?"

"Saudi Arabia."

"General Atomics. They're a defense supplier, right?"

"That's correct."

"And what was in the containers?" asked Stone.

"According to Hector, a dozen high-end military drones. State-of-the-art stuff."

"That's it?"

"Isn't that enough?" asked Payne.

"Well, sure, but..."

"Besides drones, there were missiles. Lots of them."

"So, someone is giving Saudi Arabia high-tech weapons of war?"

"Sounds that way," Payne said.

"And how does the Body Man tie into this?"

"Not sure. Hector didn't know anything about Nick. He only knew the term 'the Body Man' as a reference made by this Peter Casha guy."

"And is this Peter Casha his friend or a business associate?"

"Not a friend. Casha lured Hector and his men out to the Pacific with the promise of another job, but it was simply a ruse to kill them. He succeeded in killing everyone except Hector.

During the melee, Hector said he shot Casha in the shoulder and escaped."

"Can anyone corroborate what he said?"

"Analysts back at SIOC are running down what they can and hope to have some proof in the next few hours that Hector wasn't blowing sunshine up my skirt. General Atomics has already confirmed their shipment, although they don't think it's been hijacked. They swear it's still on a container ship bound for Italy."

Stone considered what Payne said. "What if Nick learned about this transfer of material to Saudi Arabia?"

"You mean as part of his job?"

Stone pointed her finger at him.

"Are you thinking the president had something to do with this?" Payne couldn't understand why he didn't find that ludicrous on its face. President Charles Steele had always struck him as kind of a douchebag anyway.

"Dunno—but if he did, it would be the perfect reason to get rid of the Body Man, wouldn't it?"

Payne asked, "Are you buying into Zed's conspiracy theories?"

"Truth can be stranger than fiction, more times than not."

"Yes, but as much as I think Steele is a dimwit, that's a huge leap for us to make."

"I agree. That's why we need to find the Body Man. He'll blow this whole case wide open."

"If he's still alive," Payne said.

"He is."

"How can you be sure?"

Stone's face turned grim.

"It's quite simple. Because he *has* to be."

Chapter 61
Houma, Louisiana

Payne and Stone walked into the expansive hangar housing the FBI Tactical Operations Center. Polished concrete caused their shoes to squeak as they moved against the smooth epoxy surface.

Payne headed straight for the back corner of the building where he found the command center composed of seven folding tables, a dozen laptops, and two sixty-inch flat-screen televisions. Special Agent Fred Simmons turned as Payne approached, a cellphone pressed against each ear, and gave Payne a head nod.

When the first call ended, he placed the phone on the table and held his index finger up in the air, letting them know he needed another minute for the other call. When the second call ended, Payne extended his hand to the agent from the Los Angeles field office.

"Good to finally meet you. Eli Payne."

"Eli, yes. The team's been waiting for you to arrive. I'm Fred Simmons, but everyone calls me Uncle Freddy."

"Sounds like you've been busy."

"Sure have. That mystery jet is owned by a shell company," Simmons said, "but there's some threads that tie it all the way back to SteeleCorp. Whoever set up the legal entities was pretty good. And trust me, they covered their tracks well. Too bad for them the FBI hires the best and someone screwed up along the way. Left a trail our team was able to follow."

"I find that unshocking," Payne said.

"Also," Simmons said, "SIOC got back to us on the image of the man from the jet. They ran it through the FBI national facial recognition database and got a hit at LaGuardia."

"And?"

"His name is Peter Casha."

The name surprised Payne, and he put his hands up to interrupt. "Really? You sure?"

"Yeah, SIOC confirmed it. Positive ID." Simmons saw the recognition in Payne's eyes. "Why? Does the name ring a bell?"

"It does." Payne's mind kicked into overdrive as he tried to piece together the growing evidence to form a cohesive storyboard in his mind.

Simmons continued. "SIOC determined Casha is an alias and they're running down everything they can on him, including known associates. Only a matter of time until they get his real name and figure out his connection to SteeleCorp—a helicopter chartered by SteeleCorp transported Mr. Casha out to the Gulf. Based on the coordinates, it landed on the abandoned platform we're lookin' at."

"Anything else?"

"We have another interesting development."

"I'm listening."

"Regarding the platform, your source from the Agency said to look into how it's supplied."

"That's right. What did you learn?"

"Most boats operate out of Port Fourchon to resupply the countless operational Gulf oil platforms, and we connected each supplier and their ships to the major companies that operate platforms in this area. That is, all but one."

"Let me guess." Payne didn't need to finish the thought.

"You got it," Simmons said with a grin. "The platform in question is resupplied by a single boat that operates under an LLC named P. Logan Enterprises. And get this, all the payments for their resupply business originate from an offshore bank account."

"Which one?"

"They run through a Cayman account, but the bank of record is Danske Bank, with a branch located in St. Petersburg."

"Russia?" Payne asked.

Simmons smiled again. "Not the Florida one."

"Well, since the Sanctum is supposedly a Russian outfit, that makes sense. But I'm surprised they would be sloppy like that."

"I agree, but think about it."

Simmons tapped his finger on a paper map of the Gulf spread out on the table. A red circle was drawn around the nominally abandoned PIKE 84 oil platform.

"How many people ever look into resupply ships operating in the Gulf?"

"Yeah, good point," Payne conceded. "And considering how many electronic transfers occur, few get looked at with any scrutiny."

"Anyway, I have two agents watching the boat right now. People look to be stocking it. My men asked around, and the locals say the resupply ships normally depart in the morning."

Payne asked, "Do we know how many men are on board?"

"Five, not including the captain, Bradley Taylor, who is also the owner. He moved here about six months ago, but folks we interviewed don't know much about where he's from or what he did before he arrived. Keeps to himself for the most part. There's a rumor floating around he has a military background, maybe

Army, possibly a former special operator, but nobody knows for sure."

"Anyone approached him?" Stone asked.

"Not yet."

The FBI director arrived halfway through the conversation without interrupting.

Payne turned to face him at this point.

"What do you think, sir?"

"Sounds like we need to pay Captain Taylor a visit."

Stone asked, "Are we playing good cop or bad cop?"

Ludington shrugged.

"If he's former military, it probably won't matter, but we'll roll the dice. I say we go in, ask some pointed questions, and then lay down the law. He either cooperates and we forget the fact he's abetting a crime syndicate, or we seize his boat for our thing and then throw the book at him when we get back."

"When do we go?" asked Payne.

"Now. Let's load up our gear and pay him a visit."

Payne's stomach tensed as he watched the full contingent of FBI rescue operators enter the hangar as a group and one word jumped to the forefront of his mind.

Overkill.

Rows of chairs had been set up to accommodate everyone. The video monitors in front showed real-time imagery beamed straight from the MQ-1C Gray Eagle drone circling high above PIKE 84, confirming fourteen people on the platform.

Payne watched the mass of HRT muscles and brawn assembled and knew it was way too much. These guys were about as subtle as hammers. On the flight from DC, Payne had gone over the intel from Zed several times. Although he hadn't shared it with anyone, a plan had formed in his mind.

While some agents in the Bureau might sit back, keep their mouths shut, and let the subject-matter experts do their jobs, Payne wasn't one of them. If something felt wrong, he spoke up. And if nobody listened, well, sometimes he'd get their attention.

FBI Director Kendall Ludington walked to the front of the space, but before he started to speak, Payne raised a hand.

"Yes, Payne? You have a question?"

"Sir, are we planning a full-scale assault on the facility?"

The director looked back with a quizzical look. "We don't have a plan yet. That's what we're here to figure out."

"Well, with all due respect, sir, if the consensus tonight is to go balls to the wall and hit the facility with everything we have, I think we'll have a problem."

"How so?"

"We need a small tactical team to conduct a precision strike, not a full assault team."

Ludington arched his eyebrows. Payne had his attention. "I'm listening, Agent Payne."

"I mentioned when we were in the SIOC that Zed's intel indicated the facility was only staffed by maybe a dozen people."

"Yes, I read that on the flight. Thermal imaging confirmed his data. Your point?"

"My point is, if our intention is to send in boats or chopper in and fast-rope to the deck, the Sanctum people will have spotted us from miles away. Once that happens, they'll likely kill Nick Jordan."

"How could you be sure?"

"Because that's what I'd do. If I had a valuable target I couldn't escape with and the heat was coming my way, I'd cap him and get out any way I could. Like rats fleeing a sinking ship. Leave no one to testify against me in court."

"And you have a suggestion on how we should proceed?"

"Yes, sir. We only need a small team, six HRT tops. Since we've already vetted Captain Taylor, we use his resupply boat and breach the facility undetected as part of the scheduled supply drop already expected for the morning. HRT can use the schematic of the facility to plan a small-scale assault. If we move quickly, we could secure Nick before they know what hit them.

The HRT commander, Austin Chapin, shook his head. "That's

not our standard operating procedure, Agent Payne. We normally breach with a superior force, including overwhelming firepower."

"I'm aware of your SOP, commander, but respectfully, you need to adapt to these unique conditions," Payne said. "Because a superior-force approach will get Nick Jordan killed."

Commander Chapin's face turned two hues of red, but before he could protest, Uncle Freddy Simmons stood up.

"Excuse me," Simmons said." I know I'm not a part of the HRT, but Payne makes a valid point. In my previous lifetime, I was a member of SEAL Team Five. We conducted many missions, including hostage rescues, on land and at sea. I agree we need to hit them hard, but the coordinated attack needs to be small. Above all, we must have the element of surprise—something we can achieve only by exploiting the resupply vessel. Our best chance for success is to go in light and tight, and hit 'em fast before they know what happened. I think Payne is on the right track."

Ludington turned, raising the question to Chapin. "Commander, your thoughts?"

"My team is capable of executing that type of raid, sir." Chapin's gaze focused on Payne as his eyes narrowed. "I'll admit coming in heavy could be problematic in the open ocean. Agent Payne makes a valid point."

"For argument's sake, let's say we went with what Payne suggested," said the director. "Do you have five men you'd take, Commander?"

"Of course."

"All I care is that we lay out a plan that mitigates the chance of Nick Jordan getting killed during recovery. Light or heavy makes no difference to me—I care about a successful retrieval." The director looked at Chapin. "Assuming we go light and utilize the resupply boat, what would that look like?"

Commander Chapin stood. "Well, the six of us would penetrate the facility—"

"Eight. The eight of us." Payne sat in the last row of chairs with Stone and stood up suddenly.

"Eight? What do you mean, eight?" asked Chapin.

"Stone and I aren't staying on the boat with the captain."

Chapin bristled. "Who said you'd even be on the damn boat?"

"We didn't come all this way to twiddle our thumbs in this hangar while your team breaches the facility."

"Yes, you did," countered Chapin. "Neither of you are quali-fied—"

"Director?" Payne shook his head and started to protest.

"I don't see a problem with them being on the boat," said the director.

Commander Chapin shook his head.

"Sir, I think this is a bad idea."

"We want to breach the facility with the team," Payne said.

"*Out of the question,*" Chapin countered. He turned away from Payne and toward the director, eyes ablaze and left hand clenched into a fist. "Look, sir, you can make an argument that Agent Payne is qualified to accompany us. That's fine. Several of my men have trained with him, he's proficient with firearms and HRT tactics. But there's no way on God's Green Earth we can let an untrained probationary officer come with us."

Payne could see where this was going and decided to change tactics since he knew an argument would get him nowhere.

"Look, Commander, according to the FLIR images we've reviewed, the platform has fourteen heat signatures. One of them we're certain is Nick Jordan, which leaves thirteen hostiles, at most. A handful of those are support staff who probably don't even know how to hold a gun, but let's say for argument sake they're not. You have thirteen people to deal with. Now, I know your guys well and you can take them out using a team of six.

Stone and I will stay out of your way. We simply want to ensure Nick is taken alive, not get in the way, be heroes, or steal any of your credit."

"Flattery will get you exactly dick in this scenario, Agent Payne," said Chapin as he slowly shook his head. "And you can have all the goddamned credit. My answer is still no on taking her with us."

Stone glared at Payne. Her eyes shot daggers and Payne knew what that look meant. A shitstorm was about to brew.

"Can I speak?" asked Stone.

"Hold up," Chapin said and held up his hand. "No offense to you or your abilities, Agent Stone, but we train for years to learn our craft, and this isn't a normal building we're about to breach. An oil platform is a logistical nightmare even for my guys, who know what the fuck they're doing. I don't want the responsibility of an inexperienced agent on her first assignment—that would be you—getting killed on my watch." He paused, then looked at Payne. "It looks bad on my annual FITREP. I mean, shit, Payne— besides the basic course at Quantico, has she ever even cleared a room?"

"Yes, she has. With me, in fact." Payne conveniently left out the fact the house was empty.

The perturbed look on Chapin's face only intensified. "That's not good enough."

"I vouch for her." Payne knew he'd never seen Stone fire a weapon.

"Whatever, still doesn't fly with me, Payne." Chapin gave a dismissive wave of his hand.

"She'll be on my six, and we'll both stay back as your team clears the facility."

"Doesn't matter. She's a liability, not an asset."

Payne wasn't interested in getting in a pissing contest, but he wasn't backing down. He looked at the director for support.

"Sir, we're a team. You told me from the first time we talked that this was my case. I call the shots. Well, I say she goes. We didn't come down here to watch someone else go out and rescue Nick Jordan."

The director stayed quiet.

The commander eyed Payne suspiciously, then looked back at the director.

"Sir. You're going to have to make the call on this. Payne and I will get nowhere, and we really need to plan this mission."

"I know in these situations you're normally granted implicit authority, commander, but I think given the unique circumstances, they both should go. If Payne trusts Stone, then so do I."

Chapin looked at Payne and made direct eye contact.

"I don't like this, Payne, don't like it at all." He paused and stared at the front of the hangar, his eyes darting back and forth between Payne, Stone, and the director. Finally he spoke, aiming a rigid index finger directly at Payne's chest. "She's *your* baggage. If something happens to her out there, it's your ass, not mine. You got that?"

Payne nodded. "Understood. She'll be fine. Trust me."

Over the next three hours a plan was hammered out. They reviewed it time after time until everyone on the team was comfortable with its execution.

FBI Director Ludington wrapped up the night. "Godspeed to all of you. At dawn, we bring back Nick Jordan and yourselves in one piece."

As the meeting broke up, most the group went to the far corner of the hangar where cots had been set up and team could all get some sleep.

Payne and Stone lingered.

Commander Chapin approached and got right in Stone's face, close enough that she could smell his breath, feel the heat from his nostrils. He thrust something toward her. Stone's hand reached out and felt the cool touch of metal. "You know how to use this thing?"

Stone held the H&K MP5 in her right hand. "Yeah," she said, "you take the pointy part and aim it at a bad guy and pull the trigger thingy. Bang-bang, he's dead."

"Don't fuck with me, Stone." Chapin stared her down. "You're an uninvited guest at my party and I gotta know you aren't going to fall in my punchbowl."

Stone returned Chapin's glare and without looking down pushed out the rifle's rear pin, removed the stock, and the lower. Next, she pulled the bolt and carrier assembly away from the frame. Her eyes never left Chapin's as she put the weapon back together and presented it at port arms, as if for inspection.

"Look, I know you don't want any weak links on your team," she said.

He looked down at the weapon, surprise on his face. He was impressed, and this angered him even more.

"I'm not a weak link," Stone said. "I know my stuff."

He shook his head. "It's not only about the equipment, Stone. Trust takes time to build, and while you might be a fine agent, even veteran agents have been known to freeze in active-shooter situations, especially their first one. I don't know how you'll react when the shit hits the fan. But I know exactly how my men will react. That's why I trust them with my very life. I've built no such rapport with you."

The director approached but remained quiet.

Stone said, "I understand trust must be earned, not given—so give me this chance to earn it. I want Nick Jordan back alive."

"And I don't want you coming back in a body bag," Chapin

said. His aggressive tone had softened considerably.

"Well, finally we have something in common." Stone displayed a slight smile.

"As long as we're on the same page."

"We are."

Chapin paused for a moment, then raised a fist to her. Without missing a beat, Stone bumped it with her own fist and the commander went to his cot.

As Chapin left, Ken Ludington stepped forward. He put one hand on Payne's shoulder and the other on Stone's. "Commander Chapin might have a chip on his shoulder, but his main concern is the safety of his team, including you two. I'd go to hell and back with any HRT member anytime."

"We know that, sir," Stone said.

The director squeezed their shoulders and left.

Payne leaned toward her. "After what you said when we cleaned out Jordan's safe, I didn't think you were into guns. How'd you know how to field strip the MP5?"

"You assumed I don't know guns because I asked about that one weapon. And like the saying goes, when you assume it makes an ass out of you ..."

Payne completed the trite phrase, "... and *me*. Good point."

Stone smiled. "Thanks for covering for me."

"You're welcome, but if someone busts a cap in your ass, I don't want your mommy and daddy giving me a hard time. Copy?"

"Solid copy. But what if it's me having to save your butt out there?"

Payne grinned. "I'm going to risk that."

Chapter 63
PIKE 84 Sanctum Facility
The Gulf of Mexico

Peter Casha woke up with his shoulder feeling like Mike Tyson had used it for a punching bag the night before. He walked across the hall to the bathroom and the reflection looking back from the mirror revealed he looked even worse than he felt.

After a fast shower, he walked back to his room and got dressed. The sling provided by the doctor hung on the chair in the corner of his room. He decided against using it when he went in to see Nick Jordan. The sling conveyed weakness, something he couldn't afford to project when he faced the Body Man.

After dressing, he left his room and took the narrow hallway to the cafeteria. As he ate, he overheard two workers complaining about the leftovers and how the resupply ship was supposed to arrive in an hour.

He walked back to the room and his phone rang. It still amazed him that he got cell reception inside a big tin can in the Gulf. He looked down at the Caller ID.

"Yeah, what's up?"

"You talk to him?" asked Joe Lagano.

"No, headed that way in a few. Why?"

"Change of plans."

Casha hated last-minute changes. "Don't say I came down here for nothing and they want me to leave without putting him through the wringer?"

"Well, yes and no."

"Meaning what exactly?"

Lagano said, "Go see him, but there's nothing to talk about."

"Kill him?"

"Exactly."

"What changed?"

"The president spoke with Danny Frazier a bit ago. He fed Danny some bullshit story that the files Jordan had given him contained evidence implicating the vice president in a series of crimes, and that he had given Danny those files for safekeeping while they considered how to bring charges against the vice president."

"Seriously?"

"Yes."

"And Frazier fell for it?"

"Yes, but he was pretty jacked up on pain meds. The president can be a dick, but he can sell a boxcar of powdered milk to a dairy farmer."

"So, he has the files?" asked Peter.

"Not yet. I'm on my way to get them now. Frazier stashed them at three banks around the DC metro area in safe deposit boxes."

"Clever."

"Agreed. Look, bro, get in there, take care of the Body Man, and get the hell out. I got a bad feeling about this."

"In what way?"

"Frazier is dead."

Casha was surprised. "Since he talked with the president?"

"Yes."

"He crashed?"

"All I know is he was alive. He spilled the beans. And now he's dead. End of story."

"Did someone hasten his demise?"

"Not sure."

Casha mulled over the news.

"You think Junior or the president is about to double-cross us? Maybe tie up loose ends by putting us in the crosshairs next?" Casha knew the business they were in often held such reverses of fortune.

"I'm not sure, but I think we need to get this whole thing wrapped up and watch our sixes at the same time."

"Should I bounce?" Casha asked. "I can walk out of this facility and leave Nick Jordan to rot in his cell. The helo's still here."

"No, finish him off, then bounce. We'll be okay."

Casha was conflicted, but he decided to continue with the hit. "Fine. I'm on my way to the interrogation room now."

"You going to use a gun?"

"No, something a little more personal."

"The Omega?"

"Precisely."

"Is that wise, considering your shoulder?"

"He's chained to a table. What can he possibly do?"

"A caged tiger is always dangerous."

"I got this," said Casha. "I'm no snowflake."

Chapter 64
The Gulf of Mexico

It was Payne's first time on the Gulf. For all his trips to Florida over the years, he'd never ventured to the western side of the state. The closest he'd ever got was Legoland in Winter Haven with an old flame and her son.

Someone had told him the Gulf waters stayed modestly calm most days, with rather short swells.

Someone had fed him a line of crap.

The resupply vessel bobbed up and down as it powered through one wave after another, heaving up and down like a rubber ducky in a bathtub. According to the mission brief the team received before dawn, the winds had picked up overnight and the normally calm Gulf waters were acting more like the Atlantic, with heavy chop.

A storm was brewing, and the timing couldn't be worse.

As the waves rolled, Payne caught himself staring at the operator next to him. The man was slipping a worker's coverall over his uniform. A patch on the operator's left uniform shoulder displayed a bald eagle holding a broken chain in its extended talons. The Latin phrase *Servare Vitas* exemplified the reason the HRT exists: *To Save Lives*.

In the distance, Payne saw the towering oil platform as it rose out of the sea. Relatively small compared to newer platforms, it was the first one Payne had ever seen with the naked eye.

To him, it looked like the biggest thing on the planet.

The older structure was comprised of nine levels. When in service, the lower six floors were used for oil extraction while the upper three served as living quarters, maintenance rooms, and a control center. A yellow helicopter sat tied down to a helipad atop the southwest corner of the top level.

As the boat got close to the platform, Payne thought about Peter Casha and what had brought him to the facility. The analysts back at SIOC had pieced together a rough bio but were still hadn't located his real identity. Facial recognition software placed him in various countries around the globe over the past year, and several of those flights were on jets tied to the same shell company.

A security camera near one of the loading docks at the Port of Los Angeles had caught Casha's image a few days earlier, which corroborated Hector Fuentes' story about the containers. The rough dossier compiled on Casha revealed a few known associates. Flagged communications took place between Casha and Joseph Lagano, the global head of security for SteeleCorp. Also, calls had been traced to Marcus Rollings, an information technology analyst based in the DC area.

The operator to Payne's left tapped him on the shoulder and held up two fingers.

Two minutes out.

Payne rarely felt nervous, but his stomach tightened as the supply vessel approached the platform. Out of his element, Payne took several deep breaths, which helped—at least for the moment. Grateful he'd skipped the Burger King sausage croissant sandwiches Uncle Freddy had handed out thirty minutes before they'd climbed into the boat, Payne was still surprised the contents of his stomach weren't on his boots by now.

Ahead, Stone stood next to Commander Chapin. Payne regretted giving her such a hard time. Stone had proven herself more than capable. Beside that, she'd started to grow on him, like the little sister he'd never had. As attractive as Stone was, little sister is all she'd ever be. Payne had a firm policy against sleeping with the help.

The captain started turning the boat around as the vessel approached the oil platform. Standard practice dictated he back the stern up to the platform for unloading. Some of the larger platforms required compact cranes to unload gear, but this boat was a smaller-crew, transport-style vessel that pulled close to the platform to offload supplies and men.

When they were close enough, Payne could see two men on the lower metal walkway awaiting their arrival. They had AK-74Ms slung across their chests.

The captain gave a wave. The men recognized him as they returned the gesture. "Thirty seconds," he yelled to the team over the rumble of the engines.

The six HRT operators, Payne and Stone wore identical dark blue jumpsuits with the resupply ship's insignia on the upper-right chest, the same outfit the captain and his men had worn each time they delivered supplies twice a week.

Commander Chapin turned to the team and said, "Let's do this!" as the boat idled next to the platform.

Chapter 65
PIKE 84 Sanctum Facility
The Gulf of Mexico

Nick Jordan finished his hundredth push-up and stood in the center of his cell. With his head clear of the narcotics, he needed the exercise to burn off the last dregs of the chemicals the Sanctum had pumped into him.

The sound of footfalls echoed down the hallway.

The noise caused him to move back to the cot, where he'd hidden the pencil. Using the metal in the corner of the bed frame, he'd sharpened it as best he could until it had become a finely pointed weapon. If the opportunity presented itself, he'd only have one shot with the homemade shiv.

As the steps drew closer, he retrieved the weapon and placed it between his waistband and skin, careful to pull his shirt loose to conceal the shiv. Moments later, the door unlocked, and two guards entered the cell with leg and ankle restraints.

"You have visitor, prisoner," said one of the men in a Russian accent thick as potato soup.

Jordan countered, "Please tell me it's Amal Clooney. I've been waiting for her to show up and get me out of this godforsaken shithole."

The guards looked at each other and shrugged.

"Who is this?" asked one.

"George's wife?"

Nick figured neither man had a clue what he was talking about. Their blank expressions revealed they didn't get the joke.

"She's an international lawyer and human rights activist."

"We have no fucks for your rights, prisoner."

"No, of course you don't." Jordan held out his arms as the two burly men approached with handcuffs.

Jordan waited inside the interrogation room. Shackled to the floor and table facing the entry door, there wasn't much for him to do but stare at the wall and try to remember how many bad movies he'd seen with windowless interrogation rooms just like this one. The dark, filthy walls dripping with moisture, poor lighting, and the single shaded light hanging over the table. It was right from a screenwriter's fever dream.

After the guards left, Jordan confirmed he had enough slack in the restraints to reach his waistband.

Several minutes passed, the door lock clicked, and a man Jordan didn't recognize walked in. The man had a ring of keys in his right hand, and he pushed the door closed behind him with the other hand. He used one of the keys to lock the door.

Odd, considering they usually get buzzed in and out, thought Nick.

"Well, you're not Amal," said Nick.

Surprisingly, the man understood the reference. "I'm not George, either." A half-smile appeared on the stranger's face. "I'm better looking than him, though."

The man was six feet tall, maybe slightly more, with thick, dark hair and several days of stubble down his face and neck. Sharply dressed and sporting an expensive Tag Heuer watch, he spoke without a Russian accent, which set him apart from the others except Sir. Behind the polished exterior, Nick sensed a man in physical pain. The bulge under the man's shirt at the left shoulder looked to be the source, and Jordan observed the man favored that arm as if it was poking him.

He walked behind Jordan and paused, a set of burning eyes bearing down on the prisoner. After several seconds, the mysterious man continued around and took the interrogator's seat. Jordan got a good look at the hilt holstered on the man's right hip as he sat down. The blade looked a lot more lethal than the stubby pencil tucked between Nick's waistband and bare skin.

The man placed the key ring down on the steel table. Nick looked at the keys out of the corner of his eye. Judging by their location, they were out of reach of his restricted hands.

"Hello, Nick. At last we meet. I've heard an awful lot about you." The man stared straight into Jordan's eyes as he spoke.

He was surprised to hear his actual name. They hadn't uttered it once since his ordeal at the facility began. "They normally just call me 'prisoner' here."

"Well, I'm not them."

"Then who the hell are you?"

"My name is Peter Casha."

"Are you here to free me, Mr. Casha?"

Casha's left eyebrow arched higher than the right.

"Yeah, Nick. I guess you could say I'm here to set you free."

The sudden, ear-splitting sound of automatic gunfire echoed down the hallway, and both men instinctively reached for two vastly different forms of weaponry.

Chapter 66
The Oval Office
The White House

Charles Steele knew he should feel relief. After facing certain disaster, he would soon possess all the evidence damning him and he could begin the arduous process of cleaning up the collateral damage. He'd come close—too close—to not only losing his company, but also his presidency.

As he circled the Oval Office, something still felt wrong. A nagging suspicion from the pit of his stomach gnawed at him. But with Danny dead and Nick Jordan joining him momentarily, the president came up with nothing.

Dolores interrupted his pacing. "Mr. President, your son would like a word."

With a perturbed tone, Charles stopped and walked back to his desk. "All right. Send him in."

Junior entered and started talking before the president fully sat down. "Joe told me Danny provided the location of the files."

"That's correct." The president leaned back in the chair. "Joe is on his way to retrieve them."

"How about the file Marcus and Merci recovered?"

"Also on its way."

"Looks like everything is coming together."

"It almost became a clusterfuck." The president raised his voice and balled his fists in nervous anger. Junior thought he might be struck with them.

"But it didn't."

The president looked up and made direct eye contact with Junior but said nothing.

"What's next?" Junior asked. He averted the president's probing gaze and instead looked out the windows toward the Rose Garden.

"I've instructed everyone to meet me here at nine tonight. I've got a fundraiser in Charlotte that will take most of the afternoon. Once I'm back, I'll wrap up all the loose ends."

"Meeting here at the White House? Is that a good idea?"

With a sharp glance, the president replied, "Not in the building. Under it."

"The tunnels?"

"Yes. There's an incinerator in the lower level. Once I have all the evidence in hand, I'll destroy it myself. Frankly, I'm sick of the amateur hours." His eyes bore into Junior as he enunciated the last few words. "It's time to put an end to this nonsense, once and for all."

Junior ignored the jab. "I'll see you at nine."

"No. You won't."

"And why not?"

"You won't be there. Go home, Junior. And don't make any more fucking messes." The president's tone reinforced the anger his face displayed. "I've placed you in charge of a highly respected and enormously profitable company. Don't screw it up again. With Nick Jordan eliminated, the files destroyed, and hopefully soon, the transfer of the weapons to the Saudis complete, SteeleCorp will thrive in a new and profitable market. We'll get a foothold in a part of the world that few American companies can enter."

Junior wanted to protest but knew it wouldn't do any good. Once his father set his mind to something, no one, not even a higher power, could dissuade him. And on the entire Earth, at least, Charles Steele *was* the higher power.

Besides, Junior thought, he had unfinished business with two senators and a handful of congressmen before he left town. There was also the pretty little thing working for the Speaker of the House. He imagined what the afternoon with her at the Hay-Adams might entail until his father's stern expression brought him back to reality.

"Thank you for all your assistance, Mr. President," Junior said through gritted teeth, not meaning a word of it.

Chapter 67
PIKE 84 Sanctum Facility
The Gulf of Mexico

Payne watched the supply boat's stern edge closer to the platform. He felt his pulse quicken as his right foot tapped on the deck in a rhythmic beat.

Two men met the boat on the walkway located on the lowest level of the platform. They tossed over thick, braided ropes to the boat crew. The captain swung over first with Commander Chapin on his six. The two Russians bristled as they saw Chapin, clearly someone they did not recognize. The captain said something and pointed first toward the commander and then toward the boat. The two men nodded. Whatever he'd said appeared to satisfy the men's concerns. Both the captain and Commander Chapin swung back to the boat and grabbed supplies, then the rest of the team came over two at a time.

As Stone landed on the metal walkway and passed by one of the men, he gawked and leaned toward her. She could smell a foul odor of salted herring and pickled mushrooms on his mouth.

In broken English and a clearly Russian accent, he said, "So, you are captain's hot sister-in-law? And you know how to lift something heavy?"

Stone smirked, looked down toward the man's crotch and

back to his eyes. "Well Boris, I don't see anything heavy around here. But sure, I can handle very big ones."

The man let out a hearty laugh and slapped the other guard on the shoulder. "I like this one! This one is keeper."

Two large canvas duffel bags and a pallet holding a half-dozen plastic crates filled with essential supplies moved over via ropes and pulleys attached to the structure.

Payne turned to Stone as he started up the steps. "What the hell was that about?"

"Apparently dick jokes are funny in Russia, too."

Payne shook his head. "You have a way with men."

"If you can deal with a toddler, you can handle a man."

The supplies were divided up. The eight disguised members of the rescue team trudged up the fourteen flights of stairs, two sets for each level, until they reached the seventh floor. The duffel bags contained legitimate supplies but concealed under a false bottom were the team's weaponry and breaching material.

The two Russians said nothing, nor did they volunteer to help hump anything up the steps.

The metal lower stairwell was slick with seawater, but as the team climbed higher, the footing improved. Within several flights, Payne and Stone's legs grew tired, their arms ached.

The stairway ended at a solid steel door on the seventh level. With no handle or visible lock, Payne saw the closed-circuit security cameras above the door pointed downward. The two guards moved from the back and approached the door, and the larger of the two waved at the air. A buzzing sound came from the door jamb, and the door opened.

In single file, the team entered a dimly lit space.

Payne looked around the room. He didn't see any closed-circuit cameras. The space had several large drums of chemicals and a few other boxes, and it appeared to be used solely for storage.

As one of the canvas bags containing their weapons hit the ground, it made a loud *clank* sound. The two Russians exchanged glances.

The larger one said, "What is this?" He moved toward the bag.

Commander Chapin was on the Russian as the man bent over.

Randy Riggs had the other one.

Both Chapin and Riggs withdrew prepared syringes from coverall pockets, yanked off the orange caps with their teeth, and jabbed the needles into both men in a synchronized fashion. The two operators pressed the plungers, sending enough drugs into their systems to ensure neither man would be a problem for hours. The two were then flexicuffed and their ankles bound, and a length of duct tape was applied to their mouths. Both bodies were stuffed in a closet of sorts in the corner of the room.

As Chapin and Riggs secured and gagged the Russians, Dirk Benedict, the IT guy on the team, removed his laptop and plopped down on the floor to hack into the platform's network. Zed had provided the essential details for him to breach the system efficiently, but more importantly, with speed.

Benedict had expected at least a minor challenge, but what he found as he ran the IP scanner was that there was a guest entry point. He let out an audible laugh that caused the others to turn and stare.

"They didn't change the default login," he said, shaking his head with an amused grin.

"Meaning?" asked Chapin.

"The login is admin, and the password is—wait for it—password."

Even game-faced Chapin was pleased.

Payne spoke up. "Zed said they didn't put too much into security features since this joint is out in the open water."

"Russians don't have the best reputation when it comes to

work ethic," Stone said.

Within thirty seconds Benedict had identified the system file that controlled the security cameras and gained access to all video. He recorded a minute-long loop of all the cameras currently online. Next, he set those videos to continuous playback in order for the teams to move through the floors undetected.

"We own the video," Benedict announced.

Chapin nodded. "Good deal. Let's roll."

They split into preassigned groups. The A-team included Commander Chapin, Riggs, and Dan Duncan. The B-team included George Peppard, Dwight Schultz, Benedict, Payne, and Stone. Everyone removed the supply ship coveralls, revealing matching black BDUs. The canvas bags emptied, and Chapin handed out H&K MP-5/A3 10mm submachine guns with suppressors and extra mags. Beside the submachine guns, Riggs and Benedict each carried Benelli M4 twelve-gauge shotguns slung over their backs.

The weapons acted as door breaches in lieu of explosives. All members carried Glock 22 Gen4 .40-cal pistols on their hips. Everyone was also equipped with various combinations of flash bangs, knives, and explosive breaching charges for the numerous doors they were sure to encounter.

The two teams would search levels seven, eight, and nine even though the intel indicated Nick Jordan was probably on the eighth level. Stairwells in the corner of each floor were the easiest way to move among the platform's levels.

Both teams stayed together to clear level seven. Besides the storage room, the floor contained a laboratory, a medical bay, and a dozen other rooms. After they cleared floor seven, the teams would split, with the A-team searching level eight and the B-team level nine.

All three levels had identical floor plans. A narrow hallway in the shape of a square allowed access to each floor via corner stairwells. Rooms filled the center and lined the outer portion of each square, with the four stairwells allowing access among the levels.

The combined team moved down the hall in a stack, with Payne and Stone bringing up the rear. Briggs reached the lab door first. With his MP5 raised, he turned the handle and gently pushed the door open, stepping inside.

Across the room, a startled lab technician in an oversized white lab coat spun off from his barstool as Chapin, Briggs, and Peppard made their way into the long, narrow space.

Briggs saw the tech leap from the seat and lunge for a box on the opposite wall with a red button in the center. A US Navy SEAL before he joined the HRT, Briggs let his MP5 drop and reached to his right leg.

In one smooth motion, he unfastened the Ontario MK3 Navy knife and let it fly at the tech. The knife struck the side of the slender man's neck a good yard before he reached the alarm box, severing his right carotid artery below the internal and external branches and interrupting blood flow to the face and brain. His body crumpled to the ground and twitched uncontrollably for seconds while bright red blood gushed from the neck wound.

Briggs calmly walked over to the body, removed the knife from the man's neck, and wiped the blood dripping from the blade on the technician's white lab coat before he sheathed the weapon.

It took the team six more minutes to clear the entire floor.

With the seventh level secure, the teams split up, with the A-team taking the north stairwell and the B-team taking the south. They stayed in constant contact on their comms and planned to meet up when one of them acquired Nick Jordan.

The A-team ascended the stairwell and arrived in the passageway on level eight. According to the planning intel, Nick

Jordan was supposed to be in one of the three rooms to the right as they exited the north stairs. The element of surprise disappeared when two guards turned the distant corner and saw the darkened silhouettes of the team.

Both hostiles raised their weapons and fired bursts of automatic fire in the direction of the shadows. Commander Chapin, Riggs, and Duncan returned fire as they ducked into an open room and bullets struck the walls around them.

A deafening sound filled the hallway as the shots reverberated down the narrow, enclosed space. As the sounds of the bullets abated, the wailing of an alarm took its place. Commander Chapin clicked the stopwatch on his wrist. Only minutes if not seconds stood between Nick Jordan and certain death.

In the control room where all the security functions flowed, the ear-splitting sound of bullets and the high-pitched alarm startled Sergei Alexeyev from the monotony of watching the cameras. A minute before, he'd returned from his morning constitutional in the bathroom down the hall, stopped at the cafeteria, and poured himself a fourth cup of coffee on the way back to his closet-sized server room. He scowled at the array of images on the screens before him. The four monitors were split into six small screens, each showing various images throughout the facility.

As he looked at the video, there was no movement. But something felt wrong. Then the gunfire erupted.

With a few clicks of the mouse, he determined someone had gained access to the system and run a continuous loop of empty images across the system. Thirty seconds later, he disabled the unauthorized access and live images from the platform flooded his screens.

"*Dermo!*" Sergei swore as he struggled to pull a cellphone from his skin-tight pants pocket.

Chapter 68
PIKE 84 Sanctum Facility
The Gulf of Mexico

Nick Jordan watched as Peter Casha reached for the protruding hilt on the right side of his utility belt. Jordan's mind slowed the events down as if they were happening in slow motion.

At least it isn't a gun. Jordan knew he'd stand no chance against a bullet fired at point-blank range. With his hands and feet bound, he'd have no way to defend against a hollow point.

Jordan went for the pencil. It sounded like a bad joke—a knife versus a pencil. But Jordan was aware that the ability to improvise often determined life or death in an impossible situation.

Jordan watched Casha pull the knife from its sheath. His practiced motion suggested this wasn't his first dance. Their eyes locked for a moment, and then Casha lunged across the table.

With the pencil gripped tightly, Jordan swung it up and away from his body at a forty-five-degree angle. The sharpened pencil moved in an arc, and Jordan twisted his body to dodge the impending steel blade. That body English gave his thrust a bit more power.

Jordan had taken fencing lessons as a teenager, and his fast reflexes and ability to parry came as second nature to him.

The move worked, but barely, as Casha's blade missed Jordan's neck by less than a quarter inch. It was close enough that he felt Casha's hand brush past his neck hairs.

Jordan completed the arc of his swing in an upward stab, thrusting the pencil into Casha's chest. Crude but effective, the pencil pierced skin easily and slipped between two ribs, lodging halfway in the chest cavity.

Casha's eyes grew wide when the pencil burrowed deep into his flesh. His body stiffened and, too late, his hands shot out in a defensive position. The knife fell from his hand and made a metallic sound as it bounced several times along the floor, coming to rest next to the wall.

Casha fell backward and landed with a dull thud back into his chair. A stunned expression overtook his face as a blood spot formed around the wound and spread down his shirt toward his navel. The gunfire from the hallway was loud and intense and now right outside the interrogation room door.

Jordan reached for the key ring. Casha's lunge across the table had pushed them within reach. He located the one for his restraints and started with the handcuffs and then the shackles.

"I never saw that coming, bro," Casha said. A trickle of blood started at the corner of his mouth before he added, "Slick move."

"Some of that pencil is probably in your right ventricle, Peter. If you remove it, you might bleed out in the chair. Leave it in to plug the hole, and you may survive long enough to get medical attention." Jordan paused as he cocked his head toward the hallway and the sound of gunfire. "It's your choice," he said, then added, "bro."

A half-smile formed on Casha's face. He had to admit he'd been beaten at his own game. "You know who sent me, don't you?"

"Same person who had me locked up."

"He won't rest until you're dead. What are you going to do?"

Jordan unlocked the door and turned back toward Casha.

"I'm going to burn his damned house down."

Chapter 69
PIKE 84 Sanctum Facility
The Gulf of Mexico

The gunfire woke Sir from a deep sleep. At first, he thought the loud alarm klaxon and the powerful clanging sound of lead on metal was in his dream, but dreams fade to black when your eyes open.

This one didn't.

Sounds of bullets fired in rapid succession a floor below were impossible to mistake for anything but an attack on the platform. He ran across the hall to the server room and watched confirming images from the closed-circuit cameras flashing across the screens.

He yelled at Sergei. "Who the hell are they?"

Sergei shook his head. "No clue. But they are good. American special ops, I think."

"We need to get out of here," Sir said. His eyes scanned the facility and flipped among several cameras. Then he caught something on the arm of one of the soldiers. He pointed to the screen and told Sergei to pause the image.

Servare Vitas. Sir knew that patch, and in an instant, he knew who these people were—the FBI Hostage Rescue Team.

He needed an escape plan and realized the next few seconds

would determine whether he lived or died. Without hesitation, he told Sergei to flee and ran back to his room. Sir grabbed a go bag and headed down the hall to Evelyn Rhimes' room.

The sound of more gunfire erupted below.

"We've got to get out of here!" he shouted, bursting into her room without knocking.

"What's going on?" Rhimes was already getting dressed. She hastily pulled on a navy-blue shirt over her red bra and buttoned the ivory-colored buttons.

"An FBI hostage rescue team has breached the facility. They're coming for the Body Man."

"We've got to stop them."

"Us and what army? I'm an interrogator, not a soldier."

Rhimes stuffed clothes and personal belongings into a gray canvas duffel bag.

"We've got to go *now*," said Sir as he gripped her by the elbow and practically pulled her out of the room.

"Get your hands off me." She spoke in a deep, guttural tone.

"If you stay here, you die." Sir yanked on her arm harder. "I do not intend to die here."

They were at the fifth-floor landing before she came to a sudden stop.

"Listen, we have to go back," Rhimes said, stopping. All around them rang the roars of men and submachineguns.

"For what?"

"For *him*."

"Look, I told you, a team breached the facility to rescue him. We can't stop them."

"Then we do what we were paid to do and kill him."

"The SteeleCorp guy, Casha, will do that. It's why he came. We're in the clear."

Rhimes drew a weapon from the black Chanel purse draped

across her right shoulder. "We need to make sure he takes care of the Body Man before we leave."

Sir raised his hands. "Hold up, Evelyn. What are you doing?"

"If we leave here and he's still alive, we're as good as dead."

Sir didn't respond.

"If the Chief finds out we let him live, he'll skin us alive."

Sir shook his head, and he pointed above. "I'm not worried about any of that. You need to focus on the here and now. This is simple, Evelyn. If we go back up there, we will die, or they'll arrest us, which is worse than death." Perspiration formed on his forehead as he wiped off beads of sweat with his left arm.

She trained her weapon at him.

"That's a chance we'll have to take."

"Are you fucking crazy?" Sir's face grew red.

She gripped the gun harder. "Move it, man. I don't want to shoot you, but I will. Get up those stairs."

Sir turned and took a tentative step with a feigned attempt to place his hands up in the air. He felt certain imminent death awaited them if they went back in. He went two flights before he decided on his course of action. Less than six steps from the final level, he missed a step and fell hard on to the metal grated steps.

It wasn't accidental.

Rhimes lowered her gun and reached with to help him up.

A fatal mistake.

Sir pulled the concealed Walther PPK from his ankle holster and removed the safety with his thumb as he stood. He brought the weapon up to chest level, took a step closer and stared at her. "Sorry, Evelyn, but I've got a family that needs me to live." Sir jammed the barrel of the gun between her breasts and pulled the trigger three times.

"What a waste of talent," he said.

Her eyes grew wide in surprise and the life left her body as she fell backward, tumbling already dead down the steps with one sickening thud after another until her body came to rest in an upright position against the rail. Her head rested against the middle rail and her arms and legs spread out away from her body on the oily metal floor.

Sir grabbed his bag and ran down the steps, not even bothering to look at her lifeless form as he stepped over her. When he reached the bottom level, he moved toward the center of the structure and the silver control panel on one of the steel girders. He pressed the green button that lowered a motorboat suspended from a davit ten feet above the water. There were three boats, all intended to be used only in case of emergency escape.

This qualified. The whole process was supposed to take less than ninety seconds.

Two minutes till I'm free.

As he waited for the boat to lower, he saw the resupply ship idling just beyond the lower walkway. A man cloaked in darkness stood at the helm, his back toward Sir, who hoped the idling engine sound of the boat drowned out the sound of the davit.

Chapter 70
PIKE 84 Sanctum Facility
The Gulf of Mexico

Payne and Stone served as rear guards while the B-team moved up the south stairwell. They arrived on the ninth-floor landing, and the team lead, George Peppard, held up a closed fist indicating a full stop. With gunfire erupting on the floor below, the element of surprise vanished. Peppard saw movement down the hall through the glass pane and opened the door quickly, tossing two stun grenades as far as he could throw them. Even hidden behind a steel door, the three felt the concussive shockwave as it carried down the metal hallway and rattled the door, splintering the glass like a spider web.

Peppard, Dwight Schultz, and Dirk Benedict rushed inside, sending three-round bursts from their MP5s toward the two hostile targets left dazed by the stun grenades. Their rounds found flesh and eliminated the threats.

Payne and Stone waited and entered when Peppard announced All *clear!* over the comms.

Then it happened.

Payne heard a sound to their right from around the corner, the passageway no one had checked yet. He turned away from the operators and toward the noise with Stone on his six. He didn't make it two steps down the hall before a darkened figure leaped for him from a doorway.

Payne had played Pop Warner and high school football as a young man. He knew how to take a hit and instantly remembered what it felt like to have a two-hundred-fifty-pound linebacker nail him on the field.

His legs collapsed under him and he came down hard on his back and shoulders. The attacker landed on top of him as thick, python-like arms curled around his body and started to squeeze.

Disoriented, Payne didn't see the man reach to his side and remove something silver from his waist.

Stone raised her MP5 as the man tackled Payne, but in the scrum, she couldn't get a clear shot. She took a deep and controlled her breathing, letting the air out slowly as she waited for her moment. When the man dressed all in black thrust himself back and pulled a large Bowie knife, opportunity struck.

She didn't hesitate.

A three-round burst drilled the man in his chest, a nice half dollar-spaced grouping. The man's body slumped backward off Payne. Stone stepped closer and put three more insurance rounds into his forehead.

Stone reached for Payne's upraised arm and pulled him to his feet. Peppard, Schultz, and Benedict had spun around at the sound of the gunfire and were at her side by the time Payne stood up.

Peppard asked, "You both good?"

"Yeah," Payne said. "Thanks to Stone."

The voice of Commander Chapin came over the comms. "We have the package. I say again, the package is secure. What's your status, B-team?"

Peppard replied, "Still clearing the ninth deck."

"Well, get a fucking move on. Time to evac."

"Copy that," Peppard said.

"Package says there's a man in interrogation three on the eighth floor," Chapin said. "Check his medical status after clearing floor nine."

"Solid copy. On our way."

As they moved down the hallway, Payne slowed Stone with a touch on her arm. "Thank you, sis."

With a slight pause she said, "Yeah, no problem."

Payne could see her eyes were dilated and her eyelids were open wider than normal. He figured she must be in shock.

"You good to go?" asked Payne.

"I think so," she said. "This is all pretty intense."

"And you weren't even the one about to be filleted."

It took them five additional minutes to clear the floor, engaging and killing three more hostiles. Descending one flight of stairs, they arrived at Interrogation Room Three and found it empty, just a bloody chair. And no body.

"Commander," said Peppard into the comms.

"Go ahead."

"Interrogation Three is empty."

"Say again, B-team?"

"I say again, Interrogation Three is empty."

"Copy, roger that. Proceed to the boat for evac. Watch your six in case we overlooked any hostiles."

"Understood."

Three minutes later the two teams met up on the lowest level. They passed one body, an African American female on the sixth-level landing. Another dead body lie on the first level walkway.

Nick Jordan spoke loud enough for all of them to hear, pointing to the male. "That guy just went by the name Sir. He's the one who drugged and interrogated me."

Commander Chapin looked at Peppard, Schultz, and Benedict. "One of you take him out?"

They all shook their heads, and Peppard said, "Negative, not ours."

Stone pointed to the two boats suspended from the floor of the second level. "Commander, we're missing a boat. There were three hanging from the davits when we arrived."

"Looks like a rat got off the sinking ship. The guy with a pencil in his chest?"

"If he did, he shouldn't get far in his condition," said Briggs.

"What was his name again, Jordan?" asked Commander Chapin.

"Casha. Peter Casha."

"We know who that is," Payne and Stone said at the same time.

Chapter 71
Houma, Louisiana

The humid Cajun wind blew softly as Payne stood at the hangar door and wiped beads of sweat from his forehead. He watched the HRT operators load their gear for the flight home.

Payne saw Nick Jordan, FBI Director Ken Ludington, and Uncle Freddy Simmons engaged in an intense discussion. Stone approached Payne and stood close enough to brush up against his left arm.

When the conversation ended, Simmons jogged over. "I might have something for you, Eli."

"What's that?"

"SIOC called while you were on the platform and they got a hit on one of Peter Casha's associates."

"Which one?"

"Marcus Rollings."

"Where is he?"

"New York City. Facial recognition placed him outside the Plaza Hotel on Fifth Avenue."

"Interesting."

"There's more. He was with this woman." Simmons handed over a manila folder that included a full bio and several photos.

Payne scanned the pages. "Merci De Atta. Who is she?"

"One badass bitch." Freddy caught himself and looked sheepishly at Stone. "No offense, Agent Stone."

Stone laughed. "None taken."

"She's a hired assassin. Wanted by Interpol, FSB, Mossad—you name it. Lots of global agencies have warrants out for her arrest."

"Any idea why they're in the city?"

"None."

Payne rubbed his chin. "Okay. Thanks for the intel, Freddy."

"You got it, bud. Safe travels."

Payne turned away and stared off into the distance. They needed to keep digging. He only had a few minutes before he boarded the plane but knew who to call.

Mila Hall answered on the second ring. "Payne?" she asked in a slightly hushed voice.

"A bad time?"

"Kinda sorta. I'm on Air Force One on our way back from Charlotte. Grabbing a quick bite to eat here."

"Eating a salad to watch your figure?"

"Yeah, right. Pastrami on rye."

"I forgot how perfect you were," he said in a half-mocking, half-serious way.

"You call to butter me up or share something?"

"We got him."

"You got who?"

"Him ..." He let the word linger.

"Nick? You got him?" Her voice raised several octaves.

"Keep your voice down, but yes, he's alive."

"Where are you?"

"Louisiana, on the Gulf, headed back to DC soon. We'll debrief him on the flight back with the director."

"Does the White House know?" Hall asked.

"No, not yet. And Director Ludington doesn't want it to get out yet."

"Why not?"

"Because the director and the president already got into a pissing contest about investigating Nick's disappearance. He wants to debrief Nick and try to figure out what happened before we let the cat out of the bag. I'm letting you know because of what you told me, and I don't want you blindsided if ..." He paused.

"If what?"

"Nick shows up at the White House later tonight."

"You serious?"

"I think so. He wants a conversation with the president."

"Well, depending on when he does, we—and by 'we,' I mean the president—might be unavailable," Hall said. "He has something going on later."

"And what is that?"

"I overheard a call earlier that I don't think I was supposed to. Something about a meeting tonight down in the tunnels on Broadsway."

"I don't follow."

"Tell Nick. He'll get it. Anyway, the president is meeting several people."

"Who?"

Hall hesitated only a moment. "Just heard first names. Marcus, Merci, and Joe. They are meeting President Steele at nine. Something to do with files they retrieved."

Payne was stunned. "You're sure about the names, though, right? Marcus and Merci?"

"Yes, why?"

"You didn't catch the last names?"

"No. Do you know who they are?"

"Maybe," Payne said. "We got some intel a few minutes ago that is helping connect the dots. Not sure how the president factors into all this, but the meeting sounds sketchy."

"I agree. The funny thing is I'm not even supposed to be working today. A stomach virus is making its way around the detail this week, and three of MOGUL's regular agents are taking turns either draped over the porcelain throne or shitting their brains out on it."

"Lovely. Thanks for that vivid mental image. I'll pass along what you told me to Nick."

"Give him my best," Hall said, "and please tell him I'm relieved to know he's alive and well."

"Will do. Just remember to keep it on the down low for now."

"I don't need to be told the same thing twice, Elijah."

"Yes, I know."

"Does he know about Danny?" she asked.

"That he's in the hospital?"

"No. That he's dead."

"He's—wait. *What?*"

"He crashed at the hospital this morning. I figured Nick would want to know. He died shortly after the president visited him."

"Wow, we had no clue. I'll let him know when we board the flight. Look, not to cut this short, but I'm getting a wave from the director. Think it's time for us to go."

"Maybe we can meet up again when you're back. It was good to see you, Eli," Hall said. A longing in her voice, something he hadn't heard in a long time, seemed apparent in her tone.

Payne smiled as an image of her from a weekend in Tahoe suddenly materializes in his mind. Some images in life he wanted to forget, but this was one he wanted to remember always. "Yeah, I'm glad we caught up. Let's make it happen. Drinks are on me next time."

"You've got my digits, cowboy."

Payne caught up to Stone as she walked to the jet. With a firm squeeze, he gripped her shoulder and stopped her in mid-stride.

Stone turned her head sideways. "Whoa, bud. Do I need to call HR or something?" she asked with a wry, devilish grin forming at the corner of her lips.

He ignored the joke but he did remove his hand from her shoulder just in case. "You got a sec?"

"Sure."

"Look, Stone. I wanted to say thank you again for saving my ass out there."

"Sure thing. No biggie."

"No, really. It is a big deal. That guy got the drop on me, and if you hadn't reacted, well, we wouldn't be having this conversation." He extended his hand for her to shake. "I want you to know you proved the commander wrong out there on the platform and I'll never forget what you did. Every time I take a breath, I'll remember it."

Stone's smile grew wider as she pushed his hand away, and with both outstretched arms pulled him in for a hug.

"That's how we say *you're welcome* where I come from." She let go and took a step back. "That's what partners do, Payne. Through thick or thin they've got each other's six, twelve, nine, and three. No matter what."

"Thanks, Stone," Payne said. As she turned away, he said, "You'll hold this over me for as long as we know each other, won't you?"

Without breaking stride or looking back, she replied, "Oh, hell yes. At least forty-four years." The words were followed by a loud laugh that had an ominous quality to it.

"And I think you can call me Kat now."

Nick Jordan sank into the jet's plush leather seat, closed his eyes, and felt his body relax for the first time in a long time. He promised himself that after the current shitshow came to an end, he would sleep for a week straight.

The long, slender fingers of a dream state enveloped him as the constant hum of the jet engines made a rhythmic, soothing sound, pushing his recent ordeal from his mind.

A distinct sound of a cleared throat brought him back to the present.

Jordan opened his eyes to see FBI Director Ken Ludington eying him and, specifically, the clothing he wore. Jordan still wore the same shirt he had on when he was abducted.

"I can get the Body Man a clean shirt if he'd like," Ludington said with a genuine grin. He waved and an agent brought a black golf shirt with white F.B.I. initials on the left sleeve. The director handed it to Jordan, who shook his head in protest.

"Sorry, boss, the Body Man doesn't wear golf shirts."

"Seriously?" asked the director.

"We saw his closet," Stone said. "He's a *Magnum* P.I. type guy."

"Damn straight," was Jordan's smiling reply.

"Regrettably, we have no Hawaiian shirts on board," Ludington said. Then his voice got serious. "Is there anything else you want before we get started?" The director took a seat, as did the others. He sat directly across from Jordan. Stone sat to Jordan's left and Payne next to the director.

"Guess a quick siesta is out of the question." Nick raised his arms over his head and gave an elongated yawn.

"Yes, sorry." Director Ludington's face displayed a look of genuine concern. "Business first, rest later."

"In that case, a stiff drink would be nice." Nick smiled. "To refresh the synapses."

"Of course. Pick your poison."

"I doubt you have any Old Düsseldorf on board," he looked around, but it appeared nobody got the beer joke. It was Magnum's favorite brew on Tom Selleck's *Magnum P.I.* TV show. "A brown liquor would be terrific, please. Bourbon, any brand. Light on the ice, heavy on the bourbon."

The director snapped his fingers and this time a flight attendant came down the aisle. "My friend would like three fingers of Blanton's with a trace of ice, please, Abby."

She smiled and nodded. "And everyone else?"

"Just water for us, please," said the director.

Payne frowned when Ludington pointed to Jordan.

"He's officially on convalescent leave—you're on the job," his boss said as he watched Payne's expression.

Abby disappeared down the aisle and returned a few minutes later with a silver tray that carried a three-quarters full tumbler of amber liquid and three crystal glasses of ice water.

"Cheers." Jordan raised the thick glass and then took it down in two large swallows.

"Not one to sip on it?" asked the director.

"It's been a real week," Nick said.

Stone, Payne, and Ludington all laughed. *No kidding.*

"Are you ready, Nick?" Ludington asked.

"I am now." He held up the empty tumbler as proof. Abby thought he was signaling to her for a refill, so she brought him a fresh pour.

"You are an angel," Jordan said to her.

The director said, "Before we begin, Payne, you had a phone call right before we got on the plane that you wanted to share."

Payne nodded. "Yes, sir, I did." He looked at Jordan. "Nick, I spoke with Mila Hall before we boarded the plane." Jordan nodded in recognition of her name. "First, she wanted me to tell you she's relieved that you're alive and safe."

"Yeah, Mila's a sweetheart," said Nick. "And a hell of a good agent. Wait ... you're not *the* Payne, are you? The special agent she dated?"

Payne blushed slightly. "Guilty as charged."

"Mila never told me what happened between the two of you, but I hope you realize how much she adores you. Everything is still always Payne this and Payne that."

Payne ignored the compliment although it caught him slightly off guard. "I told Mila you might head to the White House when you get back. Is that still your intention?"

"Absolutely. I plan to confront President Steele face to face. Why?"

"Mila is on the president's detail today, and she overheard a call the president had about a meeting tonight with three individuals on Broadsway. She said you'd know what that meant. I might have misheard her, and maybe she meant Broadway."

Jordan smirked. "No, you heard her correctly. It's Brood*sway,* not Broad*way.* It's the not-so-subtle name of the tunnel that leads from the basement under the White House north under Lafayette Square and connects with the St. Regis Hotel. The tunnel got its name during the Kennedy administration since it was used to bring in women for the president's, ah ..." Jordan paused. "... amusement."

"This was a regular occurrence?" Payne asked.

"At the time, yes. The tunnel didn't get much use after Kennedy, but like some of the other tunnels, it's still used to usher people in and out of the White House who don't want to be seen entering or exiting for one reason or another. Usually diplomats and other heads of state."

"According to Mila, it sounded like the people who are meeting the president are bringing files to him. I'm assuming they're the ones you tried keeping from the president."

Jordan nodded.

"Yeah, that's likely why Peter Casha came to the facility to kill me. With access to the files, they didn't need me anymore."

"What can you tell us about the files?" Ludington put his elbows on his knees and leaned in closer.

Jordan sipped his second Blanton's. "I'm not sure the three of you know what my role actually entails."

"I have a pretty good idea, based on what Mila told me," Payne said.

"Well, let's make sure you know the entire scoop."

For the next thirty minutes, Jordan gave a detailed account of what it meant to be the Body Man. Mila Hall's description to Payne was spot on, but some of the specifics Jordan provided were disturbing. After some time, the director interrupted.

"So, what did you find that caused you to confront the president?" asked the director.

"The president's son, Charles Steele II, or as everyone including the president calls him, Junior, bartered a deal with the House of Saud for a dozen of our Gray Eagle drones."

"And what would he get in return?"

"Their SteeleCorp would be allowed extraordinary access to Saudi finances. They'd become one of the premier lending institutions not only in Saudi Arabia but throughout the Gulf region."

"That's possibly corrupt," Payne said, "but maybe not. We already sell military technology to the Saudis, and besides, several former presidents also gave special deals to organizations that benefited their interests while in and out of office. To my knowledge, none of them ever got in trouble."

"True enough," Jordan admitted. "But this is much bigger than the Steele family trying to acquire more wealth. You need to understand what they were selling. These are prototype drones, the newest and most sophisticated UAVs designed by General Atomics—from whom they were stolen. We don't even employ these in warfare. This is next-gen tech we don't want anybody, even our closest allies, to have. These UAVs utilize stealth technology and are virtually invisible to conventional weapons—and it isn't Uncle Sam selling them. They were stolen, and they're being sold by Junior. Besides the drones, Junior is selling plans to build their own UAVs, as well as several of our most lethal missiles. The ones specifically designed for the Gray Eagles make Hellfires look like M80s."

"Look, I'm not mitigating what Junior is doing here," Ludington said, "but your job is to make problems go away, am I right? Why gather all this evidence? Why not bury it—aren't you specifically supposed to bury it? Or you could act to prevent the sale?"

Jordan looked lost in thought before he responded. "My job is to protect the office of the presidency at any cost. Even if that means I protect it from the man who sits in the Oval Office. This weapons transfer is for the ongoing Yemen conflict with Saudi Arabia against the Houthi rebels, who receive funding from Iran. What's going on between Saudi Arabia and Yemen is nothing more than a proxy war between Iran and Saudi Arabia. Given the technological advancement, this sale would ensure the Saudis would be in a superior technology position and likely use that tech to directly attack Iran.

"That could start World War III, since we're in bed with the Saudis, and Iran aligns with Russia. What I was trying to do was not merely stop the Steele family from benefiting financially from an illegal arms sale. I'm protecting the office of the presidency from a global war. And trust me, if the Saudis get these weapons, we will be one step closer to that occurring."

Before Payne could respond, Jordan added, "And to answer the other part, I couldn't stop the transfer. If I could, I would have."

"So, you collected this evidence and then did what?" asked Payne.

"I briefed the president." Jordan laughed. "It was comical when I later thought about it. I briefed him thinking he couldn't possibly have known what Junior and his minions were arranging. I thought I was doing him a favor. I thought he would instantly move to stop the transaction and maybe get some people arrested, even if secretly. For all the distaste we have for them and their human rights record, the Saudis are still our most essential ally in the Middle East.

Stone said, "Clearly that didn't go so great."

"On the surface, he took it quite well," Jordan continued. "He denied it even after I showed him the proof. I wasn't aware until I was kidnapped how good of a liar the man really is. Anyway, he deflected and said Junior wasn't capable of such a betrayal."

"But how could he deny it if the evidence implicated himself?" asked the director.

Jordan shook his head. "But it didn't. No evidence I uncovered points back to him."

The director raised a skeptical brow. "How could that be?"

"There are hundreds of pages of documents I was able to collect, but everything points back to Junior. Nothing implicates the president."

"But if the transfer benefits his company ..." Payne said.

"Was. It *was* his company," said Jordan. "When he took the oath of office, he signed everything over to Junior. On paper, at least, he no longer has any stake in the SteeleCorp except in trust."

Payne shook his head. "But if Junior is implicated, it would still come back to haunt the president."

"You're right. There's no way his presidency could survive a scandal like this whether he still owns the company or not. But trust me when I say his ego is tied to that company, and there's not a chance in hell he'd let it be tarnished."

Jordan looked out the window as billowing clouds passed by the wing, a slight frown forming on his lips. "Look, you can't protect the office of the presidency with blinders on. You observe all of it: the good, the bad, everything. Sometimes you make a judgment call whether to intervene or not, and lots of things that happen would excite the news cycle for weeks but still be nobody's goddamned business."

Jordan took a sip of his bourbon. "As the saying goes, the public has a 'right to know.' Sure. But the public does not have a right to know *everything*. That sums up my job in a nutshell."

Ludington agreed with that. At the FBI, he had an entire office responding to Freedom of Information Act requests. Some people just want to know if they even had an FBI file. Usually, they don't have one. Other requests come from news organizations and investigative journalists, often very detailed. Many of these requests were easily found, but in the case of current and ongoing investigations, most of the records returned to requesters were obscured by thick black redactions.

"Other times," Jordan explained, "you cover up shit that nobody should have the right to get away with. Stuff that would get a citizen sent to jail. In the end, the office of the presidency is bigger than one person. And above all, it must be protected. As for the person who acts as the Body Man, well. We're human. Sometimes we make the wrong call."

"Are you saying you should have covered all this up?" Ludington asked.

"No. Unequivocally, no. Going after Junior and, by default, the president, was the right call. As for why he's not implicated in any evidence, it's simple. The president is paranoid about putting anything in writing. That's why none of the evidence I collected points back to him."

"But how did he run his business without written correspondence?"

"Face-to-face meetings and phone calls. He would sign legal contracts, of course, but he never sent texts or emails. Ever. Nothing can be traced back to him. He's technologically illiterate. Most of his presidential directives are verbal. He signs very little besides what he must and those are often whitewashed. Nothing he's signed as president can point back to this arms deal."

"I take it Junior doesn't have his father's misgivings?" Stone asked.

"Not at all. Junior has no such qualms. He's a technology whore and tracking down evidence against him was easy."

"Regarding the documents, you printed off four copies, right?'

"Correct, one was in my safe—"

"—which they got the day after they grabbed you," interrupted Payne.

"I figured as much, based on the interrogation questions I received. The other three I gave to Danny Frazier, and he was going to put them in a secure location. They took me the day I was going to read him into what was going on."

"What did Danny know?" Ludington asked.

"Very little." Jordan swirled the expensive brown liquor in its expensive tumbler. "I hadn't shared what I'd discovered with him yet."

"Did the president know Danny was in the dark?"

"Not that I'm aware of. After I confronted the president, he professed ignorance and said he would ask Junior personally and get back with me. Well, not surprisingly, the president ignored my follow-up inquiries. I knew something wasn't right, and that's why I printed off the additional insurance copies and decided to get Danny's assistance. Hindsight is twenty-twenty, and I should have realized even though none of the evidence implicated the president, he was really the one behind this deal."

Payne knew there was no easy way to say what must be said. "Nick, listen, I hate to have to tell you this, but Danny's dead."

Jordan's expression flinched only a bit. "Damn. I figured as much. But based on the questions they asked me during the interrogation, I believed they hadn't recovered the other three documents."

"It appears that changed recently, and the president will have all the copies at the White House tonight."

"He'll destroy all the paper copies," said Nick.

"That's all the evidence you have?" asked the director.

"I only printed off four copies," Jordan replied. "There's an old incinerator in the hub. That's the name of the central room where all the secret White House tunnels converge. He'll likely destroy them there."

"We need to stop him," Stone said.

"It isn't as simple as that," Jordan said. "I need to go alone."

"I'm not sure that's a good idea," the FBI Director said.

"Look, I know MOGUL better than probably anyone, well

enough to say he won't let any of you near the White House tonight. Especially if he has all the evidence."

Payne disagreed. "He can't stop us from coming."

"He most certainly can or, at the least, he can delay you until he destroys the files. But he can't stop me," said Nick.

"How can you be sure?"

"Trust me. Inside 1600 Pennsylvania Avenue, I'm safe. Outside, I'm susceptible to the assets who work for Junior. That's why they took me in my own home. They can't lay a finger on me in the White House."

"What do you need from us?" Director Ludington's expression was sincere and deadly serious.

"I need to shower and swing by my townhouse in Vienna to get a change of clothes and my White House ID."

"That's it?" Payne asked.

"Yes, I can do the rest."

"You're sure?" Payne asked.

"Without a doubt."

"What about backup?" asked Stone.

"I'll have all the backup I need inside the people's house."

"Well," Payne said, "we can help with part of that." He reached into his pocket and withdrew Jordan's White House ID badge. "I liberated this from our evidence pile." Jordan accepted the badge. "Would you like to know what Stone and I learned during our investigation?"

Jordan nodded. "All right. Read me in."

Chapter 73
Jack Brooks Regional Airport (BPT)
Beaumont, Louisiana

E ach breath felt labored, shortened, and painful.

The eraser end of the broken pencil protruded from Peter Casha's chest, and he could feel it shift with every gasp for air and he knew that caused more blood loss. He looked down at his blood-drenched shirt. Time was working against him, but help would be summoned.

He reached to the passenger seat of the Oldsmobile Cutlass he'd stolen in Port Arthur and grabbed the jacket he found in the car. It would be helpful in covering up the bloody injury.

Going back to Houma after he'd fled the platform wasn't an option. He knew the feds would scour all the local transportation hubs, air, sea, and land, based on its proximity to the coast. And he wasn't getting far with a yellow pencil arrowed protruding from a huge bloodstain on his shirt.

After killing Sir and taking his escape boat from PIKE 84, Casha sailed west and settled on Beaumont, based on the charts he'd found on the boat. Once on land, he'd used his smartphone to track down a charter plane at the Jack Brooks Regional Airport and reserved it online. Before leaving the Cutlass and getting on the plane, he'd placed one more call.

"Hey, bro, it took you a long time to return my call," Joe Lagano said. "I was gettin' worried. Everything go okay with Jordan?"

Casha paused. "Fuck no, it didn't."

"What? What do you mean?"

"As I was about to finish him off, the facility was attacked, and Nick got the drop on me."

"Attacked! By who?"

"Feds. I think an FBI HRT, based on their uniforms."

"Did they rescue Nick?"

"I believe so."

"Fuck."

"But I can't be sure. When I went to stab Nick, he got me first with a shiv he made out of a pencil." Casha took a few heavy breaths. "Every time I breathe, I bleed like a bastard. I got the hell out of there."

"He stabbed you?"

"Yeah, big time. A very slick move, too. I even told him so as he bugged out."

"Is it serious?"

Casha pulled open the stolen jacket and the blood loss was breathtaking. Literally. He knew it was only a matter of time, with or without medical attention. "Nah, I'm all good, bro."

"Where are you now?"

"Beaumont, Louisiana."

"What about the company jet?"

"There was no way in hell I was going back to Houma," Casha said. He was coughing up a little blood now. "I chartered a plane that will take me to DC."

"You mean New York?"

"No. I'll be at the Manassas airport tonight."

He took a shallow breath and almost passed out from the pain.

The blood loss seemed to have stabilized, but much had been lost.

"You ... you get the files?"

"Yes," Lagano said. At least this part of the program had gone well. "Danny hid them in three different safe deposit boxes, but I've got them. I'm headed to the White House soon."

"And after that?"

"I'm supposed to catch a flight with Junior back home. We'll meet at the Manassas airport at ten p.m. sharp."

"What about Marcus?"

"He's with Merci in Washington, at his apartment. They're also going to the White House meeting. Why?"

"I need to warn them."

"You think he and Merci are in danger going to the White House? I mean, shit ..."

Casha wondered if Lagano would live long enough to catch the flight with Junior. "Not sure, to be honest. I can't convince you to not deliver the files personally, can I?"

"No way. I've got to do it," Lagano said. "You know how ol' Charles can be."

"Sure definitely do. That's why I don't think you should deliver them without me."

"I'll be careful. Anyway, I might not be a badass like you, but I can handle myself."

Casha knew arguing wouldn't get them anywhere. Lagano didn't realize the danger he was in and, chances were, convincing him of the risk would be damned near impossible. "Be safe, Joseph. Watch your six, and I'll see you later tonight."

Lagano thought the response was odd. Casha never called him by his formal name. "Okay bro, will do."

"If things go south, you know where the money is. You've got the access code for the Cayman account."

"Bro, nothing's going south. See you at the airport. Deal?"

"Yeah, bro. Deal."

The call ended, and Casha made one more call.

Pain thumped in rhythmic pulses from his chest to his extremities as he lumbered across the parking lot and onto the tarmac.

Can I make it? He climbed inside the Cessna Citation M2.

The pilot walked back to greet him. "I'm told we're taking you to Washington, DC, tonight, Mr. Casha. Is this a business trip or pleasure?"

Casha smiled as best he could and tried to hide the pain. A blanket he'd removed from the overhead covered his chest and concealed the blood. "Let's say it will be a pleasure for me to put some unfinished business to rest."

"Sounds like the best of both worlds."

"Oh, it will be," he said, and smiled. "Thank you for asking."

Rage flowed through the president's body like meth through the veins of a junkie. A scarlet hue formed on his cheeks and grew in intensity as he took a deep breath of air in through his nose, slowly exhaled it out his mouth.

Charles Steele—MOGUL—needed several repetitions before he was able to tell Dolores through gritted teeth to call his son.

Thirty seconds later, Junior was on the secure line.

"Yes, Mr. President."

"Junior." He paused a moment and took another deep breath before he continued. "Did you hear about it?"

"What's that, Mr. President?"

The president bit the side of his cheek hard enough to draw blood. "The fucking raid."

"What are you talking about?" asked Junior.

What a worthless piece of shit you are, thought the president. *You cannot be the fruit of my loins.*

"I just got off the phone with a contact at the FBI. An HRT raided the Sanctum PIKE 84 facility a few hours ago."

Silence greeted him.

"Did you hear what the hell I said? They hit the goddamned

facility. They hit it *hard*."

Junior paused before he said, "Yes, sir. I heard you."

"And what do you have to say about it?"

"Do they have Nick?"

Unbelievable. "I don't know, but it seems like the FBI wasn't in the Gulf of fucking Mexico for breakfast. The director kept this operation close to the vest—that son-of-a-bitch kept the White House in the dark on purpose. Even the deputy director had no clue, or we would have known about the raid."

"Who else can tell us if Nick is alive?"

"You know someone who should know. Haven't you heard from Casha?"

"No. Radio silence."

"That should tell you something."

"You think he failed?"

"I think he's dead. If an HRT raided the facility, I doubt they took any prisoners. Peter Casha sure as hell doesn't strike me as someone who would let himself be taken alive."

"What do we do?" Junior was sounding scared now.

"Where are you?" the president demanded.

"Still here. I had a few things to wrap up. Joe is catching a ride with me after he delivers the files. Should I change my plans?"

The president grew quiet and paced around the Resolute desk. "No, I need time to think. I've got a few hours before they arrive."

"What are you going to do?" Junior asked.

What *was* he going to do now? "I don't know yet."

"If Nick is still alive—"

"I'll handle the Body Man," said the president.

"And, in the meantime, you expect me to do what?"

"Clean up this mess, starting with Joe after he brings me the rest of the documents."

"As in eliminate JoJo?"

Charles Steele ignored the question as his instruction was abundantly clear. "Marcus and Merci need to be neutralized as well. They all know way too much." His voice transitioned to an angry growl.

"They're professionals. How do you expect me to take care of them?"

"With others who share their unique skill sets," the president countered.

"And where do you expect I find them?"

"Be resourceful—but in God's name be discreet."

"What about Ken Ludington? He must know what's going on."

"Not sure what he knows, but I've got ways to keep him quiet."

"Meaning?"

"I have leverage over him."

Junior paused for a moment. Then, "How did this all go to hell?" he asked. He was dejected that a plan he thought foolproof wasn't. And he was certain his father thought he was the principal fool.

The president's voice had regained a measure of confidence.

"I let inferior, weak people do my dirty work instead of shoving my hands down into the shit and doing it myself. Never again. Do you hear me? Never."

"I trusted these people and paid them handsomely for their services," Junior said in his defense.

"Not talking about them," said the president. "I'm talking about *you*, you fucking moron. I place the blame for this failure squarely on your shoulders, boy."

Junior tried to respond but couldn't.

The president disconnected the line, walked into his study, and poured a tall glass of Macallan 1947 Highland single-malt Scotch whiskey. He sat down and took the first sip to clear his mind and pacify his shaking hands.

Chapter 75
St. Regis Hotel
Washington, DC

Joe Lagano sat on a plush red sofa in the lobby of the St. Regis Hotel and looked up at the gold-inlaid ceiling. Decadent was the word that came to mind as he counted the chandeliers and marveled at the opulent display of prosperity. He glanced down at his watch.

They're late.

As if on cue, Marcus and Merci strode confidently into the lobby. Lagano stood, the three of them exchanged pleasantries, and they made their way to the concierge desk.

"George is expecting us," Lagano said to the formally dressed concierge who sat behind the desk radiating authority. The man nodded, said nothing, and slipped out using a door to the right of his desk.

The concierge returned a minute later without a word. Before Lagano could say anything, the concierge motioned to his left by tilting his head.

A tall man with a dark bushy beard, dimpled chin, and rugged good looks advanced to the desk. Dressed in a similar fashion as the man behind the concierge desk, he walked toward them with a purpose. Lagano thought he looked more like an operator than a hotel worker. The dark, wraparound sunglasses looked entirely out of place indoors.

"Follow me," the man said.

"Are you George?" asked Lagano.

"I am," he said with a warm smile and a look at the Rolex watch on his wrist. "You're a few minutes late, and he's expecting you."

George, if that was really his name, led them down a series of hallways until they came to a nondescript door at the end of the hall, identical to every other door they had passed. Instead of a key card, the door had a touchpad to the right of the door frame. The man entered a six-digit code, the lock mechanism disengaged, and the door swung open. They descended four flights of stairs ending at another door.

Unlike the door upstairs, this one resembled a bank vault door with another keypad, on the left this time. A new code was entered and a light above the door turned green, and a *hisss* sound emanated from around the frame as pneumatic pistons pushed the heavy door aside. George stepped aside as the door pivoted, then waved his arm, indicating they all should step inside.

"He's waiting for you on the other side," he said.

"Who is?" Lagano asked.

George paused, uncertainly. "If you don't know, you are most definitely in the wrong place right now. Proceed, please."

Reluctantly, the three of them stepped inside the darkened space and the thick door closed behind them. They were all alone in a mysterious tunnel with only one direction for them to go.

Before they could say anything, a figure emerged from down the tunnel and approached. The spaced-out lighting made it difficult to see much more than twenty feet ahead with clarity.

Nick Jordan emerged from the shadows and a stunned expression formed on all their faces.

"Welcome to Broadsway," Jordan said.

"Guess you're not dead after all." Lagano wasn't sure what else to say. Wasn't the Sanctum supposed to have killed this guy?

"No, I'm not dead—but the three of you will be if you're not careful."

"Is that a threat?" Merci's eyes darted around the tunnel looking for a weapon, or something she could wield against attackers.

"No threat, simple fact. The three of you are smart enough to know when someone is cleaning up after themselves."

"I take it you know who we are?" Joe's eyes narrowed.

"I do, indeed. I read all of your bios in the dossier created by the FBI on the flight from Houma." Jordan smiled with a sincerity that didn't reflect his burning desire to kill all three of these people in cold blood right where they stood.

But that wasn't the plan.

"You came here to do what? Warn us?"

"The enemy of my enemy is my friend."

"Who says we're the president's enemy?"

Nick shook his head. "In any logical scenario we would be against each other. However, Charles Steele is systematically eliminating all the evidence, and all of the operators—that's you three. Trust me. He definitely is your enemy."

"And if we told you this was all Junior's plan?" Rollings said.

"Oh, Junior is also guilty, for sure. But a dog always has a master. And the four of us know who pulls the strings. Pinocchio only goes where Geppetto leads."

"Do you know what we're bringing him?" asked Joe.

"I do. You have the files I compiled, and possibly other things."

"And do you think you'll take them from us by force?" Merci's body tensed, ready to attack.

Nick shook his head. "No, of course not. Quite the contrary."

The Body Man had a calm, almost disinterested demeanor. It

confused Merci. She kept waiting for him to snap and come at them. But he didn't. His tone remained relaxed, almost serene.

Lagano took a baby step forward. "What is it you want?"

An unmistakable fire suddenly rose in Nick's eyes.

"To light the powder keg."

"You're coming with us?"

"I'll be along shortly after you conclude your business with MOGUL—with the president. But I'd prefer he not know I'm here yet."

"What assurance do we have you won't kill us or have us arrested after we meet with him?" Merci's head was swimming as she listened to Nick.

"You have my word." Nick answered truthfully. "My word is my bond. The three of you should be more worried about the president. You're merely pawns on his board. I'm not interested in pawns."

He paused.

"I'm here for the king."

President Steele and two Secret Service agents rode the elevator from the West Wing down to the hub. Lost in his thoughts, the president stared at the red carpet and mahogany walls of the elevator as the squeak of the pulley and a slight jerk announced their arrival to the basement.

Steele walked out with an air of confidence in his step, like a prizefighter strutting into a ring against an opponent who stands no chance.

A relic of a bygone era, the twenty-five-by-forty-foot hub contained an old boiler, several large printing presses, and an incinerator. The latter item still functioned and currently spewed forth enough heat to turn the expansive room into a sauna.

Earlier in the day, the president had requested the incinerator be fired up. The White House staff thought the request was odd but did as the president requested without question. They learned early in his presidency to question none of his actions. Poking a bear rarely worked out well for the one with the stick.

The president stood in the center of the brightly lit room with his arms crossed and tapped his left foot against the tiled floor. Beads of perspiration formed on his forehead. With a smug expression plastered all over his face, Charles looked down Broad-sway at the sound of footfalls approaching from the direction of the St. Regis Hotel.

Marcus Rollings, Joe Lagano, and Merci came into view as they turned the corner. They walked toward the president with brooding looks clearly displayed on their faces.

The president looked at the two Secret Service agents. "That will be all for now, gentlemen."

"Mr. President?" asked the senior agent.

"I'll take it from here, Chris." He pointed toward the gold eagle cufflinks on his white dress shirt. "If I need you, I'll let you know."

"We can be here within seconds, sir."

"I know. It will be fine. The meeting won't take long, and my guests will show themselves out the same way they came."

"As you wish, sir," said Agent Chris Albanese, complying with the president's request.

They were all alone. Only five feet separated the president from the threesome.

"Welcome to a place few people see. It's not on the self-guided White House tour."

None of them responded.

Charles almost felt like he could smell the fear from the three of them. "Did you bring what I requested?"

All three nodded. "Yes, Mr. President," Rollings said.

Steele pointed to Lagano. "You're up first, Joe."

Lagano stepped forward, removed three brown legal-sized folders from a black briefcase and handed them to the president.

"Did you open any of the folders?" The president tapped the top file with his index finger.

"No, Mr. President. I did as you instructed and retrieved them from the three safe deposit boxes. They never left my sight."

"Not even a peek inside? Curiosity can get the best of anyone."

"No, sir. I know what curiosity did to that cat."

President Steele let out an audible chuckle. "You and your sense of humor, Joseph. Well done. I won't forget your efforts and will reward your loyalty."

"Thank you, Mr. President."

The president took the three brown file folders, undid the clasps, and flipped through the contents one at a time. It took a few minutes, but once he felt confident everything was in place, he put them down on the floor.

"And the other item?"

Rollings stepped closer and handed the president the black over-the-shoulder bag they'd retrieved in New York City.

"Same question Joe got."

"We didn't look, Mr. President. Never opened the bag."

"Good to hear."

The president tapped the bag as a wide smile spread over his face. "This one will come in quite handy in the coming days and weeks. Thank you both for retrieving it."

Rollings and Merci nodded but said nothing.

"And you, Merci," continued the president. "Very good job taking care of James Fowler. The man was a pompous ass and got what he deserved."

The president said nothing about her failure to kill Danny Frazier.

Merci smiled on the outside although, on the inside, she seethed. "All in a day's work, sir," she said through gritted teeth. She could read people well. "Are we free to go?"

"Of course. Again, thank you all."

Merci's bullshit meter flew past the number ten as she recognized the deceit in his eyes.

"But before you all leave," said the president, "let's put these files where they belong." Steele reached into the bag, withdrew the files, and walked over to the incinerator. As he got close to the heat source, the elevator made a screeching sound as it descended to the Broadsway level. The president held the files tightly as it reached the bottom and the doors slowly opened.

Nick Jordan stepped out of the elevator and with a slow stride walked toward the president.

Without missing a beat, the president smiled and said, "Ahh— the prodigal son, returned. I was wondering when you'd join our little soirée."

"Your biblical doctrine is off, as usual, Mr. President. The prodigal son left of his own accord. I did no such thing."

"True story, but he did come back."

"I came back not out of desperation, but out of necessity."

"Was it necessary to betray me, Nick?"

"My oath is to the office, not the occupant. You know that, sir."

"And that loyalty nearly got you what you deserve."

Jordan ignored the dig. "Based on your smug look, I take it you're not surprised to see me alive."

"Of course not. I have eyes and ears everywhere. You are here just in time, though," the president said. He took additional steps toward the incinerator. "I've already destroyed the copy we found in your safe, Nick." He raised the envelopes. "Destroying these will close the book on this matter."

President Steele pulled on a pair of heat-resistant gloves and opened the thick incinerator doors. They made an awful sound, like fingernails down a chalkboard, as they crept open. Even fifteen feet away, a roaring wave of extreme orange heat licked at everyone's faces.

"Bon voyage," said the president and he tossed all three brown folders into the flames. After closing the incinerator doors, he walked back to where the black bag lay on the floor.

"It's done then?" Jordan asked.

The president smiled, but it wasn't a warm, friendly smile. "Not quite. I don't like loose ends, and there are still many to tie up."

"Are you planning to kill me here in the White House, sir? Yourself?"

"Of course not. But I can assure you these grounds are where you will take your last breaths."

"Do you think my fellow agents will finish me off?"

"I didn't say that."

"Mr. President, I only did my job—the job I'm trained for and the job the taxpayers pay me for. And the thanks I got was a trip to the Gulf of Mexico, where I was tortured and almost killed."

Steele shrugged. "It's likely we'll agree to disagree, Nick."

"My job wasn't to make all of your sins go away. It's to protect the office of the presidency. Even if that means I must protect it from a man like you and your piece of shit son, sir."

"We can go back and forth all night, Nick. The bottom line is you and others without the foresight to see several moves ahead have failed. I'm still in power, and without any evidence, the Saudi deal will go through. You can't stop it at this point."

"Is that so?"

"Yes, it is."

Jordan shook his head before a smile formed. "Mr. President, I'm not sure who is feeding you intel, but the transfer of the drones and missiles won't happen." Jordan glanced at his watch. "As we speak, a Tier One assault unit should be boarding the cargo ship. They'll take possession of the containers, and the Saudis won't be getting our drone tech. Meaning the SteeleCorp will not be entering the lucrative banking industry in that part of the world now, or ever, for that matter. It also means the Middle East won't catch on fire if any war between Iran and Saudi Arabia turns into a full-scale global conflict."

The president's smile receded as his face tensed. "You're bluffing. Or deranged. Either way, you couldn't possibly know which container ship the weapons were on."

"You're right. I didn't get intel on that before you ordered my abduction. But Peter Casha knew. And he paid Hector Fuentes to make the switch. Casha was supposed to kill Fuentes but failed. Like so many of your programs, public or private, Mr. President, this one has failed too."

"Bull-*shit*," The president's lower lip twisted into a snarl.

"Remarkably, Hector survived the attack in the Pacific," Jordan said. The FBI interviewed him yesterday, and he sang like an audition on *America's Got Talent*. All it cost was an immunity deal …" A smile curled up the side of Jordan's mouth. "… a deal that was reached."

The smug look the president's face wore most of the time had now disappeared. "That isn't possible."

"You're finished, Charles."

The president's face grew crimson with rage as he swung his pointed index finger toward Rollings and Merci. "This is *your* goddamn faults! If you had killed Danny Frazier like you were supposed to, none of this would have happened."

Merci's her body tensed as the president blamed her errant shot for the entire mess. Her hands were behind her back, and she turned the ring on her finger so that the jewel faced her palm. She flipped back the ruby to reveal the small needle.

Jordan saw her hands move behind her back. He knew what she was capable of when cornered. At that moment, despite training to protect the president ingrained in him at the cellular level, he decided to let things play out.

"I should snap your neck for killing Danny," Jordan said, his voice raised to a thunderous level as he took a step toward the president.

The president's reaction surprised them all.

He laughed.

A maniacal sound from deep down coming not from a place of confidence but desperation. The tone reverberated down the corridors leading from the hub. "You? You're nothing more than a junkyard dog looking for a reason to pounce."

Jordan lunged toward the president. Steele's resolve faded as he reacted to the sudden movement. He stumbled and lost his balance, falling backward.

Merci moved with the speed of a cat evading water as she caught the president and broke his fall. The palm of her hand cupped the back of his neck, and an invisible pinprick broke his skin.

That's all it took.

The president didn't notice the small puncture to his neck and quickly gathered himself as he pushed Merci away and stood up. "Get out of here. All of you. This is my fucking house, and none of you have the right to be here."

None of them responded.

Nobody moved.

"I said get out!" He screamed louder as spittle formed on his lips and flew out of his mouth.

The four of them turned away, but Jordan motioned for them to follow as he walked to the elevator.

"No!" screamed the president as he pointed toward the Broadsway tunnel. "You'll leave the same way Kennedy's whores left my house."

They ignored him and continued toward the elevator.

Jordan turned to face the president as he reached the elevator doors. "Like hell we will, and this isn't your house—it's the people's house. You're only a temporary resident of the office who doesn't deserve the honor and privilege to call the people's house your home. Besides, we'll walk right out the front door, and there's not a goddamn thing you can do about it." Jordan handed White House visitors' badges to Rolling, Lagano, and Merci.

Steele snarled and his hands shook. Rage took him to a level where he could no longer find the words to respond.

"And another thing." Jordan stepped into the elevator with the others and turned to face the president. He bent over, slipped off his left shoe, and slid the wooden heel to the side to remove a 128gb SanDisk micro-SD card. "A piece of advice. When you destroy evidence that you think can bring down your family business and your presidency," he said as he held the tiny red and black flash drive up for the president to see clearly, "you should destroy all the evidence, dumbass."

The president stood in a paralyzed state as the doors closed.

Jordan looked at Merci inside the elevator.

"How long does he have?"

Merci looked back with an icy glare. "For what?"

"Don't bother with the act, Merci. I saw what you did with the ring. How long does he have?"

A wry half-smile raised the corner of her pert mouth.

"Fifteen minutes. Maybe a little less."

Jordan asked, "Is there anything that can reverse the poison?"

Merci shook her head. "Not according to the Agency."

Jordan paused for a moment. "I'll escort the three of you out the east gate, then I'll go back to have a final word with MOGUL."

Five minutes later at the east security entrance, Jordan waved to the guard, who knew him well. The man looked at the Body Man like he'd seen a ghost.

"These three are with me, Frank. They can go."

The guard looked down at his clipboard.

"Their names aren't on there—they're with me," repeated Nick.

"But how did they—"

Jordan cut him off with an upraised hand.

"Please, Frank. It's okay."

The guard nodded and waved them past the checkpoint.

Lagano, Rollings, and Merci stopped on the sidewalk and looked back. The Body Man stood and watched them leave.

"I don't want to see any of you again. Ever. Understood?" Jordan said.

The three of them nodded.

"How long do we have?" Rollings asked. He believed terrible retribution would follow them until it was ordered to strike.

The Body Man ignored the question. Better they should live in fear.

"Have a good life somewhere far, far away from the United States," Jordan said. He turned and walked back into the White House.

President Charles Steele stood in the west sitting hall of the official residence taking large gasps of breath, each one harder to draw than the last. *What the hell is happening to me?*

Chris Albanese, the protective detail SAC and the agent closest to the doorway, took a step into the room and saw the president clutch his chest.

"Mr. President, are you okay? Should I call for your doctor?" Albanese raised his left arm to call for help on the comms, but a voice startled him. The agent pivoted on his heels.

"That won't be necessary, Chris." Nick Jordan walked into the room and put his hand on the agent's shoulder.

Albanese's eyes grew wide in disbelief.

"Holy friggin' *shit*—Nick ..."

President Steele slurred his words. "Get this son-a-bish outta here. Call my doctor ... basard ... poison me ..."

Albanese looked back and forth between the president and Jordan.

"Chris," Nick said. He squeezed the agents shoulder a little firmer. "*Alpha seven.*"

The unexpected code phrase staggered Albanese, and he started to protest. "But the president—"

Nick cut him off. "Alpha seven, Chris. I'll take it from here."

"Yes, sir," Chris said, and he turned and left the room.

President Charles Steele tried to call out, but his voice failed him. The acutely toxic tetrodotoxin was blocking nerve transmissions in Steele's lungs and cardiac system. His body was basically turning off.

Unable to draw a breath, he fell to his knees, both hands now grabbing at his chest in futility. Sweat poured from his brow and started to flow from all over his body.

Nick Jordan approached him and leaned down. He came face to face with the man whose presidency would meet a spiteful end.

"You stood too close to the fire, Charles. But fear not. I guarantee you won't be alone for long."

Steele's eyes grew wide when the last bit of oxygen escaped from his lungs. The shock on Steele's face would be his epitaph.

"Junior will join you soon enough. I'm sure of it," Jordan said.

The president fell forward to the ground and rolled onto his back, and his body jerked about like a fish thrown onto the shore. After about thirty seconds, his erratic movements stopped, and his body grew still. The piercing eyes that had been filled with life seconds before now stared toward the ornate ceiling in an empty gaze.

"Godspeed, Mr. President," Nick whispered into his ear. Then he reached down and closed Charles Steele's eyes for the last time.

Chapter 77
Manassas Regional Airport (HEF)

Joe Lagano stepped out of the car and looked around. Like a dark blanket, a thick fog obscured everything beyond a few feet. Lagano turned back to his driver.

"You going to be okay?" Rollings asked. A hint of concern evident in his voice.

Lagano paused and squinted toward where the fog-shrouded aircraft idled. "Yeah, I'll be fine. And you?"

Rollings exchanged a glance with Merci before answering. "We're good. Transportation is waiting for us at Hyde Field. Someone Merci knows can get us out of the country fast and easy tonight." Rollings' face softened. "There's room on the plane if you want it."

"Appreciate the offer, but I'm supposed to meet Peter here tonight."

"Okay then. Well, best of luck to you, Joe," said Rollings as he shook his friend's hand. "If you need us, we'll be ..."

"... in an undisclosed, non-extradition country sipping fruity drinks with little paper umbrellas." Merci sounded like a teenager about to sneak out the bedroom window to meet her boyfriend.

"All right. Take care, you two." Lagano turned away and headed to the big private jet whose bright anti-collision lights pierced through the fog.

Rollings watched Joe walk down the tarmac in darkness on all sides, only the lights from the jet cutting through the gloom. About twenty-five feet away from the now visible airstairs, he paused. A gnawing feeling inside took over. At that moment he realized meeting Junior was a mistake and he should have left by some other means, even if that meant being a third wheel with Rollings and Merci.

But he couldn't leave. Peter Casha said he'd meet him here.

Junior and two men from his security detail, men Lagano had hired personally, descended the airstairs.

"Well, well, well," said Junior. "So, you finally made it, JoJo."

"Yes, I'm here."

The look on Junior's face confirmed Lagano's suspicions. He froze, but he knew going back wasn't an option. With the 1911 tucked in his waistband against the small of his back, he calculated his odds of drawing and dropping all three of them.

The odds were not in his favor.

"Did you know Peter failed?"

Lagano didn't say anything.

"You did know, didn't you? His failure risks everything."

Still Lagano remained quiet.

"The only thing I take away from the debacle on the platform is at least Peter is dead," continued Junior.

Lagano knew better. Clearly Casha had not reached out to Junior after what occurred on the platform.

Where are you, bro? Lagano thought.

"We can talk about this back in New York," Lagano said, stalling. "I'm sure we can work something out. I can make this right."

"You don't get it, do you? Peter failed, which means you

failed."

The two security guards stepped to either side of Junior, raised their carbines, and pointed them at Joe.

Shit.

"My father said don't leave a mess on the tarmac, but I figure we can clean everything up and bury you out at the Quantico tank course. You won't be the first body rotting in those woods, nor the last."

The first bullet rang out with a loud *crack*. Lagano watched blood spray across the side of Junior's face when a guard's face exploded without warning. The man's body dropped to the ground. Joe reached for the 1911 and, crouching, held it ready. Another shot came out of the fog a second later and a massive hole appeared in the throat of the other guard, almost decapitating him.

The man reached up to the wound as blood streamed out like the flow of water from a drinking fountain. The blood streamed for another fraction of a second before another slug struck the guard's forehead.

Peter Casha stepped forward from the darkness directly behind Lagano. "On your knees, Joseph." Casha's voice sounded raw, his tone gruff.

Lagano dropped to one knee without hesitation.

Junior panicked, frozen in place and unable to move. He closed his eyes as a sudden wetness covered the front of his pants and worked its way down his leg.

A third guard emerged from the plane and fired a burst from an AR-15 in the direction of Casha and Lagano. Most rounds missed wildly to the left, but two rounds struck Casha in the upper chest. Lagano's life was spared on his knees as the rounds flew over his head in the dense fog.

Casha stumbled and almost lost his balance as air rushed from his lungs, but somehow he willed his weapon back up and fired three rounds at the guard. One sailed high, but two of the bullets struck the guard in the chest and he somersaulted down the airstairs, landing still on the tarmac. The pilots in the aircraft cockpit looked out of their windscreen with wide, frightened eyes, their hands up and pressed against the glass.

As the shots ceased, Junior opened his eyes and yelled out. "How much money do you want, Peter?

Casha stumbled forward and emerged from the darkness. With each step, his coordination worsened as he walked like a drunk trying to keep a straight line during a sobriety test. The arm that held the raised gun started to point toward the pavement.

Unsure if Casha had heard him, Junior yelled out with more force. "I said how much money, damn you! Name your price. It's yours."

With surprising speed, the gun came back up.

"Fuck you, Junior ... *and* your money."

The pistol lit up the fog bank three times as the muzzle flashed brilliant hues of reddish orange.

Junior's face exploded and his body slumped to the ground.

As the last round split the sky, Casha fell to his knees. His white shirt, still under the stolen jacket, was soaked all around with his blood. The blue nylon jacket itself had turned black with all the blood it had absorbed.

Joe turned and ran to his friend. "No, *no, no,*" he pleaded. "Don't do this, bro. You can't go out like this. We're gonna get you back to the clinic and get you fixed up."

A bubble of blood escaped from Casha's mouth and dribbled down his chin. Within seconds his head slowly turned toward the dark sky.

Lagano knelt and brought his friend's head to his chest.

Casha pointed past the plane to the dark fog above. "I see him, bro. I see the warrior."

Tears flowed down Lagano's face.

"Go to him. Go to the warrior, my brother. Go home now."

Lagano smiled and tears made traces down his cheeks.

"Till Valhalla."

He held the lifeless body of his best friend for several minutes. Long enough to say goodbye but not long enough to process what happened. The distant sound of sirens pulled him away from his powerful grief.

He lay the body gently to the tarmac and removed a pistol from Casha's holster. The 1911 his friend carried was a duplicate of his own. He stuffed Casha's weapon in his belt and, gripping his own pistol, bounded up the airstairs of the idling jet. Lagano knew the pilots. A powerful look of fear covered both men's faces as he stepped into the cockpit.

"Miss … mister Lagano?" one of the pilots stammered.

"Do you have enough fuel for the Caymans?"

The pilot nodded. "Ye-yes, sir."

"Go there."

"But our flight plan is for New York."

Joe clicked back the hammer of the Kimber and pressed it to the man's temple.

"Change of plans, Matt. Make it happen, please."

The pilot nodded, careful not to put any undue pressure on Lagano's trigger finger.

"You got it, Mr. Lagano."

The pilot reached forward and pressed a switch, announcing to the co-pilot, "Starting number one …"

Payne and Stone sat on bar stools at the Old Ebbitt Grill on 15th Street, east of the White House. The bartender handed each a perfectly poured draft Guinness complete with a shamrock drawn in the foam, and they clanked together the rims of the tall glasses.

"To Wes." Payne raised his glass skyward.

"Till Valhalla," Stone said and threw back a large swig of her dark stout.

"Got room for one more?" asked an approaching figure.

Payne turned and saw Nick Jordan.

"For the Body Man? Anytime."

Stone moved a stool to the left. "Ignore him, Nick. I do." She patted the empty seat between her and Payne. "Here y'go, bud. Kept this one warm for you."

"Well, thank you, pretty girl."

Stone's fair skin flushed instantly.

"Are you sweet-talkin' my partner, Jordan?" Payne asked.

"Oh, so now I gotta be your partner?" Stone mocked. A surprised look spread over her face.

"What are you talking about? Where is the ambiguity?"

"That's the first time you've ever referred to me as your partner," Stone said, incredulous.

"Seriously?" Payne gave her a quizzical stare. "It is?"

Payne laughed loud enough to turn a few heads of other patrons scattered around the bar. "I'm only kidding. You became my partner the moment you climbed into my car."

"Yeah?"

Payne said, "Okay, maybe when you saved my ass on the oil platform."

"Jeez, let's not relive that moment again," Stone protested, raising both hands. "You gonna cry on my shoulder?"

Jordan laughed, a hearty guttural sound from deep within. "I love this. Are you two married?"

"Tell me about it," Payne said.

The bartender placed a napkin on the bar in front of Jordan. "What's yours, sport?" she asked.

"Oh, I'll have what they're having."

"Put his on mine, Robbie. These are all on me," Payne said to the bartender. "Plus, let's get three Irish Car Bombs when you get a sec, please?"

"Wait a minute. How the hell will we get home if all of us get shitfaced?" asked Nick.

"I'll be the DD," Mila Hall said, sliding from nowhere into the empty seat next to Payne.

"Is this a double date or something?" asked Jordan.

Stone kicked him in the shin and wagged her finger back and forth. But she grinned happily and wondered if there were any other secret meanings to the title Body Man.

The sight of the new president—last week's vice president— on the television screen above the bar caused all four to stop and pay attention.

"After what went down with Steele, how is he?" Stone pointed to the screen. The new president was eulogizing the recently deceased one.

"Who, PREACHER?" Mila Hall used the Secret Service code name for the man elevated from vice president to president only five days before. "We always liked him, long's he stays off the pulpit in the office. I'm not on his detail, but after MOGUL, I can't imagine he'd be worse."

Jordan raised his glass. "I will drink to that."

Everyone raised glasses and drank.

"Not to mix business with pleasure," Jordan said, "but do you guys have a lead on Marcus and Merci?"

Payne shook his head. "You mean after you let them walk right out of the White House? The most secure eighteen acres in the world?"

Jordan frowned. "I like to believe I gave them a professional courtesy. Anyway, I knew the FBI could track them down anytime it liked. Like they did me." He rolled his eyes at the last phrase.

Payne smirked. "Their trail went cold. They took a chartered jet from DC to Paris. From there we got a probable match from Interpol via surveillance cameras that placed them on a commercial flight from de Gaulle to Singapore. But they fell off the grid once they arrived at Changi Airport. No hits in the past twenty-four hours. Interpol is looking for them, but we all know how well that typically goes."

"How about Joe Lagano?"

"Same deal, essentially. Story is he forced Junior's pilots at gunpoint to fly him to the Cayman Islands. Once they landed, he knocked both of them out. When they came to, he was long gone. It appears Mr. Lagano emptied a bank account in Peter Casha's name and disappeared. The working theory is he fled by boat to parts unknown, but no hard evidence to substantiate that yet."

"How much money did he get?"

Stone piped up then. "A *buncha* million dollars, is the guess. Enough to fall off the grid for now, but he'll turn up sooner or later. Oh, and this morning we got a positive ID on the female body found on the stairwell outside the platform. Her name is Evelyn Rhimes. And get this, up until six months ago she worked in the communication department at … drum roll, please …" Payne started tapping his fingers quickly on the oak countertop in a weak imitation of a drum roll. "… the White House."

"Really?" Jordan looked surprised.

"Yeah. Ever heard of her?" Stone asked.

Jordan pondered the name. "No, name doesn't ring a bell."

Payne said, "It's likely the Sanctum either has or had a mole inside the White House. Rhimes was at least part of that operation."

Jordan stroked the side of his beer glass. "I'll flush them out if there's any left. Thanks for the heads up."

"What about the Sanctum?" asked Stone. "What will happen with them?"

Nick's eyes narrowed. "PREACHER started a task force called Red Star and placed me on it."

"Its purpose?"

"To find the members of the Sanctum and take them down."

"That didn't take long—he's only been POTUS for a few days," Payne said. "He's hitting the ground running."

"There's plenty of running to do. He realizes the existential threat we face with a crime syndicate of the Sanctum's reach operating in the United States so brazenly."

Stone nodded. "Interesting. And has a new apprentice been named to replace you?"

The serious expression faded, and a thinly veiled smile crept over Nick's face as he cocked his head toward Mila Hall.

Payne saw the look. "Oh, *hell* no—you are *kidding* me."

Hall reached over and rubbed her palm over the top of Payne's right hand. "Don't worry, Eli. I'm not interested."

"I might be able to convince her otherwise," Jordan said.

"Watch it, Jordan. You were starting to grow on me," Payne said.

"I'm just playin', man. So, what's on the docket for you two?" He gestured to Payne and Stone.

Payne smiled. "Tell him, partner."

"New case," Stone said. "We just got a call on the way over here. Some blowhard US senator might be missing."

"Then why are you in here drinking with me? Shouldn't you be out finding him?"

"Well," Stone said, "the Capitol Police are still doing the prelim to make sure he isn't in a drunk tank somewhere or in some prostitute's photo studio before they send up the balloon for real. But for now, we have a few questions for you."

"How so?"

"You're privy to intimate details regarding the senator," Payne said.

"Am I?" Jordan asked, his right eyebrow raised, Spock-like.

Stone nodded. "Yeah. That's why we're here."

Acknowledgments

A novel might come from one person's imagination, but others lurk under the surface and are involved in the overall creative process.

I am humbled, grateful, and happy to share in this lifelong aspiration with so many who have supported me since I completed my first novel, *Vengeance*, in 2014. It has been a long and strange road with many bumps along the way. However, as I often remind my kids, others, and especially myself, "Life's a Journey, Not a Destination."

These acknowledgments are in the back of the book, but I don't want the people mentioned below to think of themselves as an afterthought—my publisher decided this section should go here because I wanted to recognize a lot of folks. Those I thank are part of the reason you get to read the story you just finished.

Above all, thank you to **I AM** for the gifts you have bestowed upon me.

Bruce and Noelle. My loves. When I get down, you pick me up. When failure seems right before me, your unconditional love helps me overcome what seems impossible. What I do, I do for both of you. Writing a book is exciting, but being your father is my joy, my sacred honor, and above all my greatest privilege in life.

My Mom – Patricia (Patty). You have always been my first fan and biggest supporter. God blessed me beyond words for putting me in your care. I love you, always.

My Dad – Thomas (Tom). Not sure I would write books if you didn't instill the love of reading when I was young. Your tattered Tom Clancy, WEB Griffin, and Dale Brown paperbacks made it into my hands, and I emulated the writing style of the authors you enjoyed.

Jackie, Shawn, & Brett. Distance often separates us, but I'm grateful for the time we spend together. Go Red Sox!

Aunt Sue. You've been a constant in my life and treated me as one of your own from Day One. I love you.

Ray & Barb Tanguay (Gramm & Grumpaw). You were second parents to me growing up, and even though I still don't like the sound of a timer; I'm grateful for all the goodness and virtue you helped instill within me during my impressionable years. By the way, I'll never eat peas thanks to you, Mom #2.

I miss you, **Nanny.** You'd be so proud of what I'll accomplish in my writing career. PIKE 84 is for you.

To the rest of **my Family.** There's a whole lot of you, and you know who you are. Thank you & much love.

Max Council. The Pope. From the hiking trails of SC, to the streets of Rome, with a snowball fight atop the St. Bernard Pass in Switzerland, and all the way to the Sacré-Cœur steps overlooking Paris with a Coca-Cola in hand, you've been there for my highest of high's to my lowest of lows. Not only my closest friend but a true brother. *No soup for you!* Thanks for everything and enjoy the gravy train.

TC Thompson. Mr. President. I need a sense of balance at times, a calm, reassuring voice when the waves get too high. You've been that person for many years. Our brainstorming sessions have been invaluable, and I appreciate you giving the MS an early read to help right the ship. Still waiting for that guy's trip to Patagonia.

Kathy Lubin. My very first editor and dear friend. You're the definition of positivity, compassion, and determination. Your friendship has made me a better man and father. Make sure you take Charlie's call next time the phone rings.

Adam Hamdy. Without question if it wasn't for you, I would not have the ability to write these acknowledgments. A superbly talented scribe with limitless potential, a true friend, and generous supporter of other writers. You championed *The Body Man* and believed in me even when I struggled with self-doubt. I am grateful and humbled for all you've done for me, Adam. By the way, sorry we dumped your tea in Boston ... *not!*

Laurie (LA) Chandlar. One of the strongest woman I've met along my literary journey, you have proved whatever life throws at a person is no match for tenacity, resolve, and courage. You have been there with a helping hand, sage advice, and valuable insights along this journey. And you are the best damned tour guide in NYC. Period.

Brad Meltzer. My favorite author and a man who leads not by words, but by example. *Ordinary People Change the World*, but you, my friend, are extraordinary. And you were 100 percent correct. Don't Let Anyone Tell You No! I listened to you, and I didn't. Thank you for blazing the trail, I'm grateful to follow your lead. Onward and Upward.

Jack Carr. Patriot, veteran, and #1 NY Times Bestselling Author. Thank you for believing in me and offering both encouragement and positivity. I'm a *True Believer* in what you create and how you treat others. It's exciting to watch your ascent to the top, and I raise a pint of Guinness to your continued success. Keep crushing it. Still waiting for our drive in a 308GTS.

Lori Twining & Colleen Winter. The first scribes I befriended at Thrillerfest in 2017. I'm grateful for your support, laughter, and positive vibes. I owe you both a fancy dinner. And Colleen, congrats on the release of your second book, *The Disruptors*.

I write novels in large part thanks to the immersive and mesmerizing tales told by both **Tom Clancy** and **Vince Flynn**. Two of my literary heroes who inspired and impressed me. #RIP gents.

The Body Man protects the office of the Presidency. The current Body Man and those that came before would like to thank these men: **#46 Joseph Biden, #45 Donald Trump, #44 Barack Obama, #43 George W. Bush, #42 Bill Clinton, #41 George Bush, #40 Ronald Reagan, #39 Jimmy Carter, #38 Gerald Ford, #37 Richard Nixon, #36 Lyndon Johnson,** and **#35 John F. Kennedy** (the man who started it all).

Scott Swanson. Thank you for the technical insight, solid advice, and support along the journey of getting TBM published. I'm grateful you nominated me to take the FBI Citizens Academy class, which proved to be an invaluable resource and a true privilege to attend. Most of the F-bombs in this mss are dedicated to you. But I did save a few for **Josh Hood.**

Brian Andrews. Thanks for early support of TBM, and great advice.

Brad Taylor. Early in the process of writing TBM I hit a snag. You were kind enough to answer my (numerous) texts and offered a simple solution for a vital scene that gave me fits. I toast an R&C to you.

Tony (AJ) Tata. I appreciate the explanation on Middle East conflicts you provided me while working on plot points for TBM. I was honored to learn from your experience. Above all, thanks for your service and leadership to our amazing troops.

My thanks to **The Crew Reviews** guys (www.thecrewreviews.com)—**Sean Cameron, Mike Houtz,** and **Chris Albanese.** I wish you all much success with TCR, and your writing endeavors.

Don Bentley. Thank you for the early read and kind blurb for TBM. Congratulations on your writing success, and major props on the foray into the Clancy universe.

Bono. We've never met, but I hope one day we do. Your music has been the soundtrack of my life. Thanks for inspiring others to be better versions of themselves, showing the world charity, and pro-claiming your beliefs without regrets. I am your fan *Until The End Of The World*. One day we will break bread together.

I'm beyond blessed to have a great group of friends who've encouraged me on this journey. It's an honor to do life with all of you and my sincere thanks for all you've done to enrich my life: **Dave Richards (Ravid Dichards), Jim Latina, Fudgie, Brian Wohnig, Andrew Reinertsen (Rino), Simon Fraser, Dony Jay, Chris Miller, Jim Gaston, Noah George, Mickey Messick (Face)** my aviation guru, **Ryan Fogarty, Mel Puckett**, and **Stan Yoder**.

I do have a day job, and I'm grateful for the incredible team I have the privilege to work with. Special thanks to **Carolynn Tolbert, Shawn Cassidy, Kathy Lubin, Kim Marquez, Loretta Uribe, Cynthia Ehlers**, and **Diane Torres** for your constant support of my "hobby."

Joe Lagano and **Matt O'Hara**. We met after the **Warrior** left you, but **Terry**'s still here in spirit. Thank you for the dinners, texts, and words of encouragement. Hope you like your characters. Sorry they weren't the "Playboy billionaires" you requested.

To my **Troop 610 Dads**. You listened to many of my tall tales and ideas around the campfire and explored the great outdoors with me on many occasions: **Bud McCall, TC Thompson, Marty Thomas, Scott Taylor, Mike Webb, Radar**, and thanks to "Mountain Dew Man" **Wes Russell**, for uttering your last words so I could immortalize them for all time.

Thanks to the enthusiastic review team at **Best Thriller Books** (www.bestthrillerbooks.com). The 5 Angry Men: **Stuart Ashenbrenner, Chris Miller, Todd Wilkins, Derek Luedtke**, and **Steve Netter.** As well as **Kashif Hussain** (*Kashif's Corner*), **Ankit**

Dhirasaria, **Sarah Walton** (*Sarah Says*), **David Dobiasek** (**The Voice**), and the man who toils in the shadows, **James Abt**.

Many authors provided advice, ideas, kinds words, and above all support along my literary journey. The interactions may have been small but the words were lasting. I'm grateful for the encouragement from **JT Patten**, **Joe Goldberg**, **David Darling**, **Kyle Steele**, **Jack Stewart**, **David Temple**, **J.B. Stevens, G.P.**, **S.L. Shelton**, **KR Paul**, **Chris Hauty**, **Kyle Mills**, **Jamie Mason**, **Steve Stratton**, **Ben Coes**, **Simon Gervais**, **Steve Urszenyi**, **Dr. Jason Piccolo**, and **Jeremy Miller**.

My sincere thanks to **amazing beta readers** who read a very rough version of *The Body Man* and had to deal with an unedited (and sloppy) manuscript. I'm sure you questioned what the hell you signed up for, but thanks for sticking with it **Jim Cooke** (who also provided early edits), **Vikki Faircloth** (my #1 superfan), **Debbie Sabatini**, **Austin Chapin** (a skilled writer as well), **Mike Goodwin**, **Julia Hogenmiller**, **Frank Meints**, and **Doug King**. Thanks to **Frank Fitzgerald**, whom I met while taking the FBI Citizens Academy, for taking *The Body Man* copy to with him Nepal.

In memoriam: **Doug King**. RIP. A friend and encouragement to me both in my personal life and in my writing endeavors. I'll miss loaning books to you and hearing all your tales. Still not sure which one were true or not, but from the bottom of my heart thanks for believing in me. I'll continue to make you proud.

Thank you to the staff at **Force Poseidon** (forceposeidon.com) and in particular **Daniel Charles Ross** for believing in me and making my dream of publishing *The Body Man* a reality. Thanks to **Marc Lichter**, executive editor at FP, for all his efforts on my behalf. Also, thanks to **Adam Sydney** for the initial edit of *The Body Man* to get it ready for prime time.

Thanks to **Brandi Fugate** for my author photos. You worked magic to make me look presentable! You have a beautiful family.

To you, **the Readers** ... I'm grateful for every person who takes a chance and reads my words. I hope the story entertains you, excites you, and teaches you a thing or two. Above all, I want my literary journey to reinforce my belief that anyone can accomplish any task they put their minds to.

No matter what you try in life, the only thing standing in the way of success is you. Don't be a hindrance to your dreams. Life is short, our books have a first page and a last. Fill those blank pages to the best of your ability, give thanks for the blessings provided from **I Am,** and above all treat one another with kindness, compassion, and love.

One more thing. You are reading this book because I followed one simple philosophy ever since I wrote my first novel: *Never quit!*

Onward and Upward,
Eric P. Bishop
July 2021

About the author

Eric P. Bishop grew up in Connecticut, and relocated to the South after college. Moves to the Rockies and the Pacific Northwest occurred before finally heading back East to raise a family.

After many years in corporate America, he chose his passion for the written word and chased his dreams of crafting a novel—and today you hold his debut novel in your hand.

He lives in the foothills of South Carolina with his children, where they explore the great outdoors most weekends while he dreams up his next adventure. See ericpbishop.com for more about Eric and his work.

For more information on this and other exciting new authors, please see ForcePoseidon.com

FORCE POSEIDON

Made in the USA
Columbia, SC
11 January 2022